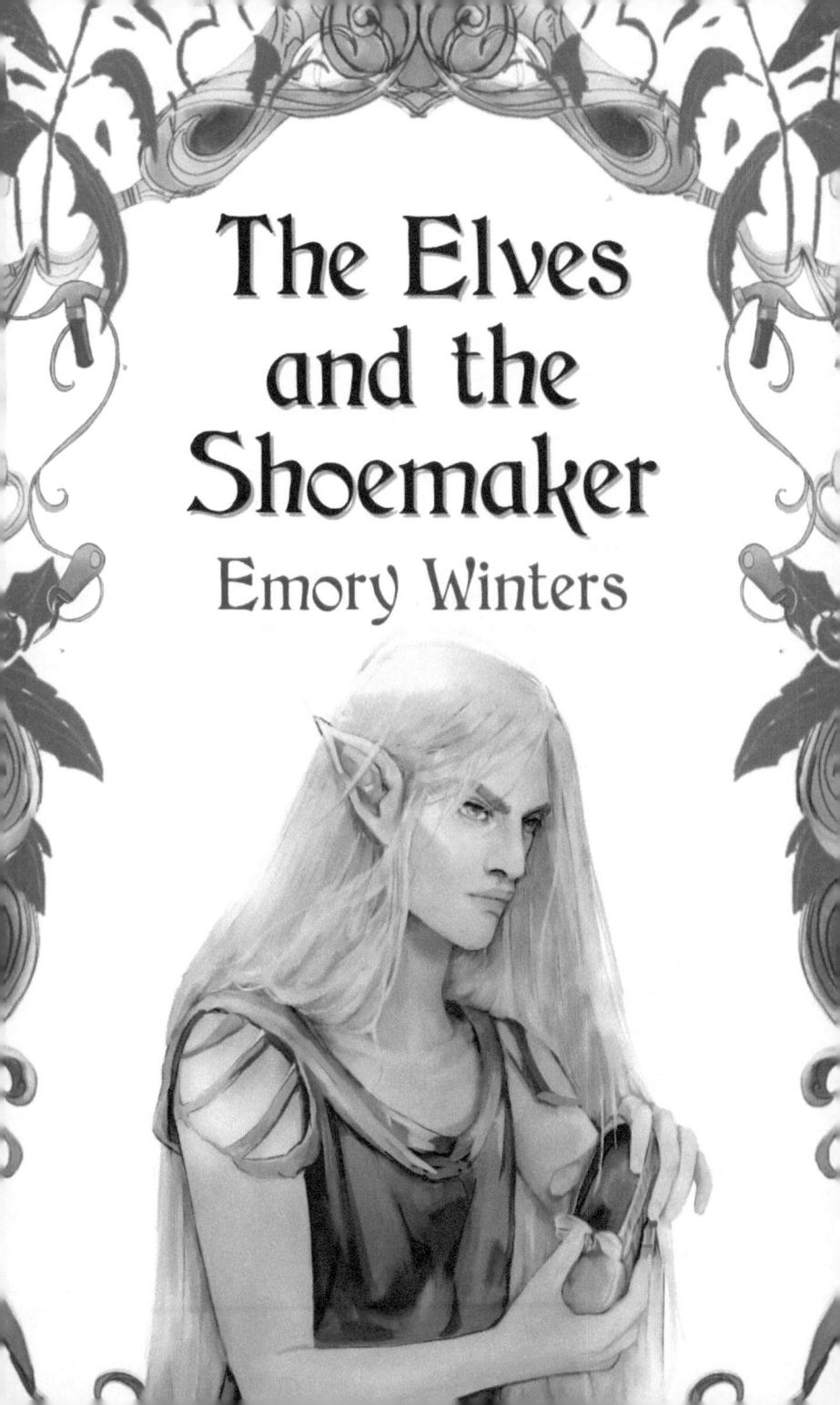

The Elves and the Shoemaker

Emory Winters

ISBN 978-1-7390946-8-3

CONTENTS

Author Note

In The Elves and the Shoemaker, one of my main characters, Johan (the shoemaker) struggles with situational (also frequently referred to as selective) mutism. Johan's situational mutism stems from an anxiety disorder that primarily makes it difficult for him to speak in front of strangers and at times even people he is familiar with. During the course of writing this book I spoke to several people who experience situational mutism and every single person had a unique experience. I have done my utmost to treat Johan's disability with care and consideration and I hope this is reflected in the story.

This romance is about two elves and a human in a closed triad. They practice polyamory as kindly and thoughtfully as three characters with no resources or frame of reference are able and this is not intended to be a reflection of the healthiest way to manage a triad.

I have been in these character's heads for the best part of eight months. They are the best and the worst parts of me and I'm both so excited and terrified to send them out into the wild, but here we are. Find your inner Johan and be gentle with them, they've been through a lot and they really are just trying their best.

Enjoy,
Emory <3

CONTENT ADVISORY

There are some elements of this story that may be challenging or unsafe for certain readers. While the focus of this story is on healing, it covers some difficult topics and I would recommend reading the content warnings.

This book contains instances of th`e following:

- Panic attack on page

- An MC with an anxiety disorder (situational mutism)

- Internal and external ableism

- References to slavery and captivity (some of the language surrounding this is appropriate for the time period but might not be terminology we would consider best to use today)

- References to violence experienced during slavery, including an instance of urination and an instance of flogging (off page)

- Trapped in a confined space

- Descriptions of violence and murder (including deaths which take place in a fire)

- Instance of magic used against an MC without consent

- Group sex within a closed triad

- Unsafe sex practises due to the time period

- Historical death of parents

- Family abandonment

- Self harm (an MC hitting themselves while frustrated)

Varinien↑

Hallin

Hallin Castle

Cinder's Estate

Frog Prince's Lair

N
W E
S

The GriMM Tales

Falchovari

Evil Queen's Castle
(Rumpelstilzchen's Haunting Grounds)

Shoemaker's Shop

Pied Pipers Music Shop

Sorcerer's Tower

Dark Forest

The Candy House

Miners' House

Old Oma's House

Mines

For the people who hear us, even when we don't have the words.

Prologue

ELIAS

The rough patch of road they travelled along made for a particularly uncomfortable journey. Elias' now-too-frail frame ached fiercely as the carriage rocked, rattling his bones. He took a deep breath in and exhaled, reminding himself that no good came from dwelling on his ailments. It wouldn't make the pain go away, and it would only cause his mood to plummet. Henrik was miserable enough for the both of them, and he needed to keep them alive long enough to escape the hell they'd been thrown into.

Elias and Henrik hadn't thought it could get much worse than the silk mill, but when it shut down due to their owners' bankruptcy, the two of them and several others were sentenced to an even worse fate.

Bought and paid for, they, along with two dozen other slaves, were on their way to serve in the Queen's castle, forced to bend the knee for the cold and unforgiving ruler herself.

The only things Elias knew about the Queen were based on rumours, but none of them were good. While a famine was starving her people, she supposedly imported food from other lands and lived lavishly in her ivory tower. She was infamously cruel for no reason beyond her own entertainment, and Elias felt sick at the thought of himself and Henrik being in her clutches.

The ten other elves, crammed into the small cage atop the carriage with them, were silent for the duration of the journey. Only two of them, Hans and Ansel, had also come from the silk mill; the others appeared more recently captured, their cheeks yet to become gaunt and their skin not yet sallow.

Equal numbers filled the second carriage; their transporters unconcerned with packing all the elves so tightly into a confined space for over a full day with neither food nor water.

By the time they entered the Dark Forest, darkness had fallen. The slavers driving the rickety carriage began ringing a bell. Despite not knowing its purpose, the eerie sound made all the fine hairs on Elias' body stand on end.

He peered through the bars that trapped them inside. The moon cast a silver glow through the tree branches, creating the illusion of glittering spiderwebs covering the road before them. For a second, when Elias glanced ahead to the bushes in the distance, he was sure he spotted a flash of red fabric, but his eyes must have deceived him.

They hadn't been in the forest long when they came to a sudden stop, and the slaver driving the carriage shouted, "Halt! Ten-minute break!"

The greasy-haired man stepped down from his driving seat, jostling all the elves inside in the process. He rattled the cage bars as he passed them, sneering before heading to the bushes to relieve himself.

As they waited, a warm body pressed extra closely against Elias' side. He glanced at his begrudging companion, Henrik, and smiled.

Rik had spent less time than Elias in captivity, and it showed. He still retained some muscle on his exposed arms, and his face wasn't quite as gaunt. Despite the deep scowl that marred his face on a near-permanent basis, Henrik was stunning. His pointed ears were unusually smooth where they poked out from his long, pale-white hair, and Elias frequently soothed himself by running a fingertip along them.

Predictably, Rik frowned at Elias' wide smile. He rarely welcomed Elias' endless optimism in the face of their dire circumstances, but Elias was fairly sure he would collapse under the weight of fear and dread if he didn't cling to any shred of hope that he could.

Henrik had hoped for a while, too, but Elias remembered the night it'd died all too well—could still feel the way Henrik had shaken in his arms as he'd sobbed. A year prior, Henrik had been captured upon returning from a fishing trip in the early hours of the morning back in their home country, Varinien.

During the first several months of his captivity, Henrik had regularly explained to Elias that his family would discover what had happened and rescue him at any moment, saving Elias as well. Elias had agreed it was a nice thought but had never given it the weight that Henrik had, and so when nobody had appeared to rescue them a year later, Elias had been considerably less devastated by the fact than Henrik had been.

Elias pushed the memories of that night away and returned to peering out between the bars at their surroundings. There was an unnatural stillness to the forest. Overseers at the mill had spoken of how empty the land had become in recent years—that hunters returned empty-handed more often than not—but witnessing the lack of life where there should be an abundance unsettled Elias.

The slavers laughed and bickered amongst themselves with a lightness that had anger burning like a furnace inside Elias. He hoped he would never understand how a person could reach the point of being so callous about the lives of others. The fact that the scariest things in this world were not the monsters from the frightening tales he'd been told as a child, but simple, ordinary men who would sell their souls for some coin, chipped away at Elias' resolve that there were still good people to be found in this life.

"One minute, folks! Get ready to move out!" the slaver yelled to the others, startling Elias back to reality.

Elias shuffled from foot to foot in an attempt to ease the shooting pains that reverberated up his legs.

Another slaver approached them; Elias recognised him as the man who'd shoved them in here in the first place by the sinister smile revealing a mouth of mostly rotten black teeth.

"Thirsty, little elf?" he sneered.

Elias narrowed his eyes but didn't reply.

"Here, have a drink," he added before tugging his cock from his breeches and spraying a stream of piss through the bars. Elias grimaced as it landed mostly on his bare legs.

Elias seethed in silence, one more act of degradation to slice into whatever was left of his soul.

"Do not give him a reason," Henrik whispered. *Reason to kill you* is what he meant.

The rest of the men were returning to the carriages when some sort of growling came from nearby.

"What was that noise?" Elias whispered to Henrik. He was certain it could only have come from an animal. He felt almost relieved at the sign of life, and his ears twitched, searching for the sound. As if to confirm its presence, the animal let out the loudest howl Elias had ever heard, and Henrik tugged Elias away from the bars, embracing him protectively.

"Wolf," Henrik replied, his voice shaky.

"You are sure?"

Elias felt more than saw Henrik's nod in response. "They would often circle our village in the night when they ran out of food in the winter. I will recognise that sound on my deathbed." Henrik gulped.

The horses began going wild, and the men were shouting things Elias couldn't quite decipher, as fear made his brain feel like it had been stuffed with cotton.

There was a commotion outside, and Elias watched on as the slaver who'd been in charge suddenly collapsed to the ground when an arrow struck through his neck. Blood poured from his mouth until he choked on it. His body twitched a few times, and more blood pooled around his head before a stillness that only descended with death overcame him. Elias stared in numb shock at what he'd just witnessed, although he was certain that a man as cruel as this one surely deserved a more prolonged death.

More yelling from the other slavers stole his attention, but then Elias spotted an arrow coming right for them and grabbed Henrik to duck down in the cage. Despite the misery that surrounded Elias' existence for the last few years, his impending death only seemed to spark a stubborn flame within him.

He was not prepared to die yet. He refused to allow for his life so far to be the grand total of his existence. Much to Elias' surprise, though, the arrow struck the rope that bound the cage shut, severing it in two.

"Rik, Henrik! Now is our chance; we need to move quickly!"
Elias yelled through the pandemonium. All of them within the cage
threw themselves at the bars until they gave way, and collapsed off
the carriage, freeing the contained elves.

Elias grabbed Henrik's wrist and tried to drag him off the track
towards the trees, but Henrik resisted.

"The wolf, Eli. There is a wolf out there. We can't... we—"

"I'm taking the risk, Henrik. I... I will not survive our next owners,
I know it. We need to run. Now!"

Elias sprinted for the trees, and he could only trust that Henrik
would follow him. From what he could see in his periphery, the freed
elves had all scattered in different directions. Their arms and legs
remained chained in heavy irons that clanked noisily as they ran.

Elias knew that the adrenaline fuelling him would expire quickly;
he needed to find somewhere to hide. When a familiar hand slid into
his, it gave him the boost he required to keep running. Henrik had
followed him.

Henrik tugged Elias in a change of direction, as one of the slavers
who'd sprinted after them had almost caught up.

"Rik," Elias panted. "I don't know how much farther I can run.
I'm so weak." Tears ran down Elias' cheeks as they raced for their
lives. He knew Henrik could keep going and escape, but he wasn't
sure that he could.

Henrik must have heard the exhaustion and panic in Elias' tone
because the next thing he knew, he was being dragged into a large
overgrowth of shrubs. Once inside, they crawled farther in, as far
and as quietly as they could. Thorns and twigs scratched and tore
at their skin, but it was a small price to pay for their freedom, and
adrenaline pushed Elias far beyond his body's limits.

When they reached a point deep within that was large enough for the two of them to curl up, they held onto each other and tried to catch their breath, all the while praying that the slaver had lost track of them.

It had been near silent for a while, except for their breaths; they hadn't even dared to whisper to one another. And then they heard, "You can either come out now, or we'll be back with the dogs, and they'll drag you out." It was the man who'd urinated on Elias just minutes earlier. "It won't take them long to track your stench, elves!"

No thanks to you, Elias thought dryly.

Elias' own heartbeat was a loud pulse in his ears as they held their breaths, clinging to one another in complete darkness. The sound of twigs snapping underfoot eventually became fainter, and they had to strain to hear the slaver's voice in the distance.

Elias wasn't sure exactly how long they remained there. But several hours at least passed before either of them dared to utter a word. They would have to move deeper into the Dark Forest soon because Elias did not doubt that the slavers would follow through on their threat and be back with the dogs.

"Is this real, Eli? Did that really happen?" Henrik whispered eventually.

"We're... we're really free, Rik." Elias choked on a sob at the thought.

One

JOHAN

A shoemaker, through no fault of his own, had become so poor that, at last, he had nothing left but enough leather for one pair of shoes.

The Great Famine had taken its toll on the entire kingdom of Falchovari, but while many had resorted to horrifying solutions like kidnapping and enslaving elves, Johan knew he would sooner die than thrive at the expense of others. His parents may no longer be alive, but they had raised him to be a kind and good man. They hadn't been able to leave him with much beyond a shoe shop that was a struggle to keep afloat, but their legacy was Johan himself, and he wouldn't let them down.

The sound of the door to his shop opening made his skin prickle. It was a never-ending cycle for Johan; he needed customers to keep the shop running and to maintain a roof over his head, and yet, the presence of strangers stole his voice from his throat.

The woman who entered was a short, thin woman with fine, straw-coloured hair and sharp features. Her cotton dress was frayed along the bottom, and he spotted several previously patched-up holes, exposing her frugality.

Johan swallowed the pool of saliva gathered in his mouth and tried to clear his throat. No words came, unfortunately, so he offered her a warm smile instead.

The lady inspected several pairs of shoes from the display near the window before bringing over a pair of leather boots that lent themselves to practicality over vanity.

"Do you have these in a size that will fit me?" she asked; her voice was raspy, much like Johan's own when it made a rare appearance.

He held up a finger, indicating for her to wait a moment, and then fetched the board he used to measure feet. She followed him over to the small bench and sat down, removing her old disintegrating shoe. Johan quickly set to work measuring her foot and then left to check his shelves.

Fortunately, he had a similar pair of boots in the woman's size, and she paid him her money with a grateful smile on her face despite the fact that he'd been unable to muster the words for even a mere thank you. And it cut Johan up because he was incredibly grateful. The coins from the sale would go a long way towards buying some supplies for making more shoes, plus some left over for a little food if the market had any. His stomach grumbled at the thought.

When she left the shop, Johan let out a deep sigh of relief.

"Thank you," he muttered quietly now that he was entirely alone, like the words might carry down the cobbled street for her to hear.

She turned out to be his first and only customer that day, but it was better than nothing.

Later in the evening, Johan locked up the shop and entered his workshop at the back. Scraps of material that he cut off and cast aside during the shoe-making process littered his beech worktop, and he brushed them to the end in order to make room.

Taking a seat, Johan laid out the last remaining leather and carefully measured and cut it up to ensure minimal wastage of material. The sound of his sharp scissors slicing through the leather was a soothing balm.

Shoemaking was something Johan had always excelled at. His shoulders relaxed at the familiarity of the process, along with the relief of knowing he wouldn't have to attempt interacting with strangers again until the next morning.

Once all the pieces were cut to size, he laid them out methodically onto the workbench, ready for the following day. He would get up early in the morning and head to the market to spend the money from his sale on some more supplies. The prospect of the busy market was simultaneously a little thrilling for Johan and gave him a stomachache.

After collecting his oil lamp from the side near the door, he left his workshop and headed up the stairs to the place he called home.

The door to his little flat creaked as he opened it. His oil lamp cast a faint glow when he entered. His flat wasn't big, and at times, it was hard to recall how he'd lived here with both his parents. A few years after they'd died from a severe case of Winter Fever, he'd finally moved to sleep on their much larger mattress over the smaller one he'd outgrown by full age.

Johan was both poor and not especially materialistic, which led to his home being quite sparse. He liked it that way, though, because when the noise of the outside world got to be too much, his little home was his sanctuary. There was nobody here to get frustrated with him when he lost his words at inopportune moments, nobody here to make unexpected noises that made him jump. But there was also nobody here when he was cold and lonely. Nobody to talk to about his day when he was able to. Nobody to share a meal with.

At the thought of food, Johan despondently made his way to the small kitchen in the corner of the room. He took a slice of bread that was going stale and the last chunk of cheese, eating the two mechanically, nothing more or less than as a necessity for staying alive.

Will I be alone forever? He thought. Johan had had one friend as a child, a boy called Christoph. He'd been accepting of Johan's quiet nature, speaking up for him when needed, but unfortunately, when the worst of the famine had hit, Christoph's parents had no longer been able to afford to live in the town and had left to be labourers on some land too far away for even the possibility of Johan visiting.

Six winters had passed since Johan's parents had died. Six winters since he'd been hugged or even touched beyond a passing brush of fingers as money exchanged hands in his shop or at the market. At times, the loneliness felt almost too much for Johan to bear, a heavy debilitating weight that he couldn't climb out from underneath.

Sometimes at night, when he would take himself in hand, he wished it were someone else's hand wrapped around him instead. But mostly, he wished just for someone to hold during the cold nights. Someone whose hair he could stroke, whom he could maybe even whisper things to in the darkness if he were able. It felt like an unattainable dream, but was a comforting one regardless as he drifted off to sleep that night.

Two

Henrik

In theory, Henrik was aware that he should be relieved to no longer be held captive and forced to tolerate working endless hours until his fingers bled in exchange for scraps of food. However, with both his and Elias' magic still bound by suppressing copper cuffs that required a sorcerer to remove them, they were now homeless and forced to resort to begging for coin or food. Both of which Henrik firmly believed were beneath what any living being should be expected to endure as a means of survival.

Henrik woke that morning to Elias shivering in his arms. They had nothing to wear except the hessian sacks they'd been dressed in at the silk mill and a small cotton sheet to cover them at night that must have dropped to the ground from one of the high washing lines in the housing district.

Due to having to remain hypervigilant lest anyone opportunistic attempt to capture them again while they were weak and vulnerable, Henrik and Elias were spending their nights inside the Dark Forest. When they'd escaped their captors only a few weeks prior, Henrik had built a den out of sticks and moss for them to sleep within, and they'd cleaned an entire blacksmith's forge from top to bottom in exchange for having their iron shackles removed.

Henrik wrapped his arms more tightly around Elias like he could gift him some warmth that he didn't even possess himself. Elias turned in his arms and smiled at him like he wasn't, in fact, on the brink of dying from exposure.

"Good morning," Henrik whispered to his best friend and some-times lover. They had never really had need to discuss exactly what they were to each other.

"Morning, Rik," Elias replied, pecking a quick kiss to Henrik's frigidly cold lips.

Elias had been free with his affection for Henrik ever since they'd first lain together.

A few months into their time at the silk mill, Elias had—through no fault of his own but sheer exhaustion—made a mistake that had cost the mill a yard of expensive silk.

Elias had panicked, almost unable to breathe as he'd held the ruined fabric in his blistered hands, and Henrik had been over-whelmed with the need to protect him. Protect the elf who had been nothing but kind to him since he'd found himself dragged into the depths of hell, the elf who had taught him what he'd needed to know in order to survive. So when the overseer had returned, Henrik had snatched the silk from Elias' hands and confessed to the error himself, receiving twenty lashings across his back as punishment.

The pain had been excruciating, yet Henrik had been sure that witnessing Elias endure that same fate would have hurt one hundred times more.

When he'd returned, Elias had been incensed but had procured a salve from somewhere and tended to Henrik's wounds with a degree of care Henrik had never experienced before.

"Why would you do such a thing?" Elias had whispered furiously.

"I have more meat on my bones, Eli. I will survive this, but you might not have," Henrik had explained matter-of-factly.

Elias hadn't replied with words. He'd pressed his lips to Henrik's with a fierceness that Henrik had returned, and being careful of his wounded back, they had lain together, taking each other in hand until release had burned through some of the passion that had been building between them.

They had lain together like that infrequently. Pain, exhaustion, and starvation had made them unable to yearn for more than food and sleep. But they had slept in each other's arms ever since, and both had gone to sleep and awoken with a kiss that had reassured Henrik that he had, in fact, had a reason to stay alive. Because, despite having had no real desire to endure that life anymore, Henrik would never have left Elias to fend for himself in this cold, unforgiving world.

"What are you thinking of?" Elias asked, stroking a finger down Henrik's nose and bringing him back to the present.

Henrik blushed a little and a mischievous grin lit up Elias' face in response.

"I... um... was recalling the first time you kissed me. And also *after*... you kissed me." Henrik stumbled through his reply.

At first, Elias pouted because he did not enjoy the reminder of the lashings Henrik had taken on his behalf, but never one to let negative thoughts bring him down for long, Elias found his smile again.

"I was so mad at you, I thought I might strike you. But then my hands gripped your shoulders, and I found my lips pressed against yours, and it was all I could think about." Elias spoke calmly, never embarrassed by discussing such matters. They'd been raised quite differently in that regard. "May I touch you now?" Elias asked, as if to prove Henrik's point.

Henrik nodded his head to give permission, and then Elias pushed up the fabric that covered him, reaching underneath to stroke the soft flesh to hardness.

An "mmm" sound escaped Henrik's lips unbidden, and then Elias suddenly had the two of them pressed together in the vise of his fist. Elias kept his hair tied up with a string of leather atop his head, but several strands had come loose during sleep and framed his face now.

Elias stroked both their lengths slowly while he gazed into Henrik's eyes, lips slightly parted. It had been some time since Henrik had found release, and his balls ached for relief.

Speeding up his rhythm, and tightening his grip, it wasn't long before Henrik was panting, pure arousal flooding his senses as he fell over the precipice and spilled over Elias' hand and cock, shuddering all the while. Elias joined him moments later, his eyes widening as he let out a small gasp of pleasure when he came.

Afterwards, Henrik held Elias close, their messy, softening cocks pressed together in a reminder of the moment they'd just shared. Having Elias in his arms like this was the reassurance Henrik needed—that while he didn't have much, he had *him*.

A few days earlier, Henrik had overheard a few locals gossiping about some travelling merchants setting up in the market the coming Saturday and how everyone would be heading there to peruse their wares. With this in mind, Henrik and Elias had decided their best bet for collecting some coin would be to spend the day near the entrance to the market.

They huddled under their cotton sheet, which did little to ward off the chill since the temperature had dropped suddenly again a few days ago. Using some willow branches, Henrik had woven a small bowl to place in front of them in the hope that passersby might be feeling generous and drop some change.

The rumours had been true that the market would be busy that day; unfortunately, though, everyone seemed inclined to keep every coin they had for shopping, and they'd barely collected enough to buy some of the stale leftover bread from the bakers. The market would close soon, and Elias' teeth were already chattering from the bitterly cold winds that seemed to come at them from every direction.

Footsteps sounded nearby, but by this point, Henrik didn't even look up, expecting them to continue on inside, not giving them a second glance. Only, the footsteps stopped, and he could feel eyes on him.

Elias looked up first, and when Henrik saw a tired but gentle smile on his face, he turned to face the same direction. Standing just a few metres away was a tall man; a beard and a flat cap hid most of his face, but the first thing Henrik noticed was that he had kind eyes.

Reaching into his pocket, the man pulled out two silver coins before approaching them. Instead of dropping them into the bowl, he held out a coin to each of them and smiled.

"Thank you," Elias said.

The man looked at them with a concerned frown on his face before scanning their surroundings. He then pointed to himself with his thumb, then at the market entrance with his index finger and held up two fingers to them as if to suggest he'd be back in two minutes. Henrik wasn't sure what he was coming back for but found himself nodding anyway because this had been the first kind interaction they'd had since arriving in Falchovari.

Once he left them and entered the market, Elias turned to Henrik and asked, "Do you think he is unable to hear, like Frida?"

Frida was another slave they'd known back at the mill. She'd been born unable to hear and relied on hand signals and writing things down to communicate, although that was difficult with how few people could read. He shrugged at Elias, still staring at the doorway the mysterious, kind man had disappeared through.

A stab of guilt pierced through Henrik's stomach when he realised he'd been admiring the man. The first and only person he'd really admired since long before he'd met Elias. Making his behaviour even more suspicious, Henrik overcompensated and pressed a brief kiss to Elias' cheek—in public, at that. Which he never did, and now Elias was looking at him like he'd grown a second head.

What was wrong with him?

Before Henrik could truly spiral, however, the man returned with a small bag in his hand and pulled out a sheet of parchment and some graphite. He scribbled something on the piece of paper, poking his tongue out between his lips slightly as he did it, which Henrik did *not* find kind of sweet.

The man passed the parchment to Elias, who sat closer, eyes widening in surprise before showing it to Henrik. He'd drawn a rough sketch of a house, then pointed to the two of them before miming going to sleep.

Henrik was fairly certain the man intended to offer them somewhere to sleep rather than inviting them into his bed, but he wasn't certain enough to agree.

"Are you able to hear us?" Henrik asked, a little louder than was probably polite, if the man could, in fact, hear him.

The man nodded his head. Then, surprising them both, he croaked out, "Johan." And pointed at his chest.

"Speaking is difficult?" Henrik asked, that time at a far less hostile volume.

The man nodded again, and Elias looked confused.

"Are you offering us somewhere to sleep tonight?" Henrik asked, earning another head nod. "In your bed?" he added tentatively.

This time, Johan shook his head vigorously enough to reassure Henrik that his intention wasn't to offer them a place to sleep in exchange for sex.

Before Henrik could even reply, Elias said, "Yes, please. We're so cold, and we won't be any trouble."

In response, Johan reached out a hand to each of them, helping them to stand, and they picked up their cotton sheet along with the few coins they'd collected. Realising suddenly that Johan had already given them money, Henrik tried to return it, thrusting the silver coin in his direction. Johan just closed Henrik's hand with his own, trapping the coin inside and shaking his head, refusing to take it back. Henrik struggled to believe anyone was really that generous without expecting something in return, and a seed of suspicion began to grow in the pit of his stomach.

"Are you sure?" he whispered to Elias.

"I don't know how much longer I can last in the cold, Rik." Elias' words were a heavy weight on Henrik's chest as he really looked at his friend. He was so thin; his face had grown more and more gaunt as each day passed, and he couldn't ignore the truth of it.

They could either take a chance on the kindness of a stranger or risk dying of exposure as they neared winter with no regular sustenance or shelter.

Henrik made the only choice he could live with.

Three

Johan

Johan wasn't entirely sure what had come over him. When he'd spotted the homeless elves looking starved and scared outside the market entrance, the urge to help them had overwhelmed him. He'd never seen elves up close before. The carriages that held them occasionally passed through town, and he knew there were a few who'd had the wealth to remain with the upper classes, but most were enslaved in the large factories behind closed doors.

They were smaller than he'd realised, and their pointed ears poked through their long, silky-white hair. Despite their current state of malnourishment, they were striking to look at. Alert amber eyes contained shadows that told of a life endured rather than lived, but they were not the eyes of people who had given up.

It wasn't safe for them there; they were too vulnerable. All it would take would be for one desperate man to spot their weakness and capture them into the slave trade that had become rife in this kingdom. Leaving them there to fend for themselves felt as awful to Johan as offering them a death sentence himself.

My parents would have offered them a safe place to rest.

When Johan stepped into his shop, the floorboards creaked under his weight, but the elves trailed in silently behind him. Their gaze darted around the room, wide eyes taking in every detail, and as Johan tried to see the place through their eyes, he was suddenly not entirely sure what he could actually offer them. He was no knight in shining armour, nothing but a poor shoemaker.

Glancing at the two elves once more as they shivered, Johan could admit that while he didn't have much, he could still help, and that was more than anyone else was offering.

After holding up a finger to indicate that he'd be back in a moment, he jogged up the stairs to his home to retrieve the spare mattress and his warmest wool blanket.

Upon his return, he found the elves exactly where he'd left them, huddled together near the door. Johan beckoned for them to follow and guided them towards his workshop in the back. It wasn't warm, but it was warmer than being outside, and the wool blanket would help considerably.

He placed the mattress in the corner, topped it with the blanket, and managed to whisper "For you" to the elves.

Johan was quite proud of himself for having accomplished getting any words out at all to them. It had been a long while since he'd been able to speak in front of strangers, and this was an unusually tense situation, after all.

"Thank you, this is very kind," the smaller and thinner of the two elves said to him. "Elias." He pointed at himself. "Henrik," the other elf said, his expression remaining understandably suspicious.

Johan offered them what he hoped was a friendly smile and stepped towards the door at the back; he opened it and gestured

to the outhouse. Thankfully, they both peered outside to look, and
Elias said, "The toilet?"

Johan nodded.

The sun had set, and with only the moon lighting the twilight
sky; Johan lit two lamps to brighten the dim room. He left one
for the elves and took the other before pointing to himself and
up at the ceiling to try to explain that he was going upstairs. He
couldn't imagine that the elves would feel safe or comfortable with
him looming over them.

Both elves nodded in understanding. "Thank you," Henrik and
Elias said at the same time.

Upstairs, Johan pottered around, restlessly cleaning and tidying
his home as he fretted about the two elves in his workshop. He'd
only been up there for an hour, though, when it suddenly occurred
to him that he hadn't offered them anything to eat or drink, and he
smacked his forehead with the palm of his hand, annoyed at himself
for the grievous error. His mother would turn in her grave if she
knew he'd been so remiss.

Not wasting any more time, Johan located his bag from the market and pulled out the small loaf of bread and wedge of cheese. He
cut two pieces of bread and placed some thinly sliced cheese on top,
assuming that, given how they had been living, eating too much at
once would probably upset their stomachs.

Johan took the stairs quietly so as not to startle them, food on a
small wooden tray in one hand and his oil lamp in the other. He
knocked gently on the door to his workshop but got no response,
so he eventually poked his head in.

The two elves were curled up together on the mattress, nose to
nose as they slept. Johan wasn't entirely sure why he was surprised

by what he saw. He knew, though, he was witnessing something extremely intimate that wasn't for his eyes and immediately felt guilty for intruding.

As quietly and quickly as he could, Johan placed the tray of food on a small table near their mattress in the hopes that mice wouldn't come looking for it and filled up two cups of the home-brewed beer from the barrel in the corner of the room. When he returned to place the cups on the table, Henrik's eyes were wide, staring at Johan with guilt and fear written all over his face.

Johan placed the cups down and held his hands up in a gesture he hoped told Henrik that everything was okay. He smiled and pointed to the food and then to the two of them, and Henrik audibly swallowed before thanking Johan in a whisper.

With a final glance at the sweet elves, Johan made his way back up the stairs before helping himself to a little food and climbing into bed.

He tossed and turned for a while and found himself blushing when he thought of the way the two of them lay together, a tangle of limbs.

Johan knew enough about the world to understand that there were men who lay together, even if people didn't talk about it much. He knew, for example, that the baker and his wife had some kind of arrangement where she spent her nights with Miss Klein, the local teacher, and he frequented one of the alehouses that was infamous for the rooms they kept upstairs with young men available as "companions" for an evening.

One thing Johan had learned to appreciate over his life was that, despite his difficulties with speaking in public and to strangers, his quiet nature meant he often went unnoticed. It was as though people thought he couldn't hear, either, their secrets spilling from their lips all around him.

Johan never did anything with the information he acquired; he merely enjoyed observing people and their relationships, even as he longed for one of his own.

The ache he felt at seeing Henrik and Elias together was a confusing one. He knew he had no right to feel envious of the comfort they got from each other—people who had endured what they must have deserved all the comfort they could find in this life—but the ember of envy was alive in his stomach all the same.

The confusion came from a second feeling, one that almost made his heart swell like he could take his own contentment just from seeing them together. It was a strange sensation, and one that Johan decided he would shove to one side for the time being as he couldn't quite decipher what it meant.

Sleep evaded him, and he spent a long time pondering his situation. He had very little money even for himself, and now that he'd taken on providing food and shelter for two others, he needed to come up with a plan. For once, though, the thought of needing to improve his prospects had some fire behind it. Rather than just a heavy, daunting burden, he felt motivated, and he was fairly sure that he had Elias and Henrik to thank for that.

Four

ELIAS

E lias stirred, momentarily confused about his whereabouts. He was warm in a way that he hadn't been since the summer, and it almost made him feel boneless. Reaching out a hand, Elias began to panic when he was met with an empty bed. Had the man, Johan was his name, done something to Henrik? He sat up quickly, searching for Henrik in the dimly lit room. The lamp was still burning on the workbench, illuminating a figure sitting before it. Elias relaxed at the familiar sight of Henrik's silhouette.

"Rik?" he asked, still a little bleary-eyed from sleep.

Henrik turned suddenly, startled. "Sorry, did I wake you?"

Elias shook his head. "No, I think I'm just no longer used to sleeping alone." He smiled sheepishly.

Henrik came to join him, sitting on the edge of the mattress and lifted something from the small table nearby.

"Here, you should eat something," he said, passing some bread topped with cheese to Elias.

His stomach growled with interest, but Elias felt quite sick. However, when Henrik continued to stare at him encouragingly, he took a small bite and chewed for a while. When he swallowed, Henrik was already there holding out a cup of something for him to wash it down with. Elias couldn't help but smile. At times, Henrik could be distant and frequently told Elias that his endless optimism made him want to gouge his own eyes out, but then, in moments like this, when Rik would act like a mother hen, Elias' heart grew ten sizes.

"How come you aren't sleeping?" Elias asked.

"I felt restless, and then I found some materials cut out to make a pair of shoes. Johan is a talented shoemaker, but his fingers and thumbs are too large for them to be truly intricate," Henrik explained matter-of-factly.

"You're making them for him?"

"I thought that if he could see what I can make, he might be inclined to let us rest here for a little longer," Henrik said softly. "Give us time to gain some strength before we decide where to go next."

Henrik returned to the workbench while Elias took a few more bites of the bread and cheese now that he felt less nauseated.

"Let me help," he said, joining Henrik. They sat side by side, the wool blanket wrapped around their shoulders as they worked together on the pair of brown leather shoes. It was familiar to work this way; they had done so in the mill on countless occasions, only there was a weight lifted now.

"It's different, isn't it?" Elias said, breaking the comfortable silence.

"What is?" Henrik replied.

"Working and creating things when it is your choice. When there is not a whip waiting for you if you dare to pause for breath."

Henrik pressed his shoulder more firmly into Elias'. "Yes," he choked out. "It is freedom. It is... everything."

The next morning, Elias woke with a sore neck. The two of them had fallen asleep at the workbench, leaning on one another. A soft knock on the door had woken him, but Henrik was still dead to the world.

Elias gently nudged him.

"Rik, wake up. Johan is here," he whispered.

Henrik startled with a gasp and looked around in fear just as Johan peeped his head around the door.

The large shoemaker waved at the two of them awkwardly before heading for the door towards the outhouse. By the time he returned, Elias and Henrik had made their way back over to the mattress and sat in the far corner nervously.

In one hand, Johan held a pail of water and fetched a cloth with the other. He placed the water on the floor near them and held the cloth out. Elias reached for it and said, "Thank you."

Johan nodded and appeared about to return back upstairs when he glanced towards his workbench and strode over. He picked up the right shoe first, looking at it closely before doing the same to the left. With both shoes in hand, he turned to face them with a perplexed expression.

Elias had expected Henrik to explain since it had been his idea, but he remained silent next to him.

"Elves are gifted craftsmen," Elias began. "Even with our magic bound." He held up his hands to show the copper bangles that prevented them from using magic. "If... if we could stay here a little longer, we could help you. If you let word get out that your shoes are elf-made, they will sell for more coin."

Johan looked back and forth between them and the shoe before reaching for something in his pocket. He pointed at them, then at the shoes, before holding up a silver coin.

"No, not for money. Only a place to stay until we can get back on our feet," Elias said, but Henrik elbowed him hard in the ribs. "What?"

"How do you expect that we get back on our feet without coin?" Henrik asked in a hushed tone.

"I don't know, but Johan is already doing enough for us."

Johan pointed at Henrik insistently and held up the coin again.

"What if you pay us coin for working for you, and we use some of the money to pay you for lodgings and food?" Henrik suggested.

Elias thought it was an idiotic idea. What was the point of Johan giving them money only for them to return it again? But Johan looked thoughtful and then nodded his head in agreement as though he understood something about Henrik that Elias did not, and it made his stomach clench.

Johan stepped towards them and held out his hand, first to Henrik, who shook it and then to Elias.

"Why are we shaking hands?" Elias whispered.

"It is how people in this kingdom make deals," Henrik explained. "It is your way of telling us we have a job and somewhere to sleep, no?"

Johan nodded and smiled before pointing at the water and the cloth again. He quickly scuttled from the room as much as a man that size was able to scuttle, leaving them to their morning ablutions.

Five

JOHAN

For once, Johan had a smile on his face when he headed towards the front of the shop to open up for the day. He'd spent a long while during the night trying to come up with a way to help the elves get back on their feet, but it had never crossed his mind that they might wish to work for him.

Money would be tight, but Elias had made a good point; elf-made shoes were not available currently anywhere in the kingdom, and if he was able to get word out to the wealthy parts of town, possibly even the castle, then the three of them stood a chance at making good money.

Getting word out was the problem, though, because words were always a problem for Johan.

While Elias and Henrik were using the outhouse, Johan grabbed a few supplies from his workshop and began making a sign to put up outside the shop. Most folks in this town weren't able to read, so it would take Johan the best part of the day to whittle an elf figurine to show to passersby that he was selling elf-made shoes now. It wasn't a hardship, though. Johan enjoyed whittling, and he no longer had a pair of shoes to make that day since Henrik and Elias had already made a pair far better than he could ever dream of during the night.

Johan was making good progress on his little wooden elf when Henrik and Elias peered around the door to the shop, scanning the place with fresh eyes now that the sun was out. Johan smiled at them but then frowned when he spotted them wearing those flimsy, dirty potato sacks again. He knew full well that he didn't currently have the coin to buy them new clothes, but then he remembered what Elias had said: *Elves are gifted craftsmen.*

With that thought in mind, Johan motioned for them to wait and hurried up the stairs. The wardrobe in the corner of the room had become an untouched relic in the years since his parents had passed. He'd never been quite able to part with all their belongings, but he felt good about giving the clothes to Henrik and Elias. His father's clothes would be much too big, and his mother's were skirts and dresses, but he was certain that with a sewing kit, Henrik and Elias would be more than capable of turning them into comfortable things for them to wear until they could afford something nicer.

Back down in the shop, Johan passed them the bundle of clothes and then rooted through his belongings in the workshop to locate his mother's old sewing kit and passed it to Elias.

"These clothes are for us?" Elias asked.

Johan pointed to the sewing kit to try to explain that they could alter them.

"We can use the fabric to make our own clothes?" Henrik said, seeming to have an uncanny ability to understand Johan despite his lack of speech. Johan nodded and smiled.

"Wow, that is incredibly generous. Thank you," Elias said, a grin stretching across his face.

"Yes, thank you," Henrik added, eyes lighting up at the bundle of material in his arms.

They rummaged through the bundle of clothes with covetous eyes that made Johan smile. In no time at all, they'd organised it all into various piles, and he was fairly certain they'd forgotten he was still in the room. So, Johan left them to it and returned to whittling the elf in the shop. He felt good about the new home for his parents' clothes, and he was now glad that he hadn't parted with them sooner.

Several hours passed by and Johan's carving was beginning to resemble a figurine, but his stomach was growling, so he closed the shop up for lunch.

When he stepped into the workshop with a tray of bread and dried meat for them all to eat, he'd expected to find Henrik and Elias under a mountain of fabric, but Elias was already wearing a pair of billowing wide-leg brown trousers with a tight cotton shirt and appeared to be adding the finishing touches to Henrik's outfit.

Henrik's clothing was more subdued than Elias', which seemed fitting for him. They'd tailored his breeches in a way that Johan had only seen among the wealthiest men in the kingdom, and his shirt, while looser fitting than Elias', seemed to complement his wider frame. The item Elias was adding the finishing touches to was a waistcoat made from the same fabric as the breeches.

It was fascinating to Johan how the clothes transformed them. While they were both still too thin, they were clean from bathing that morning and in fresh clothes that fit them like a glove; they looked refined in a way that made Johan's tongue stick to the roof of his mouth.

A tiny voice in Johan's head told him the word he was looking for was *handsome*. The two elves, though dressed completely differently, looked handsome in their new clothes, and the realisation made Johan blush furiously beneath his bushy beard.

"Is this okay?" Henrik asked when Johan had obviously been staring at him for longer than could ever be considered polite or respectable for a man to stare at another man.

Johan nodded and tried to busy himself by holding out the offering of food for them to see.

"Just one moment," Elias said before snipping some thread and freeing Henrik from the needle.

"This looks delicious. Thank you," Henrik said when they sat around the workbench to eat. Somehow, Henrik managed to frown and appear happy at the same time. Johan suspected that was just his face and didn't read too much into it.

Johan smiled and noticed that, despite Elias being the much thinner of the two, he reached for far less food, and he worried that Elias didn't like the dried meat. He pointed at Elias and the meat, then raised his eyebrow in question, but it was Henrik who spoke up for him.

"Elias has gone much longer than I have with little food. It will take him longer to adjust to richer foods like this."

Johan felt a deep need in his bones to understand why that was, but the words got stuck as usual, and his shoulders slumped in defeat.

Six

ELIAS

E lias' cheeks bloomed with embarrassment, but he had no reason to be. It wasn't as though he'd chosen to be starved for however long he'd endured this hunger for. "I enjoy the taste, though," he added.

"Why?" Johan coughed and pointed at Elias. "Longer?" he asked, and it looked like a strain for him to force the words past his lips, more so than usual.

"I wasn't taken like Rik was. My family was extremely poor, and so they sold me." Elias gulped, trying to force down the pain that spread like a poison to his heart at the memory of his parents standing at the door of their small hut while a slaver dragged him down the path as he kicked, screamed, and begged them to reconsider to no avail. While his big brother, Bjorn, had wept silently in the window, and the neighbours he'd known his entire life, looked the other way. Discovering you were disposable was a degree of anguish that Elias didn't wish upon anyone.

"I spent my first few years enslaved in a factory that made offensively ugly clothes," Elias joked to try to lighten the tale where he could. "Through nothing but sheer dumb luck, I was bathing in the outhouse when one of the other captured elves found a way to set a fire in the factory. The entire place went up in flames at a speed I didn't know was possible, but it killed almost everyone inside."

Elias nearly gagged and had to put down his food as the story of his past unearthed the memory of that smell—the stench of burning flesh as he watched from outside, unable to do a single thing to help. Even still, sometimes he would close his eyes, and the light from the flames would dance behind his eyelids, haunting him in his dreams.

"Anyway, a handful of us survived, and the owner's son sold us on as the factory was too destroyed to repair. Fortunately for me," Elias grinned. "I was bought by the owner of a silk textile mill."

"Fortunately? You cannot be sound of mind, Eli, to consider that turn of events fortunate." Henrik shook his head in disbelief.

"Well, on the bright side, my talents were finally being put to better use, and... there is the small matter that I met you, Henrik. I do not regret my time at the mill."

Elias could tell that Henrik didn't know what to say or where to even look in response to that. He also knew that Henrik didn't necessarily feel the same way. Which was okay. He couldn't hold it against Henrik that, given the choice, he wouldn't have been enslaved and therefore never would have met Elias. Okay, maybe it stung Elias a little, but he knew it wasn't rational.

"And that, is the cheery tale of how I ended up a sack of bones with the appetite of a baby bird."

Neither of them even cracked a smile, and Elias once again had the sinking feeling that he'd missed the mark with his sense of humour.

Henrik turned to look out of the window, his jaw tense and his lips tightly pressed together. Johan, however, reached across the table and took Elias' hand between both of his and stared into his eyes with an intensity that did something weird to Elias' stomach. Without any words at all, Johan's eyes managed to say, *I'm so sorry that happened to you*. And, more to Elias' surprise, *I will never let that happen to you again.*

"Thank you," Elias said quietly, no longer pretending to be so jovial about the worst years of his existence.

The rest of their lunch was quiet and a little awkward, but Elias felt lighter for having shared his story with Johan.

Later in the afternoon, Elias joined Johan in the shop as he continued whittling his elf figurine. Only, Elias couldn't help but take the carving and began including more intricate details, making the elf look almost the spitting image of Henrik. He made the long-pointed ears smoother, the elf's nose and chin a little sharper. Elias enjoyed the juxtaposition of Henrik having a slightly severe, sometimes harsh-looking face with such a soft, timid heart beneath.

They sold only one pair of shoes that day, but they were a large pair of leather boots—one of the more expensive items for sale, Elias noted—to Willhelm, the local blacksmith. When Willhelm had entered the shop, Henrik had scurried off into the back, but Elias had remained out front, curious about how Johan sold shoes to customers without his voice. It turned out to be a good thing, too, because evidently it was a significant struggle for Johan, so Elias stepped in and answered Willhelm's questions, putting his charming personality to good use. Elias could tell from Johan's soft smile that he was grateful for the assistance, and it made Elias feel like he actually had something to offer the shoemaker in return.

That night, once the three of them had eaten their evening meal together and Johan had left them for the night, the two elves returned to the bundle of clothes and the sewing kit. They quickly set to work using a few of the softer cotton items to make themselves some simple shirts and shorts to sleep in at night.

"We could embroider some flowers onto the shirts?" Elias suggested.

Henrik gave him an exasperated look. "Not everything needs to be a work of art, Eli. These are just for us to sleep in. We are the only ones who will even see them."

"What is wrong with wanting to look good for each other?" Elias asked, already retrieving the thicker threads from the sewing kit and going ahead with the embroidery regardless of Henrik's sour mood.

"Fine. Do as you please. I don't know why you bothered to ask me."

"Be careful, Rik. One day the wind will change, and you'll be stuck looking like you're sucking on a lemon for the rest of your life. And what a shame that would be because you're quite stunning when you forget to scowl for a moment," Elias said as he began using a black thread to create a sprig of heather over the chest pocket of the shirt.

Henrik huffed, blushing in embarrassment, Elias presumed. Despite the drastic turn in fortune for the two of them, Henrik seemed as miserable as he had been in the mill, and it infuriated Elias. What would it take for Henrik to be happy, he wondered?

They continued in silence after that, but Henrik waved the white flag first by passing his own garments to Elias so he could create similar patterns with the threads. Elias smiled smugly.

When they climbed into bed that night, with food in their stomachs, their own nightclothes, and a warm blanket, Elias realised he couldn't remember the last time he'd been so happy and content.

He snuggled into Henrik, who pressed a gentle kiss on his lips. For once, the fire that burned between them didn't feel rooted in a fear that it could be their final night. It felt to Elias like it came from a place deep within him, a place of want.

Elias brushed his lips in a featherlight touch to Henrik's, at first, letting their breaths mingle and the heat build. He luxuriated in the freedom to take his time, to savour the sweet taste of Henrik's mouth. The larger elf's wandering hands teased Elias under his nightshirt, stroking the sensitive parts of his skin, over his peaked nipples and down his ribcage. Elias shivered, but for once it wasn't from the cold.

Over the teasing, Elias passionately kissed Henrik, who opened his mouth wider, letting Elias press in with his tongue and tangle them together. Elias was so stiff and aroused his hips moved of their own accord, pushing his groin against Henrik's and groaning at the sweet friction against his already aching cock.

Henrik tugged down both their shorts and took—in Elias' opinion—his sweet time removing their shirts. But once they were skin on skin, all was forgiven. Elias would freeze time in these moments if he could. The intimacy of nothing between them, every bead of sweat shared, not even a breath of space separating them, it was what he longed for, eased the ache of loneliness and abandonment that Elias carried with him.

Henrik flipped Elias onto his back, and for a moment, Elias wondered if Henrik planned to enter him. Unfortunately for Elias, neither of them had been brave enough to sneak off with some of the butter from lunch, so they would have to forgo that for now.

Desire flooded Elias as Henrik loomed over him, kissing him hard and rutting against him. The feel of their cocks rubbing against one another as precum leaked from them both was enough to completely shut off Elias' brain. He wrapped his legs around Henrik's waist, chasing all the friction he could get. They both moaned, and probably not as quietly as they should with Johan upstairs and not wanting to get caught.

Well, mostly didn't wish to get caught. Elias couldn't deny that it was a little thrilling to think of Johan hearing them down here. When he got really excited, Elias could picture Johan walking in on them, hardening at the vision before him. Maybe he would reach into his breeches and tug on himself a little for relief. He might lick his lips and step closer, the need to see them overpowering propriety.

Elias whimpered, reaching down and rubbing the skin behind Henrik's sack, causing him to buck even harder than before. Gripping Henrik's hips, Elias tugged him as close as he could, getting the pressure he needed to find his release, and he'd never felt so alive. Henrik let go like he hadn't ever before. He rutted against Elias with an energy and passion Elias hadn't seen in him until now, and it was as though Elias was feeding off it.

Lost in a tangle of heat, limbs, wet lips, and the perfect pressure against his length, Elias erupted between them. A few more thrusts later and Henrik followed, their releases combining and covering their stomachs like icing on a cake.

Henrik flipped onto his back beside Elias, panting from the exertion, and they both took a moment to catch their breath.

As they lay side by side on the small mattress, Elias lifted Henrik's right hand and began playing with his fingers, making swirling patterns on his palm with his fingertips.

"I love your hands," Elias said mindlessly. Henrik's hands were bigger than his own and still looked refined despite the hard labour of the mills. Elias had been unaware that he could find hands to be so erotic, but he didn't question it too much.

"I suppose it's a good thing I didn't chop them off, then," Henrik replied dryly.

Elias turned his head to face him with a confused expression marring his features. "Why would you have chopped them off?"

"There was a time when we were at the mill that I thought if I were redundant to our captors, maybe they would set me free." Henrik's voice was solemn. He'd really considered chopping his hands off in a bid for freedom? The thought made Elias' stomach churn, grateful that he had evidence of Henrik's hand in his own as reassurance.

"So in this scenario where you've chopped off your hands, where was I? You were going to leave the mill handless, and I would remain?" Elias tried to make the question sound a little playful, but he couldn't deny that his feelings were hurt.

"No. If the price of freedom had actually been our hands, I would have chopped yours off, too. However, I realised quickly that the reward for doing so would have been death, and I wasn't quite ready for that form of freedom yet."

Elias let the words sink in; they were macabre but also oddly touching. "That's quite romantic in the most horrific way imaginable." Elias chuckled.

"Is that what we are to each other? Romantic?" Henrik asked, only, his tone was almost belittling of the fact, like it was an absurd suggestion.

Elias sat up on his elbow and looked down at Henrik. "If we are not romantic, then what are we to each other? Do you kiss me and touch me to pass the time? Is that all this has been to you?" Elias rarely found himself angry, but he was furious now.

Henrik's eyes widened, and he looked panicked. "I don't know," he said.

"You don't know? We are never apart, Henrik!"

"And what choice have we had in that? Is it truly romantic when we have had no other option than to rely on one another to survive?"

Elias was certain that if you opened up his chest in that moment, you'd find his heart clawed to pieces, blood seeping out, and the wounds preparing to fester because he couldn't imagine how a heart could heal from such a thing. How could he have been so wrong about Henrik? What else had he been wrong about?

"There were over one hundred elves in that mill; I chose you, Rik. I thought you chose me, too." Tears streamed down Elias' cheeks, and he climbed off the mattress, retrieving the nightshirt and shorts that Henrik had stripped him of not even an hour before.

He hated himself for crying right then. Hated that Henrik could see how much Elias had let him in, let him get too close. All so that Henrik would have a warm body to share his bed with. Elias felt sick.

"Where are you going?" Henrik asked.

"Anywhere else but here. I will not lie with you again, Henrik. I deserve more than to be a convenient *thing* for you to rut against," Elias spat.

"I—I never said that, Elias. You are twisting my words." Henrik retreated to the far corner of the mattress, bringing his knees to his chest protectively.

"No, you only told me this is not romantic to you while your release dries on my stomach. Damn you!"

Once Elias had shoved on his clothes, he stormed out of Johan's workshop without glancing back at Henrik. The only downside to his plan was that he really didn't have anywhere to go. He eyed the stairs, which led to Johan's home, and decided it was preferable to returning to Henrik's side.

At the top of the stairs, he pressed his ear to the door, trying to hear if there were any sounds coming from inside. There were faint footsteps, which at least reassured Elias that he wasn't waking Johan from sleep. He knocked gently on the door.

The footsteps got louder as Johan approached. He opened it and peered down at Elias, looking understandably surprised to find him there.

Elias took Johan's quizzical look as an "Is everything okay?"

"Henrik is impossible. I cannot stay down there with him. I will find somewhere to live tomorrow, but I wondered if I might sleep up here. Just for tonight? Not in your bed, of course, just in the corner somewhere. I'm quite small. I won't be a bother," Elias rambled on at Johan, who looked worried.

Johan pointed down the stairs towards the workshop and tilted his head to the side in question.

"Henrik is fine. Now we are free, he doesn't want me around anymore, so I refuse to burden him with my company any longer." Elias tried to puff his chest out with confidence, but he hiccupped at the end of his speech and then burst into tears again.

Glancing down the stairs once more with a concerned frown on his face, Johan pressed a warm hand to Elias' shoulder and guided him inside.

Johan's home was small but clean and tidy, and he pulled out a chair at the table for Elias to sit down. Once Johan had fetched them both a drink, he dipped his chin at Elias in a way that he assumed was asking him to explain what had happened.

Elias took a large gulp of his drink and then some steadying breaths. At first, he wasn't sure how much to say since he knew that men being with men was generally kept behind closed doors in this kingdom in contrast to the norm of it amongst the elves back home. But then he looked into Johan's kind, warm chestnut eyes and trusted his gut. Henrik had already told him that Johan had seen them curled up together the night they'd arrived here, and he had been nothing but kind to them regardless.

"Henrik has been... more than a friend to me?" he phrased it like a question, and Johan nodded in understanding and, thankfully, without judgment, so Elias went for it. "Well, I love Henrik. I thought he was my... my forever, you know? But it seems he was with me because he thought I was the only option." Elias hiccupped again.

Johan looked sadly at Elias and shook his head.

"It's the truth," he tried to explain.

"Your truth," Johan rasped out. Elias was momentarily shocked by hearing anything at all come from the silent man's lips that it took him a few seconds to register what he'd said.

"No. *The* truth," Elias insisted.

"No," Johan spoke again and wrapped his big hand over Elias'.

Somehow, Elias knew that Johan had reached his limit on words, and so he merely huffed in response. They finished their drinks in silence before Johan guided Elias over to a large mattress on the floor.

"I can sleep on the ground; it's okay," Elias tried to argue.

Johan just shook his head, and Elias found he was too exhausted to really put up a compelling fight. He crawled into the far corner of the bed, leaving the blanket for Johan on the other side.

Johan, however, picked up the blanket and placed it over Elias, tucking in the edges and making him feel like a cocooned caterpillar.

"Thank you," Elias whispered.

A short while after, Elias could hear footsteps fading and the front door closing.

Why was it that Henrik could rip out Elias' heart, crush the only thing that had kept him alive the last few years, and yet he was left to comfort himself while Johan sought out Henrik? How was that fair?

Elias almost laughed. Nothing in his life had been fair. Why would life change its mind now?

Seven

HENRIK

A tight fist closed around Henrik's lungs, stealing his ability to breathe as he watched the door close behind Elias. Still naked and suddenly shrouded in shame, he wrapped the blanket around himself and tried to take a breath. Only, he was fairly certain that he must have been struck by a spontaneous, deadly illness because he couldn't breathe!

Henrik's heart began beating as if it was attempting to burst free from his chest, and his vision blurred. All concepts of time warped, leaving Henrik unsure of how long he'd gone without breathing.

He was sure he should have met his end when large, firm hands gripped his shoulders. The persistent ringing noise in his ears had drowned out the sound of approaching footsteps, but the big hands shaking him were the least of his concerns. Evidently, this deadly illness included sudden blindness as he couldn't get his eyes to focus, and to top it off, he was no longer able to feel his legs.

Anguish held him in its clutches as he lamented over how he'd hurt his love, and he could never make things right with him because he was going to die from this; he had no doubt.

The hands persisted and cupped his face, making shushing sounds. Arms that were much too large and strong to be Elias' wrapped around him, squeezing around his chest so tight it ought to be suffocating, but instead of making it harder to breathe, they somehow made it easier.

When the familiar scent of leather and musk broke through the haze of panic, Henrik deduced that it was Johan who was holding him and rocking him from side to side. Instead of Death coming for him, only Johan had. And Johan seemed to have some kind of connection to magic himself because as he rocked Henrik like you might a babe, he found that the fist around his lungs loosened its grip slightly, allowing him to finally fill his lungs, and as he calmed, his vision slowly came back into focus.

Eventually, Johan relaxed his arms from around Henrik. Shame and embarrassment almost threatened to send him spiralling back into panic as he absorbed what Johan had just witnessed. What he'd thought was some kind of sudden illness was clearly a ludicrous response to his argument with Elias. He shuffled away from Johan then, trying to hide within the thick wool blanket as though that would make him appear less foolish, or at the very least, protect Henrik from seeing what must be a look of judgement on the shoemaker's face.

It wasn't successful because Johan patted his back through the blanket until Henrik eventually gave in and poked his head out.

"Is Elias...?" was all he could get out, his voice raw from his hysterics.

Johan nodded his head and pointed up the stairs to where he lived. Henrik had assumed as much, given Elias didn't really have anywhere else to go.

Henrik was grateful that Johan didn't press for more. He just sat next to him on the mattress, patting his back occasionally, but his presence was like having a calm, immovable rock nearby that made all of Henrik's fears seem a little less scary, and the judgemental expression he'd been expecting was nowhere to be found.

After a while, Henrik found he did, in fact, desperately need someone to talk to.

"I said something hurtful to Elias that I didn't mean," he confessed, barely above a whisper.

Johan merely nodded in a way that suggested this was not new information to him.

"I was worried that Elias was only with me because we had been trapped together, but what I said made it sound instead like that was why I was with him. I doubt I will ever understand why Elias cares for me—"

Johan cut him off there with a derisive snort that Henrik chose to ignore.

"But Elias is easy to love. He's like the sun in the sky, and I am the rain. The rain is wet and miserable. Nobody with any sense likes the rain," Henrik said mournfully.

There was a beat of silence, and then Johan rasped, "Plants do."

Henrik let out a wet laugh at that and wiped under his eyes with the back of his hand. "You're a good listener, thank you."

Johan chuckled sardonically.

"I don't mean because you hardly speak." Henrik gave him a scornful look. "I mean, you are able to say a lot, even without your words. It's a gift few men possess, in my experience. I can't claim it's a strength of either Elias or myself," Henrik added dryly.

Johan's smile was warm, and Henrik felt less like the miserable rain. He pondered that maybe Johan was an umbrella, well equipped for the relentless drizzle that poured from Henrik's soul.

Standing, Johan reached out a hand for Henrik. Only, when Henrik stood, the blanket fell off him, leaving him naked. Johan stared for a moment at Henrik's exposed body before blushing and quickly turning away. Henrik wasn't ashamed of his body; there was no room to be shy of it working in the mill, but he was rather embarrassed when he remembered that his stomach and now-soft cock, still contained the evidence of his and Elias' earlier release.

Henrik grabbed his nightclothes and hastily changed before wrapping the blanket back around himself and following Johan up the stairs.

Johan led the way into a sparsely decorated home, which was unsurprising to Henrik. The place had what Johan needed and was taken care of, though.

In the far corner of the room, Henrik could see a lump under a blanket, and he gulped. He was suddenly not so sure of how he was supposed to make things right with Elias, and waking him from his sleep didn't seem like an excellent start, but Johan nudged him forward and indicated to Elias with his chin.

Henrik slowly approached the lump on the bed as if one wrong move might lead to him having a limb bitten off. He took a steadying breath before lying down on his side to face his love.

"Eli?" he whispered.

Fierce amber eyes shot open and glared back at him in the dim room. Henrik bit his lip.

"I'm sorry," he began, but Elias stubbornly turned to face the other way.

Unsure of how to proceed, Henrik looked back over to where Johan stood, begging him with his eyes for help. Johan sighed but came over and gently shook Elias' foot to get his attention. Once Elias glanced his way, Johan pointed at him, then tugged on his ear and then pointed at Henrik.

"No," Elias replied before returning to his spot facing the wall. Henrik sighed in defeat, but Johan had clearly had enough of the elves' antics that night and grabbed a damp washcloth from where it was drying on the back of a chair and—very accurately—launched the cloth at Elias' face.

Elias sat up angrily at that, throwing the cloth onto the floor. "This is abuse," he squawked indignantly. Johan just rolled his eyes before once more pointing at Elias, tugging his ear, then pointing at Henrik and making a talking motion with his hand. With that, Johan left them to it and busied himself over in the kitchen, clearly clattering around to give them the illusion of privacy.

Henrik tried again. "I didn't mean what I said. I'm so sorry, Eli. I think there's something wrong with me where I just spoil things. I'm like a poison, and you deserve better than me." Henrik nervously worried his fingers.

Elias huffed. "Why did you say it, then?"

"I... I worried that was why you were with me. Like with everything else, you were stuck with me, so you made the best of it. And now that we could go our separate ways if we wanted to, I thought you might. Like... like if I pushed you away first, it might hurt less when you left me," Henrik confessed with a degree of vulnerability he'd never before offered to a single soul in his life. But if anyone deserved the raw honesty, it was Eli.

"You are an imbecile," Elias responded to Henrik, exposing his tattered heart.

"I am. But... I... I do love you, Elias. There is not a day of this life I don't wish to spend with you, and that's quite terrifying," Henrik admitted.

At that, Elias finally turned to face him, and most of the anger had melted from his expression. "Do you really?"

"Love you?"

Elias nodded.

"Like I've never loved anyone." Henrik swallowed the lump in his throat.

"Such an imbecile," Elias muttered again, only this time, he pressed his lips to Henrik's for a gentle kiss.

The gesture was as familiar to Henrik as breathing. He adored the feel of those soft lips that so often stretched to blind him with his favourite smile in the world. The smile he couldn't live without and that would have haunted him forever if he'd really destroyed what they had. He loved the little puff of air that Elias let out after they kissed and treasured it now, breathing it in and keeping it safe in his heart.

He hadn't ruined everything after all, and the relief almost brought him to his knees. They still had each other, and they would be okay.

Elias lifted the blanket he was wrapped in, inviting Henrik to join him. Henrik didn't hesitate, snuggling in as close as he could get and kissing Elias on his neck where he smelled divine, the perfect combination of masculine and feminine that was so perfectly him.

Exhaustion weighed heavily on Henrik now that the turbulent events of the evening were resolved, and keeping his eyes open was a struggle, but he needed to look into Elias' eyes once more to be reassured that his affection remained there. Glittering amber eyes gazed softly back at him.

"I love you, too, Rik," Elias whispered, pecking another kiss to the tip of Henrik's nose.

Eight

JOHAN

J ohan wasn't sure what to do. Sitting on a wooden chair at his dining table, he waited until Elias and Henrik finished resolving their quarrel and the sound of soft snores drifted across the room. The only problem was they were snoring softly in *his* bed. And he had no desire to sleep downstairs on a mattress that was too short for him to lie out on.

In the end, Johan deliberated on it for almost an hour before he struggled to keep his eyelids open. He grabbed the other blanket Henrik had discarded when he joined Elias and slept on the far end of his mattress. The elves were wrapped so tightly around one another that they took up very little room anyway.

Johan would like to think he was a better man than to go to sleep with the image of Henrik's naked body behind his eyelids, and that he was *definitely* above replaying the soft moaning sounds that had floated up the stairs earlier that evening, but he wasn't in the business of lying to himself.

After Elias had lain down to rest, something had tugged at Johan's gut, telling him to go and check on Henrik. He'd seen how Henrik was around Elias, and it left him with no doubt whatsoever that the elf loved him. Johan had observed enough people interacting to have quickly deduced that there had been a drastic misunderstanding.

He hadn't, however, expected to find Henrik having some kind of fear attack. They had happened to Johan quite frequently when he was younger. There were more occasions than he could bear to think about where his determined parents would try to force him to speak to strangers in an unsuccessful attempt at having him overcome his "curse," as they called it. The endeavour almost always ended with Johan in tears and struggling to breathe. The feeling was so familiar to him that seeing Henrik experience it had hurt his heart and ripped open old wounds.

He was grateful in some ways that the two of them were sleeping up here where he could see them. Johan would have worried about Henrik otherwise. Despite Elias being the physically weaker of the two, Johan didn't worry about him in the same way. There was a re-silience and fight to Elias that Johan imagined would burn eternally; it was something not even the cruelty of slavery had snuffed out.

Johan tossed and turned for a while, unable to get himself to sleep as he usually would, with his fist wrapped around himself. In the end, he settled for lying on his side and listening to the soft, even breathing of Henrik and Elias as they slept. It was dangerous how much Johan could get used to this. How something so foreign could feel so comfortingly familiar only he knew it wouldn't become so. He knew that this was an exception, and they hadn't intended to spend the night in his bed, so he promised himself he would appreciate it for the rare gift that it was.

J ohan scrubbed at his eyes with his knuckles when he woke. Only, when his sight came back into focus, there were two sets of amber eyes staring back.

The two elves lay on their sides facing him. Elias was in front, Henrik tucked behind him with his head resting in the crook of Elias' neck, peering at Johan with wide eyes.

"We're sorry we took over your bed," Elias whispered, but the way his lips quirked up in the corners indicated he wasn't all that sorry, and Johan couldn't help but smile, his heart feeling full at not waking up alone for the first time in over six winters.

"Can we make you breakfast to thank you?" Henrik asked.

Johan almost said no, because he didn't need them to thank him. But then it occurred to him that maybe it would make them feel less indebted, and it would be nice to have a meal he hadn't had to make for himself, so he smiled and nodded.

Henrik looked relieved. "We'll go wash up quickly and then come and make something to eat."

Elias blushed, and that made Johan recall why they probably wanted to wash up right away, which in turn made *him* blush. Only his reaction seemed to give away to the elves that he knew they'd been intimate last night, and now they were all as red as tomatoes and avoiding eye contact.

Thankfully, Henrik quickly grabbed Elias' hand and tugged him out the door, which gave Johan the opportunity to get himself together before they returned.

Johan kept himself occupied by tearing up some newspaper and building up the kindling and logs inside the fireplace. By the time Henrik and Elias came back, there was a roaring fire, and Johan was less at risk of standing to attention in his breeches by recalling the soft moans of the two—entirely too handsome for his health—elves he lived with.

Johan pointed to the cupboards and gestured for them to help themselves while he left to use the outhouse.

As he walked back up the stairs afterwards, he could hear light giggles and gentle ribbing between the two elves, and it made him smile. Inside, he found them side by side in front of the fire, keeping an eye on a small pot they'd placed on the flames.

Johan poured the three of them each a drink of water and placed three forks on the table. A lump formed in his throat at the image of three place settings before him. In recent years, he'd even begun avoiding eating at his table altogether, finding it a painful reminder of how alone he was—but not that morning.

Elias trotted over from the fireplace with the pot in hand and a bounce to his step, and Henrik grabbed some slices of bread from the kitchen. Johan tried to reach for the pot, but Elias shooed him away. "Where we're from," Elias explained, "the people who cook the meal, serve the meal, especially when a meal is a gift. This isn't a very good gift since you bought all the food yourself, but next time, it will be better." He grinned and began scooping eggs out of the pot and onto the slice of bread Henrik had placed on Johan's wooden plate.

They were about halfway through their meal when Johan managed to whisper, "Thank you." He spoke so quietly, in fact, that had the elves not had exceptionally good hearing, they probably would have missed it.

But they did hear, and Henrik said, "No, thank *you*, Johan."

"For everything," Elias added.

After breakfast, the elves returned to the workshop, claiming it needed reorganising in order for them both to be able to work efficiently at the same time. Rather than take offence that Elias clearly didn't think the space was ideal, Johan was mostly relieved that someone other than him was taking some responsibility for the shop and left them to it.

Johan stepped out onto the cobbled street, taking a moment to notice the weather. It was his favourite kind of day—the air was cold enough that his breath puffed out ahead of him, but the sky above was a cloudless cerulean blue.

Johan nodded and smiled at the neighbouring shop owners as they set up for the day, and he used a wooden step to affix the little wooden shoe and elf figurine to the shop sign.

Across the street, Mr Müller, the baker, was arguing with his delivery boy, who'd once again turned up with a fraction of what the baker had ordered. Food really was becoming a sparse commodity, but it was a worry Johan stubbornly ignored due to its being so far from his control. If things got dire in the spring, he could return to his family's hunting cabin or go fishing to get what he needed. There was no way that the forest could be as barren as the townsfolk implied.

Johan distracted himself by stepping back to admire his and Elias' whittling efforts, and he was hopeful that the rumour mill would do what they needed it to.

That afternoon, a man dressed in smart, tailored clothes entered the shop. His attire suggested he was from the wealthier part of town, and Johan had butterflies fluttering in his stomach.

The man didn't say hello; he just walked in and looked around somewhat disapprovingly. "Your sign outside. Your shoes are elf-made?" he asked.

Johan stepped forward and picked up the fine leather shoes from the shop window and passed them to the man to inspect. "Hmm. But how do I know they *are* in fact made by elves, since you are clearly not one?" he asked as his gaze raked judgementally up and down Johan's form, which couldn't be *less* elf-like.

Johan held up a finger, asking the man to give him a moment, and went to look for Elias and Henrik in the workshop.

In an incredibly brief span of time, they had transformed the space and set up three workstations. The sight made Johan's chest warm. Each time he witnessed them carving out space for themselves in his little world, it reassured him that there was a sense of permanence to their presence in his life.

Sitting on one of the chairs was Elias, with Henrik standing behind, braiding his long white hair. Elias beamed when he spotted Johan in the doorway.

Johan pointed in the direction of the shop and beckoned for the two elves to follow him out; thankfully, they obliged.

The customer looked shocked to see Elias and Henrik appear behind him.

"You made these?" he asked, holding up the brown leather shoes.

"The left one," Elias replied.

"I made the right," Henrik added.

"Do you take commissions?" The man directed the question at Johan, clearly assuming that he owned the elves rather than employed them since a free elf was rare and practically unheard of among the poor, but he just waited for Elias to answer.

They looked at each other, clearly having some kind of silent conversation before Elias spoke up. "We take commissions, but fifty percent of the price is required up front in order to cover the cost of the materials."

"What's the total cost for one pair?"

"That would depend on the shoe, sir." He turned his attention to Henrik. "Could you find me some parchment and graphite?"

Henrik didn't reply; he dashed into the back quickly, clearly not comfortable speaking to customers like Elias was. Johan could relate.

When Henrik returned, Elias set to work asking the customer questions and sketching designs on the parchment while Johan and Henrik both stood there looking bewildered. Eventually, Elias came over to the counter to charge the man for his order, and Johan's eyes nearly popped out of his head at the number of coins the customer seemed more than happy to part with. It was twice what he'd made the entirety of summer.

"They will be ready to collect three days from now, Mr Von Baden," Elias said, bowing his head respectfully.

The man looked surprised but pleased. "I look forward to it. Good day." He tipped his hat to them all before leaving the shop.

Henrik said exactly what Johan was thinking. "How?"

The look of deference on Elias' face for the customer vanished instantly to be replaced by a mischievous glint in his eyes. "He's trying to woo a princess from a neighbouring kingdom. I convinced him that three different pairs of uniquely designed shoes would be the most effective way to display his wealth and style. He is not a bright man, but he is a rich one." Elias stacked the coins and grinned at the pile gleefully.

"And people think you're the sweet innocent one," Henrik said fondly.

"What do you think, Johan? Do you think I look sweet and innocent?" Elias peered up at Johan through pale-white lashes, a playful look in those amber eyes.

Johan appreciated that Elias had made a habit of including him in conversations with yes and no questions, but he found himself wanting to try to reply anyway.

He took a gulp of air and pointed at Elias, blurting out, "You're trouble."

Henrik burst out laughing, holding his stomach as he cackled while Elias clutched his chest in mock offence.

As though the sun was beaming down on him alone, Johan's chest filled with so much warmth and happiness he could hardly contain it. A giggle bubbled out of him, and he slapped a hand over his mouth at the shock of a sound he couldn't recall falling from his lips since he was a child. This *thing*, this forever unattainable thing for Johan, was finally in his grasp, and it flooded him with joy. He had actual friends, people who laughed and joked with him, not just in front of him.

It was like taking off an invisibility cloak he'd never meant to wear in the first place.

J ohan studied Elias where he was perched atop the workbench, his chin resting on one knee with his other leg tucked under him. He looked like a ball of yarn to Johan, who couldn't fathom how it was a comfortable way to sit, yet Elias had been contorted that way for some time.

It was more fascinating to Johan than it ought to be when Elias' tongue peeked out from between his lips as he concentrated on the parchment in front of him. Elias wrote with his left hand, which Johan had been taught was a sign of the devil, but as he deftly twiddled some graphite in his devil hand, Johan decided that heaven might be overrated after all.

Despite being the thinner of the two elves, Elias was softer looking. The way he kept his slightly waved hair tied up loosely atop his head so strands would escape and frame his face made Elias look more approachable somehow.

Elias must have felt Johan's obtrusive gaze because he glanced up and smiled.

"Would you like to look at my designs for Mr Von Baden?" Elias asked.

I would like to look at you *more,* Johan thought.

Johan was caught in a distressing dilemma where if he found himself showing too much interest in Elias, he was overcome with guilt because Elias' heart belonged to Henrik. And then he would catch himself thinking of Henrik's beautiful naked body and be overwhelmed with remorse because it was Elias who Henrik chose to give his naked body to.

The whole thing left Johan in a terrible loop of arousal, shame, guilt, and lust. But like a moth to a flame, Johan stepped closer and peered over Elias' shoulder to look at his designs.

"I am having some trouble with this," Elias pointed to his measurements.

The mathematics was questionable, to say the least. Johan held out his hand, and Elias passed him the piece of graphite. Their fingers brushed, and Johan had to fight the shudder that travelled along his spine. It wasn't only that the feel of another person's skin touching his was rare; it was that it was Elias' skin. Perfect, soft, and warm, it left Johan with what he could only describe as a slightly sick feeling in his stomach. It was a *good* sick feeling, though.

Johan made quick work of correcting the errors in the measurements before returning the graphite to Elias so he could continue with the design.

The impish elf grinned at Johan. "We make a good team, kjære."

Johan had no idea what kjære meant and didn't have the words to ask, but Elias had said it kindly, so he was fairly certain it was a good thing.

Elias may not have been skilled in mathematics, but his designs were mesmerising. They were unlike anything Johan could have even imagined, let alone put onto parchment. The most incredible part, though, was how at peace Elias looked in his element. It made Johan want to carve out a corner of the earth where Elias could safely design beautiful things and nobody could ever hurt him again. And for the first time, Johan thought that maybe he *could*.

Nine

ELIAS

The following day, after Elias had finished designing the three pairs of shoes for Mr Von Baden, he decided to clean the shop while he waited.

Henrik and Johan had left for the market to buy material while Elias minded the shop. Johan hadn't been able to fully explain, but Elias suspected he worried about him and Henrik being spotted in public and someone attempting to take them, so he didn't like them to go out unaccompanied.

In the shop, however, Elias felt surprisingly safe. He liked it here a lot and was grateful to discover that his experiences in the mills hadn't killed all the joy he found in creating beautiful things.

Turning the old clothes that Elias assumed once belonged to some of Johan's family into garments for him and Henrik to wear proudly had reignited Elias' passion. Because Elias loved beautiful things. He loved the journey of an idea to a design, to a tangible thing he could behold.

Elias was cleaning one of the window displays and humming a tune to himself when he spotted Johan and Henrik walking down the street together. He watched them curiously. Johan smiled and laughed at whatever Henrik was saying to him, and when he saw the way they looked at each other, Elias prepared for a stab of jealousy—only it didn't come. After the argument he'd had with Henrik the other night, he felt more reassured of what they had together than ever before.

But Elias couldn't deny what he could see with his own eyes. Would it bother Elias if Rik also had feelings for Johan?

He was sure it should, although he wasn't entirely convinced that it would, because he was looking at two men who clearly held affection for one another and the only feeling he could muster right then was a degree of fondness for them both. How bizarre. As with most things in Elias' life, he chose not to question it too much. Life had given him enough reasons in the last few years to feel genuine misery; he wasn't going to prematurely invite any unnecessary sorrow.

The two of them had barely stepped inside when Elias asked, "Notice anything different?" He flourished his arms to their surroundings.

Henrik looked predictably suspicious as he stared around the room, but Johan smiled and whispered softly, "Clean."

Elias beamed before quickly getting distracted by the smell of warm cheese pastries. His stomach growled so loudly that he blushed.

Johan passed Elias the brown paper bag, which contained the new fine scratch awl he'd requested along with plenty of leather.

"The man in the market where we bought the supplies said he would spread word that we're selling elf-made shoes," Henrik explained as he led the way into the workshop with the bag of pastries.

"I'm excited to get started," Elias replied. "I thought it might feel too similar to the work in the mills, but I feel free. Even with these." Elias waved his bangled wrists in the air, and Johan frowned at them before silently leaving the room and returning with two handfuls of coins that he dropped onto the table. He pointed at the pile of money and then at the bangles on Elias' wrists.

Elias tried not to be miffed that Johan had just dumped all his carefully stacked coins. "I'm sorry, I don't understand," Elias said.

"You think we should use the money to get them removed?" Henrik asked, as if he could read Johan's mind somehow.

Johan nodded emphatically.

"We would need a sorcerer, and we won't use any of your share," Henrik said sternly.

Johan pointed to himself and then tapped his index finger to his temple.

"You know of a sorcerer?" Elias asked, fairly sure he understood Johan that time.

Johan tilted his hand from side to side as if to say "sort of."

"It's worth a try, don't you think, Rik?"

Small flames of hope lit inside Elias' chest, but he dared not stoke them just yet.

"It would be a relief to be rid of them. Plus, if we were able to make shoes infused with magic, we could charge more than double the current fees." Henrik was always the pragmatic thinker.

"Let's wait until we get the rest of the money from this sale because I've no doubt it will be costly," Elias said, forcing himself to be patient, and both Henrik and Johan agreed.

Elias swallowed the lump of emotion in his throat at the thought. Five years. Five years since he'd been able to speak to magic, feel her thrum through his veins with beautiful light energy. He ached for it like he'd never ached for anything in his life. Without it, he often felt like a guest inside his own body.

A sorcerer had created and used spells to make the bangles unbreakable. Would they even be able to find someone strong enough to undo such magic?

"It was our pleasure," Elias said to a grateful Mr Von Baden a few days later when he collected his commissioned shoes—parting with a hefty sum of money in the process.

It was enough that the three of them could finally begin preparing for their trip into the Dark Forest to locate a sorcerer.

Elias and Henrik had offered to go alone, but Johan insisted that it wasn't safe, and so the little shoe shop would be closed for nearly a week. Elias hoped that the sorcerer wouldn't require all the coin they'd earned because he wasn't convinced Johan could really afford to be shut for so long.

While Johan packed bags with whatever they would need for the trip, Elias and Henrik busied themselves in the kitchen preparing food for the journey. Johan had warned them that even keeping up a fast walking pace, it would probably be almost four days each way, which meant they would have to set up a camp each night. Elias felt a strange mix of excitement and trepidation about the trip because the temperatures had dropped significantly, and he and Henrik still didn't really have the body mass to withstand any truly bitter weather.

Elias glanced at Henrik, whose tongue poked out the side of his lips while he concentrated on the sandwiches he was making. Overcome with affection, Elias smacked a big kiss to Henrik's cheek, which startled him.

"What was that for?" he asked, a pink blush blooming across his cheeks.

Elias didn't reply, merely shrugging with a big grin aimed at his lover. Sometimes he just wanted to squeeze Henrik until he popped. *Lovingly*, of course.

Once they'd finished, they found Johan in the workshop with the knapsacks, two of which were considerably lighter and one which looked so heavy a donkey might struggle with it; however, Johan hoisted it over his shoulder and fitted it across his back with a reassuring ease that, frankly, Elias found quite attractive. Judging by Henrik's expression, he agreed. Elias' bag was large but light, presumably filled with the wool blankets to keep them warm at night.

"Ready?" Johan asked, his voice raspy. The shoemaker's voice sent a shiver down Elias' spine. It was gravelly and raw and its use such a rare gift that the effect of it always took Elias by surprise.

"As ready as we'll ever be," Elias replied, and he and Henrik shifted the sacks onto their backs.

They were just about to leave when Johan held up a finger, asking them to wait while he dashed back up the stairs. He reappeared a few minutes later holding out two sets of knitted hats, scarves, and gloves.

Johan gave the green set to Henrik and handed the dark orange to Elias. The elf's fingers trembled at the sight. Elias didn't cry. He wouldn't cry over a hat, scarf, and gloves. His eyes were merely watering from the frigid cold air.

"Let me?" Johan asked.

Elias nodded, not trusting that his voice wouldn't warble.

Johan picked up the hat and placed it snugly on Elias' head. Where he expected it to trap his pointed ears uncomfortably, it did not.

"You... you got these made for us?" Henrik said, staring at how Elias' ears poked out of the sides where it had been designed to fit an elf perfectly.

Johan appeared bashful as he nodded. Busying himself, Johan wrapped the matching scarf around Elias' neck and tucked his slim, fine fingers into the mittens.

Nobody had ever bought Elias a gift before, let alone something as thoughtful as this. Johan couldn't possibly understand what this meant to Elias, but as he glanced at Henrik, his expression was a mirror of his own. There was something incredibly overwhelming about receiving so much kindness after years of unrelenting cruelty.

Elias didn't want to dwell on that, though. He smiled down at his warm, cosy hands and let the comfort of being cared for into his heart.

Both of them choked up as they thanked Johan profusely. When they all left the shop, so early that the sun had yet to rise, they were even more grateful for the added warmth.

In companionable silence, Johan and the elves walked down the dark, quiet streets until they reached the edge of the forest. Elias and Henrik hadn't set foot near the Dark Forest since the night before they'd accepted Johan's offer of a place to stay, and it felt strange coming back. The forest was where they had found their freedom, where they'd sought refuge but also where they'd feared being found by dogs each night and where they had both been on the road to starvation.

Three hours had passed by the time the sun finally rose high enough to breach the tree canopy above. Elias found it easier to relax when they were no longer shrouded in darkness. The light formed all sorts of patterns on the ground, which Elias focussed on as he trudged down the path.

Henrik was walking well ahead of him, which Elias was bitter about. He was a long way off his full strength, and several full days of walking were going to be a challenge. Every step felt as though Elias were once again in leg irons, and he'd never felt such resentment towards his own body.

In the mills, Elias had become an expert in ignoring his pain and discomfort, and he was determined he could do so again, gritting his teeth as each foot forward sent shooting pains up his legs.

Johan was keeping pace with him, and he appreciated how he did so without drawing attention to the fact. For once, Elias was grateful for the silence that came with keeping company with Johan, because if he spoke now, he was sure he couldn't hide from the perceptive shoemaker how much pain he was in.

A while later, they found Henrik perched on a tree stump waiting for them to catch up with him. Elias glared at him, but Henrik didn't seem to notice, which only set to aggravate him more.

"I wasn't sure which way to go next," Henrik said to Johan.

Johan pointed to the pathway that was mostly straight ahead.

"Are you sure you know where you're going?" Henrik asked, looking sceptically at the track.

In his defence, it was the least well-trodden of the three currently available to them.

Elias looked at Johan for his response and burst out laughing at the incredulous look on the shoemaker's face, which gave all the answers they needed. Without words, his face said "Of course I do." Elias was grateful for the distraction.

"I was merely checking in case you were too embarrassed to tell us we were lost," Henrik said in an attempt to defend his question.

At that, Johan turned to face Henrik with his hands on his hips. "I'll... I'll lose *you*," he sputtered out.

Then, in a moment of absolutely perfect timing, an animal growled somewhere in the distance, and Henrik leapt at Johan, who managed to catch him in his arms, and buried his face in Johan's chest while he quivered.

It was a little cruel of Elias to take enjoyment from Henrik's panic, but on this occasion, it felt quite deserving of his petulant attitude, so he didn't feel bad.

Johan laughed as he held Henrik in his strong arms. A thick vein bulged along his meaty forearm, and Elias decided he'd never given enough credence to how attractive a forearm could be.

"Why are you both laughing? We're going to be eaten by wolves!"

Elias should probably have been more concerned by the growl himself, but for some reason, Johan's dismissal of the noise was reassurance enough to him that they weren't in any immediate danger. It shocked him a little to realise how much he trusted Johan.

Watching him now as he cried with laughter, Elias' lover in his arms, scowling like an angry kitten, he began to wonder if maybe Johan had needed them as much as they had needed him. That maybe fate had given them the missing pieces of themselves that day outside the market.

Once Henrik was returned safely to the ground, he kicked a rock and sulked. "What is it, then, if it is not a wolf?"

Johan placed a hand on Henrik's shoulder, smiling at him gently as he whispered, "Badger."

Henrik's cheeks pinkened as he registered how much he'd over-reacted to a little badger in the woods, but Johan merely moved his hand to Henrik's back and encouraged him to keep walking.

For the remainder of the day, Henrik walked between them instead of ahead.

E lias was fighting tears when Johan finally gestured for them to stop and began setting up their camp for the night.

Johan connected a rope between two trees and used a rolled-up hide to create their shelter for the night. Clenching his jaw, Elias forced himself to help when Henrik began collecting firewood, but when he tripped over a tree root, the floodgates opened and he burst into tears.

"What's wrong? Are you okay?" Henrik ran over, then started rubbing a hand over him as if to search for injury.

"I'm f-f-f-fine," Elias stuttered and then hiccupped.

He wanted the earth to swallow him up. Too exhausted to do anything with the fury that swirled like a wild storm within him, he just wept angry tears.

Elias had barely been a participant of his own life. He was weak because his parents had sold him to evil men. Evil men who'd starved him and overworked him like he was a machine instead of a person.

Elias seethed at the injustice before pushing it down, down, down like he always did. There was a well of anger in Elias that might be enough to tear a kingdom down one day, but for now, his fury joined the rest because it was the only way Elias could put one foot in front of the other.

Johan came over to them at a more sedate pace but looked at Elias with such a piercing stare he felt as though he were being laid bare. Instead of fussing, Johan walked back to where Elias had dropped his bag and pulled out a blanket. He placed it down gently under the shelter and pointed at Elias and then to the makeshift bed. "Rest," he rasped.

Henrik helped him over because there was no disguising his limp. He'd been stubborn and pushed himself too hard today.

"Tomorrow, you need to say if we need to slow down or take more breaks. You need to let us know, Eli. If it takes longer, so be it."

Elias knew that Henrik meant to be kind, but he felt scolded nonetheless and was feeling quite sorry for himself as he plonked down onto the lumpy blanket.

He sat uselessly as Henrik and Johan built a fire together. Elias wasn't entirely sure why it was bothering him so much. The last five years of his life had been far worse, and yet right then, he felt more broken than ever.

Johan smiled warmly at Elias as he passed him a mug of hot water with mint leaves.

"Thank you," Elias whispered.

He sipped the mint tea and let the warmth seep into his bones and tried to convince himself that he was not, in fact, in agony. Unfortunately, minty water could only do so much.

Once they'd all had some dried meat and cheese for their supper, the three of them sat huddled together under the shelter but close enough to the fire to watch as the orange tongues slowly devoured the wood.

Although Johan being so near was helping, being back in the Dark Forest reminded Elias of all the nights they'd spent terrified that their captors might return to claim them once more. Every sound in the forest began to resemble footsteps, and Elias couldn't take the silence anymore.

From a place within himself he'd long forgotten, he began to sing. It was a song his elder sister had sung to him as a child to lull him to sleep at night. The words spoken in his mother tongue weaved a mental tapestry of ships returning to the fjord, lovers reuniting, and fortune favouring his people. He sang despite his throat feeling like raw sandpaper from not drinking enough water that day; he sang despite the memories it dredged from a place he couldn't afford to recall. He sang until Henrik's face reflected his own, cheeks wet with tears and an anguish neither of them had let themselves feel in a very long time.

"You — you sing... in your language?" Johan asked.

"That song is in the old tongue, yes," Henrik replied. "Now we all speak many different dialects."

"Although we can mostly understand each other, overseers would beat elves who spoke with their mother tongue. We got out of the habit," Elias explained.

Elias didn't add that he hated speaking his own dialect. He connected it too closely to his own parents and could barely stand to hear it now, but he still loved the songs in the old tongue.

Wordlessly, Johan wrapped his arms around them, pulling them close on each side until they were tucked up against him. Elias hoarded every morsel of comfort the shoemaker offered, having learned the hard way that comfort was not a guarantee in this life. He'd always found it where he could, though.

A while later, when both Elias and Henrik were struggling to keep their eyes open, they crawled under the blanket and went to sleep, clinging to each other as Johan watched over them like the guardian angel he'd been since they met.

Ten

HENRIK

The following day, neither Henrik nor Johan trusted Elias to speak up and ask for help, and so they stopped to rest at least every two hours. With everything they'd endured, Henrik had never seen Elias' positivity waver, and so witnessing him break down the night before had shaken him.

That night, they had set up their camp down by the river. Elias had fallen asleep as soon as they'd eaten supper, but Henrik's brain wouldn't quieten enough for sleep, so he'd wandered a short way to the water's edge and sat down. Their camp was still in view, so he wasn't surprised when Johan joined him. They took their shoes and wool socks off and both gasped when their feet plunged into the icy water, but it was refreshing on Henrik's blistered feet.

"I love water that startles you it's so cold, it reminds me of home," Henrik said.

Johan didn't reply right away, but Henrik got the sense he was trying to find some words, and so he sat patiently with his feet dangling in the water.

"T-tell about it?" Johan blurted out eventually.

Henrik smiled a sad smile.

"My home in Varinien was beautiful growing up. My family were fishermen, we lived near the fjord. Imposing mountains with deep-blue waters. At the right time of year, you could spot pods of dolphins leaping from the surface." Henrik sighed wistfully. "But elf families are huge, and people began to struggle to feed so many mouths. When the famine took hold and we could no longer procure imported food, things went from bad to worse. Brothers and sisters turned on one another, or like in Eli's case, parents turned on their own kin. It was as though this place, which had always had soft edges, was suddenly lined with blades. I dream of returning home, but that place no longer exists."

Johan reached over and squeezed Henrik's thigh in a way that felt as if Johan was taking some of his heartache and the weight that came with it. Henrik had never realised how empty words could be until now. How much a person could speak without saying anything and how much a person could say without speaking.

"I know you disagree with me, but you're good with people, you know? You are a bright spot in a dark world, Johan. And I've seen some of the darkest corners it has to offer. Don't ever underestimate your light." He pressed his leg against Johan's, who hooked his foot around Henrik's under the water. Henrik could barely take a breath at the contact, and he merely stared at where they were connected until a short while later, when Johan pointed back to camp and said "Fire" before reluctantly getting up to tend to it.

Henrik waited a moment before returning. Guilt churned in his stomach because his foot touching another man's shouldn't make him feel like this. But it was as though tiny wings fluttered inside his stomach, and he wasn't sure how they'd got there. Like being scared, but not quite. Scared for something good, maybe. Only, that was wrong of him, wasn't it? Henrik rarely dared to hope for good, but these tiny wings seemed determined to betray his logical mind.

On the fourth day, there was a buzz of life in the air. Excitement laced with fear accompanied them every step until, eventually, they entered a clearing where a tower that must have been at least five stories tall loomed over them. It possessed only a single window near the top, and a large wall wrapped around it protectively.

There was an eeriness to how still and quiet the clearing was, and Henrik couldn't fight the feeling they were being watched, the fine hairs on his arms standing on end in warning. Henrik stepped closer to the stone barrier to see what was lying across the bottom.

"Gaaah!" Henrik leaped back from the skeleton-like husks that littered the base of the wall. If that wasn't an ominous sign, he wasn't sure what was.

"What is it?" Elias asked, trying to peer around him.

Henrik gulped. "Some questions are best left unanswered. Where is the entrance?"

Just as Henrik asked, the stones in the wall began to shift on their own, slowly creating an entryway for them. It had been a long time since Henrik had seen magic in action, and it sent a thrill down his spine.

Johan stepped forward and through the gap in the wall but motioned for the two elves to follow closely behind. Not that they needed telling; they were practically glued to Johan's back, frightened of both entering the tower and of being left behind in the creepy clearing.

Johan seemed to be searching for something near the base of the tower. Both Henrik and Elias were his shadows until they came to a spot where something was growing.

The plant had bright green leaves with gold stems, unlike any-thing Henrik had seen before. As they stared at the plant in wonder, stones within the tower stole their attention as they shifted on their own, creating another entrance.

Nobody greeted them from the gap in the tower, and all Henrik's instincts told him to run, *run far away*. But they hadn't come all this way for nothing, so Henrik gritted his teeth and followed Johan and Elias inside. Silently, they made their way up what felt like a never-ending spiral staircase before reaching their destination.

The room they entered was luxurious in comparison to the en-trance and stairway, and Henrik was surprised to find a beautiful man with long golden hair sitting lazily on a fabric chair.

"We've met before" came a voice from somewhere else in the room.

The owner of the voice stepped out from behind a large bookcase. He was as equally stunning as the man in the chair, but with a dark-ness that emanated from him. Something about him was predatory and made Henrik feel like prey.

Johan nodded at the man.

"I assume that the predicament you and your parents came to me with is still unresolved, then?" the man asked.

Johan confirmed with another nod but appeared embarrassed. Henrik instinctively knew that Johan and his parents had come to the sorcerer to try to help with his difficulties speaking, and it sent a pang of pain through his chest.

Life must have been difficult for Johan without his words, but if he'd spent his life any other way, would he even be the man he was? Would he have stopped outside the market on that frigid-cold day and offered two starving elves a place to stay? He didn't know, but he knew there was *nothing* he would change about Johan.

"Shame," the sorcerer replied. "What brings you to darken my doorway today, then?"

Henrik had expected Elias to speak up like he usually did but he was staring at the golden-haired man in the chair like he hadn't even heard the question.

"We escaped captivity," Henrik began to explain. "But these"—he held up his wrist to display the bangles—"still suppress our magic. We're looking for someone who can remove them for both of us."

The sorcerer snapped the book in his hand shut, startling Henrik. He stalked towards Henrik and, without asking, grabbed him by the wrist. The sorcerer stroked his index finger along the bangle with his eyes closed, and Henrik shivered under the phantom touch.

Johan and Elias' proximity as they stepped closer to see what the sorcerer was doing was a comforting warmth at his back.

The mysterious man hummed quietly to himself, and it felt like the copper band was heating up around the sensitive skin underneath. When it became so hot that it began to burn, Henrik snatched his hand back out of his grasp.

The sorcerer looked unapologetic as Henrik cradled his hand and glared at him.

"I can remove it... technically," he said.

"What do you mean by that?" Elias asked.

"I mean that I'm capable. But if I'm going to expend my resources on you, I'll want something in return."

Johan took the leather coin pouch out of his bag and handed it to Henrik, who in turn, tried to pass it to the sorcerer. "This is everything we have."

The sorcerer looked at the bag with disgust and snorted derisively. "Your petty coin collection is meaningless to me. I am not in need of money."

Henrik's stomach practically dropped out of him. This was all they had. He looked to Elias and Johan, who appeared equally distressed. Elias was rubbing at the copper band on his right wrist helplessly, and his eyes began to well up.

"Zel, do you know much about elves?" the sorcerer asked the golden-haired man sitting in the corner.

"Not much, other than what I know about you," he replied.

Now that he said it, Henrik's attention was drawn to the sorcerer's pointed ears. They were indeed elf-like, but there was something not quite right about him at the same time.

"You are lovers, no?" the sorcerer asked Henrik unexpectedly. He stood with his mouth open, and his stunned silence answered for him. "It is extremely common among elves for men to desire only lying with men, and the women with other women. Do you know why that is, little elf?"

Henrik did know, but Elias spoke up first, "No. Why is that?" he asked.

It surprised Henrik a little that Elias was unaware, but he had not received the education that Henrik had as a child.

"I know it is common and not met with judgment. But not why," Elias continued.

Henrik answered before the sorcerer could, beginning to understand what he might be after, "It is because elves were blessed by the Gods to be unusually fertile. It is a biological imperative for our people that we are not all... inclined to reproduce. It would be unsustainable, and people would starve. People already do."

Elias looked shocked. "Why don't I know this about my own people?" he asked.

"Some elf families believe to openly discuss the gift, risks the gift. There are nearly entire generations who will not speak of it out loud," the sorcerer explained with more knowledge than Henrik had expected.

Elias' expression was both confused and thoughtful before he blurted out, "You want a baby elf?"

The sorcerer snorted a laugh at the question. "No, little elf, I do not want any offspring from either of you."

Henrik could practically see the cogs turning in Elias' mind. "So you want this gift, then?" Elias asked. "The fertility gift from our Gods?

But that didn't entirely add up for Henrik. "Why, though? You are also an elf, are you not? You must possess the gift already, surely," he said, gesturing to the sorcerer's pointed ears.

"I am not what I once was, and it has been a long time since I met others of my kind. A rare find, you might say, and a useful gift to barter with. That's my price for removing the bands."

"Take mine," Elias rushed out, not even pausing to consider the consequences.

"Wait!" Henrik darted forward, grabbing Elias by the arm and spinning him to face him. "You need to think this through, Eli. You risk angering our Gods by doing this. It was gifted to our people. Think carefully before you give it away."

Elias raised his hand and stroked Henrik's cheek with the tips of his fingers.

"Have you ever thought that maybe they angered me first, Rik? During all the years of slavery that I needed them, what use to me was this 'gift' as they call it? I've been cut off from magic for five years, and I'm taking it back. Our Gods owe me, not the other way around." His voice fiercer than his gentle touch.

Henrik didn't argue. He let Elias' words percolate through his mind. Lifting his head to Johan, he asked, "Would you do it? Would you give the gift away?"

Johan didn't answer, but he stepped forward and squeezed the back of Henrik's neck with one hand and pressed the other over Henrik's heart.

He didn't need to hear Johan's words to understand. Johan was telling Henrik to follow his intuition and heart. He also knew that whatever he decided, Johan would understand, but when he looked at Elias, with the stubborn and determined set of his jaw, he knew what he needed to do.

"Okay. You may have it," he whispered.

Elias went first with an almost feverish desperation to have it done. Unfortunately, the process caused a repeat of the earlier burning, only far worse. The skin underneath the bangle bubbled and blistered as the sorcerer held it, his eyes closed as he performed his spell. It was gruesome to watch, and Henrik gagged when the smell of burning skin wafted towards him.

Elias remained stoic through it all, concentrating on his wrists until he appeared lightheaded from the pain and began swaying.

Johan wrapped a large arm around his waist, holding him upright until the sorcerer had finished.

Henrik could see the second it was done, even through the pain, Elias smiled a smile Henrik had never seen on his lover before. It held contentment and relief that made him appear younger somehow. Johan squeezed Elias and pulled him into a hug that seemed to release a valve in his love.

Powerless to help, all Henrik could do was watch as Elias sobbed, a torrent of tears and emotion pouring from his soul as he felt magic for the first time in over five years. Magic which had been stolen from him.

"Damn my Gods," Elias hiccupped. "Keep your gift. This is what it means to—to—to live again."

It was difficult for Henrik to swallow past the lump in his throat. He'd had no idea that Elias had been burying so much pain under his optimistic facade. It hurt his own heart just to witness it. The sharpness of it stung the air that surrounded them like thousands of pinpricks against Henrik's skin.

"Come here," the sorcerer said, entirely unmoved by the life-altering moment for the elves.

A bolt of fear lanced through Henrik, but he stepped forward, heartbeat racing, and his hands began to sweat. He feared his Gods in a way that Elias did not, but he'd made his choice. Swallowing down his trepidation, he straightened his arms to present the sorcerer his wrists.

It felt like his skin was being flayed open, so he scrunched his eyes shut and panted through the pain. The heat of it spread into every crevice of his being like he'd been set on fire from the inside. It seemed that he'd endured the agony for an eternity, but then when it stopped...

Oh, when it stopped, he could hardly believe it.

Magic. Lighter and brighter than the summer sun, it rushed through his veins like a tsunami of ecstasy. How could he have forgotten what this felt like?

Henrik suddenly understood Elias' reaction as his own face was saturated with tears of pure joy. He stumbled into Johan and Elias' embrace and wept.

How had he forgotten what it felt like to be whole and truly alive? What had he ever done to deserve having this stolen from him?

Like the needles they used to make fine shoes, magic began the arduous process of sewing the fractured pieces of Henrik's soul back together, and he could take a deep breath for the first time.

Eleven

ELIAS

They thanked and bid farewell to the sorcerer and his golden-haired friend in a daze. When they made it back into the forest, Elias could hardly recall how they'd got there.

He had magic back.

Once, back at the textile mill, Elias had dreamed of this very thing. He'd been free and walking through a meadow filled with wildflowers. The grass-covered earth beneath his bare feet had felt so incredibly tangible that it had never occurred to him he was dreaming. Wrists free of magic-suppressing bangles, he'd felt the thrum of magic tingling beneath his skin. Only now that he could really feel it, did he understand what a poor mimic his imagination had been.

He was also fairly certain that in his dream state he wouldn't have hot, white pain lancing through his feet with every step.

They took a break a couple of miles from the tower, having all walked in a sort of stunned silence up until that point.

"Pass me your shoes?" Henrik asked both Elias and Johan.

Elias smiled, having a good idea of what Henrik planned to do and kicking himself for not thinking of it sooner.

Henrik accepted Elias' pair of battered leather boots and clutched them close to his chest before his eyelids fluttered shut. Elias could feel the air shift as Rik used magic for the first time, and it sent a shiver down his spine.

When Henrik finished, Elias beamed. All evidence of where the sole of the boot was beginning to come away after four days of hiking was gone, and Elias knew the moment he slipped them back on his feet they'd feel like walking on clouds.

Confused, Johan frowned but still obliged when Henrik asked him to hand his own boots over.

Henrik worked magic once more, and Johan's eyes widened like a shocked deer when he slipped his feet back inside. "In-Incredible," he whispered as he took a few cautionary steps.

Elias took pity on their bewildered shoemaker and explained, "Rik has woven magic into the shoes, which will stop them causing any pain and also allow us to walk much faster." The small elf wriggled his toes happily in relief.

It could have been the buzz of finally having magic back, or the spell Henrik had put on his shoes, but Elias hopped and skipped along the path with a bounce in every step, no longer weighed down by the burden of having magic constricted.

Even Henrik, whose expression usually appeared as though he's chewed on a bitter dandelion, had a soft contended smile on his face as they began the long walk back home.

T hat night, they set up their camp by the river again. While Henrik and Johan built the shelter and the fire, Elias wandered down towards the riverbank, needing a moment alone with his thoughts.

The river was a dark blue, lit up by the silvery reflection of the bright moon that night. It had yet to rain that week, and so the water was slow moving, meandering invitingly past Elias.

He couldn't fight the temptation to strip off his clothes and immerse himself, cleansing his skin of the dust and sweat from days of walking through the Dark Forest.

"Ahh!" he yelped when he'd waded far enough that the icy water reached his balls. A few steps farther and it hit his chest, peaking his nipples and stealing his breath all at once. Goose bumps danced over his arms and legs. All the fine hairs on his body stood on end and glittered under the moonlight, and Elias twisted his arms in the faint glow to admire the simple beauty of the moment.

It would use too much magic to maintain it for long, but he squeezed his eyes shut and mentally reached into the well of magic at the core of him. He pictured himself carving some of it out and shaping it into what he needed until it travelled through his body and reached his fingertips. The moment he released it, the water surrounding him heated up to a more ambient temperature, and he almost sobbed with joy.

From his spot in the river, he remained in full view of Henrik and Johan who were busy tending the fire in the distance, so he turned to face away from them when he could no longer hold in the torrent of emotions that had grown into a volcano that threatened to erupt.

It had been merely a fissure at first, silent tears spilling from his eyes and down his pale cheeks. Only, when he tried to swallow, it was as if a fist squeezed his throat. Even as he desperately tried to push it back down. Push it back inside the locked box he never opened. It was no use.

The noise he emitted was that of an animal injured beyond repair. An anguish no living thing was built to withstand, but *he had*.

He sobbed for the years he'd lost, the years that access to magic was stolen from him. He wept for Henrik, knowing he'd suffered as he had. But the true grief of it all for Elias laid in knowing that while he was free, possibly thousands of his people were not. They remained chained, magic bound, and maybe would never swim naked in a river with magic thrumming through their veins ever again.

Elias had been so lost in his pain that he was startled when slim, pale arms wrapped around his middle and held him.

"Shhh. You're okay," Henrik soothed. "We are okay."

Elias couldn't find the words to explain to Henrik why *that* was the problem. Why it hurt so much. He expected to see nothing but happiness in Henrik's eyes, but when he twisted to face his lover and glanced up, it was all written there. He did understand. Because in those amber eyes he loved so much, a tornado of relief, hope, and joy swirled paradoxically with grief, regret, and despair.

They just held each other in the water until Elias' energy began to wane and the temperature of the water dropped low enough that their teeth were chattering.

Together they waded back to the riverbank and clambered out. Patiently waiting for them was Johan, carrying the large wool blanket, which he wrapped around their naked shoulders. Elias smiled weakly at him, exhausted from the outpouring of emotions, and it surprised him when Johan cupped his face and pressed a gentle kiss to his forehead.

The two elves settled themselves in front of the heat of the fire while Johan busied himself with boiling water for some hot tea to warm them up.

Elias felt raw and flayed open, and yet, for the first time in his life, he felt that, between Henrik and Johan, he would be cared for and be safe. And that was no small thing.

The remainder of their trip home had been uneventful in the best way. It had been filled with gentle smiles, harmless ribbing, and singing by the fire in the evenings. Despite Elias' boots being enhanced by magic, the walk was still long and arduous, and he was tired down to his bones by the time they stepped foot into the familiar comfort of Johan's shoe shop.

Elias was too exhausted to address it, but he was almost bereft as he watched Johan's retreating back when they parted ways to go to their respective beds that night. It felt wrong.

There was no fighting sleep that night, though. Elias had barely hit the mattress when his eyelids fluttered closed and he slipped into a deep slumber.

The next morning, the elves lay side by side in companionable silence. Elias had woken with a busy brain as he tried to process what it meant to have regained magic and to finally have found freedom.

Eventually, Henrik cut through the silence by whispering, "Eli, there's something I must confess to you. Only, I'm scared you will hate me, and I couldn't bear that."

Despite his empty stomach, Elias suddenly felt quite sick, but Henrik only clung to him more tightly. He fought back against the icy dread that tried to spread through him.

"Wh-what is it?" Elias forced out, knowing that delaying whatever Henrik had to tell him would only drag out his suffering.

"Can I ask you a question first?"

Elias didn't like that one bit, preferring Henrik get to the point, but he managed to say, "Okay..."

"Do you think it's possible to... to love... more than one person?"

Elias was surprised to find that Henrik's question melted away most of the panic that had been churning in his stomach. He'd seen how Henrik and Johan looked at one another, and he would be a liar if he didn't at least admit to himself that he'd also been admiring Johan. Had in fact bloomed under the shoemaker's warmth.

Johan was... steady. And solid. In a way that Elias and Henrik were not. Elias often felt like the two of them were feathers that might lose each other if a strong wind blew them up into the sky. But with Johan, it was like he'd safely store the feathers in his pocket, and Elias didn't have to worry about any of them getting lost. Because Johan looked after his belongings, he wouldn't misplace them or treat them as replaceable.

"Eli?" Emotion laced Henrik's voice, and Elias realised he'd been lost in his thoughts for too long.

"I think Johan is hard not to love," Elias answered.

Henrik audibly inhaled, evidently shocked by the response. "How—how did you... how?" he stammered.

Elias turned to face him. It was still predawn and so dim in the workshop that he could make out little except for his lover's eyes.

He reached out and found Henrik's hair, tucking the long strands behind his ear before cupping his cheek.

"I love you, Rik. Too much, I think sometimes. But... you and Johan understand each other in a way that you and I do not." Henrik opened his mouth to interrupt him, but Elias continued on. "We've been through too much, and we lean on one another even when the other cannot bear the weight. But Johan can bear our weight... I think."

"You feel for him, too?" Henrik whispered.

"I... When I really consider it, I suppose that I do, yes. He is attractive in a rugged sort of way, but I don't think that's it. He makes me feel like I could launch every disastrous, broken part of me at him and he would... treasure it all. Take care of it all. It doesn't lessen what I feel for you. It's just different, I think."

Henrik lowered his gaze like eye contact with Elias just then was painful. "I'm sorry that I'm not strong enough to bear the weight for you, Eli. I wish so much that I could. But... these last few years have changed me. I fear I won't ever be truly strong again." Henrik's voice cracked with emotion, and Elias wrapped his arms tightly around him.

"Maybe we won't have to be. Maybe we just need someone else to share the burden."

"What if Johan doesn't care for us, the way we care for him?"

Elias pondered that thought for a while, letting ideas seed and sprout in his mind.

"I think we just have to show him what we can offer him in return. Show him what it means to be loved by an elf. There are two of us after all, that's a lot of love to give, Rik."

"Johan would be lucky to be loved by you, Eli. I know that I am."

Elias kissed him and poured his heart into it all the while his brain began buzzing with plans and ideas for how they could woo their lovely, big, and strong shoemaker.

Twelve

JOHAN

Henrik and Elias had been behaving very strangely ever since they'd all returned from their visit to the sorcerer to remove the elves' magic-suppressing bangles. So much so that Johan was mildly concerned that he'd missed something much more significant taking place during the exchange.

Yesterday evening, after they'd closed up the shop, Elias had insisted upon giving Johan a haircut and beard trim, claiming that he must "Stop hiding his handsome face from the world." Johan had been grateful then for his beard because it hid the bright red flush that had warmed his cheeks. Afterwards, when he'd stared at his reflection in the mirror that was now clear thanks to some tinkering magic from Henrik, Johan had admitted that he did look far smarter and more like the true business owner he aspired to be.

Today, however, the elves were taking it in turns to assist Johan in the shop while the other would disappear off into the workshop. When they'd swap, they had a disconcerting habit of sneaking glances at him and whispering to one another. Not in a mean way.

Johan wasn't concerned that they were conspiring against him, but still in a way that left him a little on edge.

At lunchtime, he closed the shop and made his way into the workshop to pour himself a drink, only, when he tried to open the door, it appeared to be locked, which was especially suspicious because Johan didn't have a lock on his workshop door.

Without many options, he knocked and waited. There was the sound of some shuffling and wood scraping before Elias called out, "Just a minute."

Johan huffed with impatience. While he generally found the elves' antics to be rather endearing, he didn't much appreciate being locked out of his own workshop.

A few minutes later, the door swung open, and a beaming Elias stood before him. It was hard to remain annoyed when Elias smiled like that, so Johan just gave him a quizzical look before scanning his eyes around the room, trying to spot what they might be up to.

Everything looked normal, which somehow only made Johan even more suspicious. He pointed at the two of them and raised his eyebrow.

"What? We've just been... coming up with some new shoe designs," Elias replied, batting his eyelashes at Johan in a way that, while distracting, continued to alert Johan to the fact the elves were hiding something.

Johan approached the bench where the parchment for drawing on was and found no sign of any designs at all. "Where?" he managed.

"Oh, erm. We were discussing the designs out loud. We haven't got to the drawing portion of the design process yet. We'll... do that after lunch," Elias rambled, and it was then that Johan noticed the two of them were standing strangely in front of a wooden chest like they were guarding it.

Johan stalked towards it and nudged them both out of the way. Only when he tried to open the chest, he heard the snick of a lock and then stood back to glare at them.

The elves had previously informed him that elvish magic was good in nature, light in a way that meant it didn't really work for nefarious purposes, but locking Johan out of his own belongings didn't feel very "good."

He stood with his hands on his hips and narrowed his eyes at Elias, instinctively knowing it was him who used magic to lock things away. Johan pointed at Elias and then at the chest. "Open," he rasped.

Elias began attempting a conversation using only his eyes with Henrik. After a moment, Henrik glanced up at Johan before telling Elias to open it.

When Johan heard the snick of the lock again, he stepped forward and opened the chest gingerly, as if a wild animal might pop out of it.

What was actually inside the chest was no less confusing. It appeared to be a nearly endless supply of clothing and shoes. But most of the items were so fancy that they were practically fit for royalty, and Johan couldn't figure out why they were here.

He inspected the items carefully since they were so finely made, and he came across a pair of nightclothes that matched Henrik's and Elias'. Only, over the chest pocket was the letter J embroidered using a thick green thread. With the nightshirt clutched in his hand, he looked between the two elves. Elias was wide-eyed like a startled deer while Henrik bit at his fingernails.

"Mmm?" Johan hummed in question.

"It's not all quite finished yet," Henrik said.

"But... it's for you. We... both of us," Elias emphasised, "made these for you. As a... *gift.*"

Johan was grateful then that he was unable to blurt out the first thing that came into his head because he would have asked them where on earth they thought he would be wearing such fine clothes, and that would have been incredibly rude.

Instead, he looked through the clothes again with a different eye now that he knew they were for him. He could appreciate that, while beautiful, they were not impractical clothes.

Elias and Henrik closed in on him, peering over his shoulder with curious looks, like they were waiting on his reaction.

"Thank you. Very kind." Johan had been finding that it was slowly getting easier to speak in front of the two of them when they were all alone. He hoped that maybe one day he'd be able to speak around them as freely as he had his parents when he was a child.

Both of their shoulders dropped in clear relief before Elias declared, "Excellent. Then you must try them all on and show us!"

Henrik also appeared cautiously hopeful at the suggestion, and Johan knew he would probably do nearly anything they asked of him, although he still groaned when Elias added, "Can I dress you like a doll?"

Despite the blue skies and sunshine, the way the wind rattled the glass panes told Johan that a storm was coming. He kept glancing out the window, waiting for Henrik and Elias to return from the bakery where they were picking up some food for lunch.

Johan found himself agitated when the elves were out of his sight, and he was aware that he worried about them far more than was normal.

As he waited, the door to the shop opened, and a finely dressed man and woman entered.

"Good morning," the man said. Johan offered his friendliest smile but hoped Elias would return soon to be able to speak to the potential customers. "You sell elf-made shoes?" he asked.

Johan nodded and picked up a pair from the shelf to show them. He pointed to the fine stitching, which no one but an elf could achieve. The woman clutched the shoe, and her eyes glinted with a covetous glee.

"They really are... my goodness. I must have a pair," the woman declared, to presumably her husband.

"To try," Johan managed in a whisper, pointing at the ruby-red slipper she was holding.

"These?" she asked. "They will be much too small."

Johan shook his head and pushed them towards her. She looked sceptical but then sat down and began to unlace her fine leather boots.

Elias and Henrik had been working on this particular pair of shoes for half the night, getting reacquainted with magic to create things Johan didn't even know were possible.

As the woman began to slip her foot into the shoe, which at first did appear to be much too small, they all watched in awe as the shoe expanded until it fit her perfectly.

"This is surely not possible... How?" she asked Johan.

Johan found he had no more remaining words left and could only smile apologetically.

"You have *free* elves?" The man sounded incredulous at the idea, but Johan nodded his head with a big grin, thinking of his free elves.

Well, not *his* elves. He wasn't entirely sure why he'd just thought of them that way.

"That's certainly a first. I didn't think anyone had found a way to get the elves to work when their magic was not suppressed. This is incredible," the man said. "We are the Queen's ambassadors over in Hallin, she will be extremely... curious, I'm sure, to hear about these."

Johan feared that if the Queen ordered shoes from his little shop, he might faint from the shock of it, but he was starting to believe that with Elias and Henrik as his business partners, he wouldn't have to worry about how to pay for another piece of leather or his next meal again.

The couple parted with what Johan thought was an obscene amount of money for a pair of shoes and a down payment to commission three more pairs that, in total, would earn Johan and the elves more than he usually made in an entire year.

It was so unbelievable that by the time Elias and Henrik returned from the bakery with lunch, Johan was counting the coins for the third time just to be sure.

They were both rosy-cheeked from the gusts of wind when they entered, and the sight of them made Johan's stomach flip in a way he was unfamiliar with. It wasn't a terrible feeling per se, but it was unsettling.

"Now, don't be cross," Elias began. "But to celebrate the fact we're now actually free and we didn't end up giving all of our money to the sorcerer, we may have been a little... indulgent at the bakery."

Johan wasn't cross at all. In fact, with the money he had stacked in front of him, he thought it would be a while until he had to be concerned with Elias' and Henrik's spending habits anywhere, let alone the bakery, which rarely had much food stocked these days anyway.

"What's all this?" Henrik asked, pointing to the coins.

Johan coughed a few times before finding his words. "Sale. Plus," he held up two fingers and pointed to the parchment with the rough sketches for the design. The elves grinned widely and nearly bashed their heads together trying to both look at the drawings at the same time. "Queen's... ambassador," he squeezed out.

But then the look on the elves' faces suddenly changed like the wind outside had blown through the shop and taken their joy with it. Elias and Henrik both stared at each other, going white as a sheet, and Henrik audibly gulped.

Johan scrunched his brows together in question at them.

"The Queen can't know about us being here," Henrik practically whispered.

"When we escaped, we were travelling to our new owner, two dozen of us," Elias explained, and the direction this conversation was heading already made a tight fist around Johan's heart.

The slave trade as a whole made Johan sick to his stomach, but whenever he had to face the fact that Elias and Henrik had been stripped of their freedom and treated like replaceable cogs in a machine, anger would burn through him like a furnace. As he always did, he swallowed the feeling down, but it was bitter on his tongue.

Henrik continued on from Elias, "The person who had bought us... was the Queen. If she knows about us, it won't be hard for her to connect that we are her slaves who escaped. It... might not be safe for us here anymore." Henrik looked as devastated as Johan felt at the idea of the two elves not being here anymore.

Johan shook his head. "No. I'll... I'll... I'll make sure. Safe." And Johan meant it. He didn't know how, but he meant it. Johan knew with every fibre of his being that he would die before he let anyone take Elias and Henrik back into captivity. They might not be his. But they were his to protect. And he'd be damned if anyone harmed even a strand of long white hair on their perfect heads.

L ater that night, Johan was lying in bed, wide awake as he tried to come up with possible solutions for keeping Elias and Henrik away from prying eyes and getting them to safety. A permanent kind of safety. He was shivering because the gales from earlier that day had turned into a full-blown storm with the temperature dropping significantly.

Wrapping himself in the blanket, he scrubbed his hand over his face before trudging over to the fireplace; he wasn't going to be able to get a wink of sleep without heating the place up a little. He hoped Elias and Henrik were okay downstairs, the workshop could get bitterly cold in winter, and there was no way to heat that room.

Maybe he could make them some hot tea, that might warm them up?

Just as Johan had placed a pot of water onto the now-blazing fire to boil, he heard the soft pad of feet coming up the stairs. He got up and headed for the door, opening it before they even had a chance to knock. They were standing with the blanket wrapped around their shoulders, shivering violently, and Johan ushered them inside and towards the fire.

"We're... s-s-s-sorry. It got... t-t-t-too c-c-cold downstairs," Elias stammered out.

Johan grabbed the other blanket and wrapped it around them both until only their heads were poking out.

"W-w-w-we tr-tried to use m-m-magic to stay warm. But n-n-no energy left," Henrik explained. They both looked quite drained, and Johan was concerned that they might put themselves at risk if they kept burning through magic for things like this.

With the hot water boiled, Johan took three teacups from the cupboard and began straining the water through the tea leaves. He hadn't needed all three teacups in so long, and the action which was once so familiar made his chest ache. Especially for his warm, kind mother, whom he missed every day. She had often made the three of them tea on cold nights like this, when they'd huddle in front of the fire.

Elias and Henrik thanked him when he passed them the tea, and they were shivering far less now. Once the room had warmed up enough that Johan thought he'd be able to sleep, he took himself to bed. Only, he'd given his blanket to the elves. He felt bad trying to take it back, so he curled up on the mattress without it.

After only a few minutes with his eyes closed, Johan felt the weight of the thick wool being draped over him, and he smiled. Just when he was about to try and sleep again, though, he was abruptly sandwiched between two little bodies. His eyes flashed open to find Elias curled in front of him, his back flush with Johan's chest, leaving him to deduce that it was Henrik pressed into his back.

Johan wasn't sure what to do. It had been cold, yes, but with the fire going, the room was now warmer than usual. And Johan wasn't entirely sure why the two of them wouldn't just cuddle up together instead of on either side of him.

It took him a few minutes to try and relax again, but then Elias wriggled, pressing his bottom into Johan's groin, and he was fairly certain that his heart had stopped for a moment and he suddenly had too much saliva in his mouth. Johan held his breath, willing himself not to harden and give himself away. He wasn't sure why Elias seemed to be trying to torture him to sleep, but he was just about panicked enough by what was happening to only stiffen halfway.

Johan's next predicament was his arm. He wasn't sure what he was supposed to do with it, and it was beginning to ache holding it straight down his side. This was not conducive to getting any sleep. Eventually, with Henrik's face pressed between his shoulder blades and two sets of heavy, even breathing on either side of him, Johan risked draping his arm over Elias and, by some miracle, Johan finally drifted off to sleep.

Thirteen

HENRIK

Johan and Elias were still deep in sleep when Henrik woke up with his head resting on Johan's chest, a large arm wrapped around him. Elias was mirroring him on the shoemaker's other side, only he appeared to have his leg hiked up over Johan's thigh.

Henrik dared not move a muscle because he was incredibly conscious of his own hardness pressing against Johan's hip, and he hoped it would go down before they woke up.

Elias and Henrik had both agreed on coming upstairs last night in search of warmth; the cold had made their bones rattle in a way neither of them had felt since captivity, and Henrik had known that Johan wouldn't mind their intrusion.

However, climbing into Johan's bed and settling on either side of him had been entirely Elias' idea.

Henrik had been certain at first that his and Elias' attempts at courting Johan would have been obvious to the man. I mean, they had made fine clothes and shoes, Elias had trimmed his beard and hair, and yesterday, Henrik had massaged Johan's hands after several hours of making shoes in the workshop. But then it occurred to

Henrik that Johan wasn't an elf, and maybe he was unfamiliar with their traditional courting rituals and possibly only thought they were being unusually generous.

Elias was undeterred when Henrik had pointed this out, deciding then that an escalation was required; only Henrik hadn't realised that would entail the two of them climbing into bed with Johan and essentially trapping him until he cuddled them all night long.

Not that Henrik was complaining. Henrik was more comfortable than he could ever remember being with a large arm keeping him close and a big warm body to press up against. The fact that he got all of that with the view of his beautiful lover's soft, parted pink lips as he gently exhaled in sleep was the icing on the cake.

Henrik watched as Elias' pale-white lashes began to flutter until he blinked owlishly, sleepy amber eyes peeking through. Elias glanced up at a sleeping Johan, and his lips twitched into a contented, if a little smug, smile.

I told you, he mouthed at Henrik, who rolled his eyes in return.

The blanket still covered them from the waist down, but Elias lifted it slightly, peering underneath until his eyes widened and he licked his lips.

"What?" Henrik said, barely a whisper.

"Look," Elias replied just as quietly.

Henrik lifted his head slightly to see what Elias was staring at, and his face immediately went red at the sight.

Johan's nightshirt had ridden up his hairy stomach, and his trousers were slung low. His morning stiffness appeared to be trying to escape the confines of his nightclothes because Henrik could very clearly see the swollen pink head of Johan's cock poking out of the waistband.

Henrik gulped and found his own length hardening to steel at the sight.

A pink flush travelled down Elias' neck and chest, the telltale sign of his lover's own arousal, and Henrik's skin felt like it might actually be on fire.

A small cough startled them both, and they stared up at a now-awake Johan, whose gaze was flicking frantically back and forth between the two of them until he saw where the blanket was lifted and presumably the sight of his own swollen tip looking back at him.

The three of them just sort of froze in place, not moving a muscle until Henrik couldn't bear the silence anymore. "We're... sorry for looking," he mumbled like that made the situation any less awkward.

"Here, I'll help," Elias said, reaching for Johan's waistband and pulling it up to cover him. Only, it became clear that the waistband had been trapping Johan's erection, and it was now tenting his trousers in a way that really displayed every inch of his impressive length. Henrik couldn't seem to keep his eyes off it.

Johan groaned and lifted his arms that had been wrapped around the elves up to cover his face with his hands. Henrik really didn't like embarrassing Johan, but it was like he was trapped in a maze and wasn't sure how they could all find their way out unscathed.

"It's okay," Elias insisted. "Look, it's completely normal. See?" Elias then knelt beside Johan and tugged his hand from his face so he could see where Elias was equally hard.

Henrik was fairly certain he'd entered into one of his more absurd erotic dreams involving the three of them.

"I bet Rik is just as stiff," Elias added unhelpfully. "There's rarely a morning I don't wake up with his cock prodding me in the back."

This time it was Henrik's turn to groan. What had gotten into Elias today? They were supposed to be wooing Johan, not frightening him off with their morning erections.

"Johan?" Henrik croaked. Johan peered at him between the gaps of his fingers, and Henrik blew out a breath. "Would you like us to leave your bed?"

Elias made a noise of protest but quietened when Henrik gave him a stern look.

Johan shook his head but was still hiding his face.

"Does it bother you, when we're... like this?" Henrik nudged his hips forward slightly into Johan's hip to explain what "this" was.

Johan slowly shook his head again and swallowed.

"We could help. If you wanted?" Elias suggested.

"Help?" Johan rasped.

"We could touch you. Make you feel good." Elias' voice was breathy, and his eyes were hooded with lust.

Henrik was certain the same words from his own lips would sound stilted and silly, but from Elias they were a warm, inviting promise.

Johan whimpered but dropped his hand to peek at Elias.

There could be no doubt as to what they were asking permission for. "Touch you here." Henrik pressed his palm over Johan's cock and dared to leave it there. "Is this okay?"

Johan nodded and Henrik pressed down a little firmer, gently rubbing him through his nightclothes until the larger man whimpered.

Elias, the impatient little elf that he was, batted Henrik's hands out of the way so he could tug down Johan's trousers and free him.

Henrik had always found Elias' cock to be quite beautiful, it was long and slender like he was. Johan's cock wasn't beautiful, it was mouth-watering. It was slightly thicker at the base, and a prominent vein ran along the shaft, leading to a swollen red tip that Henrik wanted desperately to taste.

"Wow," Elias said, echoing Henrik's thoughts.

As Henrik began to stroke him, Elias reached down and tugged gently on Johan's balls. Johan moaned so loudly that he bit down on his own hand to stifle it.

"You don't need to be quiet, Johan. You should hear Eli when I stroke him. Back in the mill, I had to cover his mouth with my hand to keep him quiet," Henrik explained.

"I... I have," Johan said. "And... and you," he added.

Henrik couldn't help but chuckle at that. He and Elias had thought they were being quiet when they'd lain together this way, but evidently not.

"Did you ever... touch yourself when you could hear us?" Elias asked even as he continued to play with Johan's sack.

Johan groaned and covered his face with his hands again, which was all the admission they required.

"The thought of you up here stroking yourself while you listened to us makes me ache." Elias practically panted and pressed a palm down on his own erection. "Can I put my mouth on you?"

"Yes," Johan whispered.

Elias didn't hesitate, shuffling down so he was practically strad-dling Johan's leg before he wrapped those perfect pink lips around the tip as Henrik continued to stroke him. Elias moaned and then turned to face Henrik. "You have to taste him, Rik," he said before kissing him. Elias' lips and tongue were salty and musky, and he was right, Henrik did need a taste.

Mirroring his lover, Henrik lay against Johan's other leg and bobbed his head down at least half of Johan's length and sucked him hard. His mouth was so full, and he loved it. He loved watching as Eli ground down on Johan's leg, chasing friction to make himself feel good as he pressed his tongue to Johan's sack. The two of them took it in turns, alternating between taking Johan's hard length into their mouths and sucking and swirling their tongues around his balls in a way that made Johan buck his hips.

Henrik savoured every little sound that fell from Johan's usually silent lips and hoarded them in his mind like a dragon who coveted gold. A thrill shot down Henrik's spine at how the two of them were able to make the usually stoic shoemaker come undone.

Eventually, while Henrik had his lips wrapped tightly around the tip of Johan's cock, Johan threaded his fingers through Henrik's hair and held him there. He didn't apply any pressure, and Henrik could have pulled off if he wished. It was Johan's way of asking him to keep going, to stop teasing him and take him over the edge into release.

Elias reached out his hand and threaded it with Henrik's as he rutted against Johan's leg in a desperate rhythm. Without meaning to, Henrik's own hips had begun to thrust, chasing the friction of Johan's firm thigh against his length as he sucked and moaned around Johan's delicious cock.

When Elias had finally run out of patience, he tugged down his shorts and stroked himself furiously until he erupted and his release shot all over Johan, some spurts even landing on Henrik's hand, which he lapped up.

Evidently the sight of Elias letting go was Johan's undoing because his cock swelled and pulsed until Henrik's mouth was filled with Johan's warm seed, and he gobbled it down greedily.

Johan and Elias were both panting from ecstasy but Henrik's cock still ached painfully. Before he even had a chance to stroke himself, Elias tackled him to the mattress and crawled down his body. Suddenly Henrik's night shorts were gone and his cock was engulfed in the warm heat of Elias' mouth.

It was familiar and wonderful and Elias could play Henrik's body like a fiddle. He took Henrik deeply, letting his cockhead hit the back of his throat before swallowing around him and tugging on his balls just roughly enough to hurt Henrik the way he loved.

Henrik knew he wouldn't last long, and he was correct; it felt like Elias had only had his lips on him for less than a minute when his body began to shake and tremble. Henrik grunted and grabbed for Johan's hand as he came, flooding his lover's mouth with the evidence of his complete bliss.

Henrik went boneless as Elias rested his head on his thigh. Johan's other hand began to stroke the sweaty hair from his face like Henrik was his to cherish. He wasn't sure what this would all mean for the three of them, but right in that moment, Henrik was content with feeling whole and bone-deep happiness for possibly the first time in his entire life.

Fourteen

JOHAN

Johan was fairly certain he'd died and gone to heaven. And he was not perturbed by the thought, if this was what eternal life looked like.

A few years earlier in the summertime, Johan had been unable to sleep one night and had taken a walk through town. When he'd heard strange noises drifting from a narrow alleyway, he'd peered around the corner and seen a man on his knees hungrily swallowing down the cock of a passing tradesman who'd been in his shoe shop the day prior.

He'd stood there for a few seconds in stunned silence before he'd practically sprinted home with a pounding heart.

For years, Johan had wondered what it might feel like to have someone's mouth on him that way and his imagination hadn't done it justice.

Regardless of whether anything happened between the three of them ever again, the feel of Henrik and Elias using their skilled mouths and tongues to pleasure him was a warm, wet ecstasy that would be burned into Johan's mind until he died.

Johan was aware that people had sometimes found him attractive, he could feel the way their eyes raked over him, but nobody had ever remained interested after they'd discovered he couldn't actually speak to them.

Having people you cared about who'd taken the time to know you even without your words was a revelation to Johan, and even as the sweat that covered his skin began to cool, Johan had never felt warmer.

Elias shuffled up from Henrik's thigh until he was squished between his lovers, and he felt a little chilled now, so Johan reached for the blanket and covered them all.

"Was that okay?" Elias peered up at Johan from where his head was resting on Johan's chest.

Johan snorted at that. He was fairly sure he'd never been more okay in his life. But he also felt like he should confess something to the two of them, and in the afterglow of release, he found his words weren't quite as stuck in his throat as they often were.

"I've never... Before," he confessed.

"With a man?" Elias asked.

"Anyone," Johan admitted.

"Do you regret it?" Henrik sounded timid.

Johan shook his head. He would treasure this moment with the two of them forever, he knew that much.

"Why... me?"

The two elves sat up slightly at the question, four amber eyes stared at him incredulously like he was the most oblivious man in the world.

"We like you, Johan. You're a kind and beautiful person. Inside and out. Why not you? And well... we tried to court you," Elias explained. "But I don't think you noticed."

Elias threw the words out so easily, and yet they rooted in Johan's heart and bloomed into the brightest flower. Tried to court him? He spent his entire days studying these two men, there's no way he would have missed that. Unless...

"These?" Johan tugged at his nightshirt.

"Yes! Elves do not make clothes without payment unless they're courting. Or in slavery, I guess," he added.

Johan pointed at himself. "Not an elf."

"No. Rik pointed that out when you didn't seem to understand what we were doing. I thought this might be obvious enough, though, no?" Elias beamed, and Johan laughed until his shoulders shook. Only Elias would leap from making clothes to sucking Johan's cock with nothing in between.

"This was his idea, not mine," Henrik hastily added, which only made Johan laugh harder.

"I know." He stroked the strands of hair that had come loose from Elias' hair tie and smiled up at him fondly. How did a person go through what he had and remain such a ray of sunshine?

Johan's gaze dropped to Elias' lips all of a sudden, and it felt very important that after everything that had just happened, they couldn't leave this bed without having kissed.

Johan tapped on Elias' full bottom lip with his index finger, but the elf didn't understand and tried to playfully bite it.

Luckily, Henrik seemed to always manage to read Johan's mind. "You'd like to kiss Eli?"

Johan nodded but pointed to Henrik too, wanting it to be clear that he didn't only desire Elias.

"Kiss Henrik first," Elias said. "He's been patient for you."

The implication that Henrik had desired this for a while wasn't lost on Johan, and he filed that information away to think on later.

He sat up and tugged Henrik closer, but he still had a worried look on his face like he wasn't entirely sure if Johan really wanted to kiss him.

Johan couldn't have that.

Grabbing him by the hips, Johan lifted Henrik and placed him on his lap so they were face-to-face, Henrik straddling him. A blush creeped over Henrik's cheeks because neither of them had anything on below their nightshirts and their soft cocks pressed together in a way that somehow felt more intimate than what they'd just done.

Johan reached up and cupped Henrik's face. He stroked his thumbs along his high, sharp cheekbones all the way to his pointed ears. Johan continued, running his finger to the tip of his ear. They were beautiful, just like Henrik.

Johan took a moment to really study Henrik's face. His usual slightly stern expression had given way to something so vulnerable that Johan wanted to bundle him up with blankets and protect him forever. His chest ached with the need.

With one hand, Johan pulled Henrik's face towards his, the other pressed over Henrik's heart. For some reason, Johan needed to be able to feel the rhythmic beating of it under his palm.

Johan had never kissed anyone before, and the first press of Henrik's soft pink lips against his sent what felt like a bolt of lightning through his chest.

Henrik sort of melted into him, suddenly relaxed in Johan's arms with his hands sliding from his shoulders to his chest as they tasted one another.

Henrik's tongue swiped at the seam of Johan's lips, and he opened for him without hesitation. The moment their tongues touched, Johan began to harden again. It occurred to him that the unfamiliar taste on Henrik's lips was his own release and the thought only served to arouse him more.

When Henrik started to pull away, Johan couldn't help but chase his lips for more. Henrik was smiling, though, a smile so soft that Johan hardly recognised him with it.

Henrik reached for Elias then, and pressed their lips together briefly before guiding Elias' face to Johan's.

"Rik has magical lips, doesn't he?" Elias whispered, nothing but space for breath between them. "When he kisses me, I feel like I could take on the world. Can I kiss you, too?"

Johan didn't answer with words; he reached for Elias and pushed his hands up the back of his nightshirt to tug him closer before taking him in a fierce kiss. He was rougher with Elias in a way that felt right for them.

Elias moaned into Johan's mouth, and he wanted to swallow every sound he made. The musky taste of Henrik's cum still on Elias' lips made the kiss even more intoxicating.

In true Elias style, he arranged himself so that he was sitting on Johan's lap in front of Henrik, who peppered kisses along Elias' neck. Elias quickly returned to pillaging Johan's mouth with a ferocity that Johan could only expect from the fierce elf.

Once Elias' chin was reddened from the friction of Johan's beard, and they were both panting for breath, Elias collapsed forward, pressing his pointed ear to Johan's heart like he could hear how fast it was beating. Like a mirror, Henrik rested his head on the other side, facing Elias. He lifted Elias' hand to his mouth and began leaving gentle kisses to each of his fingertips in the most adoring way.

As arousing as it had been to hear the two of them when they were intimate downstairs, seeing them so affectionate and loving to one another was something Johan couldn't peel his eyes away from.

By lunchtime that day, Johan was fairly certain he'd never been touched so much in his entire life. They had taken it in turns for one of them to mind the front shop, which had a steady stream of customers all morning, while the other two would busy themselves making shoes in the workshop.

Johan wasn't sure if this was an elf thing or an Elias and Henrik thing, but they kind of rubbed themselves against him a lot like cats. When they passed Johan, they'd press into him and butt their heads against his arm. While it bewildered Johan, he found their affection towards him adorable, and like a dehydrated plant, he lapped it up.

Stomach grumbling, Johan closed up the shop for lunch and headed back up the stairs to where his elves were putting some food out. They both grinned at him when he stepped into the kitchen, as though his mere presence brightened their day, and Johan was becoming increasingly certain that he'd bashed his head and this was all a very vivid dream.

Taking a seat, Johan watched them as they navigated their way comfortably around his kitchen. Henrik sat next to him, but Elias took him by surprise when, instead of taking the third seat, he walked around, lifted up Johan's arm from the table and settled himself on Johan's knee.

Henrik smiled conspiratorially with Johan. "Eli is very needy. You have to tell him very bluntly when you require space."

"It's true, I am. I cannot fathom why anyone would want space from me, but alas, I have pushed Rik to his limits on more than one occasion." Elias continued to eat his lunch, content to use Johan's lap as a chair.

Johan couldn't quite imagine ever being sick of having Elias in his space, but his words were gone. In fact, he'd been struggling a lot with them that day. Instead, he wrapped his arm around Elias' waist and kissed his shoulder. It wasn't lost on Johan that how they were acting with him and the words they used implied a continuation from what had begun that morning. Something Johan yearned for more than sex. Companionship and intimacy. To be seen and understood and maybe even one day, loved.

While the two elves chatted happily about this and that—shoes they wanted to design, areas of the shop they could apply magic to for improvements—Johan just basked in the warmth of it all as he ate.

A short while before they usually shut up the shop for the day, Elias and Henrik had excused themselves and headed upstairs to Johan's home. *Their* home now, Johan supposed. They hadn't talked about it, but Johan had spotted them throughout the day taking their belongings upstairs.

It made him smile. He wasn't sure if they thought he wouldn't notice or that they just knew him well enough to be reassured that he wouldn't mind. Either way, the thought of his home being their home, a wardrobe filled with their clothes and signs of life beyond his own, soothed the ache of loneliness Johan had felt in his heart for so long.

When the shop was closed and he'd swept up and tidied everything away, Johan was not disappointed with what he found upon opening the door to his home.

Elias and Henrik were both naked, standing by the fire as they washed each other from a pot of warm water. Johan held his breath as he watched them in the soft glow of the oil lamp.

They were both stunning in their own way. Henrik was taller and sharper looking with lean muscles that covered his body. It was as though he considered every single movement he made, and it was purposeful, graceful.

Elias, on the other hand, was less inhibited. Johan could see how comfortable he was in his own skin and how he moved without any self-consciousness. While still slim, he'd gained weight since they'd met, and it had softened him.

Johan sucked in a breath when Henrik pressed the damp wash cloth between Elias' cheeks causing him to moan softly. Henrik had a knowing smile, and Johan felt a pang of envy at how well Henrik knew Elias' body, and he didn't.

A bone-deep thirst made Johan desperate to know every single thing that made them feel good. He wanted to know where and how they liked to be touched. What made them whimper, what made them moan. He wanted to taste their skin and feast on them both.

Elias opened his eyes and smiled at Johan. "Come join us," he said.

When Johan was within reaching distance, Elias began unbuttoning his waistcoat and lifted his undershirt while Henrik undid his trousers and pulled them down. They efficiently had him naked in under a minute. He didn't feel exposed or vulnerable, though. The way their eyes devoured him made him feel like a prized painting. The roaring fire had the room at an ambient temperature, and Johan was pretty thrilled to be standing there naked with two beautiful elves.

They both took a cloth from the basin, and Johan blinked back tears when Henrik rubbed the cloth against the skin of his chest, just as Elias did the same on his back.

He kept expecting to feel self-conscious. Johan looked nothing like the elves; where they were small and slight; he was big and bulky. They had smooth, nearly hairless skin, whereas Johan's chest and stomach were covered in soft brown hairs. But Johan was used to communicating without words, and the hunger and desire he saw in both of their eyes was louder than if they'd shouted it to him.

They took their time washing him. Gentle roaming hands caressed him from head to toe until he feared his skin might actually set alight from the blaze of arousal in his stomach.

After, when they were all clean and dry, Elias took Johan and Henrik by the hand and guided them to the bed.

Elias lay down on his side and Henrik tucked himself in behind him. Johan wasn't sure where he was supposed to be but Elias patted the bed to his front, so Johan lay and faced them.

It was nothing shy of surreal to have two stunning, naked elves in his bed, staring at him with bright, eager eyes.

Henrik reached over Elias and brushed his fingertips over Johan's cheek. "We need to find a way for you to tell us if you feel uncomfortable when you cannot find the words."

Johan's immediate reaction was that they would never make him uncomfortable, but then he thought maybe they needed the reassurance that he could let them know if that was the case.

Johan clicked his fingers twice and nodded at them.

"If we need to stop or pause, you will click your fingers twice?" Henrik confirmed.

Johan gulped nervously but nodded again.

"Do you know how men sometimes lie together?" Elias asked, trailing a finger down Johan's chest.

Fifteen

ELIAS

"I ... think so," Johan replied.

It had been a long time since Elias had been intimate in the way he most enjoyed. He and Rik had attempted it once during captivity, but without oil or magic to create a smooth glide, it had been painful, so they hadn't tried again.

"I would like for Henrik to find his pleasure inside of me. But I'd also like to kiss you and touch you at the same time. I'd like for us all to feel good together," Elias explained, already stiff from the thought alone.

Johan nodded. "I'd... I'd like that."

Elias smiled. He was never happier than when he got exactly what he desired.

Henrik kissed and licked down Elias' neck to his shoulder. He reached forward to lift Elias' leg and hike it up over Johan's hip. Elias loved being manhandled, loved being positioned like a doll and taken.

Elias leaned forward to capture Johan's lips and groaned into the larger man's mouth when Henrik rubbed his fingers over his hole.

It had been so, so long.

Closing his eyes, he concentrated on magic, shaping it and forming it in his mind until he felt some of the slick substance leak from him. Henrik must have felt it because he didn't hesitate to press his finger in, slipping in easily and lighting Elias up from the inside. After so long, it was both too much and not enough. Completely overwhelmed, he lightly bit into Johan's full bottom lip until the shoemaker whimpered.

Elias bucked his hips, which bumped his erection into Johan's. He kept going, rhythmically gyrating and chasing after any pressure that felt good until Henrik added two more fingers and rubbed that spot inside Elias that had him writhing.

"Yes, Rik. Right there, please." Just as he begged, Henrik stopped, and he let out a frustrated humph.

When Elias felt the tip of Henrik's cock nudging against his entrance, though, he gripped Johan's arm to brace himself, his fingers leaving little white marks on Johan's skin.

Henrik pushed in slowly, and Elias loved every moment of it. The stretch was blissful, and the intimacy of having his lover deep inside him soothed a part of Elias' soul.

This was something else he hadn't even realised had been stolen from him, and reclaiming it had Elias soaring. He deserved this. Deserved to make love the way he desired, deserved to have his lovers make his body sing for them. He deserved to feel *good*.

"How does... it feel?" Johan asked.

For once it was Elias who struggled to find the words. "Like... Like I could"—Elias grunted when Henrik thrust into him—"fly. Like I'm... finally alive." Elias gasped and let his head fall forward against Johan's chest.

He kissed the shoemaker's chest and flicked his tongue against his stiffened nipple. Johan gripped the back of his head and held him there. Encouraged, Elias kept going, licking and sucking on Johan's skin and nipples until all he could do was cling on for dear life when Henrik finally gave him what he wanted. Henrik drove his hips forward, ploughing into him over and over again, hitting that perfect spot.

Johan reached between them and took Elias' and his own length into his tight fist, rubbing their cocks together in a way that made every thought Elias had ever had, empty from his head.

He came suddenly and without thought, spraying his release over Johan's cock and hand while Henrik continued to chase his own pleasure inside him. His entire body shook and trembled at the force of it.

"You feel... incredible, Eli. Gods, how are you real?" Henrik garbled out as Elias' hole clenched around him. It didn't take long before Henrik groaned, and Elias felt the warmth of his seed filling him.

Johan let go of Elias' length and reached between the elf's legs until he could feel where Henrik and Elias remained connected. Johan scrunched his eyes shut and whimpered before using his other hand to take himself roughly, furiously stroking his cock until he joined them in ecstasy and shook through his orgasm. He was beautiful like that. All the usual strain of worry nowhere to be found and replaced with blissful rapture that transformed him.

Henrik began to pull out, but Elias reached back and stopped him. "Wait, friðill. Stay inside me a little longer," he asked. After waiting so long, he wasn't ready to be empty again so soon. Wanted to relish in the feeling a little longer.

Henrik obliged, pushing back deep inside him and wrapping an arm around Elias' chest. Johan leaned forward and kissed them both, smiling shyly before pulling them both into an embrace.

"Will you take me like this one day?" Elias asked Johan.

He looked worried and opened his mouth a few times, but he clearly didn't have his words just then.

"You won't hurt him," Henrik reassured, always able to read Johan's mind apparently, given the relief on his face. "If you go slow and he's aroused enough, he could probably take us both," Henrik joked.

"Now, that is the best idea you've had in a long time," Elias said before yawning and nuzzling his face into Johan's warm, furry chest.

That is a very good idea, indeed.

A week later, their blissful bubble burst and the elves discovered that they'd become a little too comfortable.

Johan, who had been down the street collecting some food from the butcher's, burst in through the front door of the shop, gasping for breath.

"Queen's. Carriage," he blurted out.

"Where?" Henrik asked, his voice laced with panic.

Johan pointed down the street, and Elias rushed to the shop window to take a look.

Sure enough, a golden carriage was being pulled down the main street by four huge black horses. The pavement, which had been bustling with people just moments before, was a ghost town now.

The only evidence of some children who'd been playing on the corner was an abandoned skipping rope on the ground.

Johan gripped Elias by his upper arm and pulled him into the back, shoving him and Henrik into the workshop.

They didn't remain in there for long. Once Johan had gone back into the shop, the two of them snuck into the hallway that connected the two spaces and listened in at the doorway.

The front door jingled, alerting them to someone entering the shop. It could have been anyone, but when all the fine hairs on Elias' skin stood on end, he knew that it was her.

"You are the owner of this establishment?" she asked. Her voice sent shivers down Elias' spine.

Johan must have nodded.

"I see. And your... workers?"

There was a beat of silence before a man spoke, "I believe the owner is what they call, a 'mute.'" He said it disdainfully, and Elias hated it. He wanted to go in there and tell them how much Johan says without his words. He wanted to hide Johan from anyone who's ever treated him as less than, but Elias feared exposing Henrik even more.

"Well, if you are selling elf-made shoes, then you have elves working for you in some capacity. Do you not?"

Silence once again. Elias glanced behind him at Henrik, who had gone white as a sheet, sweat gleaming across his forehead as if he had a fever.

Elias realised there was no avoiding this entirely, but maybe he could spare his love.

"Wait here, do not come out, Rik. Do not follow me," Elias whispered to him.

Taking a deep breath for courage, Elias squared his shoulders and peered around the door.

"I—" he coughed, and the Queen, plus her entourage of four men, turned to face him. "I am the one who assists in making the shoes."

Her gaze raked over him curiously. "This man here, is your owner?" She pointed at Johan.

The question alone made Elias feel sick. He wasn't sure whether lying would help or hinder him. If he declared Johan as his owner, she could easily force his hand into "selling" Elias. But if he admitted he was free, there was nobody but himself protecting him.

"No." He gulped. "He is not my owner. I am free." He showed his wrists, bare of the copper bangles which had suppressed his access to magic.

She narrowed her eyes in what Elias worried was suspicion.

"Interesting... What does he pay you?"

"One-third of each sale," Elias answered honestly.

"I have never had an elf in my... employ. But I have witnessed your talents and would be prepared to pay you double if you came to work for the palace," she offered.

Elias could taste the lie in the air he breathed.

"Thank you for such a... generous offer, Your Highness. But I do not plan to remain in this kingdom for long, so I will have to decline." Elias bowed his head, dropping his gaze to the floor in what he hoped she would take as deference.

"And what about your friend?"

Elias' head snapped up to look at her again in panic.

"My friend?" he practically squeaked.

"Yes. I was reliably informed that there were at least two elves here. Maybe your friend would be interested in my offer."

Dread sat heavily in Elias' stomach, knowing in his gut that this was all a farce, all a trap.

Elias didn't even hear the door open, but suddenly Henrik appeared at his side, hands shaking, and Elias wanted to scream at him for showing his face to the Queen.

"Th-thank you, but when we leave this kingdom, we will leave together. S-so, I must also decline," Henrik said.

Johan had moved closer, too, his large frame a fraction away from being pressed into Elias' side.

"I see," the Queen said through clenched teeth. Even her footmen glanced worriedly at each other. They were all frozen in time, waiting in suspense for her next move.

"I suppose I shall not impose on you for any longer."

That couldn't be it, could it?

Without another word, she and her men emptied out of the shop, leaving an air of dread in their wake.

The three of them remained in stunned silence until her carriage was long gone and folk had begun returning to the main street.

"This isn't over, is it?" Henrik asked.

Both Elias and Johan shook their heads. *This was definitely not over.*

Sixteen

JOHAN

The following week was a weird combination of welcome touches, full hearts, and worried looks over their shoulders every minute of the day, waiting to see if the Queen would return.

Unable to shake the mental image of the Queen's men storming into his shop and snatching the elves from right under his nose while Johan watched on helplessly, he'd insisted that he spend the majority of the day minding the shop while they remained busy in the workshop, keeping them away from prying eyes as much as possible.

He was taking a look at what stock he had and marking it down on some parchment when the front door jingled.

It was late afternoon, and the sun was already low, casting the sky in a haze of pinks and oranges.

Johan stood to attention when he recognised the woman. She was the wife of the Queen's ambassador in Hallin, their neighbouring kingdom.

"Good evening," she said, her eyes darting around the room nervously.

Johan dipped his chin to greet her in response.

She went over to the window display and picked up the nearest pair of shoes before bringing them over to the counter.

Much like her previous visit, the ambassador's wife stood out in her refined clothing, although Johan secretly thought that Elias and Henrik could both make finer clothes still.

"There will be people watching your shop right now," she murmured. "It needs to appear that I am purchasing some shoes from you."

Johan quickly took the pair and looked them over as the woman continued.

"The enslavement of elves has always left a bitter taste in my mouth. The reminder of what elves are capable of when they are given the freedom to create outside of chains solidified that view. If you wish to keep them safe"—she pushed a silver coin across the counter to Johan and took the shoes— "you need to get them far away from here. The Queen covets them. And what she covets, she gets."

Johan gulped.

She looked out of the window nervously. "My husband and I... We were... misaligned on our views on this matter. If he were to stop by, I would be grateful if my visit were not mentioned."

Johan so desperately wished his throat didn't feel as if it was swollen shut just then. He wanted to thank her and ask her how much time she thought they had, but all he could do was nod his head and hope that his eyes shone with how grateful he was for the warning.

And with that, the ambassador's wife took the shoes and left the shop, leaving Johan's brain a tangled mess of yarn.

That evening, Johan lay in bed with Henrik and Elias, each tucked under an arm.

After the ambassador's wife had left, he'd waited an hour to keep up appearances —in case what she'd said had been true and there were people watching the shop— before he'd closed up for the day and told the elves what she'd told him.

"Maybe we need to consider going home, Eli," Henrik said, causing Johan's stomach to plummet.

"This is my home, Henrik. My only home," Elias replied, sounding more exhausted than anything else.

"Well, where can we go, then? Or do you suggest we remain here where she can pick us off like apples from a tree any time she wishes?" Henrik sat up and folded his arms across his chest.

Johan's stomach was in knots as the elves argued about something so serious. His brain whirred a mile a minute in an attempt to come up with something. Some place he could take them to and protect them, but who was *he*, really? A mere shoemaker who had only recently begun to pull himself out of poverty with the help of Elias and Henrik. What did he have to offer them?

That night, they were not physically intimate with one another. The elves clung to Johan all night long as though he were the anchor keeping them on the ground. The weight of the responsibility to care for them was a heavy one on Johan's shoulders, but he would do whatever it took to keep them safe and be worthy of their love.

In the early hours of the morning, long before the sun had risen, an idea came to Johan. As quietly as possible, so as not to disturb the elves before necessary, Johan wiggled his way free of their embrace. The gap he left behind was quickly closed as they reached for each other in sleep and became a tangle of long, slim limbs. Johan smiled softly at the sight.

He stuffed a bit of food into his knapsack, along with a skin of water, before dressing in his warmest clothes.

When he was ready, he knelt on the mattress and nudged the elves' shoulders.

"Hmm? What's wrong?" Henrik rubbed his knuckles into his sleepy eyes.

"It's okay. Follow me?" Johan asked.

Henrik nodded and shook Elias with a bit more zeal.

Elias blinked his eyes owlishly before looking around the room. "Absolutely not. It is dark and cold, and the house is not on fire."

"Come on, Johan wants us to follow him," Henrik explained.

"Johan must learn appropriate waking times, then." Elias glared at Johan as he spoke.

Johan chuckled and rolled his eyes. "Please?"

"That right there is emotional blackmail." Elias pointed at Johan, who just reached out a hand and pulled the elf up to standing.

Elias huffed until Johan bent down and kissed him softly on the lips, and Elias became pliant. It was always remarkable to Johan how quickly Elias could go from acting like a hissing cat to a puddle in his arms. Johan liked the effect he had on Elias a lot, and he was probably guilty of using it to his advantage more than he should have.

Henrik snuck up behind Elias and kissed his neck.

"This is bullying. I'm being bullied with affection," Elias whined.

"However will you endure it?" Henrik teased.

Elias begrudgingly got dressed and stuffed his woolly hat onto his head before following Johan and Henrik down the stairs.

Instead of leaving through the front door of the shop, Johan led them through the back, where the outhouse was, surrounded by a stone wall.

Elias opened his mouth, and his expression told Johan he was about to complain, so Johan quickly held a finger to his lips. Johan felt a little guilty because Elias immediately registered his reasoning and looked frightened, his wide scared eyes staring up at Johan.

The shop was being watched; that's why they were leaving this way.

Elias shivered and reached for Henrik's hand while Johan stacked wooden boxes in an attempt at some makeshift steps to help them over the wall.

Near silently, Johan went first and landed with a soft thud on the other side of the wall. The jump was a little more challenging than he remembered it being as a boy.

Johan heard light footsteps on the boxes before spotting Elias' head pop up at the top of the wall. Elias stared down at the drop and grimaced.

Elias was evidently not a fan of heights. Or rather, he was not a fan of jumping from great heights.

Johan stood ready and gestured for Elias to make the leap.

Elias took a deep breath and closed his eyes before leaping from the top and landing in the safety of Johan's arms.

He blinked up at Johan as if surprised he had survived, and Johan smiled.

"You caught me," he whispered.

"Of course," Johan replied.

By the time he'd helped Elias to his feet, Henrik was at the top of the wall, looking down. Not wasting any time, he made the jump and landed in Johan's arms before Johan had even registered catching him.

Henrik hopped down and brushed off his clothes, as though being caught had diminished his pride. Johan shook his head fondly before picking up his bag and leading them quietly away from the shop.

Surprising them all, Elias had remained quiet right up until they reached the tree line of the forest, when he whispered, "Am I allowed to speak yet, or must I suffer in every regard?"

Johan chuckled before gesturing for Elias to go ahead.

"Thank the Gods. Where are we going? Why are we going? And why are we going in the middle of the night?" Elias bombarded Johan with questions.

"You'll see," Johan managed.

"It's harder for us to be followed if we leave during the night," Henrik said, and Johan nodded his head in agreement.

Although helpful, it was a little unnerving how frequently Henrik seemed able to crawl inside Johan's head and verbalise what he was thinking. He was grateful it was Henrik and not Elias, because Elias would not use those powers for good.

"Do we have a long way to go?" Elias asked.

"Few hours," Johan replied. It lit him up inside that when he was alone with the elves, his words were coming much more easily.

"I'm already bored," Elias said.

"You are annoying, is what you are," Henrik sniped.

"I'm sorry that I enjoy being entertained in my life and don't spend my days perpetually occupied by my own miserable thoughts."

Johan hated when they got like this. They could be so mean to one another, and despite the fact neither seemed to ever hold a grudge, Johan always felt sure that their harsh words must leave festering burn marks all over their hearts.

He stood between them. "Stop."

"He started it," Elias muttered like a petulant child.

"You... you always escalate it," Johan said, raising an eyebrow at him.

Elias evidently couldn't deny that fact and so huffed in annoyance before kicking a pebble along the path.

Henrik looked a little too smug for Johan's liking.

"He's right. You do start it," Johan said.

Henrik opened and closed his mouth a few times before clamping it shut and looking in the opposite direction, like the bushes were suddenly the most fascinating thing he'd ever seen.

Johan pondered whether all elves were quite as dramatic as the two he was falling for.

The sun still hadn't risen by the time Johan took them off one of the main paths and onto an overgrown track.

"How much are you dying to ask him if he's sure this is the right way?" Elias asked Henrik, who was eyeing the long grass sceptically.

"I'm certain that Johan is certain he knows the right way," Henrik replied, and when the words registered, Johan snorted a laugh.

They walked a little farther and then broke through a tree line into a clearing of sorts. In the spring, it was quite beautiful, filled with wild flowers, but right then it looked neglected. Johan supposed that it had been really. How long had it been since he'd last come here?

On the far side of the clearing was a small hunting cabin. The sight of it brought back bittersweet memories for Johan, and because he'd learned the grief of loss never really went away, being here poked at the wound until he ached to see his father again. Ached to be able to ask his advice or receive a reassuring squeeze to the back of his neck. He took a deep breath and steeled himself.

"I never doubted you for a second," Elias gloated. "But what is this place?"

Johan swallowed past the ball of emotion in his throat as some of the greatest memories of his life bombarded him.

"Mine," he said barely above a whisper.

Johan approached the cabin with the elves trailing closely behind him. He lifted the wooden latch on the door, and it creaked loudly as it swung open. A thick layer of dust showered them when they stepped over the threshold.

Inside was much the same as it had been the last time he'd come, only in desperate need of a clean.

By the door were his and his father's bows and quivers filled with arrows. He ran his finger along his father's bow; the two of them had always struggled to connect, but hunting and fishing together had been the exception. Hunting was the one place where Johan's silence was a benefit instead of a hindrance, and one of the rare times he'd felt worthy of his father's love.

Elias and Henrik remained quiet, clearly recognising that Johan needed a moment to gather himself.

"It's... small. But the land is mine," he explained. "We could build."

Seventeen

HENRIK

H enrik blinked in surprise, taking in his surroundings. He could hardly believe what Johan was suggesting.

Although small and in need of cleaning, the cabin would have enough space for the three of them to sleep and a little left over to provide a modest kitchen/dining area. While not much to look at right now, Henrik could see the potential.

Glancing behind him back through the front door, Henrik eyed the clearing critically. There was more than enough space to gradually build themselves a larger dwelling, especially with both the elves' using magic to assist. There was arguably enough space to build themselves a workshop, too, as a means to earn money when they needed it.

Henrik was hopeful, an unfamiliar feeling to the elf who had lived so much of his life always braced for the next blow.

Grief sat heavy in the room, though. Henrik was sure that Johan had rarely, if ever, visited this place since his parents had died. He stepped closer and took Johan's hand in his own, squeezing it in a way he hoped said "I'm here, we're both here for you."

"Do you think we will be safe here?" Henrik asked.

"Safer," Johan replied.

"What about the shop? Your home?" Elias asked.

"Just a... a building. Homes can change."

Henrik's heart threatened to escape his chest at that. He feared that Johan might live to regret all he was willing to give up for Henrik and Elias and knew he could never possibly repay Johan for all he had done. The imbalance was an anvil in Henrik's stomach.

"We can't ask you to do that, Johan. It's your home, your livelihood," Henrik argued.

"You didn't ask. My choice," Johan said, looking a little cross with Henrik.

For some reason, where Henrik often took great joy in poking Elias until he bit, Johan being annoyed with him had a very different effect. He wanted to make the look on his face go away, tuck his tail between his legs and seek reassurance that it was fleeting and not a disappointment that would fester into resentment.

Before Henrik could truly spiral, however, Elias interjected, "No offense to your little hunting shack, but I think we might need to build something a bit larger if we're to stay here long-term."

Johan didn't reply, but his expression shifted into a sad yet indulgent smile for Elias, who began poking his nose into everything he could find in the room like a puppy in search of some ham.

The wooden chair by the window creaked when Johan took a seat. He cleared the dusty glass with his shirt sleeve, gazing out at the dark starlit sky.

Stealing a moment, Henrik approached him and asked, pointing at Johan's lap, "May I?" He nodded and smiled. Henrik straddled him on the chair so they were face-to-face, and Johan kissed him adoringly on the tip of his nose.

We're okay. He's not angry with me. Henrik's shoulders slumped in relief.

"You are sure?" he murmured.

Johan didn't reply verbally; he took Henrik's hand and held it over his heart, where Henrik could feel the steady beat beneath his palm.

Momentarily interrupting the moment, Elias announced, "I'm going to take a proper look outside so I can develop the vision," before sauntering back out the front door and leaving them alone.

Henrik and Johan both chuckled at their ridiculous lover.

"It's a big change living out here. It might even be hard to make a living without giving away our location," Henrik said.

"I like it out here. Peaceful. Safe. Will find a way." Johan wrapped his powerful arms around Henrik, pulling him close.

"You are as stubborn as Elias when you want to be, do you know that?"

"You must have a type." Johan laughed softly.

Henrik closed the small gap and kissed his stubborn shoemaker on the lips.

"Gods, seeing you two together makes my balls hurt, it cannot be healthy," Elias said from the doorway. He wandered over to them and stood behind Henrik, hooking his head on his shoulder. "Feel how hard I am." He pressed his groin into Henrik's back where he was indeed as stiff as a rod.

"How is that possible? It's freezing!" Henrik said in disbelief.

"I might have helped it along with a little tug." Elias waggled his eyebrows in a ridiculous manner.

"Can I... try something?" Johan asked.

"Anything," they both replied.

"Within reason," Henrik added.

Johan looked around the dusty room before adding, "When we get back?"

"You big tease!" Elias bemoaned. "You would leave me in this condition?"

Johan just stood, helping Henrik back to his feet before guiding them both back out the door.

On the walk home, Elias took to guessing what Johan wanted to try, which led to the larger man either smirking or blushing furiously. Both of which Henrik found incredibly endearing.

"Do you want to try and see how tight I can squeeze my thighs together and push yourself between them?" It was actually one of Elias' less-crude suggestions, and rather than blushing, Johan appeared to consider it before shrugging with a mischievous smile.

"Not... tonight," he said.

Henrik couldn't deny that the endless ideas Elias had come up with during their walk home had left him a bit hot under the collar, and it was a welcome distraction from why they were out here in the first place.

Elias was good at that. He often found ways of getting Henrik out of his own head so he couldn't spiral too much about things outside of his control.

By the time they clambered back over the wall and tumbled through the back door, Johan and Elias had wound each other up so much that Johan carried the smaller elf up the stairs with their lips fused together and hands roaming everywhere.

Henrik enjoyed the view of them together. He remained fully clothed as he watched them undress each other frantically. With every item of clothing removed, lips found bare skin and licked and sucked wherever they landed.

It was desire, Henrik thought. Desire for the body, yes, but also desire for connection in a moment where they feared for their future.

When they were both completely naked, Johan sank to his knees before Elias and gazed up at him.

"What do you want?" Elias asked, threading his slim fingers through Johan's hair.

Johan looked over at Henrik, eyes begging for what he wanted, and Henrik wondered if Johan had access to magic himself, because it was as though the words were being shouted into his head.

Henrik undressed slowly as he walked to join them. He left his breeches on, though, and barely stifled a laugh at Johan's disgruntled expression.

"You'd like to put your mouth on us both, is that right? You want to know what it feels like when Elias' cock hits the back of your throat, stealing your air for a moment?" Henrik asked.

Johan closed his eyes and whimpered, nodding his head.

"That's what you wanted to try? This?" Elias held his cock out, tapping the reddened tip against Johan's lips until he opened up and licked the bead of precum from the head.

Henrik finally undid his breeches and was about to stroke himself to his full length, but Johan dived for him, then started gobbling up his semi-soft cock like he was just too hungry to wait. The elf's eyes rolled into the back of his head. While unskilled, Johan's mouth was warm, wet, and enthusiastic.

Elias lazily stroked himself as he watched Johan, his dark eyes flooded with desire. Johan shifted and took Henrik in hand as he turned his attention back to Elias.

Henrik loved how quickly Johan had learned what Elias liked best, bypassing his length at first and tonguing and sucking on Elias' balls until he moaned.

Reaching out to take Elias' hand and interlock their fingers, Henrik grunted in surprise when Johan's mouth was suddenly wrapped around his cockhead again. Using his other hand, Henrik carded his fingers through Johan's hair, and the large shoemaker went pliant under his touch. It was a heady experience for Henrik.

Alternating his efforts, Johan would get one of them close to the edge before swapping to the other, until saliva dripped down his chin and the two elves were trembling with the need for release.

Johan worshipped Henrik with his mouth. Put aside his fears of not being good enough, not being skilled enough, and did everything he could to bring Henrik more pleasure than he could handle.

"Gods, Johan. Your tongue... Yes. Right... there." Without meaning to, Henrik gripped Johan's hair and kept him in place until he erupted onto Johan's tongue.

Henrik was still shaking from his orgasm as he watched Johan turn to face Elias with his mouth open and his tongue out as Elias furiously stroked himself to completion.

"You beautiful, filthy man, kjære. I. Love. It." Elias grunted before his own cum spurted out, landing on Johan's waiting tongue, his chin, and his cheeks.

The shoemaker's lips were rosy and swollen, cum painted his face, and he looked happier and more at peace than Henrik had ever seen him. Elias was right, Johan was a beautiful, filthy man and Henrik was falling hard for him.

O ver the next several days, or nights, rather, the three of them began sneaking out of the shop before the sun rose with as much as they could carry, moving their belongings to what they hoped would be their new home and a safe haven away from the Queen's watchful eye.

During the day, they took it in turns to sleep while two of them minded the shop. Henrik desperately missed spending his nights curled up with Johan and Elias, but he knew this would be worth it in the end.

They couldn't afford to sleep during the night, sure that if the Queen's men were to act, it would be under the cover of darkness, so the three of them remained vigilant from sunset to sunup.

Exhausted from broken sleep, suddenly becoming nocturnal, and the fear that if they didn't move fast enough the Queen would strike at them like a waiting python had Henrik and Elias sniping at each other more than usual.

"Did it not occur to you that we should be prioritising moving things like tools rather than your clothing collection?" Henrik griped as Elias neatly folded his clothes and stuffed them into his bag.

"Tell me, are a hammer and lapstone going to keep me warm and prevent me from freezing to death in a wooden hut during winter?"

"Ahh yes, because thin cotton bed shorts will be the deciding factor in your survival of the winter." Henrik rolled his eyes.

Instead of receiving the smart remark that Henrik expected, Elias threw his bag down and stomped out of the flat.

Johan sat up from where he'd been trying to take a short nap before they left for the night and gave Henrik a judgemental look.

"What?" Henrik snapped defensively.

"You pick at him," Johan said sleepily.

Shame swarmed Henrik like an itchy blanket. He knew Johan was right, but it was as though he couldn't stop himself. When scared and stressed, he took it out on Elias, and in the moment, it felt justified. Elias almost always took the bait, and their arguments would make Henrik feel less frightened for a while, giving him something else to focus on.

Elias and Johan never argued, Henrik was clearly the problem. Henrik felt like the diseased limb of their relationship and was sure they'd be better off without him.

Johan got up despite only having napped for around an hour and went in search of Elias since Henrik was too much of a coward to mend his own hurt.

Most of their belongings were at the cabin now. Henrik guessed that two more nights of this and everything they planned to take would be gone, and then would come the hard part.

Building a home and a life.

Henrik mindlessly stuffed various belongings into his bag until it was splitting at the seams and waited for Johan and Elias to return so they could set off.

Their walk that night was a silent one, and it suffocated Henrik. Why was it that he would criticise Elias for his inability to remain quiet yet despise it when he was? Elias couldn't win with Henrik, and he hated himself for it.

A deep frown marred Johan's features for the duration of their trek through the Dark Forest. Henrik knew how it affected Johan when he and Elias argued, and it was one more thing for Henrik to self-flagellate over.

The three of them put one miserable foot in front of the other, and it was all Henrik's fault they felt so terrible.

When they finally arrived at the cabin and added the rest of their belongings, the small space was full to bursting. They hadn't been organising anything, just dropping stuff off and leaving again, and now they could hardly fit themselves inside.

Elias dumped his bag on the floor and immediately left again without a word. Johan had a pained expression as he watched Elias' retreating back.

"What if I don't go back with you tonight?" Henrik suggested.

Johan frowned in confusion.

"There's not much left to bring and someone needs to sort through all this so there's actually space for us to sleep until we can build. I can spend tomorrow clearing the space and making room. Elias doesn't want to be around me right now anyway."

Henrik knew that Elias could hear him even from outside and it stung that Elias didn't disagree, not that he could blame him.

Johan stepped into Henrik's space and tipped his chin up with his thumb and forefinger, searching his eyes for something.

"Are you sure?" Johan asked.

Henrik had a ball of emotion in his throat that prevented him from answering so he just nodded.

Johan kissed him softly on the lips before peppering them all over Henrik's face.

"We'll miss you," he said.

"Don't speak for me," Elias snapped from the doorway.

Johan dropped his hands from Henrik and sighed.

"I wonder if you'll realise when you're all alone here that it is, in fact, you who aggravates you so much."

Elias glowered, and the words landed like a punch to Henrik's chest. They frequently sniped at each other, but Elias was rarely mean. Rarely spoke with the intention to hurt Henrik rather than wind him up a little.

Despite suggesting it himself, Henrik didn't look forward to the time alone. It had been over a year since he'd been away from Elias for more than a few hours, and the prospect was nauseating.

Johan held up a finger for him to wait and then left, tugging Elias behind him. They must have walked quite far because Henrik couldn't make out what they were saying.

When they returned, Elias still had a stubborn set to his jaw but said, "You don't have to remain here on my account."

Johan elbowed him.

"You should come back with us," he added, although it wasn't very sincere.

"It's fine. I'll clear some space and return with you tomorrow night," Henrik replied, pretending to already be occupied with sorting through their belongings on the floor.

Johan left the bag of remaining food with Henrik and kissed him goodbye before they went on their way.

He only got a terse farewell from Elias.

With neither the space nor inclination to be totally alone with his thoughts, Henrik chose to get to work rather than try to get any sleep. Within the hour, his brown dripped sweat from moving boxes around and organising their things. It was another two hours before he had the space to lay the smaller mattress down to get some sleep.

The sun was beginning to rise, which meant Elias and Johan would be back at the shop by now. They probably had a lovely walk home without Henrik's mood dragging them down. Elias will have happily talked Johan's ear off, and the shoemaker will have smiled the entire time because he never made Elias feel bad for his endless chatter.

Once they'd had some food and drink, they would light the fire so that the room was warm enough that Elias could forgo nightclothes as he preferred.

Henrik could picture them vividly, climbing into bed. Johan would let his hands and lips roam all over Elias' body until he was squirming beneath him.

Maybe without Henrik in the way, Elias would invite Johan into the tight warmth of his body. Let Johan chase his pleasure in a way he had never experienced before. Johan had a much larger cock than Henrik did, and he was sure that Elias would prefer it.

Henrik squeezed his eyes shut as a tangled web of feelings left him in knots of arousal, heartache, and jealousy. He wasn't even sure who he was jealous of. Maybe both of them, maybe he was jealous that they were better people than he was and were worthy of each other's love while he merely poisoned the well they all drank from.

Unsurprisingly, Henrik slept fitfully until he gave up and returned to work. By late morning, he'd done everything he could with the little hunting cabin and spent the rest of his time scribbling away on a piece of parchment, drawing designs for their new home and workshop they could build on the land.

If he couldn't be any good, he could at least be useful, he thought.

Eighteen

ELIAS

Frustration bubbled beneath Elias' skin as he and Johan walked away from the cabin, leaving Henrik behind.

"You know what really infuriates me?" he asked without pausing for a response. "He goes from being rotten to me to acting like some sort of martyr when all I want is for him to be less of a miserable shrew!"

"Sometimes... you seem like you... enjoy the fight," Johan said.

"Yes, when it's playful. But Rik knows the difference, and lately it is never playful. He only has negative things to say about everything I do, and I am sick of it, Johan. I want to enjoy my life and not be punished for that."

Johan paused on the path and pulled Elias into a tight hug.

"I'm sorry," he said.

"Sorry for what?" Elias mumbled into Johan's warm chest.

"Sorry... you feel that way."

Elias took some deep breaths in Johan's embrace and tried to calm himself down.

"Why do you put up with us?" Elias asked.

"Hmmm. Very sweet."

Elias leaned back so he could peer up at Johan. He grinned impishly. "Was I sweet when I came all over your face the other night?"

Johan turned a shade of crimson. "Sweet... and a little... wicked."

They both laughed before continuing on their way.

By the time they'd snuck back into the shop, they were both exhausted. They'd already taken the mattresses to the cabin and so had to make do with a thick blanket on the floor. It was more unfortunate for Johan than for Elias, who preferred to use Johan's body as his mattress regardless of what they were laid on.

Nothing settled Elias like bare skin against bare skin and the lullaby of rhythmic breathing and steady beats of Johan's heart under him as his shoemaker drifted off to sleep.

He couldn't help but think of his missing lover, though. He hoped Henrik was okay. Elias actually hated the thought of Henrik alone in the Dark Forest and was kicking himself for not actually encouraging him to return with them. Most of his anger had dwindled on the walk back, and now he felt sad that they were the farthest apart they had ever been since the day they had met at the silk mill.

Elias wished desperately that Henrik could find a way to be happy. For a while, Elias thought he could be that for Henrik. That he could brighten up each of Henrik's days and love him hard enough to erase some of the pain from the heavy clouds that hung above him, but he feared that only Henrik was capable of choosing happiness for himself. In the meantime, all Elias could think to do was sometimes keep Henrik company in the rain.

E lias woke to a hand clamped over his mouth, though with the
faint light of dawn peeking in through the window, he could
see that it was Johan.

"Shhh."

The sound of glass smashing made its way up the stairs, and suddenly Elias was incredibly grateful that Henrik was nowhere near.

Elias' heart pounded loud enough that he was sure it could be
heard by their intruders. If they'd been elves, they actually might
have heard. He took a deep, steadying breath. They had planned for
this.

And Elias had made his own plans too.

They shoved on their clothes and crept as quietly as possible over
to the back window, where a thick length of rope waited for them.

Heavy footsteps thudded in the shop below, and it sent a jolt of
nervous energy buzzing beneath Elias' skin, making him feel like
he could run for miles and not tire or climb a mountain without
breaking a sweat.

Despite his larger frame, Johan gracefully and near silently clambered out of the window and made the descent first. When he
reached the bottom, Elias threw him the last remaining bags before
deftly climbing down the rope himself, and he prayed this wasn't
how he would meet his demise. Near to the bottom, he jumped
into Johan's waiting arms and silently begged for the larger man's
forgiveness for what he was about to do.

Back on his feet, Elias held his hands against the brick wall that
had been his first home in over five years, possibly the only home
he'd ever felt safe, welcome, and loved in.

Yet he continued anyway. Closing his eyes, his arms trembled at
the effort as he gathered some magic to the surface and let it spread

through his fingers and into the bones of the building, weaving its way into every bit of material it met like a spreading disease.

This was not part of their plan.

"What are you doing?" Johan whispered frantically.

Elias finally peeled his fingers from the wall and replied, "Follow me."

Now with a practised efficiency, they quickly used the boxes to climb over the wall, kicking them over behind them to slow any potential assailants down. On the other side, Elias ran like his life depended on it.

Johan's heavy footfalls were close behind him, and they continued in a loop until they were at the top of an embankment that had a view of the front windows to the shop.

The ground was muddy beneath their feet as there had been a lot of rainfall in the last few days. Elias would have to be careful not to slip.

"I knew it," Elias said on a gasp.

"Knew what?"

Elias pointed to the shop window where several of the Queen's men were fighting to escape the invisible barrier he'd created, trapping them in the confines of the empty building.

A darkness took over Elias then. A part of himself he kept hidden and buried from the people he loved, lest he taint them with it. But it arose inside him then, and there was no turning back. Elias had waited for this chance. He wasn't going to let it slip through his fingers now.

"There is a man by the front window," Elias explained to Johan who could not see as far as he could. "He's a slaver. Makes his living delivering and abusing slaves... like me. He was the man who chased us the night we escaped. He used me as a... a toilet." Elias gulped past the shame which he knew had no right to belong to him. "He is the one who chased us through the forest. We thought we might die. He threatened to get dogs to track us down like prey," Elias spat. "I was sure I had spotted him watching from the alley across the road yesterday!"

Johan reached out and took Elias' hand in his own. The look on the shoemaker's face almost stopped Elias in his tracks. *Almost.*

"Please don't hate me, Johan," he pleaded.

"Could... never... hate you. But we need to leave," Johan said with some urgency.

Elias spun to face Johan and kissed him. He held Johan's face between his hands, felt the familiar rough stubble of Johan's beard against the palms of his hands, and let the magic surge.

"Forgive me," he whispered as the shoemaker's eyes closed and Elias tried his best to lower him gently to the ground. "Take care of Henrik. I know you will. But he thinks you are the soft-hearted one, but it is him," Elias added as though Johan's limp body might hear him. He knew what he risked in continuing with his plan, but he'd already passed the point of return.

Determined, he set off running back towards the shop to finish what he'd started.

What he found was surreal. The mouths of the men in the window opened and closed like goldfish. They were screaming and yelling inside, but the magic he'd imbued the building with had muted their shouts, making them appear almost comical, like mimes from a fair.

The sickeningly familiar, soulless eyes of the slaver who'd urinated on Elias represented everything that he sought vengeance for. The man, for a moment, looked like just a man. Not evil. But frightened, terrified even. And Elias almost hesitated. But then he saw the moment recognition flickered across the slaver's face, and the menacing stare that took over his features told Elias everything he needed to know. Given the chance, he would kill Elias. Kill him, and Henrik, and any elf who dared expect more from this life than to be a mere belonging. A replaceable part in a factory.

Good, that look in your eyes will make this easier, Elias thought.

Gathering every last drop of strength he possessed, tainting magic and twisting it into something it should never have become, Elias willed magic to form globes of hot blue fire in the palm of each hand. Fire not to create like it might in a forge. No, fire to destroy. Fire to *kill*.

Elias had once explained to Johan that elvish magic was inherently good. He'd discovered that it could be manipulated, though. It turned out, if their souls were as battered, bruised, and hacked to pieces as Elias' was, they could bring forth those flames meant for the forge and use them for what Elias considered justice instead.

Elias launched the flames through the open upstairs window, where the drapes immediately caught fire. Fiery tongues spread quickly, eating through the wood even faster than Elias had anticipated.

The upstairs was engulfed in what felt like a matter of minutes, and Elias was relieved that the magic he'd infused into the building earlier had worked, preventing the spread of the fire into the neighbouring shops. He'd grown fond of the baker and his wife, and Elias had no intention of making their lives any harder than they already were.

Hypnotised, Elias couldn't look away as the fire swept through the building, filling the place with smoke and devouring everything and everyone in its path.

Smoke made it difficult for Elias to see inside, but he dared not blink. The scorching heat coming from the building had sweat beading along Elias' brow.

Like the shop was angry with him, it spat hot ash out, littering Elias' skin with burn marks and dirt. But he didn't look away. Didn't move a muscle.

It wasn't until Elias spotted a flayed hand slipping down the window as the final man met his end that he finally collapsed from exhaustion onto the pavement.

He'd expected relief. But the great, chest-heaving sobs that escaped him as he choked on the smoke were a fierce storm of anger, grief, and worst of all... guilt. Not for the men inside, no. Guilt for destroying the only home he and the men he loved had ever felt safe in. Like a mantra, he'd told himself repeatedly that it would be worth it. The cost was worth it. It had to be. And it was. Wasn't it?

Part of him wished that they had suffered for as long as he had, but the closure of revenge would have to suffice. The horrific nature of their death Elias' compensation for the quickness of it.

Elias knew that he should run, that it was only a matter of minutes until people would be out in the street to see the spectacle he'd caused, but he was glued to the spot.

It was selfish of him to do this, selfish of him to prioritise his own closure over the home and shop that Johan had grown up in.

But Elias decided this would be his life's most selfish act; he hadn't had many, after all. Years in slavery had stripped him of his autonomy, but this decision, this choice, the good and the bad of it, were all his to make.

His arms burned from where the hot ash had landed on him and singed holes in his clothes. Elias coughed from the smoke until his eyes watered, then he closed them. And that was the last thing he remembered.

Nineteen

JOHAN

Johan didn't even have time to be angry when he came to. Light that didn't belong in the dead of night danced behind his eyelids, and he opened them to find a blazing fire on the main street.

He knew instantly what Elias had done.

Heart racing until he feared it might stop entirely, Johan leaped to his feet, abandoned his belongings, and ran down the embankment. Dread and fear filled his stomach like a bitter, poisonous concoction, and when he got close enough to spot the slumped, lifeless form of his love on the street, he had to swallow down the vomit which rose in his throat.

No. No you don't get to leave us behind.

Covering his mouth with his shirt to avoid breathing in the thick smoke that billowed from the place, which just hours earlier had been home, Johan rushed to Elias' side and scooped him up into his arms.

The heavens opened up, and Johan battled his way through the torrential downpour, slipping several times in the mud as he made his way back to where he'd left their belongings. Thunder cracked overhead as Johan laid Elias' limp form on the damp ground. He put his ear to Elias' mouth and stared at his chest, willing it to rise.

Johan nearly collapsed onto the ground with relief when he felt the warm puff of air against his cheek. He shook Elias by the shoulders but got no response.

Giving himself just enough time to catch his breath, Johan gathered all he could into a bag to carry on his back and cradled Elias in his arms before setting off back towards the forest. Back towards Henrik, who Johan prayed would know what to do.

Endless burn marks littered Elias' arms, chest, and face, but none looked severe enough for him to have remained unconscious. Johan feared that all the smoke Elias must have breathed in might have harmed him in ways Johan couldn't see, but he couldn't take him to the doctor since Elias had just... had just...

Johan could hardly bring himself to think the words, but he needed to. He needed to face up to what had just happened.

Elias had murdered a number of men in his home. It would be unlikely to be safe for any of them to show their faces in Falchovari again.

Regardless of what Elias had done, the only thing that mattered right then was that the small yet larger-than-life elf wake up from whatever sickness had overtaken him.

Johan prayed to any god who would listen that Elias would be well enough to brighten every new doorway with his smile once more. Johan would sooner witness Elias and Henrik argue like they had just earlier that night, every day for the rest of his life, than live a day without Elias in it at all.

"Please be okay, you need to be okay," he whispered to Elias' unconscious form. "You need to be okay, because I love you. Henrik loves you."

Johan felt like a coward but promised himself that if Elias pulled through, he would find the words to tell both of them how much he loved and adored them. How much they'd turned his life from a mere existence to this effervescent, blinding thing that Johan would go to war to protect.

The walk home felt like the longest trek of Johan's life. He stopped only to catch his breath twice, Elias getting heavier and heavier with every step he took.

Under the thick canopy of the trees, the rain had slowed to a trickle, which gave the forest an eerie quiet. His own laboured breathing, however, seemed so loud he was certain it could be heard for miles around.

By the time he reached the cabin, his arms were screaming in pain; nothing but the surge of energy swimming in his veins had pushed Johan forward in the direction of Henrik. The sun had risen at some point during his return, but he couldn't even guess the time now.

Johan had barely stepped foot inside the clearing when the front door burst open and Henrik came running towards him.

"What happened? Why are you back already? Eli? Eli?? What's wrong with him?" Henrik's voice became more panicked with every question.

Johan couldn't speak yet. He needed to get Elias inside. Once he'd gently placed Elias down on the larger mattress, he collapsed onto the floor with exhaustion.

"They. Came. For. Us," Johan panted out. "He. Killed. Them."

"Eli did?"

Johan nodded.

"Did they hurt him? What's wrong with him?" Henrik stroked Elias' hair as he tried to press the spout of a skin of water to his lips.

"I don't know."

"How? How do you not know? Weren't you with him?"

Johan glared at Elias' on the bed and said, "No."

It was then that Johan spotted the second mattress on the far side of the room, and it was like a punch to his stomach. He was too tired to even attempt to piece together why Henrik had made a bed for him so far away from theirs.

"Watch him while I get water?" he asked Henrik.

"Of course. But... what do I do? How do we make him better?"

"I don't know." Johan hated that he himself didn't know. Hated how useless he was right then.

Feeling defeated, Johan grabbed the skins and dragged his tired body the thirty-minute walk to the freshwater spring.

He'd never thought himself a coward, but after hours with nothing to focus on except Elias' too-still body, he couldn't do it anymore. The image of Elias slumped on the ground would be burned into Johan's mind for the rest of his life, and he just needed a moment to gather himself before facing reality once more.

The air was crisp, and the rain had stopped. Fortunately, the freshwater spring hadn't frozen yet and was flowing fast from the earlier downpour, so Johan filled all the skins he could carry.

Too exhausted to immediately manage the walk back, he took a few minutes to wash himself, like if he removed the sweat and ash from the smoke then he could somehow erase the events of the night.

He should be more angry at Elias for burning down his home than he was. But he'd meant what he said, homes could change. He could grieve the loss and move on, but his anger at Elias wasn't about the fire.

The fire he understood. Given the chance, he probably would also have burned alive the people who had caused his loves so much suffering. Even though the smells from the fire might haunt him for the rest of his life, it was a price he was glad to have paid.

No, what he was angry at was that Elias had used magic on him without his permission and incapacitated him to the point he hadn't been able to keep Elias safe. He hadn't trusted Johan to have his back and support him, and Johan wasn't entirely sure what else he could do to show Elias that he was devoted to him and Henrik. That he was in this for the long haul.

How did he forgive Elias for something he probably didn't even regret? Would his love for Elias be enough?

Johan was an expert in repairing damaged, broken shoes, but what tools did you use to repair broken trust?

With a heavy heart, Johan trudged back to the cabin, where he found Henrik sitting on the bed with Elias' head resting in his lap.

He glanced at the mattress set aside for Johan on the other side of the room and nearly crumbled.

Henrik must be angry with him for not keeping Elias safe.

But then, Henrik had done this before they'd even returned, so Henrik must be angry with him for something else. What if Henrik had felt abandoned when they'd left him behind? Maybe Johan was supposed to have fought for Henrik to come with them, and he hadn't realised. He'd obviously messed up somehow.

He slumped miserably onto the mattress, wondering how it had all gone so wrong so fast.

"Wake me if... anything changes?" he asked Henrik quietly.

"Of course," Henrik replied absently, gaze remaining focused on Elias' still form.

Johan curled up with his back to them so he could hide his face in the wool blanket.

Sleep evaded him for a while as he ruminated on everything that had taken place in the last few days. They'd had a plan, and now Elias was unconscious and Henrik didn't want him in their bed anymore. His chest was tight and painful as panic took hold.

Johan wiped at his eyes with the back of his hand and prayed that Henrik wouldn't hear the change in his breathing as he cried silently and alone until exhaustion eventually dragged him into sleep.

The sun was setting when Johan woke. He rubbed at his eyes with his knuckles, still groggy from sleep.

Rolling to face where the elves lay, he spotted Elias first, exactly as he had been earlier that morning. Unconscious but breathing. It was cold enough in the little cabin that Johan could see Elias' tiny puffs of breath in the air and be reassured by them.

Henrik must have fallen asleep sitting up because he was slumped against the wall, a hand resting on Elias' chest. Johan suspected that Henrik had only found sleep because of the steady heartbeat resting beneath his palm.

Johan got up and snuck out quietly to relieve himself, and when he returned, Henrik was staring at him with bleary bloodshot eyes.

"How could this have happened?" Henrik whispered.

Johan's shoulders slumped. "Should I... leave?" he asked, staring at the floor.

"What? Why would you leave?"

"I... sh-sh-should have pr-protected him."

Henrik snorted derisively at that. "The Queen and... and any man who believes they have the right to keep people as their property are to blame for this, Johan. And the rest of my wrath is reserved for this pig headed, stubborn elf in my lap."

Henrik looked as though steam might begin to shoot from his ears in anger, his eyes flashing darkly in a way Johan had never seen before.

"You don't... blame me?" he asked.

"Of course I don't blame you," Henrik said more softly. "He destroyed your shop, your home, Johan. You have every right to be angry with him."

Johan swallowed the lump of emotion lodged in his throat. "Not... why."

"That isn't why you're angry?" Henrik clarified.

Shaking his head Johan said, "Used magic... I couldn't... couldn't... reach him. He..." Johan couldn't get the words to come out how he wanted them to, and he groaned in frustration.

"Shhh. Shhh, it's okay. This isn't your fault, Johan. He used magic on you, didn't he?"

Johan wiped at his eyes and nodded, wincing at the memory of how hands, which had only ever touched his face lovingly, were used to hurt him.

"I'm sorry he did that to you. It was wrong of him." Henrik stared at him intently like he could will Johan to believe him.

"He didn't... trust me." Johan felt incredibly foolish for crying, but the tears bubbled out of him regardless.

"Elias... he only trusts in as far as he must in order to survive." Henrik didn't sound angry about it, he spoke evenly like he was just stating a fact to be considered. "Can you love him even if he never fully trusts you?"

The question startled Johan. "Loving him is not... hard." Johan swallowed. "Trusting him, though..."

Henrik nodded his head in understanding. "I think... when you are betrayed by the two people in the world who should love you without exception, it alters you. He might never trust us like we could trust each other, but he will love us. Fiercely. That is enough for me, but it's okay if it's not for you."

Johan didn't have any answers right there and then, just a pit in his stomach that felt like a disease spreading around his insides. "He will... wake, won't he?"

Henrik returned to stroking Elias' hair before planting a gentle kiss to his forehead. "Sometimes it's like our magic belongs to us, and other times, it's like magic lets us borrow her. Elvish magic is supposed to be used for good. I don't know if he just burned through too much, or if magic is punishing him for misusing her, but he's breathing, and I have to believe that she will forgive him and bring him back to us. Elias told me once that the Gods owed him, and I need him to be right."

They sat in silence for some time after that. Henrik appeared contemplative while a storm roiled inside Johan as he tried to untangle the mess of thoughts that plagued him. There were words stuck in his throat that he needed to get out but couldn't. He needed to ask Henrik why he'd made a separate bed for him away from theirs. He needed to ask where he stood with Henrik if he couldn't forgive Elias, if they couldn't move past this. The words wouldn't come, though.

For the first time in a long time, he took his frustrations out on himself. Anger burned through him, and Johan pulled his hair hard before groaning and punching himself to the side of his head.

When he tried to do it again, a firm hand gripped his wrist, stopping him. Johan's breathing became erratic as all of his fears bubbled up to the surface and threatened to consume him.

Henrik was at his side, rubbing a hand up and down his back soothingly, but Johan didn't deserve it.

"Shhhh. Shhh, it will be okay. Please don't hurt yourself."

Johan just shook his head because how could it be okay? None of this was okay. He tried to speak but nothing except a half-choked sound came up, and then he couldn't feel anything but white, hot anger.

He stood and pulled at his hair again, welcoming the painful sting. Exasperated noises poured from his lips, all the while what he wanted to say was nowhere to be found. Johan kicked a nearby box, and it went flying across the room, knocking over some books that Henrik had carefully stacked.

Like a wild animal breaking free from a cage, Johan made for the door and dropped to his knees on the grass outside. He wasn't sure how long he stayed like that, panting and trying to calm down, but it began to rain heavily, and he still couldn't move.

Johan stared up at the grey thunderclouds as rain poured from them in sheets, saturating him down to the bone, and asked the Gods, why?

Why do my words get stuck when I need them the most?

Why did you take from me the only people I ever had?

Are you going to take my new loves, too?

Thunder boomed above him in reply, and Johan wept.

All he'd wanted was to keep Henrik and Elias safe, and he had failed. Elias was unconscious, and if he didn't wake up, Johan was certain that Henrik would follow.

He gasped for breaths as shivers wracked his body and the cold seeped into his bones.

Distantly, Johan could hear a voice calling his name, but it felt far away. Like when he'd been a child swimming in the river and his father would call him back for supper.

He looked over his shoulder towards the door of the cabin, Henrik stood there shivering and his lips were moving frantically. Johan tried to concentrate.

"Please, Johan. Please come back inside. You're going to get sick. I can't do this on my own, Elias needs us both and I'm scared. I'm scared, Johan. Please, please, please come back."

Henrik was so frantic that Johan registered that he must have been shouting at him for a while with no response. He didn't want to move. He wanted the ground to swallow him up, but their Gods hadn't taken them yet, and his loves needed him. Johan was supposed to be the strong one, so he dragged himself to his feet and put one foot in front of the other until he made it back inside.

Henrik made a fuss, and his cheeks were wet with tears, but he undressed Johan, removing all his wet clothes before wrapping a blanket around him.

With nothing left to give, Johan stepped towards the tiny mattress because sleep felt like the only way to have a break from his own dark thoughts, but Henrik stopped him.

"Wait. Let me move the mattress. You are too small for that one, anyway. You were never supposed to sleep on it," Henrik muttered.

"What?"

"Half your legs hang off the end unless you curl up, it's much too small for you." Henrik was looking at him like the cold might be impairing Johan's ability to think.

"But... why is it over here, then?"

Henrik looked embarrassed and worried at his fingers. "After how I'd left things with Elias when the two of you returned to the shop, I wasn't certain I would be welcome in his bed, and so I made my bed over there because it seemed better than waiting for inevitable rejection. But now that Elias is... unwell, our argument feels rather... um... silly." Henrik burst into tears at that and Johan almost laughed at what a disastrous mess they'd all become in the space of a few days.

Johan cleared his throat. "Even when I'm between you, Elias reaches across me in his sleep to touch you. Doesn't settle until his skin is touching yours somehow."

Henrik sniffled and stared up at Johan with big, trusting amber eyes filled with so much fear and sadness it made it hard to breathe. Johan bent down and kissed him softly on the lips.

Together, they picked up the smaller mattress and moved it over to the larger one to create a bit more space for them all. Johan laid on his side next to Elias and pressed the palm of his hand to his chest, needing the reassurance of his beating heart. He kissed Elias on the cheek and took in a deep inhale.

Henrik mirrored him on Elias' other side, and when Henrik placed his hand on Elias' stomach, Johan reached over and interlaced their fingers.

One moment at a time, he thought as his limbs became heavy and he drifted off into sleep.

Twenty

ELIAS

E lias' eyelids felt like they were made of iron when he tried to
open his eyes.

Where am I?

Squinting, he was able to register that the room he was in was the
cabin in the meadow, although he couldn't recall how he'd got back
there.

He turned his head and groaned, the movement sending a pulsat-
ing pain through his head.

"Johan! Johan!! He's waking up," Henrik shouted at such a volume that Elias might have shoved his hand down his throat and
pulled out his voice box if he'd had the strength.

The banging of a door followed by heavy footsteps only added
to Elias' torment, although at least unless something drastic had
changed, Johan was unlikely to begin shouting.

"Can you hear me? Are you okay?" Henrik asked.

Elias groaned. "A corpse in a graveyard could hear you, must you
be so loud?"

"We have been worried sick about you! You stubborn, pig-head-ed—"

"Shhh," Johan interrupted what Elias suspected was going to be a rather lengthy tirade judging by Henrik's tone. "Can you try to eat something?" he asked.

Elias felt quite sick, although that could have been due to a lack of food, so he nodded. "I'll try. Rik, can you yell at me tomorrow? My head really hurts," he requested, sounding as pathetic as he felt.

"You scared me," Henrik whispered, and guilt churned in Elias' stomach.

He didn't reply but he reached out and found Henrik's hand, squeezing his fingers. Bracing himself, he turned his head the other way, searching for Johan with his gaze.

Johan's eyes were bloodshot and his hair dishevelled. Elias tried to swallow past the lump of emotion, but his throat was so dry and painful that he winced.

"Sit up and sip this," Johan requested softly. He held out a skin of water and helped Elias to raise his head enough to drink from it.

The cool water was a balm, and Elias tried to drink more, but Johan pulled it away.

"Start slow, let it settle."

Elias knew Johan was right, but he was suddenly so thirsty that he was sure he might die if he didn't drink immediately. When he tried to grab for the water skin, though, he got a stern enough look from Johan that he snatched his hand back.

For the following few hours, Elias alternated between sleeping, having small bites of food, and taking regular sips of water until, eventually, when he woke up, his head had settled to a less debilitating level of pain.

Next to him on the bed, Johan was reading a book, while in the corner of the room, Rik appeared to be mending a hole in a pair of Johan's breeches.

Elias steeled himself before sitting up fully and giving his head a moment to adjust. It was raining outside and gusts of wind rattled the window, but he was quite warm wrapped up in a nest of blankets.

Johan put his book down. "Need anything?"

"I... erm... need to relieve myself. Quite urgently."

Johan chuckled softly before helping Elias get to his feet. His legs wobbled, so Johan assisted him in getting around to the side of the cabin where the roof extended and provided a little shelter from the rain.

Elias' hands shook as he tried to undo the strings of his breeches. "Can I help?"

Elias blushed but nodded. Johan deftly undid the knot and tugged them down until it freed Elias' cock. Johan held his soft member and aimed it away from their feet.

"Unghh," Elias moaned in relief as he emptied his bladder. It felt too good to be truly embarrassed that Johan was having to help him so intimately. When he was finished, Johan tucked him away and did up his breeches before helping him back inside.

Next to the bed, Henrik had left out a bucket of fresh water and a cloth, but Elias didn't have the strength to wash himself right then, despite how desperately he wished to be clean.

Johan must have registered the conflict in his expression because he wordlessly helped Elias remove his clothes and dipped the cloth in the water.

The wet cloth was warm, and Elias was grateful because Rik must have used magic to make it so. Elias was so depleted that he feared magic might never return to him.

It had all been worth it, though, he told himself.

Johan ran the warm water all over his skin, and Elias hummed happily at the sensation.

"Turn over," Johan asked.

Elias did so and Johan continued on, washing Elias' back and buttocks in a very perfunctory way that told Elias it was the most he was going to get from the larger man for a while.

"Are you angry with me?" Elias asked quietly.

Johan sighed. "Yes."

Elias nodded, expecting as much and understanding. The difficulty he was facing was that he couldn't truly apologise because he'd really set his mind on not regretting his decision.

"For the shop?" he checked, making sure he understood, since Johan struggled to elaborate.

Johan frowned. "No."

Elias kind of wished that Johan had been angry about the shop because it seemed like a more black and white thing to make amends for.

"For using magic on you, then?"

"Partly," he said before chucking the washcloth back in the bucket and helping Elias change into fresh clothes. "You don't trust me."

The words were like a gut punch to Elias. "I d—"

"Stop. P-please don't lie to me."

Elias looked to Henrik like the man might save him, but he shook his head in a clear *You're on your own with this one.*

"So, this is what it will be like now, then, you two ganging up on me?" Elias folded his arms over his chest defiantly and scowled.

Henrik huffed before putting down his sewing, walking over to Elias and straddling his legs. Elias just pursed his lips and refused to acknowledge him until Henrik gripped each side of his face, forcing him to make eye contact.

"Two things can be true at once. You did what you felt you needed to do. And you betrayed Johan. That is for the two of you to figure out. I know these two things to be true, and I am not picking a side. Just don't be so stubborn that you make it worse instead of better. Johan is not like us, his heart is soft and his bruises last longer."

Henrik kissed Elias lightly on the lips, but he couldn't enjoy it. Henrik's words had flayed him open, leaving him exposed and vulnerable in a way that left his brain screaming at him to run and hide, but he had nowhere to go. Nowhere to run to. Elias suddenly felt quite sick.

He wasn't crying. Not really. Just a little sniffle.

Johan passed him the water skin, and Elias was grateful just to have something to do with his hands. He trembled as he lifted it to his lips, but they were kind enough not to acknowledge it.

Elias should have been glad that the two of them appeared to be putting a pin in the matter of his transgressions, but it just made his skin itch. He wanted to know what the consequences were. Need to know where he stood with them both, individually and together. The not knowing ate at him for most of the day.

Later that night, and despite a bone-deep exhaustion, Elias remained wide awake. Henrik slept in the middle, and Elias felt the gap of an ice-cold fjord between him and Johan.

This relationship the three of them were building was the most precious yet fragile thing that Elias had ever had, and he could feel it crumbling under his hands.

Fear clawed up through his stomach and had a vise grip around his throat at the thought of losing the only good thing he'd ever had. Elias' heart pounded as he clambered over Henrik and climbed on top of Johan.

"Johan, are you awake?" he whispered.

"Hmm?"

Elias tugged the blanket down and tried to reach into Johan's pyjama bottoms, but a large hand gripped his wrist and stopped him.

"What are you doing?" Johan rasped.

"Can I... use my mouth on you?" Elias knew he sounded desperate, but he felt desperate and this was the only way he knew how to get someone to be close to him, and wasn't that bleak.

Johan shook his head, and Elias almost threw up before he tried to scramble away.

Johan didn't let him. "Come here."

Large arms tugged Elias down until his head was resting on a warm, wide chest. Johan wrapped Elias up tightly in his embrace and locked a leg around one of Elias', keeping him firmly held flush against Johan's body.

Elias cried. He cried because he was embarrassed, and he cried because this was what he'd wanted and yet he'd tried to use sex to get it. He cried because when he'd woken, he'd been so sure that he had no regrets about what he'd done, and now he was worried that he didn't know anything for sure at all.

What if I can't fix the mess I have made?

Twenty-One

HENRIK

Henrik wasn't sure what it said about him that he took more discomfort from Elias and Johan being in conflict than when he himself was directly in conflict with Elias. Maybe it was because he and Elias were naturally more antagonistic to one another.

Johan wasn't like them, and so seeing him hurt and betrayed was difficult to watch. Equally, Elias couldn't snark his way through his own discomfort, and the way he begged with his eyes for Johan to forgive him every second of the day broke Henrik's heart.

It had been a fortnight since Elias had woken up from his burn-out. Magic had slowly returned to him, and he was almost back to his full strength, which was a relief. Henrik couldn't even imagine what it would have done to Elias if magic had left him for good.

Johan had had fewer words than usual and worked from sunup until sundown, building their new home. The elves had helped, too, of course, Henrik and Elias having designed most of it and Henrik adding magic where he could, but most of the physical labour had been down to Johan. He didn't seem to mind, though. If anything, Henrik had the feeling that the process of making something and wearing himself out each day was helping Johan work through some things, so Henrik tried to leave him to it.

It was close to dark outside now, and they were sitting at a small table that he and Elias had built as they ate their dinner. Johan hadn't said a word, and Henrik could see the silence eating Elias alive.

Henrik saw the moment that Elias couldn't contain it anymore, and it started playing out almost in slow motion, Elias blurting the words out. "So, are just none of us going to have sex again because Johan is angry with me? The two of you don't need to become monks on my account. I can always... read a book or something."

Henrik's mouth hung open while Johan choked on the dried meat he'd been chewing.

After a sip of water to clear his throat, Johan glared at Elias. "I... I will not have sex with you when I-I-I'm angry with you."

"Then don't. I'm not asking you to have sex with me, I'm saying that you two can!" Elias snapped.

"We don't want to have sex without you, Eli." Henrik was exasperated.

Elias huffed before grabbing a hunk of bread and stuffing it in his mouth. It was dry and so he was left chewing for quite a while.

Johan stood up and said, "I'm going for a walk," before swiftly heading out the front door and into the twilight.

"What is wrong with you?" Henrik asked Elias.

Elias stared at Henrik wide-eyed and frightened. "I don't know how to fix this Rik, and every time I try, I swear I make it worse. I don't know what to do, should I go and try to talk to him?"

"Not right now, he will have walked to the water spring. It's where he goes to think."

"See? That, right there. I should know that about him, but I don't. I could tell you exactly how much pressure to apply when sucking on his balls, but I don't know where he goes when he needs space. I-I've fucked this all up, Rik!"

Henrik realised that when he and Johan had agreed to not have sex until things were mended with Eli, that he'd made a mistake when it came to Elias.

He hoped that when Johan returned later, he would understand and not be cross with Henrik for his decision.

"Come here," Henrik held out his hand for Elias before leading him over to the bed. Henrik took his time undressing them both, and he left a trail of kisses down Elias' neck and collarbone. When they were both naked, Henrik pulled him down to the mattress, and then they faced each other, side by side.

Henrik pulled Elias' leg so that it rested over his hip and left them skin to skin everywhere they could be.

When their cocks pressed together, Elias whimpered and scrunched his eyes shut.

Henrik kissed him hard, tried to show Elias with his lips and tongue how much he missed him, how much he loved him, and Elias all but melted.

"I'm sorry, Eli."

"Why?" he whispered.

"I've given Johan an abundance of what he needed—space. But you need touch and affection, and we starved you of that. It... wasn't kind."

"I'm like an awful little leech, aren't I?" Elias asked miserably.

Henrik laughed. "No, my love. You are a person, and you have needs just like we do. We'll find a middle ground until things are mended."

Elias sniffled so Henrik kissed him on the nose, then his cheeks, and then his lips. They kissed without the intention of it going anywhere despite their growing arousal. They kissed until the front door opened and Johan stepped inside.

"We weren't... We didn't... It isn't what it looks like!" Elias exclaimed as he covered himself with the blanket.

Johan cocked his head to one side thoughtfully, and Henrik could see the moment it registered what he was giving to Elias. Henrik felt antsy until a small smile tugged on the corners of Johan's lips.

He joined them on the bed, still fully clothed but he settled behind Elias and pressed a kiss to the back of his neck.

Johan cleared his throat. "You'll sleep in the middle tonight?" he asked Elias.

"Is that okay?" Elias whispered.

Johan nodded and Henrik was flooded with relief. He could see by the way Elias' shoulders relaxed that he felt the same. The last few weeks he'd become an elf-shaped barrier between the two of them, and the middle spot on the bed had started to feel loaded. This was a step in the right direction, at least.

Henrik smiled when he woke the next morning. Elias was wrapped up protectively in Johan's arms with one hand reaching out to rest on Henrik's waist. It was the most peaceful he'd seen Elias since they'd returned.

Johan's eyelashes fluttered before he blinked a few times and smiled at Henrik.

"Morning," Henrik whispered.

Johan reached over Elias and cupped Henrik's cheek, stroking his thumb over his cheekbone.

Henrik had learned over their time together that Johan often found it most difficult to speak in the mornings, like he needed to warm up to the idea of conversing. Henrik didn't mind, though, he loved how Johan communicated through touch like this. It was louder than words.

Henrik leaned into his hand. Johan had once told him and Elias that they were like cats, and he might have had a point.

"I need to relieve myself, but I don't want to wake him," Henrik whispered, eyeing his chances of climbing over Elias without disturbing him.

Johan peered down at Elias. "He's... awake."

Elias' eyes flashed open suddenly. "How did you know?" He sounded affronted but Johan merely smirked knowingly before dipping his head to press a kiss to Elias' shoulder.

"You snort like a... little piglet when you are asleep," Johan said.

"I so do not!" Elias smacked Johan on the leg in retaliation.

Johan laughed, and it was deep and unreserved. Henrik couldn't recall when he'd last heard it, but he was grateful for it now.

Henrik filled his lungs with air and breathed out in relief.

"Stop it!" Elias squealed as Johan tickled his ribs. "I'll get you for that!"

Apparently, Elias' idea of revenge was to stick his head under Johan's nightshirt and attempt to blow a raspberry on his stomach, but Elias didn't seem able to stop giggling for long enough to be successful.

When Johan's stomach grumbled loud enough to be heard over all the raucous, they finally tumbled out of bed to have breakfast.

Henrik couldn't help but fret as he gathered some food from the cupboard for them to eat. They were getting low and had no great resources yet for acquiring more food, so they were very much on rations now.

He and Johan had discussed trying some river fishing soon, as all Johan's hunting attempts so far hadn't been fruitful.

After they'd washed up and had a few mouthfuls of food to keep them going, they bundled up and headed outside to work on their new house together.

Henrik was excited to have a larger living space and hoped they could then turn the cabin into a workshop for making shoes, giving them a way to make a living again.

"I can help today, my magic feels stronger again," Elias spoke tentatively and looked at Johan for a reaction that didn't come, he only nodded his head.

The subject of Elias' and magic had been a sensitive one. Henrik knew that Johan would never wish for Elias to lose his access to magic, but he understood the shoemaker's apprehension around its return as well.

Johan had already prepared a lot of the logs they were building with, and so when he connected them together, Henrik or Elias would use magic to create a seal which would keep their home weather-resistant.

Henrik was rather proud of himself for coming up with that one.

"Who taught you to build?" he asked as he and Elias helped winch a log up to Johan using a rope contraption Elias had designed to save Johan from breaking his back on this build.

"My father," he paused. "We built that together." He pointed to the hunting cabin. "There's a lot... that I'm no good at but... I'm good with my hands. I think... my father knew I needed that."

Henrik's heart swelled a little for a man he would never meet. Johan rarely spoke of his parents, and Henrik hoarded every morsel of information he could to better understand the shoemaker who'd stolen a portion of his heart.

"You are a skilled builder and shoemaker," Elias said. "But you are more than what you can make. Rik and I have a lot to learn from you and very little of it is what you can do with your hands."

Henrik swallowed past the lump of emotion at Elias' sincerity. He was proud of Elias. So often he resorted to making jokes or saying something distractingly outlandish, but there was vulnerability in what he'd just offered up to Johan, and it was progress.

"Thank you," Johan said, his eyes glassy and grateful.

When the sun was at its highest, they stopped for something more to eat and drink.

It was a beautiful day, cold but the sky was a clear blue and birds twittered noisily in the trees. A poignant reflection of the day as a whole, it was fresh and comforting.

They'd just finished eating and were about to head back to work when Elias cleared his throat. "Johan, would you mind taking a walk with me? It's fine if you'd rather not," he hastily added.

"I'll take a walk with you." Johan smiled softly.

Twenty-Two

JOHAN

Johan passed Elias his woolly hat before grabbing his own. Despite the blue sky and the sun shining, the temperature had dropped significantly, and the ground had been covered in a glittering frost that morning.

It was a good day for them to try and talk because Johan was feeling more relaxed than he had in weeks, and his words had been coming more freely than they usually did.

He led the way out the front door and took some water skins to fill up while they were by the stream. Elias followed cautiously. Johan could tell he was nervous, and he didn't enjoy the way Elias had been walking on eggshells around him.

At least ten minutes had passed by the time Elias finally broke the silence. A record if there ever was one.

"I told myself a lie," he said.

Johan waited for him to go on.

"I told myself I'd kill those men because then they couldn't hurt other elves, but that wasn't true. The reality is that those men were replaced within the day, and I killed them because I was angry. I killed them because I wanted revenge, and I made sure you couldn't stop me because if anyone could have, it would have been you."

Johan was oddly relieved to discover that Elias had actually taken the time to examine his decisions that night.

"I don't know if I would have tried to stop you or not."

Elias nodded in understanding.

"I'm not sure if my words hold much weight to you right now, but for what it is worth." Elias gulped loudly before continuing. "I promise that I will never use magic on you again without your consent, Johan. I cannot pretend to regret the deaths of those men, but I have come to realise that I do regret what I did to you. I understand that I broke your trust, and I really hope you will give me a chance to earn it back."

With the hand not holding the water skins, Johan reached over and wrapped an arm around Elias' shoulders, tugging him into his side and squeezing.

Truthfully, Johan had been trying to find a way to make peace with Elias without an apology because he'd been certain that what happened that night was a hill Elias would be prepared to die on.

Johan wasn't and had never been an angry man. He'd battled every day with his hurt feelings towards Elias, tried to will them to disappear. Tried to force his heart to forgive the little elf, but the wound Elias had created had refused to close.

Johan felt it closing now, though. Felt his anger and hurt begin to fade at the acknowledgement that Elias knew he'd been wrong to make that choice.

"When I woke up and you were gone, I got to you as quickly as I could. And when I saw you crumpled on the street, I... I thought you were dead. You... you aren't an island. If you'd died that day, we'd have died that day. You don't get to... to leave us behind."

Johan had to take his arm back in order to wipe where his eyes were leaking.

They'd just stepped through the tree line and made their way towards the stream where they collected their fresh drinking water from. Elias took a seat on a large mossy rock that lined the bank.

"Sit with me?" Elias asked.

Johan did, although clearly Elias felt they weren't close enough, because he clambered onto Johan's lap, clasped their hands together, and pressed his forehead to Johan's.

"I'm sorry, I'm so sorry," he whispered.

"I know." Johan gently pushed a few strands of Elias' hair out of his face and tucked them back into his hat.

"Are we going to be okay?" A single tear ran down Elias' cheek.

Johan nodded before kissing Elias firmly on the lips. He melted in his arms like butter in the sun, his lips parting for Johan and welcoming him like they always did.

Elias whimpered, and Johan swallowed the sound, kissing him more wildly than he ever had before. Feverish hands tugged at Johan's shirt, and he helped Elias remove it before ridding Elias of his own clothes.

Johan kissed the breadth of Elias' chest, licking and sucking on his nipples, which were peaked from the cold air.

"Beautiful," he whispered into his lover's skin.

The temperature surrounding them rose slightly, and Johan smiled. This use of magic he could get on board with.

"Can I... I mean, can we? Um... what are we doing?" Elias asked breathlessly, clearly overcome with arousal but aware that his previous advances had been denied.

"Whatever you want, sweetheart. You can have whatever you want." Johan reached for Elias' face and pulled his lips to his own to kiss him again.

"Will you... will you take me, Johan? Make love to me?"

"Yes, Elias. Because I do, you know, love you. I love you so much. Even when I can't find the words, it's there in my heart."

Elias released a sob at that, shaking like a leaf in Johan's arms even as he frantically undid Johan's breaches to pull his stiffened cock free.

With their lips fused together, Elias stood on his knees before reaching back to guide Johan into his warm heat. He was so tight and wet and perfect that Johan had to scrunch his eyes shut not to lose himself right away.

"Johan?"

"Mmm?"

"I love you, too. My heart is divided in two and neither belongs to me anymore." Elias gasped as he sank lower. "It is battered and bruised but it's yours and Rik's."

Johan had never experienced such an onslaught of emotion. He was sure it must be bursting from his skin because there was too much of it.

"We'll take care of it," Johan promised.

"I know."

Johan helped guide Elias up and down his length in a slow but perfect rhythm as they made their way back to one another. With Elias' magic it was like existing in a warm bubble he never wanted to leave. Johan's imagination had conjured up some vivid scenarios of his first time entering another man, but nothing compared to the reality of being welcomed into the tight warmth of someone he loved.

He hoped Henrik wouldn't feel disappointed that they'd done this without him, but he also knew that the two of them needed this. Henrik had nothing to do with what had fractured between them, and so they had to repair this between themselves. Johan had needed space, and Elias had given him that at the expense of himself.

It would take physically reconnecting and intimacy for Elias to feel secure again, and Johan wouldn't be so cruel as to deny him that, and maybe Johan needed it too. More than he'd realised.

So, he made love to Elias, he poured his heart into every brush of skin against skin, kissed and treasured Elias everywhere his lips could reach, and he lost himself in Elias' body. In Elias' love.

The friction of Elias' grinding up and down his cock was too exquisite, and while Johan wanted the moment to last forever, he knew he could only fight his release for so long.

"You feel too good, too perfect. I won't last much longer." He moaned when Elias clenched around him.

Johan feared that he might never want to leave Elias' body again, and the fact Elias would likely let him stay was intoxicating.

It was a feeling like no other. So exquisite he could taste it on his tongue, felt parts of himself come alive in an explosion of sensation.

He scratched his beard against Elias' naked chest, reddening the skin and then swirled his tongue around Elias' budding nipple.

Johan would never get over the way Elias gave himself to his lovers. Gifted them his body and trusted that they'd do everything they could to pleasure him and use him just the way he adored. It was a beautiful thing to witness.

"Let go, kjære. I want to feel it, want to—" Elias gasped as he sank all the way down. "Need you to fill me. Mark me as yours from the inside."

Elias leaned back slightly and braced one hand behind him on Johan's knee, using the other to stroke himself hard and fast, all the while continuing to ride Johan so hard he could hardly form a coherent thought.

It was all too much, too perfect, and too everything, and Johan erupted. He practically shouted Elias' name as he held him down on his cock, trapping his release inside his lover while his body trembled from what Johan could only describe as a spiritual experience.

Elias followed Johan into bliss almost immediately, cum shooting from the head of his cock all over Johan's hairy stomach before he collapsed forward, his chest heaving.

"Please. Tell. Me. We'll be. Doing. A lot more. Of that," Elias panted.

Johan chuckled a little hysterically and wrapped his arms tightly around Elias' back.

"Our new house might never get built now," he replied.

Johan enjoyed the fantasy of a life where the three of them did nothing but make love and take turns filling Elias up with cum. He wasn't sure when his imagination had become so filthy, but he was fairly certain it started around the time this particular little elf had burst into his life with his shameless perfect mouth.

Elias' magic was beginning to wane, and it became much too cold to linger, so they quickly washed up in the stream and filled up their water skins before heading back to the elf who completed them.

"Gods, what is that? Did you see it?" Elias asked as they walked hand in hand.

"Kingfisher, they are quite common by the water."

"It's beautiful. I've never seen a bird that colour before. It's like a winter sunset or something. Magical," Elias said in wonder.

Johan beamed at Elias like the lovesick fool he was. One of the things he adored about Elias was his ability to find simple joys in the world. Elias always paused to smell a nice flower or to admire a tiny ant carrying a big leaf on its back.

"They are a lot like elves. They collect things and give gifts to woo their mate," Johan explained.

"Gosh, what romantic little birds. Do they mate for life, please tell me they do?"

"Not exactly, but they do often return to their mate for more than one season."

"Kjære, if I were a kingfisher, I'd always return to you." Elias squeezed Johan's hand.

"What does 'kjære' mean?"

Elias blushed, and Johan had to fight not to kiss the bloom as it spread across his cheeks.

"Um... it means like, darling, or... or beloved."

Johan brought their joined hands up to his lips and kissed the back of Elias'. "My kjære, too," he said.

Twenty-Three

HENRIK

*T*hose *two better come back made up or be ready to duel because I'm sick of this,* Henrik lamented to himself.

He was optimistic, though. As long as Elias didn't manage to put his foot in his mouth—which now he thought about it, was a considerably high possibility—he was certain the two of them would make amends so they could all move on.

A noise outside distracted Henrik from where he was sweeping the floor of their little cabin. He looked out the window to see if Johan and Elias were smiling or crying, hoping to get an indication of how their conversation had gone.

But it wasn't Johan and Elias.

Two men were hovering by the tree line, and Henrik's heart sped faster than a rabbit's. Henrik had only spotted one of them at first, his flame-coloured hair standing out in the shaded forest, but there was a second man with hair as dark as night to his side, wielding a knife.

Suddenly painfully aware of how small and defenceless he was without Johan and Elias, Henrik grabbed the wool blanket off the bed to cover the table and hid underneath it.

As the sound of footsteps approached, Henrik's pulse pounded in his ears like the drums they would sometimes use to keep the elves working long into the night back at the mills.

Henrik held his breath when the door swung open, and he could see two sets of boots walk by him from the small gap under the blanket.

"Well, it's certainly being lived in," one of the men said to the other.

"They appear to either be cobblers or own more shoes than the Queen."

The two men wandered around the cabin, and Henrik prayed for them to leave before Elias and Johan returned, but luck was not on their side.

"Rik? Rik! I must tell you all about this bird I saw," Elias yelled as he approached. Henrik cursed under his breath.

"It seems we have company," one of the men muttered just before Elias burst through the door.

Henrik peered out from behind the blanket only to see Elias launch himself at the red-haired man shouting, "What have you done to Henrik?!"

Pandemonium broke out then. The dark-haired man plucked Elias off his friend and held a knife to his throat while Johan stood in the doorway with his hands raised defensively, unable to speak.

What an unmitigated disaster.

Henrik crawled out from underneath the table and ran for Johan, who tucked him behind him protectively.

"Where did *you* come from?" the red-haired man asked, sounding more amused than anything.

"I-I-I heard you c-coming and hid. W-we don't want any trouble," Henrik said, even as his whole body trembled in fear.

"Your friend here seems like he might want some trouble."

"In my defence, I thought you'd eaten my friend," Elias spoke as though having a knife held to his throat wasn't an especially new experience for him.

"I would never eat... your friend." He smirked in an incredibly unnerving manner.

"Now that we've established you didn't hurt my friend, could we be a bit more civilised and drop the knife?" Elias asked.

The two strangers looked at each other and shrugged before the dark-haired man lowered the knife, and Elias slowly backed away until he was standing with Johan and Henrik in the doorway.

"What do you want?" Henrik asked.

"It's always good to know who one's neighbours are. What if we run out of honey for our tea?"

Elias' entire demeanour changed to one Henrik had never seen, the lightness of his tone before gone in an instant. "We don't have any honey," he said. "Please leave our home."

Surprisingly, they were met with looks from the men that held more curiosity than animosity.

"You are running from someone?" the one with the knife asked.

"If we were, it would be unwise to discuss that with strangers who could give away our location. I'm sure you understand." Elias' jaw was clenched hard enough Henrik feared he might crack a tooth.

"Strangers? I am Hansel," the red-haired man said. "And this is my... brother Gerhardt. Now we aren't strangers. We're friends."

"You have a low bar for friendship," Henrik muttered, momentarily forgetting that being snarky to knife-wielding, probable outlaws, was not a good idea.

As if reading Henrik's mind, Gerhardt threw his knife into the air before catching it again by the handle.

"Nobody lives this deep in the forest who isn't hiding something. You never know when you might need an ally, elf." Gerhardt somehow made it sound more of a threat than an offer, but there was no malice in the strange man's expression, so Henrik dipped his chin in deference.

"Consider us acquainted," Henrik replied.

"Indeed," Gerhardt said as the three of them stepped away from the doorway to let the two men past.

"Farewell... for now," Hansel added.

When they left, Johan shut the door behind them, and they all watched through the sash window until they were no longer visible in the dense, dark trees.

"Will we ever really be safe?" Elias whispered, and dread pooled in Henrik's stomach.

Was he destined to forever look over his shoulder? To never sleep peacefully again?

Johan put his arm around Elias and kissed the top of his head, the gesture reminding Henrik of why the two of them had been gone in the first place.

"For now," Henrik said. "We'll need to sleep in shifts again to keep a lookout."

"I hate that," Elias replied.

"I really thought... we'd be okay here." Johan sounded bereft almost.

Henrik shuffled in closer, wrapping his arms around both Elias and Johan and took a deep breath to centre himself.

"Gods! You two had sex without me." He scowled up at Johan before pinching Elias on his upper arm.

"More crucially, though, we have made amends, Rik."

That was a relief, at least, although Henrik was a little bitter that he'd gone weeks without sex only for them to finally do it without him.

"We'll make it up to you," Johan said, tilting Henrik's head up by his chin for a kiss. Most of his annoyance left him at the press of Johan's soft lips against his own followed by Elias crowding him from behind and nibbling on his ear.

"You better," he grumbled anyway.

Twenty-Four

JOHAN

Johan's head was spinning from the events of the day. He'd been nothing short of elated to make amends and reconnect with Elias, but his elation was subdued now.

Elias caught him biting his fingernail and tugged Johan's hand away from his mouth.

"There will always be something," Elias said. "Life will always give you reasons to be scared or sad. It will try to break your spirit, Johan, but we have a choice. We get to choose to live, choose to be happy in spite of it all. And we have so much to fight for now," Elias said.

Johan tugged the elf down onto his lap and pressed his head to Elias' shoulder, breathing against his soft, perfect skin.

"Tonight, we choose each other. Tonight, we show Rik what he means to us, and if we do it well enough"—Elias smirked—"he'll hardly remember his own name, let alone have time to fret."

Elias' optimism was infectious. Johan knew it often drove Henrik mad, but he could see how they would so easily spiral into misery without it.

Taking Elias' lead, Johan fetched some water from the barrel outside that collected rainwater. His well of magic now replenished, Elias held his hands over the full pail of water and heated it up a little.

Henrik waited for them on the bed, looking unusually shy and nervous, and the effect somehow left Johan feeling more confident.

He and Elias worked together to peel off all of their clothes, and they showered Henrik's body with attention as they washed him.

After they were all cleaned, Johan licked, kissed, and bit every sensitive morsel of skin on Henrik's body until he was panting.

Feeling bolder than usual, Johan manoeuvred Henrik onto all fours. The elf gasped when Johan swiped his tongue over Henrik's hole, pulling noises from him that rarely spilled from the stoic elf who tried so hard to keep his feelings locked away.

Johan had discovered that he enjoyed doing this a lot. He loved the gasps of pleasure he could pull from Henrik and Elias by using his tongue in such a forbidden place.

"You are so beautiful, Rik. Especially when you let go. I want to paint a portrait of you like this," Elias said reverently, all the while stroking Henrik's length with a lightness that Johan imagined was torture.

Johan could see Henrik battling to stay in the moment. Unlike Elias, he never loved being the centre of attention, preferring to be the one making them feel good than to be their sole focus.

Henrik reached out for Elias, tugging him close and devouring his lips as a distraction. They were stunning like this, with their lips fused together.

Johan began to trail kisses along Henrik's spine until he reached his neck and plucked up the courage to ask, "Would you... would you lie with me... as you do Elias?"

Henrik stiffened for a moment, and Johan worried that it was wrong of him to ask that of him. He was much larger than the elves, and maybe it was odd to want that? He didn't know, and his stomach flooded with something awful. Something like *shame*.

"Like... you mean... What do you mean?"

"It... it... doesn't matter. Forget I asked." Johan was surprised he was still hard given the way all the blood in his body rushed to his burning cheeks.

"No. If... if you're asking me to be inside you, then I want that. But is that what you are asking?"

Johan nodded but couldn't make eye contact.

Henrik gulped. "You are sure?"

"Of course he is sure, look how hard he is." Elias smirked, and Johan tried to cover his cock where the evidence of his arousal was impossible to ignore, beads of precum already leaking from the tip.

Henrik licked his lips, nothing but desire in those intense amber eyes. "Okay... lie on your back, I think," he instructed, and Johan was grateful to the elf for taking charge.

Johan kind of just wanted to lie back and be made to feel good, but maybe that was a bit selfish of him. He lay in the centre of their bed completely naked and was surprised to find a lot of his nerves had sort of evaporated. Henrik stared at Johan with such hunger that any doubts about whether Henrik really wanted to do this were nowhere to be found.

The first time Johan had seen Henrik take Elias this way, it had altered something in his brain. Elias had almost turned into this vessel of pleasure, nothing to think about aside from feeling good and allowing his lover to chase that same ecstasy inside him.

Johan *wanted*.

He'd envied Elias in that moment. It had planted a seed of desire in his mind, and he'd finally found the words to ask for it, trusting Henrik with his entire heart and body to take care of him through it.

"Eli, can you roll up the blanket?"

Henrik stroked gentle hands up and down Johan's thighs lovingly while Elias did as he asked.

"Lift your hips," Elias instructed before stuffing the rolled-up blanket under Johan. "Are you comfortable?"

Johan nodded.

"Can I use magic on you? It will make you kind of wet inside so that I don't hurt you," Henrik explained.

There was a pause as Johan momentarily recalled Elias' hands on his face as he used magic to put Johan to sleep, but he pushed the memory away. They'd made amends. Neither of them would use magic against him again.

"Yes," Johan replied.

Placing his hands on Johan's hips, Henrik closed his eyes and concentrated until Johan began to feel a warm liquid in his passage.

"Oh... that feels... strange." Johan blushed, but Henrik looked pleased that it'd worked.

"I've never done that for someone else before."

"You will be very glad of it." Elias chuckled as he carded his slim fingers through Johan's hair in a way that made Johan feel cherished.

Rubbing his finger over Johan's hole until some of the liquid leaked out, Henrik massaged it over his rim. It felt nice—tender and loving.

"When he pushes his finger in, try to push it out. It will help," Elias explained.

Henrik pressed a slim digit inside, and Johan scrunched his face up unhappily. It didn't feel like he imagined it would.

"Am I hurting you? Should I stop?"

"No... just... um... odd? Distract me?" He directed the latter question to Elias.

Elias grinned mischievously. "I would love to distract you. I could use my mouth on you?"

Johan shook his head and blushed again before he asked, "Can I... use my mouth... here." He brushed a finger down Elias' crease, and the elf's eyes turned molten.

"Oh kjære, that is no hardship." Elias sort of wiggled on the spot in excitement before hooking a leg over Johan's head and taking a seat on this throne.

Johan immediately began showering his hole with attention, and Elias moaned out, "Gods, yes!"

He loved the way Elias' pucker would try to clench around his tongue. Loved squeezing his cheeks apart to delve in as far as he could.

With Elias to focus on, he found his mind less conscious of the slim finger penetrating him.

Once Henrik was able to slide one finger in and out with ease, he added a second, which actually felt a little better than one.

Henrik did something with his fingers then, changing the angle until he was rubbing a spot inside him repeatedly that had Johan trying to buck his hips. He could hardly breathe with his face smothered by Elias' behind, but who needed to breathe anyway?

"Are you ready, Johan?" Henrik asked, his voice husky with desire.

Elias lifted slightly off Johan's face, and he took a deep inhale.

"Yes," he gasped.

"Would you like to be inside Elias while I'm inside you?"

Johan looked between both of them in surprise because he didn't know that was something they could do.

"We are going to blow you away," Elias said, grinning.

Johan nodded enthusiastically and that was all the encouragement Elias required before he scrambled to straddle Johan's hips.

Elias closed his eyes, a brief look of concentration indicating his use of magic to lubricate himself and then he was reaching back to line up Johan's cock with his hole.

Johan whimpered as Elias lowered himself, taking the larger man's length with ease. Johan could hardly believe it was only earlier that day he'd had Elias this way. The sensation of the elf's tight body wrapped around his cock was somehow already familiar and something Johan was certain would always take him by surprise.

When Elias was fully seated, he remained still and gave Henrik the opportunity to get into position.

The other elf kneeled in the space between Johan's legs and caressed a hand down Elias' back before gripping Johan's thigh with one hand and using the other to push the head of his cock inside Johan's entrance.

Johan liked it, the swollen tip of Henrik's cock gave him the sensation of fullness without the discomfort of knuckles, and he knew then that he was going to enjoy this a lot.

"Is that okay?" Henrik checked in.

Johan nodded reflexively but found some words after all "Yes. Better than the fingers, I think... maybe I don't like fingers," Johan muttered before gasping as Elias suddenly rose up his shaft and bounced back down again, sending little bolts of lightning all through his body.

Henrik pushed all the way in, then, and he and Elias took it in turns, driving Johan wild as they alternated between Henrik thrusting in and out and Elias riding him.

Johan could hardly think. It was overwhelming. "I don't—I can't—Oh!" Johan clamped his hands on Elias' hips, holding him down and stilling him with his eyes scrunched closed.

"Too much?" Elias asked, reaching out to massage Johan's hairy chest and rubbing a thumb over a peaked nipple.

"I..." Johan nodded his head, then shook his head, then made a frustrated growling sound as he struggled to get his throat to form words.

Elias climbed off him and Johan's cock slapped against his stomach aggressively. "Turn onto your side," Elias instructed.

They rearranged themselves so that Johan faced Elias on his side, and they kissed until Johan was finally able to think again. Henrik slid in behind Johan, kissing the back of his neck and shoulder as his hand reached down to rub over Johan's hole.

Johan moaned when Henrik replaced his fingers again with his cock and sank into him once more. It felt different this way, still amazing but slightly less intense.

"Can you use your hand?" Elias asked Johan. "Mine won't fit around us both."

Johan reached down and took them in hand, both of them moaning in relief when Johan tightened his grip. As Johan worked them closer to release, Henrik continued to rock into Johan with a steady rhythm, stroking a hand down Johan's flank before kissing his shoulder with such tenderness that Johan could have wept.

"You feel so good, Johan. I don't ever want to leave your body."

The praise did something to Johan. By letting Henrik in, emotionally and physically, he'd given his lover something he'd never given anyone, and Johan felt so many things at once that he couldn't even name them all.

He turned his head, searching for Henrik's lips. It was a sloppy kiss, desperate and uncoordinated as their arousal was ramped up high, but he tried to tell Henrik in that moment how much he meant to him, how grateful he was for this gift, how thankful he was to have these two chaotic elves in his life.

"I'm close, so close," Henrik muttered into Johan's mouth, their breath mingling.

"Yes," Johan whispered, barely audible, but Henrik sped up, losing himself in Johan with such abandon that if Johan were a smaller man, he'd have been shaken like a doll.

When Henrik finally found his release in Johan's body, the warm liquid filled him up in a way he'd never been filled before and the image in his mind's eye alone was enough to have him following Henrik into heaven.

Johan groaned loudly as his entire body tensed at once before going lax with relief, his cum spurting out of his hand and coating Elias' already leaking cock.

"Yes, Gods, yes!" Elias grabbed for Johan's face and fused their mouths together as he shook, his chest blushing pink and the tendons in his neck taut and bulging. Elias' cum joined Johan's, some shooting far enough to be tangled in the hair that covered Johan's stomach.

When Henrik softened and slipped from Johan's body, he winced, he didn't like that part so much. Turning to face Henrik and kissing him hard was the perfect distraction, though.

Elias flopped onto his back and declared, "I am dead. I have been sexed to death. What a way to go."

Johan and Henrik chuckled at their ridiculous lover before kissing each other some more.

"Was that okay?" Henrik asked.

Johan nodded. He opened his mouth and shut it again, repeating the motion but unable to get any words to leave him. Instead, he reached for Henrik's hand and held it over his heart, trying to tell Henrik with his eyes what he wanted to say out loud.

"I—" The rest of his sentence got stuck, but Henrik looked at him like he'd heard the words anyway. Like they'd travelled from Johan's mind into the elf's and made a home there.

Johan's heart pounded beneath the palm of Henrik's hand.

"I love you, too," Henrik whispered, and a tear tracked down Johan's cheek.

How had he got so lucky as to find lovers who could hear him even when he couldn't speak? Using his thumb, Henrik wiped the tear away. "So much, Johan. Both of you." He smiled up at where Elias had appeared, resting his chin on Johan's shoulder.

"I love you both, too," Elias said.

They lay in a comfortable peaceful silence together for a while, luxuriating in the calm that followed all three of them finding what they needed in one another.

Eventually, though, Elias broke the silence. "You two sleep first, I'll keep watch."

Elias retrieved the pail of water and a cloth from next to the bed for them.

Once they were all a bit cleaner, Johan and Henrik curled up under the blanket. Elias kissed them both on the forehead and whispered, "I would do anything for you both, I hope you know that," before grabbing a blanket and taking a seat near the window with a thoughtful but determined look on his face that for some reason had a pit forming in Johan's stomach.

Twenty-Five

HENRIK

Henrik woke to find Elias still sitting by the window as the rays from the rising sun slowly filtered in, lighting up the room with a soft glow.

"Why didn't you wake us?" Henrik grumbled.

Elias smiled, looking a little sleepy. "The two of you looked peaceful, and you know me, Rik. I can sleep anywhere. I'll catch up on my sleep today."

Henrik was still scowling at Elias when he realised he was being ungrateful for getting a full night's undisturbed sleep, so he tried to rearrange his features into something softer.

"Thank you," he said, pecking a kiss to Elias' forehead when he passed by.

Henrik headed for the cupboard where they kept their food, and a near-empty shelf stared back at him. They had enough to eat for two days tops, and even that would mean sticking to small rations.

Elias had made his way over to the bed and was snuggling up to Johan, who slowly stirred awake.

"Morning, kjære," Elias said.

"What's... wrong?" Johan asked, spotting Henrik's worried expression.

"We are running very low on food now," Henrik explained.

Johan looked thoughtful. "Fishing?"

"It is our best option, I think?" Henrik replied. "Will you come, Elias? I don't like the thought of you here alone."

"Absolutely not," Elias mumbled, already buried in the blanket with his eyes closed. "I cannot even fish, and I plan to sleep the day away."

"What if those men return?" Henrik said.

"They are unlikely to return to cause harm in broad daylight. If they meant to harm us, why not just do it while they were here?"

Henrik didn't like this idea one bit, but short of dragging an exhausted Elias all the way to the river so they could have something to eat, he didn't have much choice but to concede.

"We... won't go far," Johan said, his voice raspy.

Elias began snoring softly, so Henrik kissed his stubborn lover on the forehead before getting wrapped up warm for the cold day ahead.

Elias was still dead to the world when Henrik and Johan were ready to leave, and Henrik had a pit in his stomach as they got on their way.

They walked together in near silence for around forty minutes before arriving at a spot along the river that Johan seemed satisfied would be a good place to try.

Henrik watched carefully as Johan showed him how to set up the lines and dropped a few nets into the fast-flowing water. While Henrik was an experienced sea fisher from his life before captivity, he'd never fished in rivers.

"The rivers have been overfished," Johan explained. "Since the Great Famine. But folk tend to not bother with the smaller catches."

"So, if we can catch enough of the smaller fish, we should be able to get by?" Henrik asked.

"For a while. I will need to try and hunt again soon, but I haven't even seen a rabbit since we arrived."

Henrik nodded thoughtfully. "I wonder if me and Elias can use magic to search the forest for animals. It's worth a try, no?"

"Definitely."

The temperatures had dropped even lower, so they were both bundled up on the riverbank as they waited and hoped for something to bite.

Henrik stood in front of Johan, who wrapped his arms around him in a tight hug.

"Henrik?"

"Hmm?"

"I... know you know. But I want... to say it. While I can"

Henrik smiled and twisted in Johan's arms so he could gaze up at him.

Johan blushed. "I—I love you," he blurted out.

Henrik stood on his tiptoes in order to reach Johan's lips, stealing a kiss in the frigid air. "I love you, too."

They kissed leisurely for a while, tasting each other and basking in the warmth of being completely in love until Johan said, "We should be watching the lines." He spun Henrik back around, still keeping him in his embrace.

"It's probably good that Elias didn't come fishing," Henrik said.

"Why?"

"It's peaceful but nothing much happens. He would be bored within a few minutes and scare the fish off with his endless chatter." They both chuckled.

"Yes, that is true."

It took several hours before they finally got a bite, and Henrik was thrilled at what was a much bigger catch than he'd expected.

"Trout," Johan said as he pulled the fish off the hook.

The top of the fish was sort of spotty, appearing almost covered in frogspawn with an orangey underbelly. It would be more food than the three of them had eaten in a while, and Henrik's stomach grumbled in anticipation.

With a substantial catch already, they lifted the nets that had a few smaller fish in them and packed away their things.

"We should make Elias gut them when we get back since he didn't have to spend all day in the cold," Henrik muttered, shivering now.

His nose was so cold he feared it might turn black and fall off. He wasn't convinced he had the features to remain beautiful without a nose.

They returned to their home in companionable silence, their breaths turning to vapour in the icy-cold air. Their little meadow was so still and quiet, and Henrik could hardly believe that Elias had remained asleep the entire time they'd been gone.

He wouldn't be for long, though, because Henrik was excited to show Elias their trout, and so he bounded off ahead of Johan and burst through the door.

Only, Elias wasn't inside.

"Eli?" he yelled. "Elias??"

He wasn't sure why he was yelling. It was a small space and he could see with his eyes that Elias wasn't there, but panic had taken hold of him too fast to be rational.

Henrik stepped outside and continued shouting. At the alarm in his voice, Johan dropped all the fishing gear and ran towards him.

"He isn't in there, Johan," Henrik whimpered. "There's no sign of a struggle, but he isn't in there. He wouldn't have gone for a walk, would he?"

"To fetch water?" Johan asked.

"Let's go look."

They practically ran and made it to the spring in less than twenty minutes but there was no sign of Elias, and the panic overwhelmed Henrik. They were breathless and already out of places to look for him.

On the return home, they shouted Elias' name over and over again, listening out for any sign of their lover in the forest, but nothing except the birds tweeted back.

Henrik collapsed to his knees on the mattress when they got home, despair weighing him down more heavily than the irons they'd been kept in during slavery.

"What if they came back and took him?" He sobbed.

"They didn't," Johan replied.

"We cannot know that."

"He left this." Johan reached for something on the small table and passed it to Henrik.

"A feather?"

"A kingfisher's feather." It was mostly a stunning blue with a little orange, but the meaning of it was lost on Henrik.

"What does it mean?"

"He left on his own... but he will come back."

And then Johan didn't speak again.

J ohan was there, but Henrik had never felt so alone in his life. They slept each night with a space between them, as though their bodies knew Elias was missing and they must preserve his spot should he return in the dead of night.

Three days.

Three days had passed since Elias went missing and Johan had stopped speaking. Henrik didn't even know why Johan had assumed the feather would assure Elias' return. Personally, he was growing less convinced by the day.

Henrik had barely been able to eat; he was so sick with worry. Even if Elias intended to return, anything could have happened to him in the Dark Forest. It wasn't safe. And where would he have gone, anyway? Henrik had wracked his brain to think of anywhere and came up with nothing.

The forest was still and near silent as Henrik walked to the water spring. He came here every single day like Elias would miraculously appear and they'd just not spotted him before.

When Henrik had finally accepted that Elias was missing, he'd searched through Elias' belongings and found a bag, Elias' warmest clothes, and one of the blankets missing along with a meagre amount of food. The only reassurance Henrik could take from it was that it did make it more likely that Elias hadn't been taken.

Reaching the spring, Henrik cupped his hands under the small waterfall and brought the near-freezing water to his mouth to drink.

Where are you, Eli?

Why would you leave us behind without a word?

What if you don't return, and Johan never utters a single word to me again?

Henrik plonked himself down on a mossy rock and held his face in despair. He wept until he could hardly breathe. When he finally managed to clear his vision through the tears, a little bird had landed on the rock next to him.

A blue and orange bird. A kingfisher.

"Is it you who gave your feather to Elias?" he asked the bird. "Did he tell you where he planned to go?" Henrik sniffled.

The bird obviously didn't reply, it just stood there and cocked its head to one side curiously.

"What do your feathers mean, little bird?"

At that, it tweeted and flew away, leaving Henrik all alone again.

He trudged back home to a place that didn't feel much like home without Elias in it.

When he returned, he found Johan outside working on the house like he had done tirelessly every moment since Elias left.

The first day, Henrik had spoken, and Johan had responded with head shakes and nods, but the second day, Henrik had stopped bothering. Other than a sanity-questioning conversation with a small bird, Henrik hadn't uttered a word in days, and he was beginning to feel as though he might explode.

As he wrapped the blanket around his shoulders and sat by the window, he wondered who Elias was talking to right now. Henrik knew that Elias would befriend a tree before he'd go this long without speaking, and at least that thought made the corners of Henrik's mouth tug in the whisper of a smile.

O n the fifth day, Henrik woke up angry.

Angry with Elias for departing without a word. Angry with the Queen for leaving them no choice but to live in the middle of nowhere. And lastly, he was angry with Johan.

Henrik woke up alone again, the sun hadn't even risen yet and he could hear the hammering of wood outside that told him Johan had already started building for the day. He wondered if Johan had even slept for more than a couple of hours before he'd got back to work.

What was even the point of building a new home without Elias? Henrik could hardly stand to look at the new structure, resenting the space he feared would never be filled by his larger-than-life love.

After grabbing his clothes from nearby and tugging them on furiously, Henrik stomped outside.

"What if he never comes back?" he yelled. "What if he's hurt, or—or—or dead, do we just wait here forever?"

Johan stared at him startled and used the back of his hand to wipe some of the sweat from his brow. He looked pleadingly at Henrik before wordlessly turning away and picking his hammer back up, continuing on with his job like Henrik hadn't uttered a word.

Henrik lost it.

"Maybe I should leave too, then! You do not seem to care if I am here or not!" Henrik's entire body was trembling.

Johan shook his head. He stopped what he was doing but just sat there, appearing frozen to the spot.

"So, what? You will just never speak to me again?"

Johan glared at that.

"I don't even need your voice, Johan! But you do not speak to me at all, not with your eyes, not with your hands. You have both left me! Only your body is here, haunting me." Henrik collapsed to the ground, all the fight leaving him like water spilling out of a cup.

Chest heaving, Henrik dug his fingernails into the frozen earth below, begging for it to open up and swallow him because he could not do this anymore.

He'd endured slavery for Elias, he would have endured the loss of the elf who owned half his heart for Johan, but he couldn't endure this.

Heavy hands landed on his shoulders, and when he glanced up through wet lashes, Johan was kneeling in the mud in front of him, his face showing so much anguish that Henrik could barely stand to look at him.

Pressing their foreheads together, Johan wrapped his arms tightly around Henrik much like he had when they'd first met, and Henrik had had a fear attack that he was certain he'd almost died from.

Much like before, Henrik found it a little easier to breathe with the pressure of Johan's strong arms squeezing him.

"Please don't leave me too. Please, please, please," Henrik begged, his words barely coherent.

Johan didn't speak, but he did hold him a little tighter, he did run his fingers through Henrik's tangled hair and stroke his head, and he did offer Henrik everything he could in that moment, and for that Henrik was grateful.

They remained that way until they were both shivering and need-ed to go inside to warm back up again with some hot tea. Johan still couldn't speak with his voice, but Henrik soaked up even the simplest brush of Johan's fingers against his own when he handed him his mug.

Later that day, once Henrik had done his daily walk to the spring and circled a wide perimeter of their home, he put his resentment to one side and joined Johan working on the house. They worked in silence, but Henrik no longer felt ignored, so it was okay. As okay as it could be given the circumstances.

The following day, once the sun had set and Henrik had come inside after relieving himself, he found Johan sitting at the table and spinning the kingfisher feather between his fingers.

Henrik approached him from behind and rested his chin on the shoemaker's sturdy shoulder.

"I wish you could tell me what the feather means," he whispered.

As Henrik expected, Johan didn't reply at first, but then he cleared his throat and Henrik's heartbeat sped up. "If—if—if I were a kingfisher," he paused, coughing again as his voice was so raspy from disuse, "I w-w-would always come back to you."

Henrik stared again at the spinning feather. "He said that to you?"

Johan nodded and reached to grasp Henrik's hand from where it rested on his chest.

"Where are you, Elias? It's time for you to come back to us," he whispered into the air like magic herself might deliver his message to their love.

Twenty-Six

ELIAS

Elias was quite certain he might never feel his poor toes again. He should have infused some magic into his shoes to keep them warm when he'd had the chance.

His hands shook as he tried to build a fire to fight off the endless chill.

After a while, the warmth from the flames and the sheer exhaustion, were enough for Elias to finally fall asleep, clinging to the hard brown rock which he'd given it all up for.

Running on barely more than a few hours of broken sleep, Elias struggled to put one foot in front of the other the next day. He'd run out of water and couldn't find anything fresh that wasn't frozen over and so he'd made his way towards the river to set up camp that night.

He hoped it was the combination of exhaustion, dehydration, and hunger that was making him paranoid, but he'd spent the entire day so far convinced that eyes were on him. All the hairs on his body had stood on end, screaming that there was a predator nearby, but hours had passed and nothing had leaped at him from the bushes, and so he did the only thing he could and kept plodding on.

When he stopped to rest, Elias pulled a face at the colour of the river water he was about to try and drink.

What have I been reduced to?

Looking away, he reached down with his water skin in hand, which turned out to be a mistake. The water level was lower than he'd estimated, and in his tired state, he lost his balance.

What felt like shards of ice stabbed him before he even registered that he'd fallen into the icy depths of the river. The shock of it stole his breath. He tried to fight his way back to the bank, but he was weak and the currents overpowered him. He kicked and kicked and kicked, desperate to keep his head above the water so he could breathe but it felt like a hand kept grabbing his ankles, dragging him down, down, down, towards the depths of the riverbed.

If he could have, he'd have wailed in frustration.

It had all been for nothing.

He'd given it all up to protect them, and now he would die at the bottom of a river without ever having returned with the one thing that could promise safety to his loves. He would die, and they'd think he'd just left, never to return again. Nobody would bid him farewell, he would just be gone.

For some reason, he pictured his brother Bjorn then. He knew that there was no real way that Bjorn could know if Elias was alive or dead but somehow the idea of Elias becoming a nameless skeleton in a foreign land with the only family who ever cared about him never knowing, tore at wounds that Elias had spent his life carefully ignoring.

Elias didn't know which he drowned in faster, the water or despair.

"Let's go, he looks dead."

"His heart is beating, he isn't dead."

"Almost dead, then."

Something surged inside Elias, something vile, and suddenly what felt like an entire river rushed through him and burst from his mouth.

"That is... disgusting."

Elias choked on the dirty river water as his body tried to rid him of it. Afterwards, he collapsed on his back again, groaning.

"Told you he wasn't dead."

"What do we do with him?"

"He'll die of the cold out here, we should take him back."

A few moments later, Elias felt himself being lifted by strong arms and sat on something warm and kind of hairy.

"My rock, I need my rock. Can't go without it," Elias mumbled desperately.

Someone sighed. "You almost died, I think you'll manage without a rock."

"I need it. Leave me, then. I can't go without my rock. It's all for nothing without the rock," Elias practically sobbed.

"Fine, shhh. Okay, we'll go via your camp and collect your rock, then."

"Thank you," Elias whispered to the kind stranger before collapsing back onto someone's chest and swiftly passing out again.

When he came to, he was fairly sure he was hallucinating, because if he wasn't, then he was riding on the back of a very large charcoal-grey wolf. Arms wrapped around his middle were keeping him upright, and he was relieved to find his ugly brown rock nestled safely between his legs.

"Umm... who are you?" Elias asked.

"Oh, he's finally awake," the man said. "I'm Red, and this is Wim." He patted the side of the wolf they were apparently riding.

"You tamed a wolf??"

Red chuckled. "You could say that."

The wolf growled. "I have a name."

Elias startled. "Did you just talk? Are you sure I didn't die in the river?"

"You heard me, and no, you didn't die. The name's Wim, thank you for asking."

"Where are you taking me? I need to go home."

Elias wasn't even certain of how long he'd been gone now, and he felt sick at the distress he must be causing Henrik and Johan by his slow return.

"You almost drowned and you need some proper warmth and clean water. When you're well, we can help you find your way," Red said.

Elias had little choice but to comply. Despite the warmth of the wolf below him and the blanket wrapped around his shoulders, he was shivering and cold down to his bones in a way that he knew was dangerous, especially without any way to warm himself now magic had left him for good.

"Okay," he whispered, feeling vulnerable.

The next time Elias woke, he was sweating profusely. He peered around only to find himself in the middle of an entire pile of... of wolves!

His heartbeat sped up, beating so fiercely he feared it might escape his own chest, but the wolves were just curled up and sleeping. Elias was shocked to find he was outside, the cold air clearly weak competition to a heap of warm-blooded wolves. The clearing they were in was not dissimilar to where the hunting cabin was but there was an area for cooking and a large firepit, where the flames created a lingering smoky mist in the air.

Elias found Red sitting on a chair by the fire, and he appeared to be whittling some wood into arrows.

Struggling under the weight of heavy wolf limbs, Elias eventually managed to extricate himself from the pile and padded over to Red.

"Hi," he said shyly.

"How do you feel?" Red asked.

"Much better, thank you. I don't mean to be rude, but where is my rock?"

Red raised a curious eyebrow at Elias before pointing to the base of a nearby tree. Elias scuttled over and picked it up, cradling it in his hands.

"What is it?" Red asked, looking at the ugly rock judgmentally.

"It was the only way to keep my family safe. I need to return home with it," Elias explained vaguely.

"I have never met a free elf before." Red phrased it as though it were a question.

"Well, it turns out that you can escape captivity and still never truly be free." Elias stroked his index finger across the rock thoughtfully.

"How did you escape?"

Elias turned to face Red. "Luck, I suspect. I'm not entirely sure. We were being transported to the castle, and we'd just entered the Dark Forest when someone shot two arrows. The first one killed the slaver who'd been driving the carriage and the second split the rope which trapped the cage shut. We all just ran. I don't know if or who else survived aside from my friend."

Red looked astonished. He sat there with his mouth hanging wide open and a level of shock in his expression which Elias felt disproportionate to the story he'd told. How had Red imagined they'd escaped?

"You... it was you?" Red said.

"What was me?"

"Actually, I suppose it was me. I shot those arrows."

Now it was Elias' turn to stand there looking like a codfish, mouth agape.

"You? You freed us?"

Red nodded, smiling. "I cannot take all the glory. It was Wim's idea, and I thought the plan quite mad, but I did shoot the arrows and now you are here. Unbelievable."

Elias could hardly believe it. What were the chances he'd be rescued from drowning by the same man who'd freed him? "I owe you my life. Twice over."

"Let us make a deal since life in the forest can get rather boring. Wim and I will escort you back to your home and along the way, you can tell me everything you have done since you escaped. Tell me how you came to end up with a family that needs protection from a large rock. Entertain me, little elf, and we'll call it even." Red grinned and Elias decided right then that they would be great friends. He hadn't had many, but Elias knew a kindred spirit when he found one.

Itching to get back to Henrik and Johan, Elias badgered Red and Wim for most of the morning until they eventually gave in and agreed to begin the journey to take Elias home. He packed his few belongings into his bag but kept the rock safely in his hands.

Wim grumbled a little when he and Red climbed on his back, but Elias got the feeling that was mostly just his nature and didn't worry about it too much. He couldn't quite believe his luck at getting to travel home in such luxurious comfort as this. His already blistered and battered feet would thank him later.

Elias kept up his deal with Red. He talked the man and his wolf's ear off, regaling him with tales of their escape, their time in the Dark Forest, and then how they'd been rescued by the sweetest man Elias had ever known. He got the impression that Red preferred his higher action stories. Despite it being Elias' least favourite story to tell, Red wanted every last detail of the fire incident at the shoe shop.

It was a welcome distraction, though, as the closer they got, the more Elias' palms began to sweat at the reaction he was likely to face.

He was sure that Johan would once again interpret this act as a lack of trust on Elias' part and maybe there was some truth to that. He only hoped that Johan had understood his message with the kingfisher feather. That he understood Elias had every intention of returning home and had never planned to abandon them.

All the same, Elias dreaded Johan's quiet but devastating reaction more than the wrath he was sure to receive from Henrik. Henrik's anger would burn wild and bright but abate quickly—he hoped.

When the section of forest they were in became increasingly familiar, Elias wasn't sure which was worse, the dread or the anticipation.

He clutched the rock tightly, pressing it into his stomach when he spotted the overgrown track which led home. "Over there, that is the path to our meadow," Elias said, pointing to it. Elias gulped as Wim turned in that direction and continued on.

"I feel like a horse," Wim grumbled.

"You are much more handsome than a horse," Elias complimented, and he liked to believe the wolf was blushing at his words.

Over the course of their journey, he'd grown quite attached to Wim and Red. While he'd prefer never to cross paths with Hansel and Gerhardt again, he'd decided that he'd quite like it if Wim and Red came to visit sometimes. Elias had always been sociable in nature, and he knew that even with the company of Henrik and Johan, he would likely get lonely sometimes.

Elias had all but given up on the existence of his Gods, but he couldn't help but wonder if they'd tried to repay him with this gift. Delivered him safely home to his loves with his rock in hand by the two people who'd rescued him and Henrik in the first place.

Turning another corner, the clearing came into view down the path. It was like a beacon of daylight in the Dark Forest, marking the end of Elias' journey, and his stomach was a tangled web of conflicting emotions with every step that Wim brought them closer.

What if they were happier without you? the cruellest part of Elias' brain suggested.

Johan came into view first, perched atop the house, which had come a long way in such a short amount of time. Hammer in hand, he didn't notice Elias right away, too focused on his task.

Elias' fingertips bit into the rock nervously. "Can you wait here?" he asked Wim and Red.

They paused so that Elias could climb down from the wolf's back, and he continued on foot. When he'd pictured this moment, he'd imagined himself running towards the cabin without a moment's hesitation, but nerves had got the better of him, and he truly feared the reception he might receive.

When he was close enough, he called out, "Johan?"

The shoemaker's head shot round so fast it looked painful, and for an awful moment, Elias feared he might fall from the house in shock.

Johan scrambled down and ran towards Elias, scooping him up from the ground and crushing him. No words spilled from Johan's lips but he didn't let go, he held Elias like he might disappear if he lost his grip.

"Johan, lun—" Henrik called from the doorway of the cabin, his sentence cut short when he spotted Elias and Johan in the centre of the meadow.

Henrik stormed over to them and Johan put Elias down to face him.

"How could you!" Henrik shoved Elias and he stumbled back a few steps. "You bastard. How could you!" Tears streaked down Henrik's cheeks, and his hands trembled in anger.

"I'm not sorry," Elias said defiantly.

"You never are!" Henrik yelled.

Next it was Henrik's turn to stumble back, screaming as Wim approached from Elias' side, growling at the other elf.

"It's fine," Elias said. "He is right to be angry with me."

Wim huffed.

"W-w-w-wolf." Henrik pointed at Wim, his face whiter than parchment.

"He's not like the wolves in Varinien, Rik. He can talk and turn into a man."

Henrik and Johan stared at Wim with their mouths gaped open.

Embarrassed by the audience, Elias suddenly very much wanted to face the consequences of his actions in private.

"There is a freshwater spring around half an hour in that direction." Elias pointed.

Thankfully, Red and Wim took the hint and nodded their heads in understanding before leaving to give them some much-needed privacy.

Once they were alone, Elias tried to defend himself. "It wasn't for nothing. I have this." He presented the large brown rock to them.

"You left us to collect a rock? Did you hit your head on the rock??" Henrik asked in disbelief.

Elias fought the urge to roll his eyes. "We cannot spend the rest of our lives sleeping in shifts and worrying that one day either the Queen's men or random outlaws might slit our throats in our sleep. That is not a way to live. I returned to the sorcerer—"

"You did what?" Henrik screeched.

"Shhh, let him speak," Johan said quietly.

"The sorcerer from the tower gave me this rock. If the three of us drop our blood onto it and leave it near the house, it will activate a spell which prevents anyone who means us harm from being able to find us. It is the answer to nearly all of our problems."

Johan took the rock from Elias and turned it over in his hands, inspecting it before looking at Elias with the saddest eyes he'd ever seen. "At what cost, kjære?"

Elias gulped before staring down at his feet. He couldn't bring himself to say the words.

"What did you do?" Henrik choked out.

"Don't make me say it," Elias whispered.

"Eli? What did you give him?"

"I do not regret it!" Elias snapped.

Henrik practically growled.

"I gave it all up okay! Every drop. Magic no longer runs through my veins. She has left me, and I do not regret it. We will be safe now, and that is all that matters."

Elias shook his head, trying to rid himself of the memory of the moment that the sorcerer had put his hands on him and taken magic from him for good.

It was different from when he'd worn the bangles which suppressed the magic. There was always an awareness that it was there but just not reachable. Now, the well inside him was empty, and it would always *be* empty.

Elias hadn't even begun to process the grief that accompanied what he'd given up, and he couldn't handle Henrik's anger at him over it. He hadn't lied, he didn't regret it, but he would be lying if he said it hadn't left a gaping hole in his soul.

Johan carefully placed the precious rock on the ground before reaching for Elias and pulling him in close. Elias could hardly stand it, feeling himself fraying at the edges in response to Johan's gentle touch.

"How could y—"

"Stop," Johan interrupted Henrik's next tirade. "It's done. He is home. We are safe. Stop." He reached for Henrik then and pulled him into the embrace, the three of them clinging to each other in the cold.

To Elias, Johan added, "No more secrets. Enough now."

Elias nodded his head. "No more secrets."

Back inside, Elias set the rock in a safe spot, then quickly washed up and ate a few pieces of dried meat as he explained to Johan and Henrik about how he'd come to be escorted home by Red and Wim. Neither of them had been very impressed at the part where Elias nearly drowned in a river, but Henrik was as shocked as Elias had been to discover that Red and Wim were responsible for setting them free in the first place.

A little while later, Red and Wim knocked on the door to say goodbye to Elias.

"Thank you," Henrik said to them. "For bringing him back to us. And for... for setting us free. We are in your debt."

Red smirked. "Elias has already cleared your debt. He is quite the storyteller."

"Don't be strangers," Elias said. "So long as you mean us no harm, you will always be able to find us. It will be nice to have some friends in the forest."

"I'm sure we shall pass through from time to time. I hope your rock was worth it, Elias. Good luck." Red smiled before climbing onto Wim's back, cloak billowing out behind him.

"Don't fall in any more rivers," Wim grumbled in his own version of a farewell.

Elias was a little sad to see their retreating backs as they left the clearing.

"I know you are angry," Elias said to Henrik. "But it is done now, and we should activate the spell before the sun sets."

"I suppose it would be nice to sleep without worrying," Henrik conceded.

Johan patted Henrik on the back as if he was proud of him for not continuing the argument.

Elias collected the rock from where he'd stored it safely and retrieved a knife while he was at it, then they all headed outside.

"How does this work, then?" Henrik eyed the rock sceptically.

"The sorcerer said to make a shallow cut, just enough to draw blood, on one palm each, and then we all press the wound to the rock at the same time. He said we will know when the spell is done," Elias explained. "I'll go first."

Elias sat cross-legged on the cold ground and picked up the knife. He winced when the metal cut into his palm, but once satisfied the cut was sufficient, he passed the knife to Henrik.

Henrik and Johan quickly copied the action until both their right hands were dripping crimson onto the grass.

Elias gulped a lungful of air. "Here goes," he said, picking up the rock he'd survived almost drowning in a river for.

He was worried for a moment when nothing happened, terrified he'd been swindled and had gone through all this for nothing, but when Henrik and Johan pressed their cuts to the rock as well, Elias felt it then. His hands quivered a little as he continued holding it, and a tingling sensation began in his fingers and travelled through his body until it felt like his heart skipped a beat.

Henrik and Johan both stared at the rock wide-eyed, evidently feeling it too, and then right as Elias was about to say "Do you think that's it?" the previously dull, brown rock glowed like a star in the night sky.

They were silent as they witnessed the light trickle out of the rock and sink into the ground beneath them. It danced across the grass like fireflies, more and more of them bleeding out of the stone and spreading out to surround their home until finally the rock had returned to its original state.

It was unlike any magic Elias had ever encountered. He couldn't tear his eyes away from the way the light appeared to guard them, and he was so relieved he could hardly hold his exhausted body up. Because it had worked. It hadn't been for nothing. *It had worked*.

Like a reflex, though, Elias reached inside himself to brush against his own well of magic, only, it was no longer there.

Elias hadn't even realised he'd started to cry until Johan wrapped an arm around him and Henrik brushed his thumb under Elias' eyes.

"I really don't regret it," Elias sniffled.

Johan cleared his throat. "Even without regrets, you... you still get to grieve, sweetheart. We will grieve with you. To have sacrificed this for us..." Johan choked up at the end. "You don't have to mourn alone."

Henrik held Elias' hand and squeezed it tight while they sat in the quiet together for a while.

"This was quite an extreme measure to get out of doing any work, you know," Henrik said, and they all burst into laughter, bringing some much-needed levity to the moment.

"Come on, it's freezing," Johan said, and in a swift movement, which took both Elias and Henrik by surprise, Johan scooped them up and carried them inside.

They all landed on the bed, and Johan squished Elias between the two of them. "This is where you belong."

Belong.

Had Elias ever truly belonged anywhere?

"Are you okay?" Henrik asked him softly.

Elias smiled a watery smile. "I will be. The whole time I was enslaved, I only ever dreamed of escaping and getting my magic back. And when we did? It was like my anger tarnished it. I shaped it into something it was never supposed to be."

Johan stroked Elias' hair and stared at him with so much understanding it was hard to finish what he wanted to say.

"In the mills, it never even occurred to me to dream of having a family of my own. A home with people within who care deeply for me. My life with the two of you is literally beyond my own imagination, and if the price to pay to keep it safe is my access to magic? So be it. I would have paid more."

Elias blushed, feeling slightly embarrassed by his emotional theatrics for the first time in his life. Maybe because there was a vulnerability to them this time. A truth that he kept buried. Johan and Henrik had the power to destroy Elias, and he had to try and trust that they wouldn't. Not an easy thing when your own parents sold you to the worst people the world had to offer.

"Will you forgive me, Rik?"

"Johan will need to build us a bigger house just to fit your head inside if I tell you what this truly means to me, Eli." Henrik sniffed.

"Come here," Elias said to him.

Elias curled into Henrik's front like he had so many times before, tucked into the slightly bigger elf's embrace. An embrace that had been the closest thing to safety that Elias had known in years, only, this time a large body pressed up against his back as well, cocooning him.

Life would not suddenly be perfect. Food was still scarce, and they would need to find a way to make money. Their relationship had bruises that needed time to heal. But for the first time in his life, Elias was truly safe and loved. And he decided that the warmth of Johan and Henrik's love running through his veins felt even *better* than magic.

Epilogue

Elias

The following summer

While there was not an abundance of food in the forest, the spring and summer had gifted them plentiful flowers, and Elias adored the tapestry of colours they provided.

Elias had gone to collect some fresh water and took a detour on his way home to check on the little haven for escaped elves and took the liberty of collecting some pretty flowers while he was in there.

He'd come across the haven by accident, and through happenstance, they'd met one of the elves who had created the haven some years ago as a place for recently escaped elves to seek safety in the forest.

A cause close to their hearts, Henrik periodically came by to gift some magic to the spells which surrounded it, and Elias popped by from time to time to ensure it had any necessary supplies, and as an added bonus for himself, to pick bunches of his favourite flowers—blue moons and sprigs of fresh lavender.

Flowers in one hand and the water skins tucked into a knapsack across his back, Elias skipped all the way home.

Home.

Although they'd finished building their new house back in the winter, it had taken some time for it to feel like a lived-in home. Elias felt that the flowers helped considerably, even if Henrik griped from time to time that they didn't live for very long in a cup of water.

Johan appreciated them, at least.

Once they'd vacated the little hunting cabin, Johan had built them a work station inside, and with the assistance of the kind ambassador's wife in Hallin, they had found a way to create commissioned shoes for the residents of the neighbouring kingdom.

Without magic, Elias joined Johan in making the shoes, using his smaller, more dextrous fingers to focus on the finer, intricate details, and Henrik infused them with magic at the end.

They had a process, and it worked.

Aside from the occasional passing visit from their friends Red and Wim, nobody had found them, and they all slept peacefully as a result. Their rock had done as promised.

When Elias entered their meadow, he kicked his shoes off so he could feel the grass and daisies under his toes.

"I've just swept inside and now you're going to drag in all that dirt with your grubby feet," Henrik wined from the porch.

Some things had not changed.

"To feel the earth under your toes is to feel alive, Rik. You should consider removing the stick from your behind for a moment and enjoy nature."

Henrik huffed but wandered down the steps that led to their cabin and kissed Elias on the nose. He took the knapsack from Elias back and carried the water inside for him.

"Kjære! Come look!" Elias yelled as he raced up the steps. He found Johan sitting in his favourite spot on a rocking chair he'd made by the window, whittling the tiny elf figurines he'd been giving to the orphaned children he came across in Hallin. It was so sweet that it hurt Elias' teeth.

"Beautiful." Johan smiled at the handful of flowers Elias had collected. "I love the blue moons," he added.

Elias beamed before giving Johan an enthusiastic kiss and scampering off to fill a cup with water for his flowers. He placed them in the centre of the table, where he and Johan could enjoy them with the added benefit of annoying Henrik.

"Come here," Johan said, reaching out for Elias.

It was nice to hear Johan's voice. Each time he went into Hallin to deliver the shoes they'd made, he often found it hard to speak for a few days afterwards, and it was a relief when he once again felt relaxed enough again to talk to them.

Elias sat sideways on Johan's lap and began playing with his shaggy beard. It had been a while since Elias had trimmed it for him, but he enjoyed running his fingers through it, so it could wait a little longer.

Johan kissed him with a passion they usually reserved for the nighttime, not that Elias complained. The shoemaker's tongue licked at the seam of Elias' lips, demanding entrance, and Elias obliged.

"Mmmm," Elias moaned. "My cock aches, I think you must check on it, make sure it is okay," he muttered into Johan's mouth.

Johan chuckled before fondling Elias. "Oh no!" he said in mock horror. "Does it need chopping off?"

Elias glared at him. "For that comment, you must kiss it better and give it *lots* of attention."

In a movement which aroused Elias for its show of strength, Johan stood and lifted him in one swoop before carrying him into the second room they had made their bedroom.

With Elias spread out on the mattress like Johan's next meal, Johan began very slowly taking off the elf's clothing.

"Ooh, what are we doing?" Henrik asked, appearing at the doorway.

"Apparently Elias' cock is starved of—of attention," Johan explained.

Henrik snorted. "You poor thing, how long has it been, a day?"

"At least that," Elias gasped as Johan took an exposed nipple between his teeth. "My hole is also very empty if you are inclined to help a horny elf out."

Laughing, Henrik joined them on the bed, which was now raised thanks to a platform that Johan had built.

Completely stripped of his clothes, Elias writhed on the bed as two mouths kissed and licked him all over.

This was Elias' ideal situation.

He came alive under the undivided attention of Johan and Henrik when they worked together to give him endless pleasure.

Henrik pushed Elias onto his side and stroked him while Johan lifted his leg and began licking and sucking along his balls and hole.

"Oh, oh, oh, Gods! Yes!" Elias moaned.

"You like Johan feasting on you?" Henrik asked breathily.

"So much. So good."

Johan paused and asked Henrik, "Can you?"

Henrik nodded before placing his hand on Elias' stomach and closing his eyes. While Elias missed the convenience of lubricating himself, there was an intimacy to Henrik giving him what he needed so the two of them could take their turns with him. Elias loved it when they did that. Passed him between them, taking their pleasure from his body before giving him to the other. It sent him wild with lust.

Once Johan could feel that Elias was wet enough, he pushed in two fingers and plunged them in and out before scissoring them to stretch Elias open. Elias went pliant, sinking into the sensation of allowing his body to relax and welcome his loves inside him.

"Let's get him up to four today," Henrik said to Johan.

"Do you mean? Are you going to... finally?" Elias gasped when Johan added a third large finger.

Four of Johan's fingers together were girthier than his cock, which was already the largest thing Elias had taken.

"What do you think, Johan? Shall we finally take him together?"

Johan answered with a desperate strangled noise which burst from his throat.

"Yes! Finally, yes!" Elias was so excited and aroused he might burst out of his skin. He'd been asking them to take him together for months, but Henrik said without Elias' magic to help, they must take their time to prepare him.

When Johan added a fourth finger, Elias pushed back greedily. Henrik kissed him hard, swallowing all the noises of pleasure which spilled from Elias' lips as he rode Johan's fingers.

"I'm ready. Please, I'm *so* ready," Elias begged.

Johan removed his fingers and lay down on his back so that Elias could straddle his hips. Elias was practically vibrating with excitement.

Henrik held Johan's cock in place so that Elias could sink down. He sighed in relief at the fullness Johan's big cock provided him. Loved feeling stretched and stuffed.

"Ride him," Henrik instructed as he kissed Elias' neck, sucking on the skin until he'd be sure to leave little pink marks that Elias would admire in the mirror later.

Elias rode Johan with the exuberance he was known for. Occasionally, Johan would grip Elias' hips to slow him down so they didn't both come before it was over.

"If you don't... hurry... up," Elias gasped when Johan punched up into him. "I'll come before you're even inside me."

Henrik chuckled. "Lean forward and stay still."

Elias yelped when Henrik took him by surprise, spanking him.

This was it. This was finally it.

Elias very much wanted this to be a recurring element of his sex life and so he did as he was told, the only time he enjoyed obedience.

Henrik ran his hands soothingly down Elias' ribs and waist until Elias felt the head of Henrik's cock nudging against his hole on top of Johan's.

For a moment, it felt impossible that they both might fit, but Elias took a deep breath as Henrik pushed in. The elf behind him was slow and careful as he gently kept going until he was all the way in and his balls pressed against Johan's.

"Wow," Johan whispered in awe. "That feels... Wow."

Elias panted, there was some pain, but it was quickly fading into pleasure as he finally got to feel the two loves of his life take him at the same time.

His whole body trembled as he tipped his head back and revelled in the sensation of it.

Henrik held his hands on Elias' hips, and it wasn't long before Elias felt more warm liquid pooling inside him as Henrik worked his magic.

"Can I... move?" Henrik gasped.

"Yes, just... slow at first."

Henrik cautiously pulled out a little before pushing back in, and all three of them moaned in unison.

"Gods, yes! Do that again," Elias demanded.

Slowly at first, Henrik began to build up a rhythm, thrusting in and out of Elias until sweat was dripping down the small elf's spine. Henrik licked it up.

Tentatively, Johan pushed up into Elias at the same time, and the feel of them both moving inside him had Elias floating off into the sky above. He couldn't even form thoughts, he was just an object of pleasure, and he soaked up every blissful moment of it.

As Johan and Henrik got braver and chased their release inside Elias, his blonde hair came loose from his leather hair-tie and tumbled down onto his shoulders in waves.

Henrik gripped it at the root and tugged Elias' head back, twisting him to steal a kiss that was as loving as it was aggressive.

Moans, gasps, and panting echoed around the room like the finest symphony Elias had ever heard. The walls they had built with their own hands infused with it.

Unable to form words, Elias rode the high right into an ecstasy he hadn't known existed. Like a domino effect, Henrik came first, and Johan quickly followed, holding Elias down onto both their lengths with a firm grip, which had Elias so full he just exploded. He shook and trembled and tears streamed down his cheeks as he experienced a release like no other. Rope after rope of cum shooting from him and landing in the soft hairs which coated Johan's stomach.

There wasn't a spot on his body that didn't feel marked with Johan and Henrik's love, and the feeling settled into Elias' bones like the warmest blanket to ever be woven.

Henrik softened and slipped from his body, but Johan remained inside him, tugging them onto their sides so the shoemaker could wrap his large arms around both the elves.

Johan knew that Elias hated the sudden feeling of emptiness after sex and always stayed inside him for as long as he could. Elias appreciated it now as to go from being so incredibly full to empty would have left him bereft.

Henrik fetched them all some water before crawling back into bed. They were a tangle of sweaty limbs, and Elias couldn't help but bask in the afterglow of being cherished by his two favourite people in the whole world.

With nothing but the sound of soft breathing and tweeting birds outside their window, Johan whispered, "When the leaves turned brown, I asked whichever god would listen if I would be alone forever."

Elias blinked up at Johan through wet lashes.

He continued, "The next day, I found you both. The gr-greatest gift of my life. I... sometimes lose my words and can't say it. But I...

I love you both so much." Johan's eyes were a glassy mirror, and the emotion held in the depths of them stole Elias' breath.

"You show us. You show us every single day," Henrik said, his voice cracking.

"My perfect family," Elias added. "If it is the Gods who brought us together, I will find it in myself to forgive them." He snuggled in even closer. "My happily ever after."

GriMM

Thank you for reading The Elves and the Shoemaker. If you enjoyed the book, I would be eternally grateful if you could **take a moment to rate and/or review** as this goes a long way in helping other readers find out that I exist and I do exist so that's nice.

Other books in the series:
Little Red Riding Hood by TJ Rose
Zel by Amanda Meuwissen
Hansel and Gerhardt by W.H. Lockwood
The Elves and the Shoemaker by Emory Winters
Cinder by D.N. Bryn
The Frog Prince by A.M. Rose
Rumpelstilzchen by Sam Northman
Snow White and the Seven Little Miners by Kit Barrie

ALSO BY EMORY WINTERS

Star-crossed Betas *A Northern Shifters Novel*
Paw Prints in the Sand *A Northern Shifters Novella*
A Den Mate for Dylan *Foxwood Hollow Book One*
Scrum-Half in Heat *Rugby Omegavers Short*

Acknowledgements

This book has been a hell of a journey during the most chaotic year of my life.

Starting with a thank you to TJ Rose for organising this collaboration and inviting me to take part back when I was the freshest baby author ever. Thank you to Sam Northman for making me ask for help when I needed it and all the other GriMM authors who have been eternally helpful and kind during this process. It has been a pleasure working with you all.

As always, this book wouldn't exist without A. Knightly's endless cheerleading and encouragement. Thank you and sorry you endured this one for quite so long lol.

Thank you to my beta readers, Emma, Logan, Imi, and my sister, Beth. You were all so helpful and gave me the push I needed to get this over the finish line.

And a huge thank you to Sara Onstine of Mild-Mannered Editors for proofreading this book on such short notice. Your attention to detail with this was so reassuring and has made uploading the final copy far less stressful. Commas based on vibes for life lol.

Last but not least, a huge thank you to Lina Ganef for the most stunning cover art imaginable.

www.ingramcontent.com/pod-product-compliance
Lightning Source LLC
Chambersburg PA
CBHW050411260626
47156CB00003B/968

the slope toward the cars. Taking well-spaced steps, the farmer was soon at his side. "What in hell was that all about?"

Val's anger, however, had come and gone like a low-flying bird. Disengaged again from care, he savored Tanya's parody and suppressed a grin.

"She didn't seem to like you none."

"That's because she understands me so well. Boy, it's great to be understood. You know what she once said about me? That never in her whole life had she ever met anyone more *wholesomely depraved.*" He snickered with delight and then with a swipe snapped a green reed out of the earth.

> "'She can flourish staff or pen,
> And deal a wound that lingers;
> She can talk the talk of men,
> And touch with thrilling fingers.'"

"Who said that?" asked the farmer.

"I did just a moment ago."

"Auh, sheet."

"Hey, wouldn't it be funny if I've lost the keys?"

They had come over the bluff that leveled off to the road. With the reed in his teeth as they passed through the gate, Val rummaged in his pockets. "Here she be," he said, and tossed the ring with its chattering keys into the country air, catching them again and stopping at the muddied Pontiac to open the trunk. There they lay folded next to the pile of white, string-tied boxes which he had placed there that morning without noticing the blankets at all.

"Look-a-here. I got to tell you somethin' I heard." With his long middle finger Esra touched a spot of dried mud and flipped it off the fender. "My sister she said she heard talk of the sheriff knowin' about these here goin's on here."

After removing his head from the jaws of the open trunk, Val bounced it closed, and then again, until it clicked. "Does he have a camera? Invite him along."

"No, I mean this is a problem."

"Where does your sister get her information?"

"I don't know. I don't want no trouble."

"You never had trouble before. No one can see us from the road. This is private property. What are you worrying about? And if they throw us in jail, then they got to feed us, don't they?" He flung the blankets from one arm to the other.

"Just thought I'd mention it."

"What are we doing, over*throw*ing the damn *government* or something?"

"You're right, I 'spose," said the farmer, waving absentmindedly at a green and tan station wagon rattling briskly along Tuckabunkwac Road. "Yeh, you're right."

"Friend?"

"Yah."

Val headed back, pulling at the grass reed in his mouth as he went.

"So you think we ought to go on with it?" said Esra, catching up.

"You *do* want your cut of the money, don't ya?"

"Surenough. You got it with ya?"

"You want it now?"

"No, no. Pops always paid me later."

"Suit yourself."

"Okay, I'll skidaddle to the house now. Just lemme know when you're done."

"Aren't you going to watch?" Val stopped and removed the reed from his two front teeth.

"Pops thought it safer not to have too many guys around doing nothin'."

"Well, Pops isn't here *now*, for crysake."

"You know, it's the way he'd want it."

Val turned away and then turned back again. "Who was this joker," he asked with disgust, "some sacrosanct chieftain, some African Buddha whose ways we must follow as law? Come on, god-damn it."

"Well, ah don't know."

"Look, don't be silly. Tag along. Or you'll miss the whole show. Or maybe you embarrass easy."

"Oh, come on now."

"Broads don't appeal to you, perhaps?"

"I wouldn't say that, exactly."

"You wouldn't?"

"Not exactly."

Val chuckled, the reed wavering in his mouth like a long, reptile tongue. "Not exactly. Well don't run *riot*, for crysake. No more of these sexual outbursts; it'll upset the cattle."

"'Cept there ain't no more cattle."

"What?"

"Had to sell 'em. All 'cept one. She was sick. Ah, the whole place is going to seed."

"I'm sorry to hear that. What a shame.... Well, there you are. What you need is something to take your mind off things. There is *enough* restriction in this world. Don't add to it by inhibiting *yourself.* Come on, we'll have a ball. Besides, these things bore the hell out of me, and I want someone to talk to."

He pulled the green blade from his teeth and trotted in through the gate.

In the palm of the pasture, which was growing warmer in the morning sun, most of the men stood together half-facing one another and began, with the caution of city people, to talk. There were folded arms with shoulders held high, thumbed pockets with shoulders low, clasped belts with chests concave, and arms held behind with jacket buttons straining. As the talk livened, so did the gestures. A step forward brought the thrust of an emphatic finger. There was a drastic laugh, a nod in tempo, a cigar gone out. Someone performed the mannered tapping, the elaborate grimacing, the delicately exaggerated handling that goes into the lighting of a single cigarette. There was the jingle of pocket money, the pompous clasp of a left lapel and the furtive adjustment of trousers at the groin. A finger would pull at a tight collar, a palm would pat with vanity some wayward strands of thinning hair, and then every so often, with casual stealth, an eye would wander and check the women.

Two photo bugs were the first to begin talking. Nat DeVore, lifting his peaked cap to scratch his head, his shoulders and neck still supporting the stuffed gadget bag and the two cameras (Leica and Rolleiflex), got into a discussion over the virtues of the Heiland Strobe as opposed to the Stroboflash. The man he was talking to was Harry in the wild Hawaiian shirt, who carried a bulging gadget bag, a Contax with a telephoto attachment, plus the bulky black and gray battery box of the Stroboflash itself.

Near these two, yet showing no interest in their technical talk, stood a preoccupied Ben Reno. From time to time Harry looked his way trying to suck him into the conversation, or at least make him part of the audience, but Reno took no notice. The only things that interested him now were the green, quiet hills and the dripping forest that stood all around them. In fact, nothing else, not even Tanya, existed in his usually tireless, sex-geared mind. For him, the hills stood supreme. He studied them, turned slowly and appraised them, their humps and slopes and mysteries. Finally, his mind came down from out of the heights and he was himself again.

"Well, if Mantle would stop getting injured for a change and if they can straighten out the pitching staff...." The conversation, as it always did when Joe Jones was around, had quickly entered the world of sports.

Nat DeVore kept to himself, listening with resentment to the endless talk concerning the national sport. It bored him as always. One baseball season seemed just like another. Eternal youth was what the game offered; eternal youth to all except those who played it. Each year nineteen teams battled one another to their collective deaths, only to be resurrected the following spring when the whole business would start all over again. The great names of the game grew old and vanished, yet each new spring those who followed the treadmill were once again given a taste of past youth.

The sports-talk was being flung about like a ball in an infield warm-up. Then it came to Nat and was dropped. Did Mays or Mantle hit more R.B.I.'s last year? It was assumed that Nat might know.

"I shamelessly admit that I don't even know what an R.B.I. is," he said. Someone in the crowd gave a lonely laugh. "The fascination escapes me, this watching other men play ball."

There was a bit of floundering at this point and a pinch of resentment at his implication that this great interest in their lives was really not worth an intelligent man's valuable time. Joe Jones frowned. It was a habit of his whenever something he was about to say took thought.

"You know why sports gas me?" he began. "It's the only place these days where a guy can be heroic."

"Make a million," said Reno, "and people'll treat you like a hero."

"People who don't know any better," Nat interjected in a slow voice which was interrupted by Joe Jones trying to explain that this wasn't what he meant.

But now Eddie May was speaking. "I never heard of them asking a rich man for an autograph."

"Take it from me," Reno said, tapping his palm with a finger, "money can do anything."

"I used to think so," said Harry.

"What can't it do? Huh?"

"I'm talking about a real hero," Joe Jones insisted. "What the hell is money?"

"I was a hero once," Eddie May explained. "In a crowded subway I let a girl sit on my knee."

Ben Reno, however, had taken over. "Well, I really *was* a hero. Korea, medals, the works. Take it from me, it's nothin'. But if you got it here," he announced, slapping his right trouser pocket, "if you got it here, the rest's a lark. Nobody treats you like dirt. You get the glad hand. You get the big smile. No matter what they think of you. They'll shine your shoes and tie your laces. They'll do anything you want. Without money you're dirt and they know it. With it, you get the best. Cars, clothes, women. All yours. Hero? Famous? Tell you what you do. You're rich, see, so you give a little of the loot away and you've got that too." Slapping his right trouser pocket. "But you've got to have it here. That's all that counts."

There were despondent mumbles of agreement in the wake of this speech as Val marched up and asked gleefully: "What counts? What do you *got* to have?"

"Money," said Eddie, lifting a knee to pull up a sock, "that's what they say."

"You got to have *money?* I thought it was 'heart' you've got to have?" And marching on through to where the women were standing, he tossed the two blankets at the surprised Tanya who caught in a hug this not-quite-rudely yet not-quite-properly-thrown heap of flap and fuzz and then straightened up again as she glared. But Val had turned rearward, marching a few yards off to talk again to the farmer who, with slow, sullen strides that kept pace with Val's rapid, deliberate step-step-step, had followed him all the way down the long slope from the road.

The field was alive with the twit-twit-twiddly-twit of one bird and the switswit*sweet* of another. The air seemed to move and hum, and high up, a lonely fleck with wings flapped three times then flapped again, while several feet away a field mouse rustled grass in a flight to safety. A shake and shudder of leaves, violent and localized, bounced from one branch to another as something small and terribly alive leaped about and was gone. Living things were spying on them and vanishing while they all talked and walked in the open field, believing themselves alone.

The women reached the point near the farthest end of the field, not far from the tarpaulin-covered, broken-wheeled object with its black puddles of water now growing smaller in the sun; reached the point where two wooden poles placed five yards apart were standing mysteriously in the field of wet bent grass. A slack rope had been strung out from one pole to the other. Over this rope Tanya tossed the two opened blankets, forming from rope to ground a screen of cloth behind which the two of them disappeared.

"Why do we change here?" Honey asked.

It was faster, Tanya explained, than going to the farmhouse.

The blonde let out a relaxed giggle as she reached into her bag. "We're kinda exposed in the rear."

Tanya eyed the hills behind them with disapproval. "Leaves a lot to be desired."

"Well, what does it matter?" Honey mumbled from inside her sweater.

"I suppose," Tanya agreed. Having hung her dress carefully over the line, she brushed some thread from its shoulder.

Honey flipped her sweater carelessly over the rope. The bra that encased her buoyant breasts showed signs of frequent repair. After a minute or so of making soft, atonal humming sounds, she stopped short, having spotted the intricate purple, green and brown of a hectic butterfly.

"Oh, looklookhowlovely," she gushed. "We should catch it."

"We should leave it alone," Tanya asserted.

"But it's so beautiful. It really is. I mean just to hold it. Not harm it."

"Don't, you'll scare it shitless." Then, as though talking to a child, Tanya said: "Just watch and see the little wings. Like they're too delicate to touch."

"Oh, there's another one. Can't we touch that one either?"

"No, not that one either," said Tanya, finding her ingenuousness beyond belief. "You'd better get undressed. We can watch them later."

"Oh, yes, let's." And the blonde whipped up one side of her skirt and began rolling down a black stocking.

Tanya peered over the blanket top. "Will you just look at him. The way he talks with his body. Bouncing like a jumping jack."

Honey didn't have to look up to see who was meant. "He certainly has a lot of energy, I can tell you."

"Wasted energy," Tanya said, removing earrings from her turned-and-tilted head.

"But that's his charm. I just love the way he wastes his energy."

Tanya put her earrings inside her pocketbook which she stooped for and wiped clean before opening.

"You seem to know him fairly well," she said, checking the blonde's baby face.

"Oh, yes, I do." She shook out her skirt and tossed it on the line. "He's my boyfriend."

Tanya reappraised her at once. "You go out with him?"

"Oh, yes. I lived with him for a while."

"Did you, now?"

"Yes, at the studio. Don't you think it's cosy, fixed up the way it is? I just love it, I really do."

Honey dropped her panties to her ankles and then with a high kick she grabbed them in an overhead catch.

"So you go out with him. Well, lot's of luck. Do you have Blue Cross?"

"Why do you say that? Do you know him well?"

"Kind of."

"You do?"

"Ve vos buddies dere for a vile."

"You went out with him, too? Oh, what a coincidence. It really is."

And she gave forth with a great smile of comradeship which Tanya, in all sincerity, wanted to ram down her throat.

As the air grew warmer, Reno felt himself beginning to sweat under the arms. In Tanya's direction he saw nothing but the occasional, distant movement of Honey's amber hair. The men were assembled in a good-time circle of talk and laughter. Yet several kept themselves apart: two of them, he observed, were still at the pocket chess set, moving the tiny bakelite pieces with delicate, two-fingered care. Val, off with Eddie May and the stooped farmer, was entertaining them with another run of gestured dialogue. Glancing again in Tanya's direction, Ben Reno glimpsed the black-haired back of her head. He was impatient to make contact again. Chance had placed her in his sights, and he knew he would probably have just one more shot at her for fate had also assigned to him the role of Judas which she would learn about soon enough.

The idea of getting his hands on her and of erasing her haughtiness thrilled him. He preferred his women disdainful and stupid. What he wanted was a well-sculptured female whose evening activities provided episodes in the lives of transient men. And time was short; just one brief afternoon to schedule such a night for himself. The trouble, however, was that she kept turning human on him, revealing her anger, wit and compassion until he nearly lost hold of his fantasy. This, for Reno, was the essential misfortune of life: that sexuality and personality did not really gel. Her body spoke one thing to him, her mind quite another. She was the type who would never say what he wanted to hear nor keep silent when he wanted silence. All his life he had desired simplicity. In order to achieve it he found himself frequently misunderstood and even unjustly despised. The role of villain (a part he had no idea he was playing) was essentially one of frustration for him. The difficulty was that of communication. When intimate with a woman, for example, his excitement would often fail unless he engaged her immediately and without preliminaries. Invariably, at such moments, she thought him an animal, and how could he tell her he wasn't? Or occasionally his excitement would arrive slowly, and then he was thought of as considerate and patient, and, of course, that wasn't true either. It was his fate to have women think him crude when he was anxious, lecherous when he was playful, gentle when he was hindered, entertaining when he was indifferent, selfish when he was hurt and disrespectful when he was passionate or filled with love. It was infuriating but he became used to it, for often the pain of misunderstanding was preferable to the shame of recognition.

Two brown sparrows flapped madly across the field and were gone before Reno could see what caused the blur. Instead, he noticed the blankets again as they hung over the rope in the distance. He looked away, then back again. Behind the barrier Tanya was vigorously waving at him. He took a full step forward and his hand was halfway up, when he stopped. He turned and managed a little whistle. "She *wants* you," he said, calling over his shoulder.

Beginning that rapid walk of his, Val started toward Tanya to see what was up.

"*Guarde.*"
"How classic and gallant."
"Wait, I take it back."
"Not allowed."
"You took your other move back."
"All right, all right. Go on."
"No, I'll make it anyway."
"Take it back or I'll never hear the end of it."
"O.K., I kick you with the pawn."

"*J'adoube.*"
"Boy, that bishop of yours is really in cold storage."
"Your move."
"What'd you do?"
"Pawn takes queen's bishop pawn."
"I knew you'd do that."
"You see every move but the last one."
"Look who's talking. You're two pawns down and your king is facocked."
"I live dangerously."
"Move, will ya. Move."

The plane flew into the blinding neighborhood of the sun, and Nat, who had been following it, diverted his eyes not quite in time so that an elusive replica of the great light remained with him for a while moving into his vision again and again.

"Looks like he was brought along to supply the entertainment," said Reno.

They watched Val hurrying off toward the blankets and Nat's face hardened as he saw Val beating out a rhythmic movement with his arms, snapping the fingers of each hand and clapping them together, fist against palm, in a kind of idle snap-thump, snap-thump as he walked.

"You can always spot them," DeVore asserted, rubbing his mouth.

"Sure can. The guy's as queer as a left-handed three-dollar bill."

"That's *not* what I'm talking about. That's irrelevant. What I have in mind is far removed from something as simple and harmless as that."

"Oh? What? I don't..." Reno was cut short.

"He's one of the destroyers of this world," said DeVore firmly. "You can always spot them; his kind, anyway. Their manner is fraudulent, their gaiety false, their activity a cover-up for laziness. In my work I see so many of his kind, they become as one. Delinquent, beat, rebellious, call them what you wish. Set them free, or send them to the chair, it's all the same. They just stand there as the sentence is passed looking up at the judge with that same polluted half-smile, always the same impudent superiority as though no power on earth could touch them. They're right, too. How can you punish a man or pardon him either when he has already judged, sentenced, executed and resurrected himself? His crime? Well, in sports, when a man loses on purpose they say he threw the game. That is exactly what this one is doing in life. Throwing the game."

In another place in the pasture, two others were talking.

"I'll give you fifty cents if you can name the starting line-up of the 1935 Chicago Bears," said Joe Jones.

"I'll give *you* fifty cents if you'll go away," said Eddie May.

They were waiting as he came, only their heads were visible above the army blankets that curtained them off from sight of the men. Her chin resting on the rope, Honey Bea, with her colorless pallor, was beaming at him like a retarded baby. But as Tanya stepped up to the, rope, her displeasure was all too visible.

"Hate to pull you away, but like we've been ready for fifteen minutes. How do you want us to come out?"

"Singing 'Onward, Christian Soldiers.'"

"Hardee-har."

Val smiled: "All right, then, any song you like."

Honey giggled, the rope sagged, and there were Tanya's marvelous shoulders looking burnished in the late morning sun.

Tanya frowned: "Both at once, one at a time, or what?"

"Suit yourself," Val replied.

"You're a big help."

"Why all the fuss," Honey wanted to know, with that deadly innocence that Tanya hated. "Who cares? I really mean it."

"And I couldn't agree more. I really couldn't."

Val's mimicry of Honey's voice and posture won from her a slow, impish grin.

Tanya observed this exchange between them and then broke it up.

"Meanwhile, back at the farm. What's with Esra?"

Val snapped a reed out of the earth. "What do you mean?"

"He seems to be hanging around."

"He's keeping me company. I get a kick out of him."

"He ain't got no camera, fella. He should be off milking cows or something."

"You aren't serious?"

"Oh, yes I are."

"Look," he said, the reed quivering in his mouth. "I've few enough friends in this place. Honey's one. He's another. She's going to be working, so old Esra and I are going to be talkin'. Besides, there ain't no cows to milk. Now are there any questions?"

"About a dozen, but who needs clarity? Just tell him to vamoose."

Val seemed amused by her revolt. "You can't just make him leave. Think of the damage to his psyche, for crysake."

"I've got to worry about his psyche? The hell with that. Listen, I'm not going to pose with people standing around without cameras. Is that clear?"

"You getting prudish in your old age?"

"Pops never did things this way."

"You know something? I couldn't care less."

Her eyes had the glint of obstinacy, and even as her anger flew at him she knew that Esra was not the cause. "Look, he bugs me. Tell him. To. Take. Off."

"You tell 'im," he shot back, as quick to anger as she, and at that moment their whole past together seemed like dry timber awaiting flame.

"Me? You're mishiga. Since when am I supposed to?"

"Why can't he watch us?" Honey wanted to know. "It's just one more pair of eyes."

"Oh, shut up." Then to Val: "I'm not going out there until he's gone and that's that."

"Well up yours. You come here to direct a morality play or what? You want to get paid, you pose. Jesus H. Christ."

He marched off through the moist pasture with his quick, almost comic walk, flinging away the green reed, shaking his head and talking still. Tanya watched and felt weak and miserable. Then she looked off and saw two far-flung birds moving steadily away from her like the last hope of love.

With precise delicacy, Eddie May's right hand softly chopped a wave into his sleek hair. "All right," he said, "now I've got some questions for *you*."

"Sport questions?" said Jonesy. "Are you kidding? Shoot."

"O.K., ready? This is a toughie, Lou Gehrig, famous member of the New York Yankees, set a world record by playing in two thousand consecutive games. Why? Here's another. Ted Williams was the last player to bat .406 in a complete season. Name me at least three other players who have not done so. Last question. What do Jackie Robinson, Sugar Ray Robinson and Edward G. Robinson have in common?"

"You know something?" Jonesy told him, nodding his head in a kind of benevolent disgust. "You're sick."

"And not just lately," Eddie said.

❧ ❧ ❧

Two brown sparrows dipped low and swooped back across the open field again like frantically lost messengers with no time to spare. In the other field (that miniature replica inside his own heroic mind), hunter Nat DeVore aims an out-of-season rifle and *wham-wham* two dead birds drop into the bowing reeds. An arrow staggers him. Hostile Indians appear. His gun cracks in reply, and Indians topple from high trees, slip from galloping ponies, fall as they retreat. Then the farm is safe, the danger past. Calm and valiant, Nat sits and treats his wounded shoulder while those he saved approach with gratitude.

The obsolescence of heroism was a great loss to modern man, in Nat's opinion. Now there are law courts, speed limits, burglar alarms and thermonuclear passivity. Progress has turned the beast into the businessman. Violence is lost in a sea of litigation, and the great battlefields belong to the attorney and the congressman. Grievances are aggravated by adjudications, and angers are replaced by backaches. Lust becomes academic and eventually archaic, and the murderer even refrains from kicking the hangman.

Though Nat was dedicated to a lifetime of work for progress, privately he felt diminished by its victories. There seemed now to be nowhere to go to meet the test, to kill fear with valor and, in so doing, have proof.

The field was ready, the men were idle; what was taking so long? Someone should expedite matters, he decided. He looked at Val, who was seated against a tree. The farmer jumped away, too late, as Val pulled loose his right shoelace. Then, placing his hands behind his head, Val leaned back and rested. Clearly nothing constructive was getting done. In fact, here in the open field in the fragrance of a stalled Sunday, nothing was taking place at all.

Then, without warning, it started. From behind the blankets came the two women, one in a Mexican poncho and the other wrapped in a towel, both heading toward a little rise in the ground that was immediately half-encircled by the men. Tanya noticed her wrist watch, and hurried back to take it off. But Honey went ahead, frail and deglamorized in her bare feet, walking not proudly nor casually either through the needling grass and already oblivious somehow to all those eyes she knew were there. Then she stopped and, without a touch of staging, without so much as a sign of feeling, raised her arms, dropped the garment and stood there naked.

THERE was bending and kneeling, shifting and jostling and occasionally someone tipped forward, his knee pressing accidentally into the moist earth. Heads tilted or craned to peer one-eyed into a tiny squint-sight, or down onto a shadowy ground glass or even in under a black camera hood where a nude blonde was seen calmly standing upside down.

Blurred, almost de-atomized, she came together in colored sharpness in Nat DeVore's second-hand Rolleiflex, dispersed and congealed again as he continued to fuss with the focus. In the squint-sight of Leo's Contax, she appeared split at the waist, the upper and lower Honey sliding together horizontally making the two half women whole. A pair of immobile blondes, standing in the eyepiece of Eddie May's Yashica, slipped completely into each other so that the two chin-raised, straight-backed, knee-bent, identical twins became one.

Striding in spiked heels from behind the wall of blankets came Tanya Lando, still wrapped in a white towel that had hung that morning in Val's bedroom and which she borrowed from Honey's bottomless bag. There was a slight stir when she appeared, her face somber and guarded as she threw off the towel without theatrics and left it behind her on the grass. She didn't remove her shoes. She rested both hands upon her hips. Then, bending one knee and arching her back, she struck a totally irrelevant bathing-suit pose and beamed an equally incongruous smile.

From among the crowd came faint sounds of shutters being released (drawn out like a slow leak of air or briefly as though someone were sucking twice quickly on his teeth). Honey, the shorter of the two, maintained her posture of sober solitude, her arm held

199

breast-high and bent across her body, her head turned aside, alert yet in repose; not aloof nor even meditative, simply dramatic and immobile, a demonstration of graceful, almost poetic relaxation rather than one of conscious posturing. Embarrassment, modesty, even vanity no longer existed. What she had was that rare talent of transfixing herself into a fine, abstract nude whereas Tanya was theatrically naked. She wore stylish black shoes, a delicate ankle bracelet, her best stage smile, and it was all wrong. Those hundreds of hours, when she had posed for this or that photographer in this or that state of three-fourths undress, could not be unlearned. The combined effort to create with her erotic riches the desired suggestiveness now failed for want of having anything left to suggest.

When Eddie May had seen all there was to see he paused, caught up by a disappointing sense of neutrality; it was as though an important promise had not been kept. The result, however, was that he was able to concentrate now on the serious purpose at hand. Jonesy lowered his camera a minute to stare at Tanya and found that her eruptive beauty had become tranquilized, that it no longer implicated him in what had been inferred beneath the sheathed packaging of her dress. Even he decided to give sober thought to the job of taking some decent photographs. Nat DeVore studied the melancholy droop of Honey's breasts, her slack and joyless buttocks, the sadly exposed secret of her pelvic goatee, and he was filled with a flood of compassion. She stood there holding to the last few moments of a pose. Then, choosing another, down she went, seating herself on the green earth as happy and calm as a child being read to.

Because he had begun sweating in the heat of the late morning, Nat removed his peaked cap, rubbed his brow with the same arm, jammed the cap back on his head and began to take his first picture. He was able to catch Honey's eye, and she directed her pose right at him. He bowed, and peering into the camera, stepped back three feet and forward one. Forward two and back one. To the side, one. There, yes. No, not yet. Now he swung to and fro as though practicing an exercise of some mystic cult. He looked up at her and then down into the ground glass again which now, for some reason, had gone opaque. Frowning, he at last discovered what the trouble was: the front flap of the camera case was obscuring the lens. Once more he bowed, peering at the cloudy image of the girl stretched sideways and now frowning at him. He lifted and lowered the Rollei along the land mass of his stomach, then knelt, got up and stepped back into someone, apologized, swung to and fro, then bent over still farther as though to butt her with the top of his head. He motioned vaguely to the model to change something or other in her pose, and in response Honey flattened grass with her palm, braced the ground with her leg and shifted her sensual wealth into a different display. He looked up, nodded, dropped his chin onto his chest, steadied himself, focused some more and then ready at last, called out, "hold it!" and pressed the shutter release which responded with dismaying silence. He had forgotten to wind the crank. Nat quickly cocked the shutter but Honey, thinking the picture taken, directed her attention at someone else, blurring the image as she moved, for Nat had shot at just that moment as did Leo, who accidentally placed her in permanent double exposure with the previously recorded standing figure of Tanya Lando.

Upon the rise of grass sat the two women back to back, each with one knee drawn up. Moisture on the ground was vaporizing in the sun, giving off an enticing smell and creating a drowsy sense of warmth. Tanya avoided Reno's eye and offered up a smile to Eddie May. Honey's back shifted against hers. Longing for a cigarette, Tanya heard metallic Rolleiflex sounds: the magnifying glass snapping up, then clicking back down, the short, dull shutter click followed by the rapid forward-backward grind of the film crank. "Look this way, please." It was the little man in the loud shirt with his name stitched on. She gave him a false look of fixed passion and he snapped it, saying thank you.

An ant was exploring her thigh. She flicked it away and looked for others. None in sight but she remained vigilant. The clouds were drifting off like lost strays, and the sky became a lovely blue. Glancing about, she couldn't find Val. There he be, the bastard, talking with the farmer and getting pushed playfully at some outrageous remark. Valitchska, I see you. Valitchska, look at me. She was chagrined to find herself still attracted to his lean face, and to that small jutting shelf of his rear end. She was told to raise her chin, turn her head, move an arm, all of which she did while continuing to smile at someone's Leica. Well, me boys, here we be and guess who's posing again in her birthday suit? A half dozen manic midgets finally ceased tap-dancing in her stomach. Well, who the hell can be at ease parading about in nothing? And there was also the fight with Val after which she decided, fuck it, I need the money. It took twenty steps to reach where the men stood, the air feeling cool against the entire length of her as she moved. Look, everybody, see what nutty Tanya is doing. Looklooklook. And they did. The sun watched, the morning watched, and all things alive and moving in the woods watched. All things, that is, but him. Standing in the background, he was rolling up the farmer's sleeve. Then he mussed his hair and ducked away. Someday, she thought, someday that boy has just got to get barmizva-hed. Yet his hands moved like birds and his hair hung like wheat, and oh, those lips. Valitchska, look at me, damn you, look at me.

But he was too busy horsing around. When he grew tired, finally, of his own playfulness and the boredom of the field trip, he wandered off along the rim of the forest and with a stripped branch the size of a cane he struck at the trees as he walked. It had become a day of extravagant good weather with high cloud tracks embedded like fossils in the sky. The foliage whispered to him for a while and then spoke out in alarm as the wind pushed through the forest and through his hair. He pressed his inside pocket for the reassuring bulge and for a while thought about the money. The intake was $190 from 19 men—$30 to Tanya, $30 to Honey—$60 he owed the girls. Esra gets $35 and the food was $35. Now 60, 35 and 35 made 130. He stopped and scratched that into the ground with his stick. Plus gas made 140. Those were his expenses. The 190 in his pocket minus 140 left $50. That was his profit for this Sunday. He took another swing at a thin birch and walked away in hatred of such petty soul-squelching concerns as money. Then he stopped, fingered his hair, and walked back to where 190 above 140 left a thin 50 written into the dirt. That was Sunday. During the rest of the week he averaged about $50 each evening when about 10 men on an average showed up at the studio each night to pay him $5 each. This, after newspaper ads and models' fees, came to about 150 a week or 600 a month. Then minus the goddamn rent of $400 a month there was left a 200 profit with which to pay for food, clothes, studio repairs, dinners for broads, gas and electricity, pipe tobacco, laundering, and those endless galley-slave payments to Ulysses each week for the $3,000 owed him for the purchase of the studio in the first place. Oh, and booze. It seemed he was always shelling out for that first. Added to the 200 profit was the $50 intake each summer Sunday providing it didn't rain, which it had, of course, for the last three weekends. His maximum profit was $400 a month during the summer and $200 a month the rest of the year. And since he hadn't been too successful so far in renting out the studio during the day, this, then, was the sum total of his income. On an average this came to about... what was that last figure? He looked back at the ground and found that his bearings were lost in a scramble of scratches. Finally he cursed and rubbed out his financial existence with the sole of his shoe. What did it matter? He knew the answer. He was spending more than he was earning, and he was sorry as hell that he had been conned into this blasted business of ownership in the first place.

Pushing through the high grass, he aroused a number of butterflies, who climbed the air in a zigzag of color. With an exaggerated pucker of his lips he sent each a kiss, and at one who danced within range he swung his stick and missed. Decapitating three sunflowers with mighty blows, he wandered about, then stopped to look at his watch.

With bits of grass still clinging to her thigh, Honey started to search for another pose when someone cried: "Hold it, please. Just like that," and she froze, her every muscle waiting to be released into animation again when Val De Franco, balancing a stack of white, string-tied boxes, came down the slope from the road crying out: "Lunch, everybody, lunch you buggers, lunch."

They gathered like picnic-goers in a triangle of shady trees where the atmosphere was so jovial that even Ottomeyer forgot himself and became almost as good-natured as the others. He sat demurely on a corroded apple crate and delved into the boxed lunch on his lap. It contained roast chicken, cole slaw, potato salad, custard and a peach. He lifted a drumstick for cautious inspection and then barely bit into it as he eyed the others. Honey, again wearing her poncho, sat propped against a tree making a fist so Eddie May could sample and nod over the biceps in her arm. With a towel around her waist, Tanya sat on an old stump looking like a Polynesian native while high above them an inquisitive squirrel studied the scene as he clung upside down to one of the trunks.

Reno, his glasses in one hand, his handkerchief in the other, rubbed them together quickly in reverse circular movements. He squinted painfully in Tanya's direction with eyes that seemed to have emerged from a long spell in darkness. All morning, while she was posing, he had crouched close with an empty camera. But instead of lust, he found himself experiencing an unpleasant return of innocence. He guided the pliant stems of his glasses over both ears, and she jumped into clarity. He moved closer, circled where she sat and stopped to try again.

"It's the philosophy of 'as if,' " Ottomeyer was saying. "You *act as if* you're going to be a big success and so you are."

"I tried that," Eddie May replied as he sat down Indian-style and opened his lunch box. "I went up to this girl *as if* I was going to dazzle her with conversation."

"And?"

"And she looked at me *as if* I was crazy."

A brief pause in the conversations seemed to open a door in the forest, and out came damp stillness. Then Val continued a discussion in which he had become embroiled.

"What I don't understand," he said, "is why, if it was correct for us to have missile bases in Turkey, it's incorrect for them to have missile bases in Cuba? And why, when we have been sending U-2 flights over the USSR since '45, it's a surprise to some people that the Russians consider us warlike and dangerous."

"You sound a little pinko to me," Jonesy said, only half joking.

"How very right-wing of you to say that," Val replied with a poisonous smile.

Listening at some length to the conversation, DeVore eyed him and asked a question.

"How come you care about the world community and not at all about your local one?"

"Who says I care?" Val said, tossing a chicken bone into the woods and rubbing his lips with his sleeve. "I don't, not about either. But world affairs interest me because of the grand hypocrisy of it all. That's what's fascinating. I get a real kick out of this nationalism bit. I just love going into bars and starting political discussions and listening to people rant and pontificate. Christ, it's great. They don't know what in hell they're talking about most of the time. I ask little questions like, let me see, like what's the difference between socialism and communism? Little ones like that. Or are you aware that the United States invaded Russia with an armed force in 1918? People don't know what the fuck I'm talking about. Real political analysts, they are. It kills me." And even now he broke into an escalated series of chuckles that bent him in half.

"Man, you really are pink," said Jonesy, jovial and cutting.

"Whereas you, my friend, are green," Val shot back. "Green behind the goddamn ears. And probably wet in the pants, as well."

"And who's your agent," Reno asked, crouching beside the tree stump.

"Mike Ferrero handles me," Tanya said, forced to turn her dark eyes in his direction.

"Handles you, eh? Some guys got all the luck."

She stared in disbelief. "I've met like some pretty subtle schmucks in my time, you know? But *oh* boy."

He gave her a sordid smile. She shook her head and looked imploringly at the sky. "But oh *boy*ohboyohboy."

"Come on, you can't do that. Your king is in check."

"Ah, how true. *J'adoube.*"

"You're busted anyway."

"I fight to the death."

"Move, will ya? Will ya move?"

Leaning over, Honey bit into her peach, emitting a slow, sloppy sucking sound and then wrung both her hands as though wet. Standing beside him, she offered to share her peach just as he had once offered to share his the day they met. Val turned away from watching the chess game long enough to say, "No, thanks, sweetie," and she was left alone and hurt. Deciding to make him jealous, she set to work, for the time being, on another man. When she saw Nat DeVore, arms folded, looking at her from a few yards away, her choice was made. Approaching, she glanced into his lunch box on the ground and discovered an apple.

"You're not eating your fruit," she told him with mock surprise.

"Guess I'm not in the mood for an apple."

"Nonsense, they're good for you."

He protested. She insisted. Refusing him permission to touch the fruit, she held it out playfully, and he broke into the moist Mcintosh with his teeth. He caught himself. Had he looked foolish? Her ingenuousness, however, had made everything seem quite natural. How was it that her joyful artlessness seemed to afford her greater freedom than that which he derived from his carefully nurtured sophistication? In fact, here in the country, they all appeared to have escaped the confines of guilt and self-consciousness. He decided not to analyze this but instead to revel in the pleasure of the open air.

Honey turned away for a moment to obtain a napkin, briefly exposing her entire flank. His only surprise was feeling no surprise at all. Her body looked pale with a wholesome rump, and a cool, vaccinated thigh. He accepted her attractions with pleasure, dismissed temptation without effort and bit into another offering of the apple.

"Was it an oral or a rectal thermometer?" asked Leo Wertlieb, using his tongue on some food lodged in the back of his teeth.

"Oral," said Eddie May, walking beside him into the sunlight and wiping his hands on a napkin. "We wanted to cure him, not entertain him."

Above their heads two brown sparrows, frantic and hurried, again swooped low and back across the field. Honey was waiting on the hill ready to resume work, palming her hair and tossing away her poncho.

Jonesy glanced at Tanya who stood preparing to migrate with the others back to the center of the open field where she would become simply a nude again and no longer a stunning, half-naked native girl casually tightening a makeshift skirt around the inlet of her waist with its slit up her cinnamon thigh, her hair splashing across her face as she looked down to secure the towel, and then up again as the dark crystal of her eyes caught him watching her. He was embarrassed, then pleased as her perfect lips turned human with a smile. He was amazed, come to think of it, at how proper and serious had been the mood of the day. It wasn't what he had expected, but it hadn't been a disappointment either. Walking behind the others, cleaning his glasses once more to examine the hills, was Ben Reno. One of the chess players, with long heavy double strides, swung his way forward on yellow crutches. Beside him, still absorbed in the involved middle game of a French defense, walked his opponent with the pocket chess set in one hand as though it were a small pie he was about to push into his own face.

The cove where they had gathered to eat was now deserted of all but two, while above them the wind rattled through the forest.

"I suppose you're going to leave these empty boxes lying around?" she scolded, quietly.

Bending to pick up his walking stick, he swung it to his shoulder and moved toward her.

"I didn't know it was your forest."

She softened a bit. "It just doesn't seem right, leaving them here."

With a smooth back swing, he took a chip shot at an acorn. "So you actually thought I was going to leave them here?" His voice was chillingly calm.

She spoke up as though asking for the correct time: "Val, why are we fighting?"

"We always did. Remember?"

"That was then. This is now."

"All right, why are we fighting?"

She thought for a moment. Then, quickly, eyes wide: "Igiveup."

"Oh, now it's games. First anger. Then games. What next?"

"I don't know," she said, disarmed and hoping to sound helpless. "I'm sorry. Like I guess I was trying to communicate."

"Oh, balls. That's the theme of played-out playwrights. The impossibility of communication. What a farce. People can communicate. That's not the problem."

"What is the problem?"

"People don't *care*," he rifled back. "They are not interested. They don't want to know. They don't want to feel."

True to her femininity, she reduced all this to the personal.

"It's not so. I cared."

"Who's talking about you?"

"Well, who *are* you talking about?" She was hurt and angry.

"People," he said, tapping her left nipple for emphasis. Then before she could thrust his hand away: "*People*," he announced, swinging his arms wide to include the pasture. "*People*," he cried to the heavens, shaking his stick in mock rage.

"Oh, you're so farblungit. I suppose you cared about me when we were going together? A lot you cared. Like with pot and booze and all that shit. You cared, sure, but not so you would stop wrecking your life and mine."

He began to enjoy her anger. "Well, you weren't any good for me."

"Just what do you mean I wasn't any good for you?"

"You were kind of ratty in bed."

She gave an outraged cry. With arms akimbo, she did it again. "I am *not* ratty in bed, you fink! You know I'm not."

"Well, I didn't find you physically stimulating."

"Like hell you didn't. You're putting me on, aren't you?"

He smiled. "No, I'm not. Physically you left me cold. I mean it. Remember, in the beginning? You even thought I was queer, the way I acted."

"You got over that quick enough. You and your goddamn scissors. Or don't *you* remember?" When he laughed, she waved him off. "Schmuck." She turned away, then swung back. "Now who's playing games? Huh? You don't even care enough to be serious."

"Or too much to be serious."

"Up yours."

"Ladies first."

"You're the one who doesn't care," she stormed, her anger re-enforced by all the remembered frustrations. "It's you. Like you're whatdoyacallit? Creating the world in your own image."

She turned to leave. He, still smiling, reached out and held a piece of her towel. She took two strides into complete nudity, whirled, as though finding herself in Macy's window, and lunged to snatch back the towel. In a fury, throwing the words into his grinning face: "You're worthless. You're cruel. You play with people. I hate you."

Turning rearward, she marched off like an enraged queen, holding the towel carelessly in front of her as intermittent patterns of sunlight splashed her back and shoulders from the foliage above. She emerged into the flaming noon of the open field, gave her lustrous hair an emphatic toss and did not look back.

Honey waited as the photographers moved into position. She saw Tanya approaching in quick strides from out of the woods, and for the first time she noticed the farmer asleep against a distant tree. Lifting her head, having knelt on one knee, holding her pose, she noticed men in olive green uniforms emerging from the woods. Some kind of mistake. An error. They will see that they are intruding and turn away. Then she saw more of them descending from the road. Others appeared behind her. She stood up, alarmed. *They were police.* She could see guns, clubs. A man in dark blue was directing the others. *Oh, God, the police were closing in.* Suddenly she was caught in the act as she stood without clothes in an open field in Catskill County, New York. Panic and shame sprang upon her, and the wind against her chilled skin seemed to enter her body. She gave a whimper and dove for her poncho.

The arrest was swift and was made with the minimum of confusion. An elderly matron, hired by the sheriff, conducted the women behind the blankets again and stood guard as they dressed. The photographers were lined up, their cameras and gadget bags taken from them, their exposed film removed and then their belongings returned. The members of the field trip were marched up the slope to where an old bus stood puffing exhaust. Everyone waited his turn to climb aboard, the door rattled shut and the bus, with COLIN P. KELLY HIGH SCHOOL printed in fading letters along its side, strained out of the mud and moved up the road.

Two swift sparrows flapped in haste as though searching the vast field for something lost, while from out of the high tilting reeds a slow squirrel approached a moist apple core that was already turning brown in the open air.

DUST-FILLED rectangles of sunlight flooded the stark courtroom. A low, wooden fence separated twelve rows of vacant seats from a high, empty judge's bench behind and above which stood the flag. The only person in the room was a uniformed guard in olive green who was throwing slow, rhythmic punches at the bottom of a light cord. He threw one last left hook, faster than the others, and then moved up the aisle, touching each bench on his way, as he walked toward the sound of a bus squeaking to a stop in the street. As he passed through the large front door, the engine died, and a dog began barking in half-hearted alarm. The court-room remained empty for a time, and the only movements were the slow galaxies of golden dust. Blurred voices gradually became more distinct, and soon twenty men and two women entered in the company of guards in olive green who conducted the prison-ers to their seats.

Leading the way was Sheriff Mike Woodrow, a robust outdoor type in his early fifties with a reddish, weather-honed face and bone-white hair. He had a lively step, a quick smile and by the way the guards called him "Woody," it was obvious he was well liked. In faded blue work clothes with his badge pinned and wobbling on his shirt, he indicated the empty benches with a polite sweep of his baggy hat.

Woody was the kind of man who, though stiffly religious, could take a joke at the expense of the church and who accepted the use of four-letter words from everyone except, of course, his family. He never threw his weight around and occasionally even made fun of the job whose responsibility meant so much to him. Woody believed in the family. What he meant by this was that people should stay at home. He felt that they should provide their own entertainment and so discouraged his family from going to movies, nightclubs, museums, bowling alleys and ball games. What he did encourage was hiking, picnics, swimming, parlor games, handicrafts, carpen-try and parties for all occasions, plus dancing and bingo if sanc-tioned by the church. He was generous and a good companion to his children. He was faithful and loving to his wife, though a bit demanding and critical. He had been married half his life to the same slim, obsessively clean woman whom he had met when he vis-ited the library for the first time in his life at the age of twenty-six to hunt out a book on motor mechanics. He returned it seven days later to take out a second book which this time he had no inten-tion of reading, and then a third one, waiting a week each time because he guessed that it took at least a week to read a book all the way through and because he wanted the librarian to believe he was doing just that.

When she saw that it was romance instead of knowledge that kept inspiring his return and that he was simulating all this ruggedness and good cheer for her sake alone, she took pity on him and let him see that she was interested before she was quite sure of it herself. She had had a good education, which she was intelligent enough to play down, making sure that he got all the flattery and support that his staged manliness so clearly needed. She had a chipped front tooth and wore too much rouge on her pale cheeks, but he never spoke about this, and it didn't matter to him anyway, for he was one of those men who needed continual encouragement and approval from a woman, not challenge, competence, or even beauty.

In all of the years of their marriage, Penelope Woodrow was never disappointed by her husband except, of course, where she had always known he would disappoint her. She could never get him, for example, to appreciate good food or wine, and her love for literature she enjoyed alone. He would not go to a doctor except when he was perfectly well or to a dentist except when pain had all but disabled him. He was an adamant Republican whose right-wing views she did not dare try to temper. Rarely did he say he loved her, and he never showed any affection for her in public. She had expected this, too, and was fulfilled by knowing that his need for her was so great that he was unable even to admit it. Though he loved his children equally well, he once threw their son Ron out of the house for cheating on a college exam. However, the boy was allowed to return in four days, at Mrs. Woodrow's insistence. Their daughter Trudy was married and living in Manhattan yet the whole town remembers the winter evening of her seventeenth birthday when she was molested on the way home from a church dance by a local mechanic. He came out of a bar, followed her down the street, and pulled her into a back alley where her screams frightened him off. Trudy told her father the man's name when he arrived, summoned from home, to find his whimpering daughter being comforted by friends in the rear booth of a neighborhood drugstore.

Though Woody wasn't Sheriff yet and didn't own a gun, he went off alone to the back end of town where he stopped in front of a two-story house and checked the address. He pitched a stone at an unlit window and listened to the smashing glass. He tossed another stone and kept throwing until most of the rock garden had gone through all the up and down stairs windows. Only then did the mechanic run out the front door swinging a wrench in a wild frenzy. They fought by lamplight in the empty street, rolling and struggling for possession of the weapon, kicking and punching at each other, and then Woody stood up with the wrench in his hand and tossed that through one of the windows as well, attacking the mechanic with his fists again until many arms took hold and pulled him off. He noticed that the street was now filled with people and that the police were there with old Sheriff Bundy beside him and Trudy staring out at the scene from the back of a police car while the mechanic lay coughing blood with two of his front teeth stuck like small tablets in Woody's closed right fist.

"The worst is over, folks," said the Sheriff. "Just make yourselves comfortable."

"I wish at this time to lodge a formal protest concerning this arrest," said Victor Ottomeyer. "I demand to know your name and badge number, and I want to remind you that New York State law allows me a free phone call to my lawyer."

He had caught the Sheriff's attention by raising his hand as though he were a little boy requesting permission to leave the room. Yet when he spoke, the anger in his voice gave dignity to the devilish look of his bearded face.

"You bet," said Sheriff Mike Woodrow. "Soon as the questionin' is over with, you'll get your phone call in, all right. I'm a bit rusty at it, but then I promise I'll formally introduce myself. And if my job allows, which I sincerely hope it does, I'll even get a chance to stand still long enough for you to copy this here number offa my badge. How's that?"

Esra slumped in his seat and said: "Woody?"

"Yes, Esra?"

"Woody, would you mind if'n I strolled off to the john?"

"Not at all, Esra. But I wonder if I could persuade ya to just hold off for a little while. You know, until we get squared away."

"Kay, Sheriff. Sept ah hope it's not too long elsewise this here courtroom is goin' to be soppin'."

"Shonuff. Thanks, Es."

"Why are we all so friendly?" Ottomeyer wanted to know. "We've been arrested, and yet everyone is so friendly."

"Stop worrying," Val said. "If they arrest us, they got to feed us. What could be better?"

Val was seated one row behind, and Ottomeyer turned with angry sarcasm.

"Oh, you're such a comfort to us all."

Adjusting his rimless glasses, Ben Reno smile-grimaced at Tanya. He had made certain to sit next to her.

"Anyone spare a weed?"

The Sheriff produced a pack from his shirt pocket and tossed it to Reno, who made a sudden, girlish catch.

"Offer them around," Woody said. "It's O.K. Just so long as you don't burn the place down."

Reno extended the pack to Tanya. "Anyone for a cancerette?"

At first she pretended not to hear, but so many others were accepting the offer that her need for a smoke became greater than her need to ignore him. Allowing two of her fingers to pick out a filter-tip Kent, she gave him a grudging nod of gratitude and then was obliged to face him again as he held up the great blue flame of his lighter. As far as she could tell, he was the only lecher on the trip. But he more than made up for the shortage. The pressure of his thigh forced her to inch away with a look toward the ceiling of controlled exasperation.

Upon entering, she had confronted the courtroom with a fierce silence. Whenever she caught one of the guards looking at her, she returned a haughty glance of obvious loathing. Holding herself closed off from the surrounding police atmosphere, she sidestepped into one of the rows, pinched up her dress one inch and then, as if it were an act of angry punctuation, sat down.

Drawing in her cheeks, filling her lungs with smoke, she leaned forward and hit his shoulder with the length of her finger. Val turned in his seat, his face inches from hers, and raised his eyebrows.

"What are we going to *do*?" she whispered, demanding to know.

"You mean, what am *I* going to do?"

"All right, yes."

"What do you suggest?" He removed her cigarette to place it in his own mouth, and it occurred to her that their lips hadn't been this close in half a year.

"If I knew what to do," she replied, "I'd go ahead and like do it myself. Doesn't it make you furious to be arrested and marched off like a child, when it's they who are the children? We must act."

"Boy, you're still the same broad, all right." He stuck the cigarette back between her lips. "Always out there picketing reality. Save Washington Square, save Penn Station, save Fire Island. Disarm, integrate, negotiate. Okey dokey. But right now, let's pay the man the two dollars. You know the joke. Besides, I've never been arrested. To me this is kicks."

"Oh, balls. Hey, where are you going?"

"To the john."

"You can't. Not until the Sheriff says so," she said, hoping to impress upon him the extent of his captivity. "You heard what he said to Esra."

"Can't go to the bathroom, did you say? Can't go to the john?" He presented a stiff-backed parody of the political Tanya. "I shall march on the W.C. If refused entrance, I'll take part in civil disobedience. That is to say, I'll make in my pants."

She watched him march away, hoping that he was right, that there really was nothing to be alarmed at. And sure enough, he wasn't interfered with, not by the Sheriff, who frowned but let him pass, nor hy the deputies, who received no sign to act, nor even by Esra Willis, who typically enough said nothing, though it was he who had had first call.

As Val disappeared, the door opened from the inner office, and out came one of the young guards. He whispered a message to the Sheriff who called out: "Val De Franco, please? Mr. De Franco?"

"He's done run off to the john," said Esra.

They conferred again, and when the deputy shrugged his shoulders, the Sheriff looked around at the prisoners. "One of the women, then," he said, and his eye scanned the faces and settled on Honey Bea. She rose in shy triumph as if being called to accept an Academy Award. Sidestepping her way to the aisle, she touched her hair and smoothed her skirt. Then caught up in a roaring daydream of applause, with Woody opening the gate for her as though imitating a bullfighter making a pass, she swept by with sporty theatrics and outdistanced the Sheriff to the D.A.'s door. The Sheriff did not go with her into the inner office but sat on the gate, facing the prisoners and swiping with his hat at the mudstains that had dried in patches of light tan on his dark corduroy trousers.

Reno, in another part of the room, had not given up. "Why not?" he asked her, putting away his lighter with a lift of his shoulder. "You and me. Dinner. Dancing. What's the harm?"

"Know something, fella?" Tanya said, disarmed by her own exasperation. "You deserve a real promotion, you know that? Like from Sensualist to Second-Class Lecher."

"I asked you out six times and you said no six times. Only one thing left to do."

"Pray tell."

"Keep askin'. I'm not kidding. I got no pride, and a man with no pride can do almost anything. He don't care what happens. People think I'm common. As common as they come. Sheer guts, is what it is. Got to make up somehow for no looks and no charm. We can't all be beautiful. Hell, I'll give you a good time. Ever met guys who seemed great but turned into foul balls? With me it's the other way around. Slow starter. Can't help myself. But I've been around a lot. Know a lot of things. You could have a grand evening. What say?"

"Vell, ha'll zay von ding dare. Ya got ha great personality goin' hagainst ya."

216

"You kid around a lot, huh? I like that. But what does it mean? Do you like me any at all?"

"Do I like you? Listen, you're a real schmuck of a nice guy."

"Schmuck? What does that mean?"

"Big, you know. Like big."

"Thanks. So then, what say? You and me? Huh?"

"Well," said Tanya, trying to get rid of him once and for all, "you really wore me down. Yes, sir, you just went ahead and wore me down."

"You'll meet me in New York, then?" He seemed both elated and suspicious.

"Ah-huh. But I'm kind of a busy chick and all. Show biz hustle and like that. Haven't got much time, is what I'm trying to say. What's my schedule? Let me think. I'm free on Wednesday afternoon and maybe the early part of the evening. Got to go to Philly for a tryout," she added, searching his eyes for signs of belief. "Say, how about meeting me in Philly on Friday? We could sort of spend the weekend together. O.K.?"

As if he were in pain: "Philly?"

"Just two fast hours from midtown Manhattan."

"That the only free time you got?"

"Yep, that's about it. Hell, Philly's a very interesting place. Founding fathers and all that jazz. Then I'm off to L.A. Some big-deal producer wants to look me over. Let's see. In Philly I don't exactly know where I'll be staying, so how about meeting me at the Aquarium. Friday, twelve noon, in front of the octopus tank. O.K.?"

"Well, it's a long way off. Got to go to New York first. Then to Philly."

"Why, where do you live?"

"Here."

"Here?" she repeated, with surprise. "In Salemville?"

"Only some of the time," he added, obviously covering up. "Here on business, you might say. I'm in New York a lot. Yeh, an awful lot. Philly, huh?" He grimaced an unsuccessful look of suggestiveness.

217

"It'll be worth my—our while, you think? Getting together in Philly?"

She turned up the flame of her sensuality and said: "I mean if you think the odds aren't right, sweetie, like forget it."

"No, no. It's O.K. Philly. Twelve noon. Next Friday."

Tanya, reproachfully: "You be there, now. I'm not going to take a cab all the way to the Aquarium for nothing."

"Don't worry. It's done. We'll have a ball. Might even see some of the city, who knows?" And he grimaced at her again.

"Oh, you're a rogue, all right. Now leave me be. We don't want the others to catch on, do we? This is our little secret."

"Got ya."

He moved off, looked back and squeezed a last-minute, intimate, wink-signal forecast of things to come, and she, suppressing laughter, returned it with an exaggerated, head-tilted, expression-fixed, razzmatazz, roaring twenties, palms up, burst of joy wink-smile and then dropped it, turned away and tumbled into a depression. She felt as though she were trapped in a world of decay and indifference where she and everyone else seemed fatigued by flippancy. You will be a great actress and famous, she reminded herself, but even this did no good for she wanted to scream at the others, and she wanted to kill Val. Where were all those truly adult men whom she had been waiting all through childhood to meet? She ground out her cigarette with the sole of her shoe, recrossed her legs and just sat.

She found herself staring at the door through which Honey had gone. It had the sealed finality of the entrance of a tomb. A few moments later Val emerged from the bathroom, and after concluding some charming words with one of the guards, strolled up the aisle. Tanya remained transfixed by the office door. Then, for no reason, fear touched her, and she signaled for Val.

"We have to do something."

"What do you mean?" he asked, sitting beside her.

"They took Honey inside. She's being treated something terrible. I feel it."

"Oh, nonsense. They're just questioning her. Right? That's all."

The last thing he wanted to see was the world as she saw it. Life was palatable if played as burlesque, and for all he knew this was exactly its grand design.

"But I feel it," she insisted.

"No you don't."

"I tell him yes, he tells me no."

Then as though to prove he was right all along, Honey emerged from her interrogation undamaged and all smiles.

"There, you see," said Val.

"Well, she's pure steel wool. She'd have to be to have shacked up with you."

"Oh, you know about that," he said, obviously pleased.

"And let me tell you something else. If she knows anything that you want kept secret, like look out."

"But that's her charm. She's the only woman I've ever met who's totally without inhibitions or morals. It's marvelous."

"So *that's* her charm," said Tanya, viciously. "I wondered what it was."

"Well, don't you sound good and catty. It so happens she's a fine, good-natured, well-built schizophrenic and I would recommend her to any virile young man or bored psychoanalyst."

"She's not the only one we know who needs an analyst."

"By that, of course, you mean ... "

"Mr. Val De Franco," the Sheriff boomed, and Tanya's beautiful lips stretched into a joyless smile.

But when Val stood up, he looked vulnerable to her, and she begged him to please, please be careful. He pinched her cheek and moved in swift steps down the aisle, winking at Honey Bea who waved back. At the end of the aisle, he pushed open the gate and, following the Sheriff, went on in.

It was a small office made to look smaller with filing cabinets and maple desks. On the wall was a calendar photo of the Grand Canyon, three Scotch-taped, open-flapped birthday cards, a succinct playing schedule of the New York Yankees, grim portraits of two murderers, and a child's pale, drip-dry watercolor. The leftovers of somebody's drugstore lunch stood on a desk top with a set of keys and a checker set, its board folded shut, and the open box of red and white plastic pieces placed on top.

District Attorney Giles Keith, handsome and boyish at thirty-six, rose from his desk, tucking his murky green and black striped tie into the V of his jacket. With one hand he indicated a chair beside his desk while adjusting with the other a slash of white in his breast pocket. His suit and his manner were Ivy League, giving him a buttoned-down, three-buttons-all-buttoned brand of intense composure, of intellectual allure, of effortless efficiency and spiritless vigor. His eyebrows were a bit too heavy, and the face was surprisingly free of the scuff-lines of use. He had about him the air of a man self-instructed in the appearance and postures, the packaging and presentation of everything he was that would meet the eye and ear of others. He had that executive awareness of living always under the guise and judgment of higher-ups even when there were no higher-ups judging any more or watching at all. In the art of projecting his image, he had mastered everything but the knack of artlessness, for there was about him, occasionally, the flow of simulated sentiment; this and a chilly, geometrical exactness. Val, for his part, enjoyed him immensely.

"Sit down, please," said Keith in a gentle voice and, as though the command were a general order, all three men did so at once, the Sheriff using the edge of one of the desks.

"I understand..." Keith interrupted himself to push a pack of Kools across the desk. "Smoke?"

"Don't mind if I do."

"I understand that you're the leader of this excursion." He was glancing at some papers as he spoke. "That you took a total of $190 from these men, all of whom answered an ad in a newspaper. That you hired the girls and arranged with the farmer —I forget his name...."

The Sheriff came through with the information, for Val was busy lighting his cigarette.

"Thank you, Woody. That you arranged with Esra Willis to use his farm for these activities and that you have been doing so for some time." He looked up at Val again and saw a slow, ironical grin. "Is that correct?"

"Well, no," said Val, exuding nostril smoke like a dragon. "But I'm impressed. How on earth did you collect all that goddamn information?"

"How are these facts not correct?" asked Keith, growing firm or pretending to, Val wasn't sure.

"Well, I didn't arrange anything with Esra. That's the first thing."

"Then how did he know you were coming today?"

"It was arranged years ago."

"What do you mean by that?"

"Years ago he was told that a field trip would show up at his farm every Sunday during the summer when the weather was good."

"But you arranged that, did you not?"

"Hell, no. That was the doing of one Ulysses S. Grant Hill."

Keith gave a hard look at the Sheriff before returning to Val again. "Who is he, this Hill? Where is he? Can we got hold of him?"

Val made like a dragon again. "He went South a few months ago ... to retire ... or die or masturbate or something."

"You know where he settled?"

"I give up, where?"

"I'm asking *you*, sir."

"Oh, in Alabama, I think." Crossing his legs, Val rested an elbow on the desk, his cigarette held high. "This is no ordinary man, let me tell ya."

"Where in Alabama? What's the address?" Pen and paper were ready to record the town, the street.

"Beats me. See what I mean? Any ordinary man would have told me."

The Sheriff covered his mouth, and the D.A. bristled, or pretended to bristle. "Is he the owner, leader, or what you will of these field trips? A straight answer will be appreciated."

"Is he the owner? Boy, do I wish he were. He sold out to me and skipped. Well, what can you expect from a twelfth-generation American? Today was my first official trip up here, you know. One trip too many, it seems."

Keith leaned back in his swivel chair which gave a cry of anguish. "All right. Now—at this time—there are a few things, answers, I want from you. General information, if you will. First, what are the names of the women? There are two of them in all, I believe. What are their names and whatever else you may have, know about, by way of information."

"Ask them yourself, why don't you?" Val suggested. "What does it matter? They were hired by me. If you want to prosecute someone, I'm your boy. Me and the other clowns out there. That's if you *want* to. Don't let me talk you into anything. Hell, these are just girls working for a living, for crysake. Leave 'em be."

"I assure you, we have no intention of harming them."

"And what's the charge anyway? What are you holding us for?"

"It'll all come out in time."

"Maybe now's the time."

"No, but since you seem anxious about it, very well. We have not determined yet whether, against the others, a misdemeanor or a disorderly conduct charge will be preferred. It depends on the type of cooperation we get. It is particularly important, Mr. De Franco, how *you* cooperate. We will most probably bring against you the charge of procuring women for purposes of indecent exposure, and then release you on bail. As I said, we have not definitely made up our minds on this issue. But I would like to underline the seriousness of the situation and particularly to stress the point that our decision will be based very greatly on your attitude. Which brings me back to the names of the women. You were saying?"

From where he sat, the prisoner could see the sky gathering its final strength in the west. Beyond a clustered branch near the window, an abstract of stained and delicate clouds was floating away from the light.

"I was saying," Val answered, with angry intensity, "I was saying that these are just girls working for a buck. You should leave them be, is what I was saying."

Giles Keith shook his head. "I see we are going to have to take a firmer line with you, Mr. De Franco. Remember, if you wish this business to be kept discreet—to be kept out of the papers—we must have nothing less than your complete cooperation. Nothing less. Otherwise," a wave of his hand indicated the vast and awesome possibilities that lay crouched in the near future, "otherwise ... well, you understand. We have our duty to perform, distasteful as it may be."

"Put their names in the paper?" His amazement seemed to retard his capacity to think. "The names of the women?"

"We can. If driven to it, we will. Of course, a scandal might follow. I think neither one of us would care for that. I believe in fair play and respect for the individual. But if we are opposed, a hard line will be adopted." He presented and immediately withdrew a swift, muscular smile.

"How do I know that the names won't be given to the press anyway?" Val looked up. "How do I know that?"

"You have my word. And when I give my word—and I hope I can say this without undue vanity—when I give it, it means something. I, personally, would like to keep the whole thing out of the press."

"You already had one of the women in here. Didn't she give you her name?"

"Much checking and double-checking is necessary in this kind of work."

"Well, I'll have to go back and ask them what information they wish me to give out."

"That's impossible, I'm afraid. This is not a joint interrogation. It would lose all value that way."

"It's *their* names, *their* lives," Val insisted.

"I'm sorry."

"Well, call them in here, then. I'm not trying to confer secretly with anyone, for crysake."

"No, I'm sorry."

Val was outraged at the incontrovertible will that sat in judgment before him. Here at last was the voice of society in the pontifical role of authority. For the first time in his life Val had been presented with an ultimatum he could neither defy, ignore, nor laugh off. Cigarette ashes fell on his suit as the prisoner rose to his feet. He pushed back his hair and faced the D.A. with an expression of pain and confusion. It was as though he had come awake in an incredible place to find himself doing and saying unbelievable things.

"I intend," he concluded, in a hushed but furious voice, "to ask them anyway."

The D.A. sat forward with another swivel-chair squeak of anguish. "I would strongly advise against it."

Val looked at the Sheriff who shook his head "no" in a kind of fatherly request. For the first time Val noticed the gun at Woody's belt. Woody's right hand, on the edge of the desk, moved a bit closer to the weapon. His head shook "no" once more. Val was trapped for lack of a course of action. He sensed that they were bluffing, that they would use the gun only as a last and final move. Most probably they would call in the guards to have him restrained, perhaps even roughed up. He felt a familiar force overcoming his will; it was that old urge to smash things open, to tear apart the afternoon. Soon he was filled with a desire to make the Sheriff use that gun, to see if they would actually attempt to kill him. If he moved swiftly enough, Val reasoned, they would have to do just that, for aid might come too late. Destroy yourself and embarrass them all: that was his first thought. It gave him comfort, for it presented him with a path of defiance where a moment before there was none. The door had a bolt lock; he had only to get to it and shuttle it closed and the three of them would be alone. If the Sheriff had not pulled out his gun by then, he would have to, once the prisoner advanced on him, and he certainly would have to once the prisoner started throwing punches—as if the gun were not leveled at his chest—continuing to punch away until the Sheriff had no choice but to fire.

Later, when Val realized how close he had come to setting all this in motion and when he realized that what had come between him and the first step of action was an abrupt and unexpected return of pride, he had to smile. As if to a little boy, Tanya had said: please, please be careful. Remembering this he suddenly could not act at all, for in doing so, he would prove himself to be what she had always claimed he was, a reckless child.

So he did not act. The rage, however, and everything else in the room remained just the way they were: Keith looking up at him with formal patience, and the other, with the gun, leaning forward, resting as much on his palms as on his rump and breathing, now and then, like a man with a cold, in short, sucking snorts.

"What more do you want beside the names?" Val heard himself ask.

"We'll come to that. All in good time."

"You're choking me to death, you mother-fucker," he shouted in the hollow of his mind. "I'll kill you for it yet." But what his lips said was: "Ach, zoo."

"Will you be seated again?"

The prisoner, after gazing for a moment at the ceiling and then nodding to the window as though in a secret agreement, bent forward and, with his finger, flicked the seat of the chair he had just vacated as though testing it for dust. When it had passed inspection, he said: "All righty."

Hands on his knees, he sat down on the edge of the chair as though about to spring up again at any moment. You had better give in, he told himself, it's wiser that way. Do it for Tanya, though she has no faith in you, and keep her name out of the papers and keep her life simple and clean. In fact, do it for all of them out there in that goddamn wooden courtroom like a self-service synagogue. No choice in the matter. Better wait, cooperate, and get the bastards later. That's the strategy, wait until later.

He tried to smile at the travesty and self-betrayal of his own surrender. But it was as though his skin had been turned to glass.

"Honey Bea," he said, giving the names of the two women, one who loved him, the other whom he loved, "and Tanya Lando."

The D.A. wrote them down with a ball-point pen. He leaned back, and the swivel chair gave another cry. Then he asked for the money. Val pretended to misunderstand. His gross profit on the field trip, he was told. Val said he didn't have it, that he hadn't taken it with him. But the D.A. explained that the money —one hundred and ninety dollars worth—was in a white envelope in the inside pocket of Val's jacket.

"How the devil do you know that?" For a moment the anger was mixed with awe.

Keith smiled. The prisoner explained that the money was to pay the farmer and the models. It would be given back to him, he was told, and besides, the bail would probably be fixed by the court at about two hundred dollars anyway. Val debated the matter. The thought of being imprisoned for a month greatly appealed to him. Yet he was too much in debt now as it was, and to fall another month behind would put him right out of business.

"Well?" asked the D.A., and Val didn't answer. He stared straight ahead like a dumb animal.

The white envelope was tossed across the desk. Keith counted the bills and handed it to the Sheriff who came forward. The prisoner sat perfectly still, staring out the window.

"Now *I* want to ask a question," Val insisted, hoping to cleanse himself.

"Ask away."

"*How* were we disturbing the peace?"

Keith, writing again, appeared at first not to hear him. "What? Oh, yes. The charge." He rotated his right shoulder, gripping it with his left hand. "You were disturbing the peace because people passing on the road by the Willis farm could see the activity in the pasture. You, as the ringleader, will be held, as I said, on a misdemeanor charge, and you will return in thirty days or so for a trial. The judge will inform you of all the particulars. Thank you. That will be all, Mr. De Franco."

"That," said Val, in great excitement, "is just so much high-flung shit. You can't see the pasture from the road. That's absurd, for crysake. And indecent exposure? That's equally ridiculous. It was no more indecent than an art class. Or are they next on your list?"

District Attorney Giles Keith put down his pen with both hands. "Young man, though your manner is rude, I feel it is my responsibility to explain to you some of the realities of the law. To talk about morality—any such talk about morality—will give a false picture of how things stand here. The law is quite clear on indecent exposure. The law is quite clear on procuring women for such purposes. The law is quite clear on private and public demonstrations of this sort and on the right to arrest and prosecute. I might add that if you have anything to say on the matter, that you reserve such comment until you face the judge. Sheriff, would you escort Mr. De Franco and bring in Tanya Lando? Thank you."

When she came in and sat down, the chair was still warm. She had drawn a moist fingertip along each arm and touched herself behind each ear so that now the inner office was infused with perfume. Her face was an angry mask and, after studying its sensuality for a moment, the D.A. became equally unfriendly. She was so starched with pride, she even refused a cigarette. Keith stood with one foot on the swivel chair, and the questioning went badly. She made no effort to make it easy for herself and answered each probe in a venomous tone. When he finally threatened to expose her publicly by naming names to the press, she angrily accused them of trying to trap her with cheap threats. The Sheriff assured her this was not so. She remained adamant, and Keith's fingers touched the phone as he offered to call the press there and then. A look of childish inattention seemed to numb her face, her eyes slipping down to study the tip of her shoe.

"You don't seem eager for a showdown," said Keith, pleasantly.

"Who needs it? I sign tomorrow for one of the leads in a wonderful play. You think I'm anxious to screw up?"

"I wish you—and I'm sure the Sheriff joins me in wishing you
—the very best of luck."

"Surely," the Sheriff added.

"Wow. Like thanks a whole lot."

"You're welcome, I'm sure."

"I don't dig being threatened," she added quietly.

"I suppose not," Keith agreed, with his quick, all-purpose,
tossed-away smile. "But I'm sure a pretty girl like yourself, I'm sure
we all understand each other and that you will help us to expedite
matters with the least possible inconvenience or embarrassment to
all concerned. Am I correct? For example, you refused to give your
address before. You will please give it now."

A moment of silence; then she recited it quickly, closing her
right hand to examine her nails, straightening her fingers to examine them again.

"Your age?"

Her eyes widened. "I don't see what the hell that…"

"Your age, please." His voice was blunt-edged and confident. After a pause: "There are always the newspapers, Miss
Kretchmar."

"How did you learn my real…"

"Your age, please?"

Tanya moved as though to rise but sat back again after yanking
at her skirt to cover her knees. She looked about helplessly.

"Twenty-eight," she said, staring out the window.

"Married or single?"

At this, the Sheriff got up and strode about for a moment staring at the D.A. but failing to get his attention. He rested one arm on
a filing cabinet and continued to stare. He sniffed as though trying
to check a running nose.

"Single," she fumed.

"Have you ever been married?"

"I am not now nor have I ever been married."

"Any previous criminal record?"

She turned to Woody. "Will ya get him. He's just too much."

"I will receive from you not only the correct answer," Keith demanded, "but the proper respect as well."

The Sheriff's eyes jumped from the soft dark hair of her head to the D.A.'s face.

"Well, up yours," she salvoed in a cold strangled rage.

He lifted the phone and began to dial. She looked a bit sick and then moved her lips to say: "No ... criminal record. None."

"Remember, Miss Kretchmar, we will double-check all of your testimony."

She looked at him, at the Sheriff, at her nails. She spoke with a dull voice.

"I was arrested in 1959 in the Village. It was a pot party. I wasn't booked. I was let go." Looking up at Keith. "I was *not* one of those using the stuff. Then, let me see—then I was named as co-respondent by an actor's wife in a divorce case." Looking up again. "But that doesn't—that isn't part of a criminal record, is it?"

"No, Miss," said the Sheriff, "it isn't."

"You will please leave the interrogation to me, please."

Angrily: "I was just trying to give the young lady a break. I beg your pardon."

"The young lady, as you put it, is doing quite well."

Woody's unexpected words of mercy caught Tanya off guard and both strengthened and weakened her. She saw his face exuding health and comfort as though he were a young actor unconvincingly aged with makeup to look the part of somebody's father.

"Miss Kretchmar, I'd like to finish this interrogation, if you please."

"So who's stopping you?"

"You mentioned a party where marijuana was used." Leaning forward and pinning her with a professional stare. "Was anyone, to your knowledge, was anyone there a communist?"

Tanya looked at him, her mouth open, moronic, inert. Keith, who had been tapping a cigarette on his left wrist, stopped.

"Well, I'll be damned," she said and stood up, her tight dress wrinkled at the hips. Securing her purse under her arm, she tossed her hair out of her eyes. "I refuse to be submitted to such questioning. I refuse."

"May I remind you ..."

"I am not interested in your reminders," she stormed, marching away, turning back, firing at him again. "Now I know you for what you are. If these men with me are too cowardly to tell you off, well, I'm not. You are a John Birching, bomb-sheltering, red-baiting, atom-testing, stock-piling fascist crud."

She made for the door and Keith, with a smile, signaled for the Sheriff to let her go.

Somewhere on the way from the pasture to the courthouse the heel from Nat DeVore's right shoe had fallen off. He had trudged through the field to the truck like the captured general of a routed army, now and then stirred by some recurrent thought, pride perhaps or contempt. Without a heel, he walked his wounded walk down the aisle of the courthouse to a seat near the front and somewhat away from the others. But Honey followed, asking permission to sit beside him, and he could think of no way to dissuade her. While he stared at the vacant judge's bench, she not only talked, she seemed never to stop. Since he needed to stifle anxiety, it was to this end that the prospect of her presence seemed pleasing; it would, he hoped, distract him for a time from the grotesque comedy into which he had fallen.

As he expected, she chatted nonstop, but this time not pleasantly. Her subject was her hatred for the law, and she related first an incredible story about police brutality (a girl she knew had been raped by two policemen in the front seat of a patrol car) and of a sadistic judge (he had sentenced a girl she knew to a two-month imprisonment on trumped-up charges and saw to it that her child was taken away). Though angry, she was vague about names and dates when he questioned her further and, of course, none of these transgressions of authority had ever personally happened to her. All her hate and disgust was expressed in a kind of disjointed monologue as though it were a run-through of a high school play. Then she smiled, changed the subject, and the air was clear again.

He asked her what had happened in the D.A.'s office, and the story she related was also incredible but enough so to be true. Using a French accent, she had told Keith that she was Norma Vincent Peale, the exotic dancer. "Honey Bea? Oh, no, no. Een my business, one has ze many names. I have been at one time or ze other Ulga Boatman, Wilma Dean Howels—dis eez when I dance at ze men's college, eh?—Honey Bea, N. Joy Loving, Cherry Pepper and Ada Buoy." There was a bit of discussion over which of these was her real one. She settled on Norma Vincent Peale, and he asked her if that wasn't the name of a stripper on the West Coast.

"Dat eez ze name I am being zese days," she had replied.

When he asked her father's last name, she gave a sigh and said he had so many. "Ozerwise ze police, they would have caught heem easily."

"Oh, great. Your mother, then," Keith had asked, "what did she call herself?"

Nana Coupeau. But Honey had explained that her mother had borrowed it from a character in a French novel. Keith then got from her the admission that she had been living in this country for five years. She said she was proud to be an American citizen. He asked to see her identification.

"Oh, nonono. I nev-air. I nev-air."

"Why? Why do you never carry identification?"

"Why? Why zen people, they would know my real name, no? Oh, nonono."

At that moment a piercing ring cut through the inner office, visibly startling the District Attorney. Shaking her head as though to reprimand an unruly child, she reached into her deep leather bag to produce a large, old-fashioned alarm clock, now ringing more violently than ever. A slight touch of her finger rescued them from its mechanical fury.

"I cannot afford ze, how do you say? ze arm watch. Zo I take zees from my bedroom each day, huh?"

"Miss Bea—we'll use that name for the time being—Miss Bea, do you realize—are you aware—that what you were doing out there today in the Willis pasture was illegal and indecent?"

"Endesont? What mean endesont?"

"Indecent. Immoral. Not right. Incorrect."

"Incorrect? Incorrect? Why ees not correct?"

"Taking off your clothes. Removing your clothes so that you have nothing on so that they could photograph you—take your picture—with nothing on. Do you understand me?"

Honey collapsed with laughter. "These eez immoral? These eez endesont? Oh, Monsieur, I am so-ree. But et ez so funny. Ze clothes, et is ze clothes zat eez endesont. People, when zay are like babies, wizout ze clothes, zen, only zen, are zay mo-ral."

At this point, the D.A. stressed the seriousness of the matter, spelling out the consequences if she failed to cooperate.

"My name in ze pay-pare?" Lifting both hands and clapping them three times. "Oh, zat would be so *wonderful*. Eet would help me so much in ze work I do. Would you please? Would you? Yes, put me in ze pay-pare."

"What did he say then?" Nat asked.

"Nothing. He just said I could go back to my seat, he really did. So I took my alarm clock and left. I like him though. He's cute."

"He threatened to publicize this arrest, did he?"

"Uh-huh. Wouldn't that be wonderful? A starlet is always trying to get her name in the papers. Any old way at all. It's degrading as all heck, but that's life. Hey, you look serious. Papa-bear serious. Don't you want your name in the papers?"

"I think I might just be persuaded to pass up that honor."

"What do you do for a living, anyway? You never said."

"Let's just say I'm a businessman."

She crossed her legs and eyed him with interest. "You sure don't give nothin' away for free, do ya? I appreciate that. I kinda make everybody my analyst. Cheaper that way. You married?"

"For some years now, yes."

"Children? I love children. I always wanted a dozen myself."

"One child. A son, so to speak. He's a young painter. Name's Ethan."

"You don't sound too proud of him. I appreciate that. Parents are always so darn proud of their children no matter what they're like. Gets me sick sometimes. Is he young?"

"Well, you might say that he ..."

"Is he like you?"

"Well, as a matter of fact he's ..."

"You know, I think I'd like your son, I really do. I get that impression. He sounds disreputable. I don't know why. Is he? I go for people like that, especially men. They're so much like little boys. People who have bad reputations, who are kind of muddied up, if you know what I mean, there is always a part of them that's all clean and white. A part inside them, really. And they're better actors, don't you think? People who act bad are better actors than people who act good."

"Are you disreputable?" he asked, finding her just nutty enough to hold his interest. "What about you?"

"Who, me?" She touched him through the sleeve of his corduroy jacket. "Tell you a secret. Val once said to me. 'Honey,' he said, 'I can't even get you out of bed long enough to change the sheets.'"

Both players were in a state of anxiety. Each had made a fatal mistake after hours of work and was now worrying whether the other would find it and destroy him. It wasn't often that two men, facing each other in silent combat over the chessboard, could both be mated on the move. Neither saw the opportunity that existed for him, but only the threat against him. Irving Rubin, whose turn it was to move, had so far overlooked both the forced win that was his to execute, ending the game there and then, as well as the obvious maneuver that would protect his own king. Max Cohn saw the mate-in-one that threatened him, and he was sweating out the minutes hoping his opponent wouldn't spot it in his ponderings. What he couldn't understand was why his friend looked so worried.

❧   ❧   ❧

Taking his eyes from the two leaning, upright, wooden crutches that rose together above the benches beside the bent head of one of the chess players, Joe Jones turned back to the boy seated beside him and resumed: "Yeh, and one of the greatest of all was old Roy Campanella. What a catcher he was. In a wheelchair now. Great loss. Injuries can change the whole history of a team. It can happen to the best of them. Pete Reiser. Dizzy Dean. Monty Irvin. The whole history of a team. Terrible."

"Speaking of a loss," said Eddie May as he combed his hair, "how about our film. Think we'll get it back?"

"Sure. None of this is serious. Don't worry. They give you a scare and charge you five clams, and then everyone gets sent to the showers."

"They go to all this trouble for five bucks?"

"Five times twenty, don't forget. That's a hundred, right? And they'll probably get more from Mr. Scarecrow over there plus the telephone numbers of the broads. It's worth it, don't worry."

"Guess you're right," said Eddie, intrigued at the other's flippant attitude. "The police have to make a buck, too, I suppose. Even if it means arresting innocent people."

"Listen, it's on the innocent people they make their profit."

"I hate to be a killjoy, but isn't that kind of unethical?"

"Hell, it's a great outlet, being unethical." Jonesy brushed his lap with a few idle strokes. "Saves a lot of people from becoming downright criminals."

"A refreshing thought," Eddie said with a grin that his companion failed to catch.

"Yeh, a guy's got to make a buck. That's for sure."

"What with the rising cost of girls and theater tickets."

"You said it."

"I see what you mean. When the standard of living gets high enough, Americans have got to be unethical or go broke."

"Something like that," said a frowning Jonesy who had just noticed the frayed edge of his jacket sleeve.

"And you don't seem a bit p.o.'ed at the police taking you in like this to make ends meet. I admire that. Shows a real understanding of our economic system which allows the law to be unethical in a harmless way rather than have it become out-and-out criminal."

Jonesy stared at the young man beside him for a full two seconds before replying. "Right. Yeh. Say, how old are you anyway?"

"Eighteen."

"Well, I'm sure glad somebody of your generation understands. I guess the youth of this country aren't lost after all."

"Well, I took Earth Science in high school."

"Oh, uh-huh." Jonesy nodded with a clouded look.

"It has certainly been refreshing talking with you," the boy said. Then he added: "But dating the models. That does seem a little far out."

"It's in the bag. Don't worry. Men in uniform always score."

"Well, here's a young lady I don't think they did too well with," he declared, as Tanya came marching out of the inner office aflame with silent rage.

"Who knows?" Jonesy said, goring Eddie with an elbow in the ribs. "Maybe they scored already."

"Will wonders never cease?"

"They don't miss, I tell ya."

"God, what wisdom."

"Hey, Shoeless Joe. I forgot about him."

"I don't get ya?"

"Shoeless Joe Jackson. What a loss he was."

"But he wasn't injured playing ball."

"He didn't bust his leg, no. He only busted the law."

"Was he unethical, do you suppose? Or just crooked?"

Now, for the first time, Jonesy looked at the other with an alien frown. "Don't you get it? Only crooks break the law. The unethical are innocent."

"Of course. How silly of me. Well, here comes one of the non-crooks all set to make ends meet."

District Attorney Keith appeared from his office and was about to address the gathering. Eddie elbowed his neighbor with mock excitement. "Let's see how he preserves his nation's economic heritage by making a fast unethical buck on these nice people. You know something? This has given me a whole new view of the political scene. I can hardly wait to hear what he has to say. This is even better than Earth Science."

Standing, hands clasped, Keith smiled out at them with all the dehumanized graciousness of a maître d' or like a physician who knows all about your chances of survival but who is charmingly determined to keep this information from you. Keith spoke of his concern for the prisoners, expressing his confidence that Sheriff Woodrow had treated them with courtesy and hoping there had been no unnecessary inconvenience. The room hummed with silence. He tapped the eraser end of a yellow pencil on the low fence in front of him, changing slightly the configuration of his facial muscles as though better to present the diligence and benevolence of a District Attorney. Sliding his fingers down the length of his tie, fitting it more evenly into his jacket, he spoke of his decision concerning the charge he must present against them.

"The intention at first—in the beginning—was to book you on a misdemeanor. That would have meant," he explained with a wave of his hand to indicate all the unspoken intricacies involved, "fingerprinting and so forth. An FBI matter." IIe paused to glance at the pencil for a significant moment. "But I, we, have decided to limit the charge at this time to a simple one of disorderly conduct." He conjured up and quickly dismissed a smile. "As things stand now, as they stand at this time," he looked out over their heads and then into their midst, "that will be the only charge. A judge has been sent for." A look at Woody who nods, yes. "And I trust, I am told, he will soon be on his way." With his knees against the fence, he tilted forward and back, studying the floor. "As for those in authority—the, er, two men, the principals, as it were—involved in the field trip, as for these two, separate and individual charges will be worked out and brought against them."

His eyes were on Val who was slumped in his seat, legs stretched into the aisle, plunged in thought as though he hadn't heard a word. Esra glanced over at him from several benches away, caught the eye of Tanya instead, who looked down at Val and up at Esra again, and shrugged.

"I understand that some of you have expressed a desire to phone your lawyers," said Keith, tapping his lips with the pencil. "That is perfectly within your rights by state law and you are welcome to use the pay phone in the hall. To save you some time, though, I should explain further that with a disorderly conduct charge—if you plead guilty and pay the fine, whatever it is—you will be released and allowed to go home. A plea of not guilty—should that be your plea—you will have to return in thirty days with a lawyer and argue your case." Touching the ends of his mouth with two fingers. "I believe that is all for the time being. Once again now I'll leave you all in the capable hands of Sheriff Woodrow. Thank you."

The concluding words were delivered almost as though he were trying for applause, but the only sound, muffled pleasantly by distance and closed doors, was the vague, halfhearted warning of a barking dog. Keith moved swiftly, dropped the pencil, stooped, snatched it up and went into his office. Several of the guards visibly relaxed, now that he was gone, while Sheriff Woodrow tampered with a toothache as he stood by himself in the back of the hall. When he looked up, he found Ben Reno standing in front of him. They spoke together, and the Sheriff looked startled at something Reno said. The exchange ended with Reno giving a nod and going off to the men's room. Woody stood waiting for a moment and then strolled down the aisle, through the gate and into the office.

Keith didn't bother to look up as he continued to search for something in the top drawer of his desk. "Don't tell me you finally located our Justice of the Peace. Don't tell me Seth called on his own accord and" (looking up at last) "that he's sober, actually sober."

"No such luck."

"I didn't think so. Say I had some mints around here. You take them?"

"Gone, huh? You see, turn your back for a minute and what have you got? Corruption."

"Uh-huh," Keith mumbled, opening another drawer. "Oh, and you can send Reno on home. And try calling Seth again. We've got to have someone presiding over this court."

"Reno's what I came in here to tell you about." Woody tested his sore tooth with the tip of his thumb while Keith shut the drawer of his desk and stood up. "Seems he's gone and made a date with one of the gals. Got it all fixed up, he has. Gonna meet her down in Philly next week. If he takes off now she's gonna know he's a cop. So he's sitting it out, pretty as you please, pretending he belongs with them."

"I see he's been working on everything but his job," Keith said disgustedly while closing his tie and collar.

"Well, he never was much for takin' photo pictures. But he likes travelin'. Wouldn't surprise me none if, after one weekend, Philly becomes his favorite town."

"He doesn't keep much of his life a secret, does he?"

"He's right proud of himself about this one. Quite a coup, I'd say."

The Sheriff made for the door where he was reminded to call Seth Alden again.

"Will do."

Woody's fingers were on the doorknob while Keith stood by the window and looked out on the back of the grocery store with its empty cardboard cartons, its abandoned bits of sickly lettuce, and a muddy mongrel prowling about. "It's warm in here, isn't it? I don't think shutting this keeps out the heat." And he rolled up the window and caught the fragrance of a warm, late, country afternoon. There was a slack silence, and Woodrow turned the doorknob to leave.

"Which one was it?" Keith asked with a touch of uncertainty. Then he moved away from the window.

"Was what?"

"Philadelphia."

Woody raised an eyebrow, and Keith added:

"That stupid French one?"

"No, the other. The one who got so pissed off when you pulled that communist shit."

Keith had raised another paper cup to his lips and stopped. "You're joking. I don't believe it. You're asking me to believe that he and that…" He trailed off as though he had been personally offended.

"Well, if he's lying, he's sitting out there for nothing when he could be going the hell home right now, and I don't remember him ever not going home when he could. Go see for yourself. He's become one of them. I even think he's going to pay the fine, too. Funny thing is that his is the only evil-looking face out there."

"The actress? Are you sure she's the one. He and what'shername?"

The Sheriff tried to recall. "Tanya Landow or Land Ho or like that."

"He's got it set up with *her*?"

"Hard to believe, ain't it? A choice bit of acreage there, eh?"

Keith stood fixed with disbelief, and Woody recognized in him that thorough souring some men experience when they discover that another is succeeding with ease where success had seemed impossible.

"You know, I don't think that guy's doing his job."

"Oh, go on. Why do you say that?" said Woody, lifting a knee and fixing his cuff.

"Well, for one, he has too much free time."

"You mean this business with the girl?"

"Well, for one."

"But what didn't he do? He did everything else. He phoned us from New York when they were kinda all set to leave. And by eavesdroppin' he was able to slip me that info about her real name, remember? And he saw what'shisname stick the money in his jacket pocket, and he told us how much money it was as well. I'd say Reno has gone and done his job."

"If that's what you think, then I just don't admire your judgment. A good job, indeed. He's done a good job of sitting on his ass and staring at the women. That's about the sum of it."

"Hold up there now, you're doing it again. Whenever you're sore you attack everyone in sight. Now just hold up."

"Oh, I do, do I? Well, I never will understand how you can defend an incompetent like that. It means only one thing. That you are backward and provincial, that you have been corrupted by small-town thinking."

A muscle twitched in Woody's jaw. "And you have all the purity of a big city official scroungin' for personal gain."

"You think you're attacking me?" Keith exclaimed, greatly agitated. "You think you're attacking me, don't you?"

"I had my suspicions. Sure, I'm attacking you all right, and the personal gain I'm talking about is..."

"Is today's arrest."

"Is today's arrest."

"You think it's unethical."

"I think it's unethical, shonuff."

"Then why, may I ask, did you go along with it after five years of doing exactly nothing?"

"Not for the reason you did, I'll tell you that. I believe it's important that these here trips be stopped."

"All right, and why?"

"'Cause of what they represent. Hold up, now, let me finish. I'm against the selling of dirty pictures 'cause of the effect they have on the young. These here outings produce such pictures, and this arrest will discourage other outings like it. And kids have been watchin' from the hills Kids from my own town. My own kids, maybe. Christ, that's reason enough. And women exposin' theirselves is indecent. I don't care what you say."

"My God, you *are* provincial. The antisexed, backwooded Woody, a twentieth-century mid-Victorian. I knew you were Catholic, but I gave you credit for being a bad one."

"What you can't stand about me is I'm ethical or moral or whatever you want to call it. And I'm not as smart as you, with your college degree and all your legal twists and turns, but I sure as hell know an opportunist when I see one. You will do pretty near anything to win, and I love to watch you at work. Boy, do I just love to watch you at work. So halting and folksy and sentimental. But selling fertilizer somethin' fierce. Part grass-roots sincere and part TV M.C. But in here with me you're as direct, as sophisticated, as ruthless as ..."

"As an opportunist out for personal gain," said Keith, with a slight grin. "Well, as an opportunist out for personal gain, let me enlighten you on a few minor points." He removed his jacket and draped it over the back of the swivel chair. "Sure I'm after power. Name me an important man in government without it. You could call Lincoln and FDR opportunists. One is either an opportunist or one flunks out. That's our system. That's political America. Wake up. Either change it or live by it. But wake up."

Keith placed a foot on the seat of the chair and leaned on his knee. As he spoke, the light continued to diminish from the room, and as Woody listened all color and pleasure in the world seemed to fall from the air. Keith talked with fire and sincerity. The halting, tie-touching mannerisms were gone. The voice was flooded with feeling, and for a time Woody heard not the words but the tone, so startled was he by the change.

"My point is that there are many moral acts that cannot be performed within the law. It is the failure of our political system that we're unable to meet some of the present-day world problems. Yours is the eternal plea for ethics and morality. To me you sound like a voice calling out plaintively from a dead century. The American Revolution was illegal. The winning of the West was illegal. Civil Disobedience is illegal, even when it's hydrogen insanity that the lawbreakers are trying to outlaw. In fact, all revolutions and acts of civil disruption are illegal and always have been. The communist threat to overthrow this government from within is illegal. And the Un-American Activities Committee which sees as its duty to suppress this threat is also, in my opinion, illegal. So what the hell is the law? You raise your eyebrow again. Well, look at yourself. Because of your beliefs, you were willing to join with me in an illegal arrest. I planned it and you pulled it off, and as I remember you had no complaints. Your actions are up-to-date, but your ethics are out of style. Morals make the man, and you are lovable and courageous but obsolete."

"And you, I take it, are the modern man."

"Yes, the modern man. And drifting, as he is so often accused of, without a moral base, without deep beliefs. Yes, I am that man and rightly so. There are many like me in government. Our country is being led more and more by men such as we. Technicians to meet the complexity of problems that transcend the capacities of any one political system or moral concept. I pride myself on being one of them and hope to be one of the best of them. Flexibility, you see, is the only approach to modern times."

"You're a technician, then. A political technician."

"That's right," said Keith, taking a drink from the water cooler.

"Well, since this here arrest is technically illegal, what will be your technique if they plead innocent and all come back in thirty days with a whole lot of lawyers?"

Keith removed the paper cup from his lips just long enough to say, "They won't, don't worry," then sipped water again.

"Just supposin' they do. Say they threaten to bring it to a higher court once they lose. Just supposin'."

"Easy."

"Yeh, I'm listenin'."

"I back down, that's all. Simple, isn't it? I can't afford to get caught off base with this thing. I need a few arrests in the debit column. Election time is coming near and I want that seat in Congress. I need to be there, and the people of Catskill County need me there. I can't afford a setback now. So if it really looks like they intend to fight, I simply tell Seth to find them innocent and send them home. But they won't fight, don't worry. People don't. The one thing they haven't learned to do after all these centuries is take action. It's pathetic."

"There's lotsa things lotsa people haven't learned," the Sheriff concluded, but the D.A. had spilt some water on his lapel and was busy wiping it off.

They went over to Esra, and the blotched, bent crane of a man stood up out of a misplaced sense of politeness and was made to sit down again.

"Could anyone on the road see us in the pasture?" Val asked, crouching in the aisle beside the farmer.

"Not unless they stood on the roof of an auto-*mo*-bile with some-one else inside drivin' it."

"Don't he speak interestin'?" said Honey, who had wandered over as well. "So very—I don't know—so different. Like a foreigner or somethin'."

"You speak kind of way out yourself," said Tanya, with cheerful animosity. She sat facing Esra on the arm of the bench just ahead of him.

"This D.A.," Val continued. "What's he like? Who is he?"

"He's kinda new hereabouts. He comes down and does his attor-neying and then kinda scoots off again. He's on the move a lot, you might say. Runnin' for an election. Though he don't live no further than about thirty miles from this here courthouse. Some say he's right brilliant. Guess he is at that, since I don't think he's ever been arrested. Some say he's on his way up in the *Re*-publican Party. But he's new hereabouts, like I told ya."

"I think he looks like Dana Andrews," Honey put in.

Esra was delighted, "Why, I thank ya kindly."

"No, not you, silly."

Val touched his sleeve. "That's all you know about him? The D.A.?"

"Yep, that's about it. 'Cept they say his marriage ain't none too good. Lotsa rumors there. 'Cept you can't rightly trust rumors. They just as likely to be true as not."

"And the Sheriff?" Tanya asked. "What about him?"

"Now *he* looks like Spencer Tracy," said Honey. "Don't you think?"

"What about him?" Val insisted.

"Old Woody? Old Woody's O.K. Been around these parts for years. My brother was kinda good buddies with him."

"Was?"

"Well they still are, I suppose. 'Cept he don't get much chance to socialize no more."

"Who don't, doesn't?" asked Tanya.

"My brother. But he and Woody were right good friends. Used to fish together and all."

"And your brother, where is he now?" Tanya wanted to know.

"Not far from here actually."

"What's he doing?"

"Five years."

"Oh, my, in prison? I'm sorry."

"That's O.K. He's lucky, actually. Attempted murder ain't no mis-dimena. But he gets out soon, though. Yep. Couple of weeks, I'm told."

Honey, eagerly: "Who'd he try to kill?"

"Who'd he try to kill?" Esra gave a small, stillborn laugh. "Well, uh, me actually."

Tanya: "Oh, swell."

"And about Woody…?" Val began, but Honey cut him off.

"Why'd he try to kill you? My gosh, why?"

Tanya reprimanded her. "Why don't you ask him some personal questions? Like it's a private matter. Jesus."

"Ain't a private matter no more," Esra smiled, wringing his ear. "Got in the papers and everything. TWIN TRIES TO KILL TWIN. Brothers Battle over Naked Beauties. That's what the papers said. For a while I was quite a see-lebrity in these here parts."

"Naked Beauties?" asked Honey, deliciously.

Tanya slapped herself on the thigh. "My God, nothing's sacred with this girl." Then she looked at Esra and, with the others, waited for the answer.

"Ah, it's not what you think. It was just Pops holding his first field trip on the farm. Jonas, that's my brother, Jonas got word of it. He was out of town at the time fishin' with the Sheriff, as luck would have it, and he got right angry at me."

"So angry they sent him to prison," Honey concluded.

Tanya frowned: "What happens when he gets out?"

"I'm hopin' prison life will sort of temper him some."

"If they knew about these field trips all these years," asked Val, "how come they didn't do something about them before this?"

"That's right," said Tanya, "how come?"

"'Cause my farm is private property. That's the law."

"But that didn't stop them today, for crysake."

The farmer thought about this. "Sure didn't, did it? Bet the new D.A. had something to do with that."

"Figures," said Tanya.

Val was sitting in the aisle, arms circling his legs. "About Woody, do you like him?"

"A really good joe. One of the best."

"If he's such a good guy," said Val, angrily, "why the hell did he arrest us for something that didn't happen?"

"Oh, old Woody's all right. Guess he's doing his job. Guess that there's the trouble with havin' some jobs. Anyway, he's kinda on the moral side, you might say, if you know what I mean? He's always been for long skirts and no lipstick and one-piece bathin' suits at Jupiter Lake. You know how it is with his sort, with those types."

"What types is that?" Tanya asked, giving the sentence an immediate second thought. "Are that? *Is* that. *Are* that."

"You know. He's kinda ... Well, he's sort of ... Well, he's Catholic is what he is. Hell, nobody's perfect. But he's O.K. They broke the mold when they made him."

"Like over his head they should have broke it," Tanya added.

"Hey," said Val, "a joke. That's one in a row."

"Oh, shut up."

Honey, interrupting her engrossed and vacuous stare: "Excuse me. I've got to make a sissy."

"You know," said Tanya, watching her leave, "there are great gaps in that girl's ignorance."

"No sitting in the aisle."

Val looked up and saw one of the guards towering above him. He reached out and untied his shoe. The guard jumped back and signaled another guard.

"I said, get up," he demanded with his fierce, adolescent voice.

"Val, please." Tanya looked worried.

Brushing back his loose hair, Val got up to face his assailant, but Tanya immediately led him away. The guard, re-enforced by one of his uniformed doubles, placed a firm official hand on Val's shoulder and executed a harmless, needless, thoughtless push. It was simply a young deputy indulging his assertiveness, yet it seemed to demonstrate in a single act what the powerful forces of the law had been doing to them all afternoon and to Val all his life. Touched as though by an atrocity, Val slapped away the offending arm in a ferocious pirouette. Their two wrists crossed like swords, and both men paused awhile in pain. The guard stepped back onto the shoes of his double, and both the young deputies stood their cautious ground saying nothing.

Aware that all eyes were on him, Val moved off, carrying his rage. He slumped into an empty seat, his face tight and flushed. The small humiliation had brought back all the details of the larger one—that outrage in the inner office—and all his flippancies were crushed and useless.

"Oh, Valitchka," and she held his hand.

"Right now I could kill."

"It's all right, baby. He just touched you. He's a bad bad man."

"Not him," Val stormed, indicating the guard kneeling to tie his shoe, "*Him*," and he nodded at the door to the office.

Tanya swung around and faced him formally. "Do you believe me now? We must do something. My lungs feel stuffed. I want to fight them. Oh, Val, I want to fight them."

"You mean you want *me* to fight them."

"The two of us, why can't the two of us do it?"

"It's got to be the whole damn bunch of us doing it or it's no good." He ran his hand like a crab through his blond hair. "But how *can* we, for crysake. He gave me a big talk about cooperation."

"Me too."

"Made threats about publicity."

"Same here."

"Me, I've got nothing to lose. He took all the money anyway."

"Oh, God." She touched her face. "The profits? All of it?"

"If you ask me, the whole business is shot. Never should have gotten talked into it in the first place. I owe left and right. I'm behind in the rent. I'm behind with Pops. That bastard, he got out just in time. So now I have just what I needed, a nice little business to keep me out of trouble and in jail for the rest of my life."

Tanya dropped her head on his shoulder, the fragrance of her hair rising into his lungs. "Oh, Val."

"So how can I make a fuss? He could muddy up a lot of names if he wants to. The women particularly. You, for crysake, always so fussy with your goddamn reputation. How do *you* feel about getting in the papers?"

She lifted her head and stared at him with bedroom eyes. What began as a smile became a bitter-sweet pouting of her pretty mouth.

"Ever since we met," she said, "like almost the whole time we knew each other I kept bugging you to take things seriously, to be a mench. And so now what should I do, stop you?"

"Answer my question. What about it? You in the papers, page four, *Daily News*?"

There was a pause as she fumbled through her pocketbook. "I don't care. Who knows, it might do me good?" Looking up: "I don't care. I really don't."

"You know, I never can tell when you're lying."

"Neither can I, sometimes."

He became absorbed by the dark of her eyes and by her thinly sheathed form whose swelling secrets mocked his efforts to forget. He heard a distant lilt of an old love which now threatened to return and sing to him again. Roguishly he reached out and pressed with the tip of his finger the thrust of her hidden nipple. She pulled away, looked about and turned back aping scandal.

"Sir," said her haughty voice, "unfinger me, sir. You are here to do brave deeds like in the hardbound books. Not to hanky-pank about like in a paperback."

Val sat up in his seat. "So you're ready for a fight, are you?" To this, she nodded. "Well, first I'd like to check to see if it's O.K. with one other person."

"I trust you mean Miss Bea with the big bazzums?" she said, knowing full well he did. "She won't say no. She never once said no in her whole life."

"Say you really are on her back, aren't you, you bitch?"

With tinseled innocence: "Like maybe she's bad at a lot of things, but she sure is good at being stupid."

"So she's stupid. I like that in a woman."

"Balls."

"No, that in a woman I don't care for so much."

"Oh, how could you have *lived* with her?"

"It wasn't easy."

"You bastard. You never wanted to live with me?"

"Well, I'm allergic to cats."

"*Ha.*"

Suddenly Tanya saw what was happening.

"No," she cried, "no flippancies. Let's not throw it all away. Come on, now. We've got a job to do, no?"

"What do you mean *we've?*"

"Oh, please, Val. Please, no jokes."

The air hummed with softly tangled voices as the room full of captives awaited their punishment without anger or guilt. No one seemed to care.

"All right, let's go," Val said, without conviction.

He walked off a few steps but then sat down again, Tanya right beside him. He dug into a cuticle with his thumbnail. She studied his almost poker face and the taut line of his lip. Did she believe him capable of a rational act of protest? The answer was obvious.

Her stomach tightened when she realized that for a moment she, too, had given up.

"If we plead innocent," said Val, studying his nails, "if we get a lawyer and come back and fight it, it'll cost us more, even if we win, than if we plead…"

"When did you ever give three damns about money?"

"When one's broke and in debt…"

"Like when weren't you broke and in debt? Huh?" Then she added: "Are you giving up?"

He paused to rub his face. His voice, slow with fatigue.

"The whole thing seems like such an effort."

"I knew this would happen. Oh, the hell with it." She turned away. She turned back again. "You'd think for once in your life you'd want to act like a man. What a laugh." She swung her body away from him, crossed her legs and rammed her hand into her pocketbook before remembering that her cigarettes had long since been used up. She uttered a single syllable of fury and frustration. How she hated them, how she really hated them, down to the last living man.

Honey appeared from the bathroom. A bored deputy, slapping at a light cord, studied her careless, self-satisfied flounce and gave her a quick wink. She lifted her nose and marched past. Looking for Val and finding him slumped in thought with Tanya beside him, she shrugged and advanced toward the seat Nat DeVore occupied.

By now, one of the dusty rectangles of sunlight, filled with the abstract movement of ascending cigarette smoke, had extended its last brilliance fully across the room to where it touched Val's shoulder. A dog barked in the street. Just outside a window, a thin tree moved with the soundless wind. At that moment the Sheriff, emerging from the D.A.'s office, saw in the center of the auditorium the thin figure of Val De Franco rising decisively to his feet.

"Gentlemen, I'd like your attention for a moment, please. Gentlemen, what's happening to us today is a fucking shame. First I want to talk to you about this arrest, and then there's something

I'm going to ask you to do. What I'm going to ask comes very hard to most people. I'm asking you to fight for your goddamn rights."

The gist of his statement was this: Since the women were not visible from the road, and since no crime had been committed, they should plead not guilty, hire a lawyer and return to defend and clear themselves. Such action, he explained, would be time-consuming and it would certainly cost money. But reputations were at stake, and a legal malignancy of this sort should not be allowed to go unchecked.

The response was mostly favorable. Eddie May agreed at once. Others nodded. Esra clasped both hands in victory above his head, and one of the chess players raised a crutch in a gesture of encouragement. Joe Jones, however, didn't know if he could get free of his job to return for trial, and Reno broke in to say that they should, as he put it, "pay the man the two dollars." As for Honey, she applauded each speaker in loyal bipartisan support.

Standing before them, Val suggested that if a World Series game were being held in Salemville, Jonesy would find a way to get there quickly enough. To plead guilty and be done with it, he told Reno, might be the easiest way out. But wasn't the worst kind of moral paralysis that which allowed the innocent to plead guilty because it was less expensive to pay a fine then fight for one's rights?

Because of Val's cool eloquence, and as Tanya watched with amazement, opposition to the plan slowly lost strength. There was no real conviction in his performance, simply the enjoyment of doing what he had never done before. Yet for her it was enough, and with side comments and discreet cheers, she aided all she could. The Sheriff smoked calmly and watched without speaking. Victor Ottomeyer kept saying, "Yes, right," whenever Val made a point. Nat DeVore looked on in silence, and Honey kept applauding anything anyone said. She was having such a high old time during the debate and without the slightest concern as to the outcome, that at one point Val asked her why in hell she was cheering both sides. She looked surprised and pointed out that this was the democratic way, was it not? The laughter that followed swept away most of the opposition to Val's request. He was just about to ask for a show of hands of all those who agreed to plead innocent and return for the trial when Nat DeVore at last spoke up. It was the man's long silence as he listened to the many exchanges of opinion that made Val uneasy. He had an urge to shout no, that Nat could not speak, that he had lost his chance and that now it was time to vote. Instead, Val turned and gazed through one of the windows at the last full flush of the vanished sun as it turned the sky into an abstract painting. Its beauty seemed to draw him toward the west and away from this place where he did not belong and these endless kindergarten discussions.

"Young man, you are misleading these people," Nat growled.

In an instant, Val flew the thousand miles from the distant sunset to the speaker's face. A rash of anger spread over his neck, then vanished. He kept still, and the other went on talking, his poised voice commanding attention and respect. In a slow cadence he explained that the penalty could be more severe if they fought and failed to win. As things stood, they faced the loss of only five dollars. It would cost them each fifteen or more to hire an attorney and return for trial. Then, if they lost, the fine might be as high as twenty-five dollars. On top of this, he explained, a trial would attract publicity, and even if some notoriety were already unavoidable surely there would be more of it, the more they protracted the battle.

"Don't let him convince you that this is a moral issue," Nat told them, "because it is not. Any lawyer will advise a client that it is pointless to contest a case that will cost more to fight and win than not fight at all. And on top of that, and in this case definitely, you will lose. Believe me, you *will* lose. That, to me, is a foregone conclusion."

"Are you making this up as you go along?" Val demanded, "or are you speaking with some sort of authority?"

Nat picked a brier from the cuff of one of his trousers.

"Yes," he said at last, "I speak with some sort of authority."

"What the hell does that mean?" Val fired back. "Are you a lawyer, or what?"

The man brushed his lap with two even strokes. Secrecy or revelation? He was torn between them. His entrance into the debate was an impulsive one, for at first he had decided not to take part at all only to find himself frightened and leaping in. Once he had broken his silence, problems engulfed him.

"Yes," he said grimly. "I am an attorney. Yes."

The destructive effect this had on Val's purpose was considerable, and the young man fought it as best he could.

"This doesn't give you the right to judge our case."

"No, but I have had enough experience to know the odds. We can't be absolutely certain that we weren't seen from the road. They will probably produce witnesses to swear to it. At any rate, we could have been seen from that rise separating the pasture from the road. Children could easily and would most naturally scamper onto it or hide watching in the woods. It doesn't matter that this constitutes trespassing, such evidence would be damaging to your case nevertheless. If you were paying for this advice I assure you that you could not get a sounder opinion."

"You are mouthing law," said Val, "not voicing conscience. It isn't just a matter of winning. There *are* other reasons. But I wonder now if you understand what in hell I'm even talking about. Sounds like you want a sure thing or no contest. If you're so damned concerned about our costs, how about volunteering to be our lawyer? Then all it would take is transportation. What do you say?"

"Evidently, time is more valuable to me than money is to you. Don't you understand? It's pointless to do battle when you have clearly lost. You don't seem to understand that."

"Have you never willingly fought a lost cause?"

"Certainly," the lawyer replied, with an imperious lift to his voice. "But only when there was something, somewhere to be gained. Not otherwise."

"You haven't answered our question."

"Oh, it seems to me I have."

"About being our lawyer."

"You'll not be happy, I see, until I become as irrational as you."

"Answer the goddamn question."

"If you had any wit you'd realize the answer has already been given."

"Will you represent us next month, yes or no?"

"No."

"Will you represent us now, right now?"

"Again, no."

"You're a coward," Val shouted, "a disgrace to whatever the hell you are or were."

Sitting just three rows from where his antagonist stood, Nat stiffened and leaned forward in his seat.

"You always knew it, didn't you?" Val continued in a lowered voice that was now even more venomous. "Didn't you always know it? I'll bet you always knew it. A coward. A pompous legal coward."

"You worthless tramp. You who believe in nothing want me to believe in you and your folly. You flippant fool. And you always knew *that*, didn't you?"

"Goddamn son of a bitch," Val screamed back.

Tanya called to him in alarm.

"You shit," Val yelled, his face trembling, his lips pursed. The Sheriff rushed forward to stifle the noise. Several guards moved in as well, and Tanya stood up, desperately seeking Val's attention. One of the deputies placed a hand on the prisoner's shoulder and, as the others looked on, paralyzed with amazement, Val became a wild beast. He shoved furiously, and the uniformed guard did a wildly gesturing backward flip and hard flop over the low fence. Two other guards made a grab. Val broke free and with one cuff link lost and his flapping shirt cuff doubling out of jacket sleeve, he whirled and went for the nearest throat. Amid the loud turbulence of awkward grappling, Honey Bea rose with one long blind hysterical scream, flailing her light fists against the hated uniforms and shouting, "*They took my baby!*" while in stunned silence, Giles Keith stood in the doorway of the office holding a partly peeled orange.

THE screen door slapped shut. With both palms, Esra clamped his chest, his rump, his side pockets. No matches. He moved cautiously through the darkness, closing his useless eyes as though this gave him a kind of mystic protection. A chair jostled him. The broom toppled with spite. Some bags of garbage spilled in hate. A couple of bottles rattled and rolled. In the kitchen, he reached above his head, palmed the darkness for a while, then gripped and accidentally amputated the light cord from the ceiling plug. He recalled now what he had come into the house knowing: the electricity had been turned off for days. Carefully he extended his fingers to where he hoped the flashlight was standing on the tabletop. He fumbled with an empty can of beer, spilled an old bottle of sarsaparilla, identified wrappings from TV dinners, withdrew his hand from a bowl of borscht and cursed the flashlight wherever it was. In the darkness he wandered about the house with no purpose in mind and found himself upstairs listening to the house stillness and the farm stillness and wondering why he was upstairs at all. He stood toying with the doily on the dresser, then closed his eyes in protection as he stepped gingerly along the hall. He sat on the top of the stairs for a time, or rather on top of a hill of old laundry, and then descended and moved out through the kitchen door into the cool pale night. He stood slouched and dejected listening to the faint, timorous gossip-sounds of a woods steeped in living things. The stars had splurged their patterns. Far off stood a mountain watchtower and its single boxed-in room of light with its solitary unknown sentinel.

Esra felt like crying. He was so completely alone that he longed for either friend or foe. He would even have relived the entire day, as bad as it was, for at least it had been filled with people. Humming a few bars of "Red River Valley," the farmer shuffled along where the ground sloped downward until out of the darkness the huge colorless barn accumulated before him. A four-legged something made a spurt through the grass and was gone. As Esra entered the barn, all its good smells of manure and hay rose up to meet him. Living things moved in their stalls, massive and patient. "Hi, there," said Esra, reaching over a gate and patting a hard, hairy shank.

There was a brief blithering of nostrils. Esra entered the gate and closed it again, edging his way between horse and stall to where he could throw his friendly arm around the lean, firm neck. He stood there, doing nothing for a while, simply caressing the smooth animal who swayed a bit in recognition.

"He made a mistake," Esra said aloud to the animal. "He gave them brains to learn all there is to learn 'ceptin' how to leave each other alone. So brains ain't enough, I guess, 'cause nobody cares anyway 'cept if you're havin' fun and then they care enough to stop ya.

"Hit ain't that men is bad," he said, patting the great neck and trying to lift himself out of self-pity. "Hit would be easy if there was only good men and bad. That would be a long sight easier. Trouble is all men is good and lookit." He shook his head. "Just will ya lookit the mess."

A FAT, frightened rabbit was transfixed by a pair of moving headlights (inflaming briefly her small, saffron eyes) that splashed their way down Tuckabunkwac Road as three autos (the fourth didn't start at all and had to be left behind) began the long trip back to the city with some passengers now forced to sit on the laps of others. The procession wound its way through rustic darkness, stopping now and again at obscure road signs until they moved onto the quiet highway and, the worst seemingly over, sped off in the wrong direction.

With Val at the wheel of the Mercury, it lurched away from the Buick and was soon out of sight. He leaned forward, twisting the radio dial and muttering angrily when he remembered it was broken. Seated beside him, Tanya stole two cigarettes from Leo's pocket (he was asleep next to her) lit both and placed one between Val's lips. She brushed back his hair with two careful strokes and then dropped her arm casually around him. Directly behind the driver, who now snapped off the radio in disgust, sat a disinterested Joe Jones with a preoccupied Victor Ottomeyer, removing a pebble from his shoes, crouched beside him. On the right was Nat DeVore with Honey Bea squirming in his lap. No one spoke.

Her screams had startled Val back into a state of calm. Having stumbled to the floor, he had looked up from the center of all the havoc to see the blonde kicking and struggling in the arms of the guards and shouting about her baby. It took a long while to calm her, so convulsively did she weep, though she finally whimpered off into slumber, curled up on the bench, for three whole hours. Having extricated himself lately from Honey's love, he longed to turn about and be good to her again, to shelter and soothe that ever-changing personality which he would never understand. But she seemed not to want or need his help, not even after her outburst in the courtroom which had been, after all, an attempt to help him. In one way or another it seemed she had been helping him from the first day they met. Now, as though nothing had happened she chose, of all things, to sit on that bastard's lap despite all of Val's hatred for the man. No, he would never understand.

What Nat couldn't fathom was why Val had not been punished for his assault on the guards. The District Attorney had seemed almost apologetic over the incident; and four hours later, when they finally had found and brought in a Justice of the Peace to preside over the Court, not a word of the outburst was mentioned. Odd, indeed.

Just as odd, perhaps, though less disturbing was Miss Bea's habit of trailing after him. In court, and during the bus ride back to the farm, he could hardly have told her, "Please don't sit next to me." When one of the autos failed to start, and it was necessary to double up, she pleaded to sit on his lap, claiming there was nobody else she trusted, and again he could think of no gracious way to decline. He was also pleased that she asked and was really not disgruntled by it. If a man could not resist temptation, he thought gaily, where was his dignity? She squirmed again, not yet quite comfortable. Then, asking if she were too heavy for him, the blonde beamed her loveliness pointblank into his face. He maintained his dignity as best he could, musing, meanwhile, on those peculiarities of social lunacy that allowed her to sit almost in his arms while all the old restraints of decency remained. One arm, of course, was around her waist; all very proper. And his other hand clung to his lapel with Edwardian propriety.

That scene of her sobbing madly and Tanya rushing to her aid had been to him like some wild reversal of reason. Much later, he asked what had caused it, and in reply Honey created an unintentional rhymed couplet: "I hate cops, I really do. I also hate injustice, too." Her voice was cheerful, yet she unearthed by accident what he had been trying to hide. It was this: in the courtroom today when it was clear to him that their guilt was questionable he had, nevertheless, argued against resistance. The point was not why had he done it? He knew why and could justify himself much too easily by using conservatism's ponderous logic: that logy soul of the law. No, the point was just this: he had argued against resistance, and that took no courage at all.

Shifting his attention to less discomforting thoughts, he concerned himself solely with the passenger in his lap. Why had she cried out about her baby? Had there been perhaps some miscarriage of the law which his influence could set right? Her answer surprised him. Baby was actually "Baby Joe," a prizefighter she had loved dearly and who was now serving ten years for crimes committed by someone else. The more he questioned her the more there was need for further questioning but the less he learned. Yet fixed in his mind was their physical closeness which she accepted quite naturally, her large pretty head just a kiss away, not that he would have taken one, would have wanted one, would even have accepted had she offered one, but which reminded him of those absurd moments in the subway's rude rush when some young coed, squeezed up against him by the pressing mob, would stand and stare dispassionately at the tip of his right coat lapel for three stations, getting mashed closer at each stop. Occasionally, at such times, he would get the urge to say something witty, but of course he never did. What if she got the wrong idea, missed the joke, made a fuss? What then? Perhaps, loud and lordly scandal. Caution was best, and this time he did it himself, tricked his thoughts back into the courtroom, remembering again how he had arranged his life so that it needed no courage at all.

Several voices interrupted the dark, soft, sleepy mood of the moving car. Tanya wanted to stop for cigarettes and Harry to make a phone call. Ottomeyer asked for the third time whether Val was sure this was the right road. He seemed in an obvious hurry to get home. Jonesy was the most content of all for he had learned from one of the guards that the Yankees had won both games of their doubleheader.

When they stopped at a diner, most of them scrambled out: Tanya for a smoke, Leo for water, Nat for the john, Harry for the phone and Jonesy for food. When it was learned that they had been going in the wrong direction after all, Ottomeyer rushed about asking if there was a train back to New York. The owner told him there was, but that it wouldn't arrive until five in the morning. Until the others were ready, Ottomeyer remained out in the road by himself clutching his hands and peering in both directions as though hoping for a miracle to come barreling out of the night and whisk him away.

Val stood emblazoned by the headlights of the Mercury deciphering a road map as Honey came by carrying a coke which she immediately offered to share. Smiling blissfully, despite the pain in her unemployed mother's heart, she accepted the drink back from him and with her eyes swimming in his, closed her lush lips over the glass neck. Val, too, had to know. Why had she shouted that thing about her baby? Because it was true, she told him in a pleasant chatty voice after taking a swallow. He didn't understand: "Those guards took away *your* baby?" he asked, "took away little, what's her name, Jacqueline?"

Honey's smile showed Val that she was charmed by his mistake.

"Not *that* baby, silly."

She picked a black hair from his gray suit.

"Whose baby, then?"

"My baby," she said, lovingly.

"I don't get it. Who?"

"*You.*"

Me? was the word his pursed lips tried to say but they had become glued in amazement. He waved his hand at a moth and then pulled her away from the lights, though it was really the subject and not the insects he was trying to avoid.

"You might call it irrational," she said, shaking the drink to hear it fizz, "but when I saw them roughing you up..."

"I also roughed them up, remember?"

"Well, anyway, it was roughhouse time, and I sort of blamed them for what happened between—you know—us."

"Then Jacqueline is O.K.?" he asked, again steering away from such perishable things as love and devotion.

"Oh, yes, she's fine. Absolutely."

"You sure?"

Honey took another swig from the bottle, leaning forward abruptly to keep from spilling it on herself.

"Why did you drop me?" she asked with a fairmindedness that frightened him. There seemed to be no escaping the subject.

The map fell to the road, and they both bent to pick it up. A knee cracked loudly: his. They rose, each holding an edge of the State of New York.

"Well," he began, "you see..." Then the line came to him. "It was just one of those..." He halted, cliff-hanging over the edge of the cliché, hearing in his mind the playback of words and lyrics reminding him that what he had started to say had even been made into a song.

"Drop you?" he continued. "What makes you say that?" He gritted his teeth. What a devious bastard I am, he thought.

A car sped by angrily pushing its beams of light.

"Damn it," he said, finding himself in the mood to expose dishonesty, even his own. "Yes, I've ended it." And he slapped his thigh with the map. Ferreting around in his paralyzed mind, he sought for a way to break her heart painlessly. He could find no way, and still he searched.

"Is it... her?" she asked and then blew over the top of the bottle to make that deep, distant cyclone sound.

"Yes." How simple. "Yes, it's her."

"It's just as well, I suppose. It really is. You see, I'm leaving town anyway."

"Oh?"

"Going to Mexico to make a film. Isn't that wonderful?"

"Really?" he asked skeptically. "What film? When?"

"A Paul Newman movie in Mexico. Soon. I'll drop you a postcard."

"Sounds great."

"It's only a bit part."

"That's O.K. It's a start."

"It really is. I can hardly wait."

"Wonderful."

"Do you love her?"

"Who? Tanya?" He was bogged down again in guilt. Determined to tell the truth this time, he said: "It all depends. Some days, yes. Other days, no."

Now that he had said it, he didn't know if it was the truth at all.

"Oh, I didn't tell you, did I?" She was trying to balance the bottle on her head. "Did I tell you? I'm getting married."

"You're kidding. Who to?"

"To a great painter. Young boy. Village type. But a wonderful artist. He goes his own way. Much like you. He even reminds me of you, he really does."

"What is his name?"

"Ethan. Ethan's his name."

Tanya confronted them at this point with a jealously arched eyebrow, and the bottle, tumbling from Honey's head, though it hit soft earth, shattered.

It was another half hour before they had returned to that point in the road where they had originally gone wrong. All went well for a time until they came to a vaguely marked triple fork, and soon they were lost again, which took time to debate and set right. Ottomeyer, of course, was beside himself with anxiety, and Jonesy began to think he was mad. The two cars following them had long since been swallowed by the night, giving Val the delicious sense of their being the last wandering remnants of a shattered army. With a glimpsed road sign to guide them, Val raced across unseen terrain, the speedometer wagging a warning finger, the headlights plunging steadily into the dark to be bounced back occasionally by a patch of fog. Tanya's thumbnail explored the short hairs on his neck as her legs were repeatedly sculptured by the persistent parade of overhead lights. With Leo laboring in sleep, she leaned over and whispered to Val her great secret of the day.

"No," he said. "You? The *lead?* You aren't?"

"Yes I are."

"*The Idiot?* Dostoevsky?"

"Yes indeedy-do."

"Really? Hey, crazy."

"Like I'm so happy I could plotz."

"How wild. Great."

"All I can think of is like at last, at long last. I kept asking myself, what can go wrong? You know, like what can go wrong? Don't you dare tell me. I don't want to know from pessimism."

"I wasn't going to say a thing. I was *going* to say how happy I am for you. You'll knock 'em dead. You will. You'll be great."

"Oh, Valitchka. From you that means more to me than anything. Oh, you're a pussycat."

"We've got to celebrate. When we get back to town, you and me, we'll celebrate."

"You mean it?"

"Mean it? I insist. Us together. Two celibates celebrating. Or is it masturbates celibating. Well, whatever."

She pulled on his sleeve. He looked at her.

"Mine friend," she said. "You're ha double puzzycat vitha long tail. Vit such a puzzycat vot could go wrong, hi ask you?"

"Shit."

"What it is?"

"Your puzzycat is out of gas."

The car in a long, gentle roll came to a dead stop. For a moment, no one spoke. Three of them were asleep anyway, and Ottomeyer was too stricken to say a word just as Tanya was too flushed with joy to be concerned. Nat informed them that there was a gas station about a mile or so up ahead. How the hell did he know? was Val's question.

"Road sign," was the reply, "a mile back."

More to escape DeVore's annoying omnipotence than anything else, Val climbed out and marched off. A moment later he heard Tanya in double time coming to join him. He was tempted to leave them all stranded and keep walking until he hit New York. He wanted to club Ottomeyer for all his crabbing. His rage at DeVore had returned, and as for the rest of them, in their constant indifference, they were just so much dead wood. Except for Tanya, he would have liked to ditch everyone, just take off and never come back.

With her fingers locked in his, and swinging her shoes in her free hand, she ran for fun until she was forced to stop. Regaining her breath, she spoke for the first time of how proud of him she was and how she would never forget the way he rose in court and spoke his mind. Yet the more she praised him the more uncomfortable he became. To stop her, he slapped her rump, which he knew she hated. She chased him to the crest of a hill where they saw the station washed in lights like a landing field below them.

With a gallon of gas sloshing about in a two-gallon can, they staggered back to the road together and tried to flag a ride. Two cars growled past without stopping, and Val grew angry. He placed her where the neon was brightest, and she thumbed the air for another pair of lights but with the same results. When auto number four approached, Val stood straddling the road to Tanya's distress with his arms wide until the stranger stopped, or rather slowed down to catch their plea. "Out of gas. Down the road. Appreciate it if…" Carbon monoxide was the only reply.

"*You bastard,*" Val yelled, hands cupped to his mouth. "*Eat shit.*"

"Hey, you'll break a windpipe."

"They just don't care," he said, circling the gasoline can in stifled fury. "Did you see that? At this time of night. We could be left to die out here. People are shits. They are crud-laden, one-dimensional shits." He bellowed again at the now vanished driver: "*May you get five flats at once and crash in the woods.*"

"But not until your insurance expires," she added, pleased at his anger and puzzled at her inability to share it.

The next pair of lights didn't slow down at all, and he leaped for his life, stumbling and touching gravel with all ten fingers to keep from falling. She screamed and hurried over, but he had scampered off the road and kept on going into the darkness. She called and got no answer. He came charging back out of the woods obsessed with the idea of stopping the next car at all costs. She caught her breath when she saw the large rock in his right claw. Another pair of lights appeared, one lamp brighter than the other.

"No, Val."

"Look out. Step back."

"They'll arrest you again."

"Good, this time I'll be guilty."

"Hey, like this sort of thing never used to bug you. Laugh at it."

"It always bugged me. Step back, damn you."

"So they pass us by. Like that's life."

"That's exactly the part of life I don't like."

"Val, please."

"Get back, here he comes."

"Val, no."

But he forced his way into the road mumbling: "All right you mother-fucker." He thumbed awkwardly with his left hand, holding the other behind him. "Stop or you'll get it right in the windshield."

Plodding along at no great speed, the auto rolled wheezing to a halt at the first sight of Val's signal. A young Negro with a Band-Aid on his forehead ducked to see out of the passenger window. "How far you goin'?"

Val was so startled that Tanya beat him to the answer. They climbed in, the gasoline can between them, and noticed a woman with a child sleeping in the back seat. They chatted with the driver and offered him a cigarette as the car churned tentatively on its way. Val finally got around to ask where he was heading.

"Canada. Had myself enough of these here states. E-nough."

Tanya shook her head. "Swell. We finally find one good Samaritan and *he's* leaving the country."

"Got to," the driver said. "Can't box and ah can't sing. And ah don't think there's much of a chance ah me runnin' for governor."

"I dig," said Val.

"As you came north," Tanya asked smiling, "you didn't happen to meet a nutsy friend of ours going south, did ya?"

"A Negro," Val explained, "going South to retire. How does that grab ya?"

"Oh, I don't know," said the driver. "I understand Mexico's a right nice place to settle down."

"Ha. I'll have to write Pops and tell him that one."

Up ahead sat the Mercury, cold and still. Ottomeyer was standing on the road, looking highly agitated.

"Check that one," Val said. "He's psycho, I swear to God."

Tanya shook her head in amazement.

"Here O.K.?" the driver asked.

"Here's fine," they answered, and the Negro pulled the car to a halt as though it were a horse.

"Boy, he's getting to bug me," Val said of Ottomeyer.

"Is he the one you fixing to drop with that there rock?" asked the driver.

Val's attention jumped to his right hand. "Christ, will you look at this?"

Tanya lowered her face into her hands, then lifted it out again. "It's for elephants," she explained with embarrassment. "We use it to kill elephants."

"You meet many in these parts?" he asked, with his dry, unchanging voice.

"A few this afternoon. Like they got away."

"Well, man, there's always donkeys," the driver put in. "They're not much better."

Honey squirmed out of a dream and looked up at Nat DeVore from the vantage point of his shoulder where her head had fallen. A streetlamp bathed his face for a moment. How wise and thoughtful he looked. Would he use his influence to get back her baby? She must be patient and wait for the right man to ask. But I *will* get her back, she thought, I will. Perhaps she is back already and waiting there like a wonderful surprise. Honey moved her lips without making a sound: Please, God, have Jacqueline there waiting for me, lying there all tiny toes and little fingers in her crib in the tub. Pretty please?

She thought of Baby Joe and without effort assembled him in her mind for the first time. He was John Garfield at some moments, Kirk Douglas at others. He had adored her, made love to her and had been taken from her by the hideous police. It was a beautiful story, and as a movie it would make people cry. He was in prison now yearning for her body and mailing out great yellow-paged letters of love. He was a poet more than a prize-fighter, really, like Garfield in that movie. Poor Baby Joe. Jail is no place to be. The trick is to stay free and become famous. She wondered if any of those she had met this Sunday would remember her years later when she had become famous? How surprised they would be if they knew that at this moment they were riding in the same car with a future Academy Award Winner who will some day live in duplexed splendor with everyone recognizing her face on the street and asking for her autograph in restaurants and collecting her pictures for their walls. Fame will push away worry and make life leave her alone. Handsome men, famous men, great, rich and deeply feeling men will all strive to win her fancy. And one day with klieg lights sending up their white columns into the night to announce one of those grand motion picture premieres, the beautiful Miss Honey Bea will step out of a black polished limousine to enter a plush theater through a narrow passage forced open through a wild crowd by the straining police and suddenly she, Honey Bea, will spot a little girl (age ten) running forward crying, Mommie, Mommie, I've found you, I've found you, and then she and Jacqueline will at longlast be together again. It will be a monumental day, and the whole world will be hers like a box of candy. Even while riding on Mr. DeVore's lap, an omen, promising that all this will come true, appeared where a moment before there was nothing but night. She had been the first to see it. Lifting her head, she glimpsed her life like a lot of new clothes all waiting to be put on, her career waiting to be fulfilled, free of fear and sorrow, lined with untarnished triumphs and long high lightning strokes of love, and she would be swept up and held in a hundred million hearts, cherished by nations, honored by cities, to stand in stone and live in song and smile forth from canvas, her beauty and her greatness expanding like the dawn itself until, in a full flood of light, she would be spread upon the sky blazing like a goddess.

"Oh," she said, "the *sun's* coming up. It really is. Look. It really is."

NOT until she had unlocked her door for the two of them to enter did Val realize that this was home to him more than any place he had ever been. The posters, paintings and photographs, the fish, cats and canaries were all as he remembered them. And she continued to renounce group therapy, and Tshombe continued to be stunned. While she fed her helpless menagerie, he made two bourbons and soda and then settled into her Carole Lombard chair. She knelt, placed milk near the kitchen door, stood up, tossed her hair and sipped her drink.

"You look beat," Tanya said, crossing the room and flopping on the couch. "You look like a Jewish, cancerous, homosexual, psychotic, impotent, communist refugee with a cold."

As she kicked off her shoes, he said: "And you look like you just took on ten escaped convicts in the back of a truck and didn't get paid."

"Well," she said, pointedly, "I didn't get paid for yesterday. That's for sure."

"Neither did I, don't forget."

She stirred her drink with a cigarette holder and spoke softly without looking up. "What are you going to do, Val?" She sipped from the glass.

"I may go home to Mother."

"You hate your mother."

"That's right, I forgot." And he slumped in his seat.

"Christ, I got to get out of this dress," she announced, standing up. Then, as an afterthought. "Into zomzing more *come*-fortable."

She carried her drink into the bedroom, leaving her shoes behind. After a few moments, he stretched out a foot and tipped one over. Cat and Other Cat were lapping up the milk. Tom Tom was inside with her mistress.

"Keep talking."

"What about?" asked Val.

"About what you're going to do, you know. The arrest."

"I'm hungry."

"Are you hungry, sweetie?"

"I just *said* I was hungry."

"Ah, maybe that's where I heard it."

He shook his head. Reaching out with his foot he stood her shoe up again.

"Go inside and make us two sandwiches, why don't you."

He went inside and made two sandwiches. Twice she said something to him and twice he called back: "What?"

"I said go in and make two..."

"I am, I am."

A roach ascended the wall behind the sink. "Good morning," said Val, as he opened the mayonnaise. The roach kept climbing, then stopped. "Don't let your mistress see you, little man, Or it's *splauech* for sure."

Tanya, from the bedroom: "Valitchska, what time is it?"

"It's eight in the A.M."

"Twenty-four hours without sleep. Wow."

Balancing his bourbon upon a container of milk and with a plate of sandwiches in his other hand, he re-entered the empty living room and nearly fell over a cat. To avoid catastrophe, he grabbed hold of his drink with his teeth.

Her bedroom door stood partly open, and he decided to take fair lady in tender surprise by marching right into her secret domain like some dirty old man's skillful apprentice. With the glass still in his mouth, its rim pressing against his nose, he stepped in unannounced and unnoticed. She was standing by the dresser with her back to him, covered head to foot in a marvelous silken robe. She turned and thrust forth a hand from its enveloping sleeve and in her full theatrical voice threw herself headlong into speech.

"Hyham *gor*geous," she announced, stepping up and taking firm hold of his hair. "Hyham Nastasya Filippovona and Hyham gorgeous. Just a leetle beet insane, unfortunately. But gorgeous." She pulled him closer. "Observe my sucken, suffering cheeks. Har you observing? Goot? Hyham Nastasya Filippovona of Russia, and Hy vill be magnificent off Broadvay. Look for me. Hy vill be looking for you."

Pretending to have fallen under her spell, he stood wide-eyed, the glass suspended in his mouth. Unable to applaud, for both hands were occupied, he tilted his head back to take in some of his drink and then, balancing the glass on top of the milk container, he tilted his head back again and loudly gargled. She acknowledged his approval with a deep curtsy.

"Today I sign," she said with great excitement and in her natural voice. "Oh, Val, today I sign." Moving an invisible pen through the air she beamed at him.

"Hupla," he said.

"*Food,*" Nastasya cried, as though noticing his offerings for the first time. "Hy vant nourishment. When Hy have been nourished, Hyham magnificent."

"So, nourish already."

"Oh, Valitchska," said Tanya, putting her food on the night table. "Oh, Valitchska."

"Yes, baby?"

She took his hands in hers. "Oh, Valitchska."

"Like what?" He smiled.

"Everything," she said. "The good and the bad."

"Yes, baby. I know."

"Val, will I be O.K.? I'll be O.K., won't I?" Her tone of voice was like a spasm of pain.

"You'll be colossal, for crysake. The part will make you. After ten years of struggle, you'll be, at twenty-nine, an overnight sensation."

"At twenty-eight."

"Twenty-nine. You're twenty-nine."

"Well, you can't win 'em all."

"You'll be great, goddamn it. Just great. You are a magnificent actress, and you'll be pure genius in the part. You will dazzle, uplift, bemuse, decimate and purify. *You will be famous.*"

"Let me see if I got that right," she said. "I am a magnificent actress. I will be pure genius in the part. I will dazzle, uplift, bemuse—I like that, bemuse—and what else? Decimate and purify. Check. Oh, and I *will be famous.* Is that right?"

"That's right."

"Now, like if I can only believe it."

As they wolfed down their sandwiches, she got an idea. She would ask for an advance on her contract so he could have money to hire good lawyers for his trial. He patted her head gratefully, but a sense of helplessness in the matter rendered him silent. The entire affair, past and future, was beginning to mummify in his mind, fixed and final and beyond discussion. Like an actor in a bad melodrama whose closing notice had already been posted, he felt resigned to the inevitable, knowing that any further investment of time or money would only worsen an already hopeless condition. He felt mercifully removed beyond the need of fervor or flippancy. All he wanted now was her in that bed on top of him.

"I was so proud of you yesterday," she said, checking the sides of her mouth for food particles. "When you were angry, you were tremendous. You will go on being angry, won't you? With indignation and bulging veins and everything."

"Why does it matter so much to you? It's lost, you know. The whole stupid thing is down the drain."

"Idiot. I couldn't care less if you win or lose. Like I just want you to fight. That's what went wrong with us, Val. You never gave two damns about anything. And if you don't care about anything, then you don't care about me. A man who's always indifferent, like he's got no substance. He's not a child and he's not a man. He's nowhere. Nothin'."

Tom Tom moved across the bed and into her mistress' lap. Tanya took the milk from Val's hand and drank, her other hand stroking the cat's head. She gave back the container, frowning. "Boy, it tastes from lemons."

Struggling to get comfortable on a lopsided footrest, Val made a peevish complaint. "I don't see why the hell you keep cats. You with your goddamn emotional demands."

She hugged Tom Tom like a baby. "They balance things out."

"And I think you're getting too hot in the pants about this arrest business. You get so damn adamant you lose all perspective. You become grotesque."

"Come on. I do not."

"Like the time your plane landed in Hamburg for a stopover. You had six hours in town, so what did you do? You sat on the bench in the airport waiting room like a Neanderthal with amnesia."

"So?"

"So it was sunny out, and everyone else on the flight went sightseeing."

"So?"

"And you sat there like it was Hamburg 1942, not '62."

Lifting its head, Tanya spoke to the cat. "He doesn't understand these things. How much I love Germans."

"Turning to stone as soon as you set foot on German soil. That's a kind of grand-scale civic nuttiness, isn't it?"

"No," she said, haughty and hurt. "I just don't happen to care for their past."

"You mean, of course, Bach, Beethoven, Brahms, Wagner, Mahler, Bruckner..."

"Schmuck, their more recent past."

"Oh, you mean all those concentration camps and Hitler killing six million Jews and all? Hell, nobody's perfect."

She lurched with outrage before she saw that he was smiling. "O.K.," he said, "so some of them did a terrible thing. You're not going to hold it against all of them for the rest of time, are you? Remember, now, they didn't invent concentration camps."

"No," she grinned sweetly, "they only perfected them."

Val doubled over in silent pleasure at this retort while she gave him an exasperated toss of her head. "I hate it when you get this way. The Jekyll and Hyde bit. What brings it on? I bet you don't even know."

He laughed and removed his tie. "I just can't resist teasing you. Hell, you're always so *inflamed* about everything. If it isn't politics or The Bomb or your next role or something, then it's wicked me. If I'm a good little social-minded citizen then you let me hold hands with you. If not, zip—you're gone. Hell, that's nutty, woman. Your love rests on my voting record. Well, the hell with that noise. What if I told you that I wasn't going to appear up there on the tenth? That I was going to jump bail and screw 'em all? And Ulysses, too. Let 'em catch me. Let 'em shoot me down. What would you say to that?"

"First, I'd ask if you really truly meant it?"

"And if I really truly meant it?"

"Well, my diagnosis would be that you're like gornicht." Yet her face weakened with worry. "You don't really mean it, Val."

"I really mean it."

"Are you teasing me?"

"No, ma'am."

She pinched and rearranged her frock. The cat had deserted her. The plate beside her was clean, her drink empty. It struck him how utterly alone she looked, and exhausted. She straightened up, hands folded in her lap.

"Well," Tanya said, pertly, "you just talked yourself out of a lay."

Unable to maintain her gaiety, she shut her eyes instead. Seeing the pain his playfulness caused, recognizing her courage and recalling her concern, he became flooded with more love than he was prepared to bare. He turned away with disgust from that part of himself that was the spokesman and the stranger. Then, with a great need to give, he discovered his poverty. He spoke anyway, recklessly and then faltered.

"Once I start... don't you understand?"

She looked up, seized by the tone of his voice.

"Once, way back, I believed in God," he said. "Then it was astrology. Next, I had a grandiose vision that art stood above all else. At one time I believed sex was everything. I even believed in my parents until I realized how great they fucked me up. I don't want to believe again. It's not healthy. I don't want to burden myself with hopes and theories and then have to struggle against a lifelong tide of conflicting evidence. Bitter? No, sir. I'm not a sore loser. Man isn't evil, he's just a mistake. And I like mistakes. I'm a mistake myself. My parents arrived at the church five months late. I was a baby retroactively in good standing. Ditto my brother and sister. O.K., great. But I just don't care for crusades. To me all holy grails are filled with sludge. Don't you see? Even if I wanted to do something there's nothing to do. Nothing. That's what's wrong with being young today. The twentieth century. Like wow. Am I going to paint after what Picasso and the others did? Or write when there was a Joyce or Faulkner? And what they've done with music already is too much, and I can't even whistle. Fight a war? That's a laugh. Make a splash in business? That's finished. They've done it all better than ever before. Man has even been more evil than man can ever be again. Don't you see? Before I even start out I'm third-rate. Science? Fly to the planets? I won't live long enough, and besides I get airsick. Across the last fifty years stretch mountains of accomplishment. We're in a valley now. Let me wander in peace. I don't believe anything big can be done. Not now nor for a long while. At least not by me. All this has made me third-rate. I am right and I don't want to bother proving it. But the world's a mess, you say. Injustice, etcetera. That's the danger, don't you see? That I'll start to care so much that I'll end up hating everything including the valley I'm living in, and then I'll really be through. And you want me to get pissed off about a little tinhorn arrest out there in the woods? For what? For some extracurricular heartache and a shot in the ass?"

She stared at him with loving amazement, and he stared back, never before realizing how much he needed an ally.

"If only everybody cared too much," she said, hopefully. "Oh, then there'd be so little heartache. And less shots in that place dere what you said."

It stung him that she could be this flippant when he had been so close to the flame, so foolishly blubbering in his own sincerity. As he leaned forward to slash at her with words she, at the same moment, could hold back her feelings no longer.

"Oh, Val, I love you, oh, I do. I do."

After a moment, he sank forward until his brow pressed her knees, and in the quiet room her hand settled upon his head. Her soiled feet, uprooted from the woods, were warm to the touch. Then his palms clasped her raw calves beneath the coils of her frock and his lungs came alive with her creature aroma. She knelt beside him, wrapped in her thin, flesh-filled silk and pressed her head against his chest. Numb with joy, he heard a clock throbbing, glimpsed a painting dead with distance and felt her teeth clamp his shirt button.

He lifted and steered her by the elbows to the bed. There they renewed their love with labored kisses and together freed him from his clothes. His arm sent her silk robe into flight where it landed on then slithered off a maple cabinet. Stretched across the bed was the one woman he thought he would never clasp again, her Congo red fingernails picking lint from his white stomach. She followed his lead into languid grappling, her body's sunstained skin receiving his lips' slow homage. He had forgotten how varied were the sounds of her astonishment and how gentle were her hands guiding him into his stride.

Later he withered as though from lashes across the back. Then they lay drowned in each other while her furniture returned silently to its various places in the room.

"Krumba," she said and wiggled her toes.

"And now," he announced in somber finality, "our national anthem."

Eventually he rolled onto his back. "Well, that's what *I'd* order at the last supper."

"That and separate checks, if I know you."

Her hand on his stomach recorded a slight tremor of mirth.

"There's one thing about you I never could decide," she said. "I never could decide if you were like good or evil or what?"

"Well, I'll give it some thought."

Then, as though the last twenty-four hours had sprung on them at once, they both were asleep. Later, the phone rang. Clumsy and moronic she picked it up to hear someone speak her name. She mumbled in reply.

"Hey, baby. I wanta cavort withya in da altogether. Where do I sign up?"

"What?" She focused on the bulbless ceiling socket. The voice repeated what it had said, so she hung up. She looked at Val, who was asleep, and she thought: does the whole world know that we've just this minute been making it? A cautious glance at the window revealed as always a comforting brick wall, and she was asleep again. There was that sense of having taken a great, slow step through time when the ringing returned. "Hello," she said, cheerfully trying now to hide the fact that she had been caught asleep.

"Shame," thundered an ancient voice. "The Lord's beauty is yours in trust. It is not to be degraded in nudity or defamed in sin. You and your type are a poison in the growth of man."

"Up yours," she exclaimed, slamming the receiver down. "Swell. Must be groundhog day."

She cherished Val's narrow chest until he disgorged a thick, sudden "Wha?"

"Rest, my love. You need your strength. Look how thin you look."

"Screw you," he mumbled and shifted back into slumber.

She tried to join him but kept worrying about that call. Or had there been two calls? What the hell was going on anyway? Her anxiety was like a hammock in a high wind. Today, I sign; the armored suit of fame. And gee whiskers, all this and love, too. Happy birthday, Miss Kretchmar, happy birthday to you. Diaphragm in? No! Safe period? Yes! Happy days! Always that chill before sleep. Fame plus love. Swing, man, swing. Ah, Valitchska. Then she was gone. Back again. Gone again. A thought began clearly and became blurred. Buildings disassembled noiselessly. A vacuum. Clarity. Fuzz. The splendor of an oncoming … a clear jumble of … nothing.

When the phone rang next, neither of them stirred. Finally, she shifted her beautiful legs and made an ugly face but remained asleep. He lay in beatific serenity, plunged face forward in a fluff of blue pillow. Then, with a shrug and a snort, he jumped awake in a spasm of fear. Sitting up, his life took shape like an ill-kept file cabinet. He paused to consider the warm, dead sprawl of her as the phone made noise again. He fondled one spreading breast and kissed the other.

"Sweety-pants," he said. "Someone's ringing."

She sprang into consciousness and clubbed him with her elbow. "Sorry," she yelled grappling savagely with the black claw of the receiver and imitating a polite, receptionist's "*Nyes?*"

Val stumbled out of bed, his hand covering his right eye. Doubled over, he ambled blindly into the vanity table. Now with one hand on his eye and the other on his knee, he wobbled away grimacing and graceless.

"Hang on, Mike, will ya?" Then to the writhing apparition: "Val, are you hurt?"

"Only physically."

"You look like a crippled nudist taking an eye test."

"I'll say one thing about you," he admitted, still cupping his face. "No matter how much pain I'm in, you never lose your sense of humor."

"Poor baby. I'm sorry."

"Who the hell is it, anyway?"

"My agent."

Val just shook his head and stepped into her carpeted bathroom to examine his raw eye in the streaked mirror.

"Hello, Mike?" said Tanya's muted voice. "Sorry. Just a little morning mishagoss dere."

Val turned on the cold water and bathed his face with a wet washrag. When he shut off the faucet, there was a silence in the bedroom; then Tanya's sober voice. "What stories? What are you talking about?"

He turned on the faucet again and repeated the medication. Then her voice again:

"You've got to be kidding … *oui* … Yes, read it."

Val removed the cloth and leaned in toward his earnest face, rolling his eye, pulling down on his bottom lid. I'll live, he decided, but under protest. He squeezed out the rag and hung it away.

"Oh, God," came a cry from the next room which he took as a more or less normal theatrical outburst. Perhaps she learned of a misquote in an interview or a misspelling on a credit list, and now all at once life is a technicolor drama on the wide screen.

An Anchor paperback of *The Selected Letters of John Keats* lay on the edge of the tub. "Reading other people's mail, eh? So that's your game." And with this gag warm and ready, he carried the book into her room.

On the bed, her legs drawn in, the soles of her feet equally earth-brown, she sat with a taut shoulder blade in bas-relief as she held her tilted head against the earpiece, removing and returning it again with a twist of neck to free her hair. This lovely pose, unconscious and eloquent, excited him with its impermanence. How long now had it been since he had last used his camera? Refusing to calculate, he shrugged the thought away and circled the bed to wag Keats at her like a lottery ticket. His words, imminent and playful, were halted by her frown.

The heat of the day began to crowd the room, and a kind cerebral dryness reminded him that he was still a night behind in sleep. It was almost ten A.M. by the churning electric clock on her ill-stained dresser with its three open drawers like steps leading to a woodcut on the wall. He sat on the sinking mattress, and ran his palm along the varnished thigh of her leg. She shuddered. He drew his hand away before he realized that she didn't even know he was there. Her face was a death mask. Her left hand clutched her stomach.

"Mike," she cried. "Do something. Please do something." She rolled her head as though someone she disliked had called to her from the other room. Immediately she brought her ear back to the voice that Val couldn't hear. "He promised…" Her dark eyes flashed open. "Don't *tell* me that," she raged. "*I don't want to hear that.*" Covering her face with her hand. "I'll sue. I swear to God. She has no right. That stupid bitch."

Val moved closer. "What's wrong?"

"I don't understand," she said, her voice wavering. "Oh, Mike, tell me what's happening? I don't understand."

Val called her name softly.

"I don't want to hear that. Not from you, Mike. Mike, listen to me. This is my big chance, don't you understand?"

"What's happened?" Val spoke with a mounting sense of alarm.

"Mike, I'm not young any more."

This had a tone of despair that he had never before heard from her.

"You don't know what to say to that one," she asked the phone, "do you?"

"Tanya, hey. What is it?"

"Mike do something huh? You're my agent. *Please, do something.*"

"Baby, is it the play or what?"

"That's ridiculous." She rubbed her knee with an angry palm. "How was I to know?"

"Hey, what? For crysake." He took her hand but it flew out of his to clasp her brow.

"I was broke," she insisted, savagely. "I've got to pay the rent, too, you know…. Oh, shit. Do you think I would have, if I had known."

"Jesus, someone speak to me."

"Mike," she said, her head lowering almost to the mattress and rising again, "Mike this is terribly, terribly unfair…" and then her voice broke. "*Ohdear.*" She bit her lip. "*Ohdear.*" She sat, crushed into silence, her eyes shut, her mouth gaping, her tears streaming. She dropped her arm to the bed, and from out of the fallen receiver vibrated a droning voice like a recorded announcement of doom. Val buried his face in her thighs and, tortured by her grief, begged her not to cry. She lifted the phone to her ear once more but, unable to speak, she slammed it into the cradle.

She ran all the way into the living room before he could grab and stop her. She screamed at him that it was all his fault. Why couldn't he have just left her alone? Why did he have to re-enter her life and screw it up? Stung by the force of her own assault, she turned her back and refused to face him until he had wrestled her to the carpet amid a shriek of cats and his own growling. Then he found her hugging him instead, pleading forgiveness, even kissing him, and when he sat up with her hot tears on his astonished face, looking all too clearly stunned by the whole affair, she actually laughed, pointed at him, and laughed, then screamed again, slapping at Tom Tom who had sunk his claws into her thigh.

Val gripped her smooth shoulders. "What the hell happened, for crysake? You going to tell me or not?"

Sitting up, wrapping his jacket around her (it was within reach on the couch) she told him about the news stories (three papers had carried the arrest) and how the producer of the play, or actually his wife, had read them and decided that an actress who would do such a thing in the woods on the day before she was to sign for a Circle in the Square production was definitely not fit to appear in her husband's play and that he must find someone to replace her. Nine-thirty that morning Mike Ferraro received a call from the producer's answering service telling him that his client was not suitable for the part after all.

"So that's that," she concluded, examining the white scratches on her leg.

Val rested his head on the seat of the canvas chair and rolled the world around on his neck muscles. The ceiling shuttled to and fro above him as she wet two fingers and rubbed the damage. And here, too, the way she was sitting was a photograph, the empty arms of his jacket hanging dead at her sides with her legs exposed and her face somber. Then her bloodshot eyes looked up as though he had called her name and, like a man in shock, he rummaged among his numb and useless feelings for something to say.

"He read me some of the stories." Her tired voice was almost a whisper. "Ugly. Like the worst things possible. Just awful." She looked at her leg again, rubbing the claw marks in continual, half-hearted concern. "A couple of girls take their clothes off so it's a gonsa magilla."

"Is it really lost? The play?"

"Ha."

"Jesus, that bastard."

"Which one?"

But he didn't have to answer, and she pulled at the jacket as if she were cold. "I knew it would happen," she confessed. "For me everything works out this way, you know. I'm a tzurus collector. That's what my analyst says. Oh, fuck him, too. I was just not meant to succeed and that's it."

"That's a load and you know it."

"I'm serious. I wasn't meant to. I can feel it like a weakness inside me. Can you see yourself like famous and talked about and all that? Well, I never could. I'm serious. I think first you've got to feel it inside or something. I'm small potatoes. I came close a few times, but that happens to plenty of 'em. Fuck fame. Who needs it? Ha. Listen to me. I'm so furious, I could choke. Well, this time I'm really through. I'm twenty-nine and I've had it. When I was eighteen, I gave myself ten years to make good or check out. Well, this is it. I'm finished."

"You most certainly aren't."

"Oh, bull. You know it, too. Like don't lie. I've spent ten years in a rat race, and what the hell have I got to show for it. Nine hundred shots of me in a bikini and the world's indoor record for propositions received. That's about it. A broken ankle at summer stock. A worn-out leotard and a free trip to Europe with a G.I. entertainment show. And that really *is* it. Period."

"You had a few laughs, no?"

"Sure. None of which I can remember."

"You're making it all look pretty dark."

"I don't see any light, do you?" She pinched the rug, looked up and erupted once more. "I feel like going back up there and giving that D.A. a piece of my mind. We should have made a bigger fuss. Tsh, what's the use?"

She tried to tidy up her tear-streaked face with a few quick dabs and touches. She asked if he had a handkerchief, then smiled, for he was naked. He went into the bedroom and returned wearing his trousers and carrying a box of tissues. She was on the couch now, her legs under her, and she was wearing his jacket. Flipping her way through several record albums, she made a face and threw them down. "Ah, shit." When he settled beside her, she whimpered: "Val, what am I going to do?"

His hand, reaching for hers, disappeared into the opening of the sleeve.

"Good God, what will my mother say?" she exclaimed, slapping her brow. "Boy, this will be all she needs. Like final proof. Yeh couldn't be ha simple vife like everbuddy else. Yeh had ta be hun actress and make skendal."

"Maybe she won't see the papers this morning," he ventured, plagued with the need to speak, to say something.

"Ha. She reads the tabloids like they were supplements to the Old Testament. She never misses a rape or a robbery. She knows more about show business than I do, providing it's about whose ex-husband is sleeping with whose ex-wife. Right this minute she's waiting, my mother, to see if I got the guts to call."

"Would you like another drink?"

"I feel so cheap," she explained, and then paused to fish out two yellow theater stubs from his jacket pocket. In her hands they looked like a pair of canceled tickets to the Promised Land. She read aloud: "M 4, M 5. Three ninety. Cherry Lane Theatre." She waved them at him. "Doing the town without me, eh, buddy?" She smiled. He grinned, too, with all the ease of an actor who had forgotten his lines. "Baby, get me a cigarette." He returned with two Kents and lit them. "The great Tanya Lando," she said. "A Kretchmar to the end." He patted her knee. "Oh, Val, I feel so goddamn cheap. They'll all think I've been in an orgy."

"Listen to me," Val said, driven by a need to bathe her in love. "Little pumpkin, listen. I really think..."

"Oh, hell," she interrupted through an exhale of smoke, "the phone. This day is going to go on forever."

"Your answering service, let them get it."

"That's what I'll do, yes. Good idea."

It rang the second time, and they sat motionless like two absurd mannequins sharing a single summer suit. The ringing persisted, and finally Tanya leaped from the couch. "Maybe it's my agent. Maybe it's about—*hello?*"

Val got up as well and walked about feeling wretched. His trousers hung low on his shirtless frame, swallowing up his bare feet and clownishly mocking his despair.

"Well, well, Mr. Morganstern," said Tanya, sounding startled.

Overcome by an annoying sense of discretion, Val made himself walk out of the room. He had smashed her entire life; at least he could take care not to step on the pieces. Sitting on the edge of the bed, he heard her say:

"Yes, I read them."

You bugger, he thought, be gentle. How much can she go through?

"What do you mean, were the stories true?"

You idiot, he thought you goddamn idiot. And he snatched up Keats's letters. On the inside cover, in ink, were written the words: Dearest, We have so much in common that I thought you might enjoy sharing another little sin of mine…reading other people's mail. All my love, Dexter Morganstern.

Furious, Val threw the book clear out the window and waited for the sound that signified the end of its flight. But all that came were more of her words, rapid and reckless.

"Don't worry, I understand your question. You don't have to explain it. Like of course they were true. Don't you have any faith in the American press? It was an orgy, man. You should have been there. It would have done you some good. Like the *Daily News* was modest. They left out a whole bit about the animals. You know those farm orgies. A real bacchanal. Grapes and sheep. That's the scene and the wine, pure Manischewitz. Until yesterday like I never even knew the proper etiquette. Animals came first, did you know that? And *then* the women. I'm writing a book about it. *Etiquette at an Orgy* or *The Peaceful Uses of Sexual Perversion*. If it sells I'll follow it up with *Orgies and the Single Girl* or *A Daisy Chain Is Only as Strong as Its Weakest Link*. You like?" Something in her voice made Val go and stand in the doorway. "And I'll follow that with *The Most Unforgettable Orgy in Which I've Been Known* and then …" But her voice ran aground and slamming the receiver into its cradle and almost falling over a cat, she flew to the center of the room where she stopped and pressed her knuckles into her mouth.

"Why am I so cruel?" she wailed. He rushed up and threw his arms around her as the phone rang.

"Oh, stop that thing," she cried. "Stop it. It'll drive me bats."

Val zeroed in on its black, meddlesome presence.

"No, gimme." She sprinted up and snatched it out of his hand. "Hello?"

Val hitched up his pants and dumped his disgruntled self into the canvas chair. He thought of bourbon and bounded up again.

"Who *is* this?" she asked. "…Who?"

He entered the kitchen, bare feet on cold linoleum, and returned immediately when he heard:

"And you're calling for what reason?... *Val!*"

She was pressing the mouthpiece with the heel of her hand. For an instant he thought she had been reinstated in the play.

"Do I look different?" she asked.

"What? No."

"'Cause I'm going mad. You know who this is? One of the green guards from the filthy woods. Wants a date, he does. Isn't that too much? I'm so touched I could..."

Her sarcasm was spliced by his rush to the phone. "Hold on," she said into the receiver, "here's Daddy Warbucks."

Val snatched it away from her mouth. "Listen to me, you miserable two-bit son of a..." The line went dead like a slap in the face and he was left overloaded with his own fury. "He hung up."

"I swear to God I'll end up on the funny farm."

"What a pair of eggs he's got to go and call you." Then he looked frightened. "Honey! Is she getting this business, too, do you think?" For a moment he turned his face to the ceiling. "Jesus Christ, they must *all* be going through this. Let me see, Honey will survive anything. But Esra is stuck right there in the heart of it. And Ulysses— if I get jailed he loses three thousand dollars. And you, for crysake. I really smashed you up good, didn't I?" He pushed past her, collided with a cat, kicked at it and missed. She tried to speak, but he cut her off. "How did I *ever* let myself get talked into this? That black bastard, why couldn't he have just left me alone?" He punched his palm with his fist. "And goddamn it, I feel so responsible for what happened to you... I don't know if I can..."

"Oh, baby." She threw her arms around him, her hands emerging from the sleeves. "I love you for saying that."

The last thing he wanted was an award, so he freed himself from her tentacles.

"O.K., so you love me. That only makes it worse. I feel sick about what happened and..."

"Valitchska, you didn't do anything to me. Not a thing."

"I called you up at the last minute, didn't I? And you really saved me, boy, you really saved me. And what did you get out of it? You get a royal…"

"I got *you* back," she exclaimed, delighted by his ranting.

"Don't talk like a child." He turned away.

"Baby. What exactly are you so pissed off about?"

"I don't know," he fired back. "Yes, I do know. I want you to get your ass off the floor and *do* something. I want you to raise the roof, for crysake. None of this shit about how you always knew you would fail. Go to your agent again or see that producer or somebody. Raise the roof."

"I can't. It's out of my hands."

"Nonsense."

"It *is*." And she strode into the bedroom. He tried to catch her, but the three cats beat him to it. "I am not good at that sort of thing." She flapped her arms. "To beg for a job back. Oh, kind sir, please hire me again 'cause I'm not the slut you think I am. The hell I will."

"Try anyway," he insisted, as she tossed off his jacket and pulled on a robe. Her angry nakedness remained in his mind, sexless and threatening.

"Why should I? To relieve you of your guilt?"

"No, bitch. To get rid of your self-pity."

"Well, I *like* that! You screw me up but good, and like I have no right to feel sorry about it? Chuck you farley!"

"You're a goddamn coward, you know that?" When she indicated the open window, he continued in a strained whisper.

"You'll fight for anyone's cause except your own."

"And you'll fight for *no* one's cause except your own …. *Maybe.*"

"Boy, I don't understand you." He paced a full, angry circle, yanking up on his trousers. "I don't understand you at all."

She sat abruptly on the floor to pet one of her cats. "Why are we fighting?" she asked, softly.

"Don't pull that crap. You know why we're fighting."

"Tell me."

He was pulling on his shirt. "I said *you* know why. I don't know. How the hell should I know?" He noticed her delicious grin. "What's so damn funny?"

"Us." And she covered her mouth to bottle it in. "Oh, *no*," she cried, jumping to her feet. "*I can't stand it.*"

"Let it ring," he ordered, taking her by the shoulders. She clamped her ears. Pulling her against him, he placed his hands over hers. At the third ring she leaped away and screamed for him to get it, which he did before it could stab them again, dashing into the living room to pick it up.

"Well, could you tell me what time she'll be back?"

The voice was obsequious and deceptive, and Val scrambled through the labyrinth of memory to fit name and voice together.

"I have *no* idea, sir," said Miss Answering Service, with chilly disdain. "Would you care to leave your name?"

"Is she usually away all day long?" asked the voice.

"I have *no* idea, sir. Would you *care* to leave your name?"

"Thank you, no." And whoever it was hung up.

"Phew," said Miss Answering Service and she, too, was gone.

Val hung up as well, and while he stood there, striving to attach a face to the tone and temperament of that voice, a wet, tepid sandpaper tongue licked the big toe of his right foot.

Tanya peeked around the corner of the doorjamb as though the caller might have materialized in the room. "Who was it?"

"I'll tell you in a minute."

"What do you mean, you'll tell me in a minute?"

Val knelt and petted the Angora named Cat. "Shhhh. I'm trying to think."

Tanya strolled up to them, knelt and peered into Val's face as though down a dark passage. "*Wha?*"

"I'm trying to remember. *Shh.*"

"Remember what? So who was it? Hey, like tremendous recall you got dere."

He placed a restraining finger to his lips.

"Would you please tell me who just phoned? Val? Val, I hate to be nosey, but..."

"Ah," he shouted.

"What, already? What?"

"It was Reno. That Ben Reno."

"You're kidding. Did he give his name?"

"No, but I'm certain. It was the same cruddy nasal voice."

"You know his voice? When did you talk with him?"

"A few times yesterday. What's he calling you for, anyway? Is he hot to trot?"

"Him? Sure. Most guys have like eyes to make me. But this one, he's not to be believed. I tried to cool it with him, but he comes on like a landslide. If he calls back, say I'm dead."

"Was he coming on with you? Really? I didn't notice."

"You didn't notice? You bastard, you wouldn't notice if I was being raped by the Fourth Army Band in the center ring of Madison Square Garden on opening night."

"Depends on what you're wearing."

She gave out with a frustrated growl. "God, sometimes I wonder how I got you to stand up for yourself back there in court."

"I didn't stand up for me. I stood up for you. And had I known they were going to ruin your life, I'd still be back there fighting."

"You would?"

She smiled gratefully, and all he could think of was how good she looked. Seated on the couch, he made her curl up in his lap.

"Oh, Val, what are we going to do?"

Her frock parted, and he slid his palm along her thigh.

"Is this the answer?" she murmured with a pained look.

His reply was to tunnel his tongue into her ear with a slow moan.

"Val, I don't think this is the answer."

Five careful fingers supported her pliant breast and soon he was tongue-fluttering her jutting nipple.

"The gall of it all," she announced, angrily.

He opened his eyes and found her frown-nodding and biting her lip.

"Val, you're right. You're like oh so right."

"Huh?"

"And I *do* fight for every cause but my own. Yes, I've gotta raise the roof. Absolutely. I'm going to face these people. The hell with being pushed around. I'm going to bitch and fuss."

"Oh, great. Right this minute?"

"I'm sorry, baby, but I have to. I feel so anxious, I could die. You and me, you know, like swell but later."

When she tried to get up he held her. "But pumpkin..."

"You talked me into it," she snapped. "Like don't stop me now. *Please.* I've wasted too much time already. I've got to go."

"All right, all right. Just hold my sword so I can fall on it."

"Hardy, har." She stood up and bounced down again. "Hey, your eye *is* bad. All red, ech. I hit you pretty hard, looks like."

She was out of the room and back again with a bottle of witch hazel. He saw from her mood that she was beyond reach, her fear and resolve mounting now that she had re-entered the quick, cold world.

"Bathe your eye with this," she instructed him, avoiding the grab he made for her leg.

Leaving him stranded on the couch, alone with the cats, she hurried off to dress. He got up (when he was able) and found the bourbon. He was mad at mankind and all its foolishness and at himself, as well, for remaining neutral.

"You want me to go with you?" he called out, dropping an ice cube into his drink.

"I'd feel better doing this bit alone. But thanks."

"Do you know how to get hold of this guy? This producer?"

"Do I what? *Yes.*"

Slumped on the couch, with the bottle and the glass, he wondered if there was some way he could put her at ease. He rose and approached the component parts of the hi-fi set to examine a stack of records. He dismissed piddling show tunes, raging symphonies, pompous oratorios and chose instead the tranquillity of a Bach Partita. Back on the couch, with the cats and the music and the liquor and the futility, he waited.

She appeared two drinks later looking more sublime than he had ever seen her. In a form-fitting, high-necked white dress to off-set her suntanned skin, she stood before him, her face vivid with eye magic, lean with loveliness and fraught with doubt.

"Noo?"

"I bid eight thousand drachmas."

"Thank you, dear. You always were a big spender."

She vanished to reappear again with a white pocketbook on her arm and a pair of gloves, hand held. There was now a splash of red ribbon around her neck to match her shoes.

"I'm frightened," she told him from the center of the room above a clamor of Bach.

"Now when you get there, don't beg him. Be indignant, controlled and merciful."

"And sick to my stomach."

"Come on. You look terrific, for crysake, and you'll *be* terrific. After seeing you, I swear, he'll strangle his wife."

"He'd better or I will."

"That's the spirit. Be triumphant."

"Oh, Valitchska." And she sat beside him amid a deluge of perfume. "Will you wait for me? I don't want to come back to an empty pad. I'm terrified. Do you have anything to do this afternoon? Stay here. Please?"

"I'll be here, baby. I'll be waiting to strip off that dress and all you're wearing under it and..."

"There's not *that* much under it," she confessed, seductively.

"And I'll ravish you like some ancient warrior of old."

"Ha. Redundant. Ancient and old. Got ya."

"Isn't that what sex is, after all? A regal redundancy, and endless who-ha with a bit of onomatopoeia thrown in."

"Sir, you are a great raunch in our time." She touched his cheek. "Stay here. Huh? Until I get back?"

"Yes, go. Will you *go*?" And she was gone, her haughty heels receding along the cold tiled hall, fading into the sound of softly poured bourbon and a saraband from Bach.

He was alone to do as he wished, to pry, to make free with her secret things, to smile roguishly at himself in the mirror. He moved about with no idea of what he was after except perhaps to exploit his sense of freedom and to toy with the gift of her trust. He spied a cat curled in the canvas chair. "*I hate cats,*" he announced. "*Now it can be told.*" At the kitchen door, holding bottle and glass, he re-examined photogenic Tanya in a 2 ¼ × 2 ¼ contact print which showed her nearly popping out of the top of her dress while beaming unflatteringly into a head-on flash, with Jerry Lester and Joey Adams crowding close and gagging it up. "*And I hate show business,*" he pontificated, jiggling his ice. "*Yah.*"

Her bedroom was as still as a tomb, and he sat on the bed and thought *Oh, mighty God, please give her this job back. Don't let her end up beaten.* He sipped his drink and shut his guilt away in the corner of his mind where it waited like an unfinished tray of chocolates for him to return. Fatigue pressed upon him like the weight of the sea, and he thought of all the studio business he must attend to and the lawyer he would have to hunt up. "The hell with it," he said. And he continued with his vigil and his drink. *Give her this job back. Give her this one thing.* And he went on doing nothing.

Someone marched across the ceiling. Then silence. A pleasant shift of air inflated the drapes. He sat upright on the bed and drank, eyes closed, trying to evoke tranquillity, and then the hiccups began. He pounded his chest, held his breath, did all manner of things, but the enemy only held its fire until all was still again. He struggled with this for a while like a world-weary Bacchus until the telephone startled him. He sprang to his feet and strode away from it to the far wall. "I will not answer it. Go away. Die." It rang again and he marched back, leaned over and shouted at its dark plastic soul. "And I hate phones, too. *I hate them.*" It stopped. The hiccups were gone as well. *Give her this one thing, goddamn it.* "Goddamn it."

Then Honey plunked herself into the lap of his mind, and the box of guilt in the corner burst open. Val took up the phone and dialed her number. He hung up at once, heavy with despair. Good grief, had he forgotten Honey as easily as that? He couldn't attend to this over the phone; he would have to see her in person despite what he had promised Tanya. He got up, finished dressing, and left.

AFTER he pounded repeatedly on her plywood door, she finally, slowly, opened it and, looking out with sleepy eyes, saw him and smiled. Stepping in, he eyed the terrain of twisted sheets, a pummeled pillow and a number of undergarments lying here and there which he discreetly ignored. Her room, obviously not cleaned in months and with layers of dust everywhere, struck him as a place of decay and contamination. The photo facades of show business personalities were still there on the wall where he had seen them once before. A few new ones had been added: women, lovely in low-cut gowns or brief Bikinis and men, all handsome, with dark, carefully combed hair. As for Honey, she was dressed in the same sweater and skirt she had worn on the field trip, and he guessed that after coming home she had gone right to sleep without taking them off.

"Hello. I've come to see how you are after such a rough day."

"That's kind of you," she said. "You are a very kind person."

"Doesn't seem to me that I've been very kind to anyone of late."

"Maybe that's why you're being so good now to me," she said sweetly.

This unexpected bit of analysis caught him off guard. "Well, it's too early in the morning to investigate motives," he concluded, suspecting that, more likely, it was too late in the day.

He saw today's *Daily News* lying on the coffee table; the headlines said: REDS REQUEST HIGH LEVEL TALKS and the photograph showed a despondent schoolteacher jumping from a building ledge.

"So you've read the paper," he remarked, sitting on her bed.

"Nope, just bought it only. In fact, Mr. DeVore bought it for me along with his morning *Tribune*. He said to me, it was a pleasure to meet you, my dear. Then he put me in a cab and sent me home. He's nice, he really is."

"To blondes, maybe."

"Well, *I'm* a blonde," she explained, missing his point.

"Listen, there's a story in today's paper that I think you should read."

"There is?"

"It's about the field trip."

"Really?" Her interest became enormous.

"I'm afraid it's not too ..."

"Ou, let's see." And she dumped herself beside him, and together they opened to page four.

Photo Fans Fined For Using A Long, Wrong Exposure

Salemville, Aug. 26 (AP)—A farmer who turned out to pasture two beautiful models to serve as subjects for a group of 19 photographers, promised the sheriff yesterday that in the future he will allow only four-legged females to frolic in the fields off Tuckabunkwac Road, Salemville.

Esra Willis, 38, made that statement in the spirit of sad repentance. After he had put the damsels in his favorite dell, he found that many of the photographers were not equipped with cameras. The eyes had it.

EVERYBODY FINED $5

The 19 photographers paid disorderly conduct fines of $5 each to Justice of the Peace Seth Alden in nearby Southboro Town Hall.

The models, both from New York, were assessed the same amount. Described as a principal was Valentine De Franco, 30, of 58 West 44th Street, who was the one, the sheriff said, who arranged for the increase in Catskill County's scenic wonders. De Franco was paroled with Willis pending a hearing Sept. 9th. They were charged with causing others to expose themselves lewdly.

The damsels were cavorting in the altogether to an occasional camera click and many appreciative "ohs" and "ahs" Sunday afternoon when Sheriff Mike Woodrow moved in from behind shrubbery with his shocked troops. Not a single person escaped the field.

By early morning yesterday the arraignment of the prisoners was complete and the models were allowed to go home. They were: Tanya Lando, 28, of 87 West 49th Street, and Honey Bee, 20, of 17½ W. 16th St.

The raid was ordered by District Attorney Giles Keith as the result of an investigation of a recent ad in an afternoon newspaper plugging a photographer's excursion to Catskill County. "Many beautiful models," the ad promised.

Detective Benjamin Reno had the hardship of posing as one of the photographers after traveling with the field trip from their starting point in New York City to their destination at the Willis Farm.

District Attorney Keith indicated that this wasn't the first such affair on Willis' farm.

"There were no complaints from strangers," Keith said, "but people passing on Tuckabunkwac Road could see what was going on."

De Franco explained that the photos were taken for artistic reasons, that some were entered in national exhibitions. The sheriff said the exhibitions were taking place right there.

He ought to know.

"They always spell my name wrong," Honey complained. "Even when I warn them about it. It's so annoying."

"Jesus Christ, Ben Reno," he mumbled, wanting to smash through the flimsiness of the news story as he could the paper on which it was printed.

"I must buy up a dozen copies," she told him, "and mail clippings to agents and producers. I'm almost famous. I really am."

"You don't look too happy," she added. "Don't tell me they spelt *your* name wrong, too?"

"No, it's correct, as luck would have it."

"You look pale, you really do. Is something wrong?"

He examined her childlike face as if for the first time. "You really have no idea what's wrong? Could that be?"

"Don't you feel well?"

"The story about us in this rag," he asked, sarcastically, "does it give you perhaps a hint?"

"Don't you like what they said about you? Is that it? Well, maybe the other papers have better stories. Let's buy them and see."

Shutting his eyes for a moment: "Good grief."

"What?"

"I had forgotten about the other papers. I really must be in a state of shock."

"About what?" she asked, pleasantly, trying to be of help.

"Well," he said, getting to his feet, "I can see it hasn't touched you one bit. Look, I have to be going."

She begged to make him something to eat and when he rejected this, something to drink.

"Please stay, oh, please," she asked. Seated on the couch, hands folded in her lap, she was all apprehension and longing. "Pretty please?"

He permitted her to bring him water and allotted himself ten minutes and no more by his watch. He sat on the hard wooden chair without using the backrest and looked (he suspected) perfectly absurd. Well, the world outside could damn well wait. They would have their chance at him soon enough.

She returned with a teacup of all things (no saucer), and though she now looked as pure as sweet cream and, for all he knew, doomed to die at ninety-nine, the sight of that cup in both her hands and the cheerful acceptance of the poverty of her life made her seem to him utterly pitiful.

To reach the cupboard, she had borrowed his chair to stand on so that now the only place for him to sit was beside her on the bed. To retrieve the chair or to remain on his feet would be an obvious demonstration of platonic feelings, especially now that she was patting the mattress beside her. His first thought, after sitting down, was of Tanya, and spotting the dust-covered phone on the floor he asked permission to use it. He wanted to make certain that she had not as yet returned home.

"It takes incoming calls, only," Honey admitted almost proudly. "When you don't pay your bills, the phone company screws you in slow stages. I kind of like that, don't you?"

"Hey, you must have fallen on hard times."

"Oh, no. Just short of money. For the moment, that is. MGM still owes me a check for a small part I did in that Mickey Rooney movie. They really do. And my agent wants me to go on the road again, which I'm considering."

"On the road?"

"A road company. But I did that before, twice, and I kind of, you know, hate the traveling. I was in *Damn Yankees* and then *West Side Story*, but when it comes to the road I think I've had it. Do you want some more water? On the house?"

"Thanks, no. I didn't realize you had been m such big shows."

"Yup. Sure you don't want some eggs or anything?"

"No, no thanks."

"O.K. Just speak up if you change your mind."

"Sure."

"O.K."

Silence cluttered the room like dust.

"So," said Honey, "aren't you glad to be rid of all those policemen and everything up there in the woods? I sure am."

"I'm hardly rid of them. I've got to go back there in a month. Got to get a lawyer and go back and defend myself."

"Against what?"

"Procuring women for indecent exposure. Or some such thing."

"Well, you didn't procure me, I'll tell 'em. Anyway, I think it's awful what they're doing to you. Can I help at all?"

"Know any good lawyers?"

"No, I don't. Don't you? Oh, I hope you get one, I really do."

"Thanks," he said rather perfunctorily. "Say, let me use your bathroom, huh?" And without waiting for her reply, he headed in that direction.

The door stayed shut only with the help of a towel. Tacked up on the inside were two poems by Robert Frost that had been torn carelessly from a magazine. A battery of bottles lined the wall below a street map of Manhattan that looked like an insect floor plan for a piece of driftwood. Both white hand towels and the white sink were filthy. A mysterious telephone number was Scotch-taped to a streaked mirror in which Val appeared disappointingly, unchangeably himself. The long night, it seemed, had altered him not at all. Also torn from a magazine was a professional glamour photo of a new and improved Honey Bea, half-naked and squatting beside a swimming pool in beltless dungarees looking indolent and earthy with her head back, eyes shut, suckling the sun. Next to this was an amateur snapshot taken some years ago of her with brown hair, standing happily on a tenement stoop in a polka-dot apron, holding a Dixie cup and offering ice cream to the camera on a tiny wooden spoon. As he lifted the toilet seat, he noticed on the cluttered hamper a blue plastic compact which he recognized as a diaphragm case. Had she any secrets at all, he wondered? And as he relieved himself into the bowl, he grinned at having found someone who was not only immune to scandal but who actually embraced it.

How would they fare? he wondered—two women, a farmer and himself. Had he not meddled, had he only maintained his typical indifference, perhaps none of this would have happened. The irony, it seemed to him, was that the immoralist had stood up out of character and rocked the boat. As a result they had all suffered a loss. Yet, certainly, it was better to have made the fight. But who on earth enters every battle that confronts him? Shouldn't a man stand clear of the wrong ones? Yet which *are* the wrong ones? And who should do the fighting? He looked in the mirror for the answer, and all he saw was himself.

After washing his hands, the sight of a filthy towel made him look for another. He drew aside the shower curtain and once again saw the crib standing empty in the tub. Snapping his wet hands a few times as a last resort, he went out to settle once and for all this business of the baby. She was kneeling on the bed securing the top left corner of the Elizabeth Taylor photograph which had come loose. In her other hand she held a cigarette.

"What's a single girl like you doing with a crib?" Suspecting that he'd get no further this time than before, he added: "And don't tell me you sleep in it?"

"A single girl like me isn't doing anything with it. I'm holding the thing for a friend."

She bounced with lurching breasts into a sitting position.

"Honey, dear."

She looked up at him.

"Come on now," he said. "Straight from the shoulder."

She was busy biting a hangnail, and he thought of Tanya for some reason, and then he wanted nothing more than to hurry back to her apartment.

"Belongs to a friend," she mused.

"Belongs to a friend, huh?"

"To a friend."

Moving toward the door, he thought: why on earth am I even bothering with this? But she stopped him.

"Don't go yet. There's something I want to ask you or rather I'd like you to ask your lawyer for me. It's one of those problems you need a lawyer for, and since you're going to hire one anyway we might as well both make use of him, don't you think? It's not about me, actually, it's about her. But I figured it makes no difference to a lawyer, right? Anyway, her name is Aida."

"Who's is?"

"This girl I want to talk to you about. The girl who owns the crib. I met her in an orphanage. I was an orphan, did you know that? I had a life like Marilyn Monroe. In fact, I was once in the same orphanage as she was in. At different times of course. My father was a member of the Lincoln Brigade in Spain. He was shot a few hours before the armistice. Machine-gun bullet in the temple. My mother was given life imprisonment some years later for killing an unfaithful lover. We were living in Berkeley at the time, and she ran him down with his own car. I was four at the time and sitting in the back seat. I remember she said to me: 'Now we're going to play a new game. It's called scaring Uncle Henry. You watch Mommie drive fast and scare Uncle Henry.' She was a real pisser, my mother. She didn't give a shit about nobody. She used to say to me: 'Honey, the secret of life for a dame is to walk softly with a man who's got a big stick.'"

He didn't know whether to believe this gruesome story, though she related it as if it were a pleasantry plucked from childhood. Her hitherto soft passivity had been replaced, however, with a surprising straightforwardness. Her face looked as innocent as ever, but while he was out of the room something had changed.

"I don't know why I'm talking on and on like this. It's Aida I want to tell you about."

"Well, perhaps some other time," he said, thinking of Tanya.

"My friend is in a fix, you see. I've been buddies with her for so many years I really would like to help her. 'cause she was arrested illegally, she really was."

"Who isn't, these days?"

"Oh, my friend *is* innocent. She really *is*."

She dug at a cuticle with meticulous concern.

"This guy she knew actually raped her," Honey continued, blowing at her thumbnail, comparing it with its twin. "He just forced himself on her. No fuckin' finesse or nothin'."

"It sounds absorbing."

"When he made her submit and all, do you know what he did then? You won't believe me, but what he does is arrest her for being a prostitute. How's that for a pair of balls? I really think it's terrible."

He nodded slowly and stared at her.

"It's a terrible thing for a cop to do," she said, "don't you think?"

"Yes, it is."

"I don't want you to think my friend is promiscuous or anything like that. She owns a diaphragm, sure. But I know lots of girls who sleep around and don't own one. That's cause they don't want to look on themselves as pros. They don't want to lose their amateur standing. My friend wears one whenever she goes to a party. Oh, don't get the wrong idea. She only sleeps with people she likes. But at a party she almost always meets at least one or two people she likes."

"My friend doesn't hate many people," she added, looking up at Val.

"I'm sure she doesn't."

"But she sure hates this what'shisname Fowler. Boy, does she. He used a strap on her. Can you imagine? He just took off his belt and..."

"Fowler?"

"Yeh, he looked like Dean...what'shisname? The Secretary of State."

"Acheson?"

She nodded, the side of her face twitching several times.

"You said..." He stopped. The story was becoming too detailed to be just one more of her many fictions. "You said he used a strap?"

"He sure did."

"Do you know why she was arrested?"

"Beats me. I think that..."

"What was her full name? Aida what?"

"Aida Ginzburg. She got red hair and a pair of gams like nobody's business and she..."

"But why was she arrested? Why did he pick *her* out?"

She thought for a minute. "I give up."

He paced in silence glancing at her with uncomfortable concern. Heavy pairs of feet assaulted the stairs in a descent to the workaday world. A torn flap in her window shade allowed a blot of light on the wall. He had forgotten all about the outside world. Aida and Miss Honey Bea, he knew, were one and the same. She was like one of those people who, to cover their shame, would solicit the advice of a lawyer on behalf of a fictitious someone else. Perhaps doctors and analysts came up against the same phenomenon. At any rate he wouldn't embarrass her if he could help it. If she felt guilty about something, God knows, so did he. That was the hidden value of guilt. It really is common property after all.

"Well, he must have caused her a lot of grief," he said. How foolish that sounded.

"A lot of grief?" she almost shouted, sitting up suddenly, her face twitching. She lifted and dropped her arms like dolls. "You don't know the half of it. Not *this* much of it." And she squinted at him through her barely separated thumb and index finger. "You really don't."

"I love my friend Aida," she explained. "But what she lost is irrefutable."

"Irreplaceable."

"Something like that. They put her in a woman's house of detention, and that's no Greenwich Village coffee shop, I can tell you. You can bet your sweet ass it ain't." The side of her face kept twitching like a heartbeat. "She was a junkie, she was, Aida. And she puked her guts out in cold turkey. You ever been a junkie?"

"No, not really."

Perhaps, he decided, it was fiction after all.

"She died in that prison."

"What?"

"She. Died. In that. Prison. Cha cha cha."

"What are you saying?"

"When she got out she was like a dead person."

"Oh, for crysake."

"You should have seen her. It was pitiful. You know why it was pitiful?" She was standing, blinking through her tears. "Because she had a baby, that's why it was pitiful. She. Was. A. Mother," Honey said in slow emphasis as she approached him. "Baby's name, Jacqueline. After the president's wife. Jacqueline. The loveliest little wiggly-piggly. All fingers and toes." Tears seemed to be streaming all over Honey's face. "So frail. She was so lovely, so very…"

Val felt a constriction across his chest. "Afterward, surely, she got her child back. Surely…"

The girl lowered herself onto the floor, sat Indian-style and said: "Fuck."

He knelt with a sharply cracking knee and removed her hands from her face. Honey shook her head violently as though she were trying to free it from her shoulders. Then, with the flat of her hand, she wiped one cheek clean as Val said:

"You mean they didn't, she didn't get her…"

"Shedidnot, shedidnot, shedidnot," *was the strident reply.*

"Good grief."

"Some shitty judge. Took her baby away. By law."

"Good grief."

"Took her far, far away," she added wistfully and with a hiccup.

He found her tears contagious. Gripping her shoulders, he managed to get her to her feet and over to the bed whose sheets now seemed twisted with their joint despair. They collapsed together and, still clutching her shoulders, he made a promise. He made it to her, to himself, to the whole arid, pitiful room.

"All right. We'll get her back. We'll try to get Jacqueline back. I promise you. Do you hear me? Now, what I want is information. All the information you can give. So start now. Do you hear me?"

She smiled. "How much sympathy you have, you really have. I feel like I'm talking to a father."

"Wonderful. Now tell me about Jacqueline."

"Such a beautiful baby."

"Yes, I know."

"Want some water?" she asked, pointing to his empty cup. "It's on the house."

"Who is the mother of this baby?"

"I told you."

"You're the mother, aren't you? It's *you*. They took her away from *you*, didn't they?"

"Please don't hold my shoulder."

He shook her slightly. "You're the mother, aren't you? No need to be ashamed."

"Please." And she tried to free herself, her cheek twitching.

He shook her more forcefully, a perverse fear beginning to gnaw at him.

"Look, I've got to know. We can't just sit and do nothing, for crysake. Do you think getting your name in the paper this way is going to *help* regain your child?"

The surprised jump her eyes took in meeting his told him he had hit a nerve. Incredibly, this was the one thing she hadn't thought of. He could sense something within her fleeing from what he had just said. A little girl's look of pain dug into the corners of her face.

"Jacqueline is your daughter, isn't it? Isn't she? She's yours, damn it. Right? Isn't she?"

Honey remained immobile, her vacant stare fixed on his face. He called her name. He shook her and called her name. She freed herself and moved closer, one hand on his knee, the other falling on his thigh. Quickly he took her by the shoulders again and held her off.

"Don't do that," he said.

She frowned and hit at his hand with a weak, peaceful slap slap slap.

Ominously, as though dealing with a child: "I want you to *listen* to me."

"Huh?" she replied, startled, wide-eyed.

"Whose child is she? Come on now."

"Huh?"

"What's wrong with you?"

She gave him a smile of total surrender. "Poppie doesn't love me," she said, touching his knee again, trying to edge forward.

"Look," he grumbled with disgust, "stop your goddamn vamping. Do you hear me?"

"Poppie gonna put Honey to bed."

"Stop it, will you."

Smiling, she reached out and pinched his lips together. He freed himself and she plucked away his ball-point pen. He returned it to his shirt pocket and she reached for his mouth again, all the while beaming beatifically.

"What the hell are you doing?"

She frowned as though deeply hurt.

"Stop it now, goddamn it."

She pouted, then lifted her skirt to bury her face, exposing herself completely. Val made her drop her hands and found her grinning. Something in her face chilled him.

"Poppie," she said. "Poppie, I hungwe."

"Are you playing games?"

She shook her head violently up and down, then side to side. She giggled.

"What did you call me?" he asked. "What's my name?"

"Poppie."

"No."

"Yes."

"What's *your* name?"

"Honey. Beatrice. Nickle. Son."

Val surveyed her face with terror. "Age?"

She drew in a long breath. "Four."

"How old?"

"Howald. Can I play with Howald? Can I?"

He shook her like a rag doll until her head snapped about on her shoulders. "How *old* are you?"

"*Four*," she shouted back. "Inky dink a bottle of ink. Cork fell out and you stink."

"You're not four. You're *lying*."

"I want my mommie."

"What's your mommie's name?"

"Mommie."

"Yes, what's her name?"

"You stink."

"What *city* do you live in?"

"I live in."

"Yes? Where?"

"Detwoit."

"Jesus God."

"Poppie. Hold me, Poppie."

"Jesus God."

The plane crawled on the underside of the sky like an insect that Val glimpsed without thought. A yellow sanitation truck moved down the avenue, lashing the street with its spray and sending a diaphanous curtain of vapor against his squinting face. Keeping ahead of the truck, he marched to a glass-enclosed phone booth that stood where a couple of torn and gutted tenement buildings were in the process of being razed. Though work had stopped for the day, one structure had been completely leveled to a hill of rubble with only an empty ground-floor window frame remaining. This left exposed an entire naked wall with four floors of color schemes that had once been part of the living rooms and bedrooms of now vanished families; large, peeling rectangles of mocha and blue on one level and shit green and dull gray on another with a top floor room-patch of ugly intricate wallpaper that clashed with all the rest. A neat zigzag scar was left by the missing stairway where it rose with ghostly precision through the abstract beauty.

Val rolled shut the door of the booth gazing through the glass at the colors of the disassembled building. He dropped the coin into the slot, still staring at the wall and feeling an odd pleasure at its beauty despite his grief. He dialed once, and as the disk unwound, his view of the street was beclouded with moisture. The truck halted at the corner, its spray turned off, the nozzles dripping. A voice said to him:

"Operator. May I help you, please?"

"The nearest precinct, please."

"Is this a business or an emergency call?" asked a young woman with the Bronx in her voice.

"Emergency."

"Yes, surely," she replied, with excitement. "One moment, sir."

He heard her dialing as he watched the moisture evaporate from the glass. A phone book had been wrenched from its chain and was missing. An empty bottle of Calverts stood in the corner.

A tiny sticker had been placed crookedly on the door. PEACE IS THE ONLY SHELTER.

He heard a ringing at the other end which ended abruptly. Then a stilted, almost mechanical voice informed him that:

"The number ah-you have dialed is not a working number."

The operator, with her frightened, embarrassed, refreshing voice jumped back into his ear. "Oh, I'm terribly sorry, sir. One moment please, sir. One moment."

He heard dialing once more and realized that the booth smelled faintly of urine. The ringing continued seven times before a man's voice, dismal with fatigue and disinterest, said: "Yeh?"

"Police department?"

"Yeh."

"A girl in a room on Sixteen Street has undergone some kind of psychotic collapse. Might be temporary. Might be permanent."

"*One* minute."

Val waited for what seemed like several.

"Yeh, gohead."

He gave the information.

"Yeh, all right and who are you?"

He gave his name and address.

"Youwit dis girl now?"

"No, her phone doesn't work. I'm in a booth."

"You goin' back there?"

"No, I've got someone else now to worry about. Listen, take care of her will ya? Good care of her, huh? She means a lot to me."

"We'll send someone right over."

"Christ, send an ambulance too. That's what she needs."

"Is she that sick?"

"Yes, damn it, yes. Will she end up in Bellevue?"

"She will if we send an ambulance."

"Then send one."

"Will do."

"O.K. Take care of her. I've got to run." And he hung up. Bellevue, he thought. Well, it's better than jail. Call there tomorrow.

Be able to tell how she is. She's unfit now for anything. To be a mother, impossible. He rubbed his hand over his eyes. He waited a moment watching the multicolored wall, studying its patterns. He dialed again and waited.

Then, by itself and for no apparent reason, the top quarter of the wall, in a kind of silent dream sequence, quivered a bit and leaned out from the building, the rectangle of ugly wallpaper and a rectangle of sickly yellow both tilting away from their natural upright position until in two great halves they dropped four flights in a frightening suspension of the time it took to thunder into a hill of rubble below with an earth-quivering concussion. Up rose a great brown cloud of dust like a slow towering wave, and Val stiffened while the wave engulfed the glass booth leaving him standing inside a dim brown upright coffin with nothing around him, neither sky nor street, just earthbound darkness and fear. Following a few haunting refractions of light, the cloud parted to reveal a section of the road and a squinting, coughing grocery clerk holding a six-pack of beer. Finally, where the top of the wall had been, Val glimpsed the sky, and at that moment, as the city returned, a voice came to him over the phone.

"Miss Honey Bea?" he asked.

There was no answer.

"Is this Honey?"

There was no answer.

"Who is this, please?"

"Honey. Beatrice. Nickle. Son."

He could think of nothing to say. Finally: "Stay where you are. Just stay where you are."

"Poppie? Is that you, Poppie?"

"Yes, sweetie. Just stay where you are. Someone will be there soon."

"Poppie?"

"Yes, baby?"

"I'm unhappy."

"I know. I know. Just stay there. Everything will be all right."

"Poppie?"

"Yes, baby."

Silence.

"Yes, baby?"

"I love you, Poppie."

Though Val had begun to sweat in the booth, he didn't open the door. He sat for several minutes and did nothing; then he remembered Tanya. When he dropped another dime into the box, it didn't fall with its familiar double chime, and the phone remained dead. He pounded with his fist, jiggled the carriage, pounded some more. It was no good. Ramming the receiver down, he marched half a block to a dark cavernous bar empty of business. He entered and became blind. Waiting for change of fifty cents gave him time to perceive the dimensions of the room. An ex-boxer in a white apron returned with the coins jiggling in his fist. The *Daily News* was opened on the bar, and the man returned to it with open-mouthed scrutiny. He was on page three, Val noticed, reading about a tenement fire on the East Side.

A rubber fan turned on as soon as he closed the door to the booth at the back of the bar. The overhead light, however, was out. Val lit a match to dial the number he wanted, but the phone rang before he could touch it, the noise was like a blow to every nerve in his body. The shock even halted his breath.

"Yes?"

"Pardon me. Is Hyman Lowe there, please?"

"The place is empty," he growled and hung up.

He dialed Tanya's number and discovered with relief that she hadn't returned yet. For a few minutes more he sat in the darkness, then stood up and rattled the door open. He waited with one foot on the rail, and finally the bartender condescended to look at him. He ordered a double Jack Daniels and was left staring at the reverse newspaper. The drink was placed before him, and he stood watching the bartender read his way slowly from page three to page six. There was not a shift in the man's expression. Swallowing the last of the whiskey, Val walked out into the ocean of August light, feeling no better.

A WAKE. Eyes upon the ceiling and Other Cat upon his narrow chest. The light had changed and faded, deceiving him as once his mother had deceived him, persuading little Val, aged five, to nap at noon with a promise to wake him at one thirty—and then she left him lying there like a fool until four.

He sat up, tossing the animal rudely off the bed. Laden and cranky, he rubbed his face in his hands and checked his watch. It had died at noon. Across the room, her churning clock claimed seven. The light from the window hinted it was later still. And where the hell was she? Why hadn't she come back? And then all at once there she was stretched out beside him unnoticed and asleep. The blue sheet was bunched at her waist leaving her back and shoulders bare and her face buried.

Her stillness was frightening, for it was not like her to return with the news of her reinstatement without waking him at once and babbling her joy. Her pretty white dress had been tossed into a chair. He spotted an empty glass on the dresser. Had she stood there drinking whiskey and watching him sleep? And he recalled her once saying that she never drank alone. He turned on the radio by the bed to find his exact position in time and to give himself something to do.

"This is your city station, WNYC, where eight and a half million people live in peace and harmony and enoy the benefits of democracy."

He snapped it off. *Zugzwang.* If he remained where he was here in bed forever, he would be all right. If he moved in time, forward or back, he was ruined. So he lay still, sensing a ticking of clocks and hoping that mankind was proceeding on its way without him.

The phone rang.

Tanya rose as though she had never been asleep, reaching across his brow to drop a heavy hand upon the receiver. The wire was pulled across his chest as she said:

"Yes? ... This is she speaking ... Who?"

Her voice was heavy with primeval numbness.

"Who? ... Ben?" She frowned.

Val grabbed her arm and with a vengeful whisper, cried: "Reno."

She looked at her lover and blinked: "Huh?" as though trying to project her voice into the back row, top balcony.

"Say hello," he hissed, barely audible.

"Huh?"

"Say. Hello."

"Hello," she said to Val, the receiver in her lap. He picked it up and held it to her face. "Again."

"Hello," she said, into the phone.

"How are you?" Val prompted her.

"How are you?" she repeated.

"Tell him to hold on."

"Hold on for a sec," she said, and he jammed his hand over the mouthpiece.

"Listen, you idiot, it's him. He wants to see you. Make a date with you. Understand? Get him up here. I don't care what you say. Get him up here. I've got a plan. You're an actress. Act. Go."

He handed the phone to her and she blinked, shook her head to clear it and began to speak.

"Yes, I'm alone ... No, that was a neighbor, a girl who dropped in to borrow something ... What? I'm fine, how are you? ... That's nice." And she frowned at Val as though to say: why in God's name am I even speaking to this putz?

With convincing gesticulations, he conveyed the idea that if she didn't continue he would break her arm, and so she stayed with it chatting pleasantly about one thing and another with a hardened and ironic gaiety. Finally it happened: "Well, yes, I am free, as a matter of fact ... Well, could you come up here? We could have a few drinks and talk. We could have a late dinner, you know ... Eight? ... On ze button. I'll be ready ... O.K. Take it easy. See ya. Bye now." And she hung up as if the phone were the knife of a guillotine.

"Would you mind telling me why I had to make nice to that jerk-off?" Then, remembering, she clamped her hand to her mouth.

"So it comes back to you?" he asked.

She nodded quickly, the hand still at her mouth.

"You bought the paper when you went out?"

She nodded.

"And read the story in all its ghastly..."

She nodded again.

"And you noticed the name Ben Reno."

"I couldn't believe it."

"Reno who drove all the way up there with us and all the way back with us."

"With that creepy smile yet."

"Who even paid five bucks to the judge along with everyone else. That I can't figure."

"He thought he had me lined up for a quick killing. Guess he didn't want me to know he was like a regular Judas in disguise. Say, how'd *you* know he was one of the cops?"

"When you were gone, I popped out myself. Just for a minute."

"For the paper?"

"For the paper."

"And you came right back?"

"Came right back."

"Then I'm not angry."

Val slowly brushed some hair from his face and spent a moment in memory.

"Well, how did he sound?"

"Who?" she asked.

"Reno."

"Almost human you might say."

"Do you think he'll show?"

"Baby, when I tell 'em to drop up for drinks. They. Drop up. For drinks."

"I hope so."

"But what's the bit? Why are we being so friendly?"

"You're going to be friendlier still. You're going to put on the performance of your life when he gets here. The real come-on."

"Oh, come *on.*"

"Hero worship for the authority figure. That bit."

"You're out of your ... My God, you're out of your mind. When he gets here I'm cutting his ping-pongs off, festaysht?"

"Wrong again. He's going to get you on the couch and futs around a bit. He's going to be all hands and you're going to let 'im."

"*Val!* What are you talking about?"

"And just when things look promising. Enter Val in Richard the Third costume."

"Wha?"

"With camera in hand. From the closet."

"Are you serious?"

"What do you think? Of course I'm serious."

"So we get the photograph. Then what?"

"I don't know exactly. We talk. The three of us talk. Son of a bitch, if he's got a wife and kids, we'll have something to talk about. It certainly can't help a guy having a photo floating around showing him trying to slip the eel to some luscious babe, especially when he just arrested her for reasons of morality. Anyway, when it comes to going to court again, I'd like to have *something* to bargain with."

"Will it work, the plan?"

"Hell, who knows? But it's worth a try. Why? You want to forget it?"

"I didn't say anything."

"You willing, yes or no?"

"I'm willing, yes and no."

"You'll do it?"

"Tsh, yes I'll do it."

"Tough life, huh? Say, what happened this afternoon? When you went and talked to ..."

"Oh! Oh! Oh! I saw a drunk today and it reminded me of a very funny thing I once saw. I never told you. It was last fall and I was in the subway and in comes this young girl and her date. A little Miss

Virgin type, sixteen at least, and her gung ho, all-collegiate boy beau. And they sit down beside this drunk schlub sprawled out like someone hit him with a hammer. Only this particular drunk had an extra added attraction. Like his fly was wide open. Realismo, you know? And next to him are sitting pristine pure these two fresh grade A types. Like they've got a date to go to the Cloisters and hum hymns. Except she has this long diaphanous scarf around her neck which, when she sits down, kinda partly drops over his open fly. Get the scene? So then Mr. Dead-Drunk sort of emerges from his deep what'sits there and quite properly zips up his fly, scarf and all. At that moment, Miss Lily White and Master Crew Cut both notice their predicament. Now, moral problem. Like what do you do? Abandon the scarf? You know, write it off to travel expenses. Or do you sort of have a tug of fly. You and your date against the drunk. Or do you pull the ultrasophisticate bit. Beg pardon, sir, but I do believe I've caught my scarf in your fly. Terribly sorry, what? Wow, like I'm dyin' just watching. What happened? Well, let me put it this way. Somewhere in this city a drunk is walking around with a scarf in his fly."

The electric clock moaned steadily. Val stared at her as she sat upright, holding the sheet to her body and staring in turn at his joyless expression.

"You didn't answer my question," he said, quietly.

"I know."

"About the producer, what did he ..."

"My God. Did he say eight? Reno? It's seven twenty already. I got to get dressed and you got to get your camera."

The crisis touched him like a shock. She was already out of bed and high-stepping into her panties. He approached her with one sleeve still rolled to his elbow and the other unfurled, its French cuff swallowing his hand. As she doubled both hands behind her back to fasten her bra, he took hold of her and said: "This afternoon. What happened?"

"We're late, Val, you've got to ..."

"What happened?"

With a desperate look, she pleaded for a reprieve. On the floor, Other Cat lurched playfully into motion, halted, looked up, paused and sprang with primitive grace onto the mattress. Tanya's rib case felt sparse and smooth to Val's hand. Her eyes seemed darkened with despair.

"O.K.," he said. "Let's get dressed."

"And hurry or you'll be late."

"The studio's five blocks away. Relax. I'll get the Rollei and strobe and be back in ten minutes."

She kissed him as though he had already returned. "I love you. Oh, I love you. I never could figure if you were a good guy or a bad guy, but I love you. Hurry. Be back fast. Please."

Snatching up his tie and jacket he stumbled, cursing, over a cat and was gone, sprinting lightly down the hall. Tanya went off in three directions, straightening up all the rooms at once. She hid the laundry. She made the bed. She spilled the milk and wiped it up. She squeezed herself into her "Freud red" dress, wound on her snake bracelet, gave herself a perfume bath, wobbled into her spiked shoes, stabbed her cheek with a beauty mark and, after turning off all the lights but one and letting Rachmaninoff loose on the hi-fi, she looked at the time, saw it was twenty to eight and gave a sigh of relief.

With that the doorbell groaned like the ten-second buzzer at Madison Square Garden.

"Ah, my hero," she said, and hurried to throw open the door.

"Well, hello," he smiled, displaying his two parted front teeth. "Got here a bit sooner than I thought. Hope you don't mind?"

"YOU'RE like very early, you know?" "Sorry. Seems the old watch has stopped. How are ya?"

"Keeping busy."

"I brought you something."

"Did you, now?"

He held out a pink rose which her slim fingers took by the. stem. Her lungs expanded with the aroma. "*Gracias*," she said, and wondered if his hawk eyes could detect her fright. You're an actress, she reminded herself, so like act.

"Well, can I come in? Or are we ready to leave?"

"Oh, no. Come in. Do come in."

"Sure thing."

Pressing the safety latch, she closed the door and followed him through the foyer, the rose at her side and upside down.

"You're lookin' good, kid, all in red." Turning, he faced her from the center of the room. Then that split-tooth smile.

How would Val know that he was with her? Would he wait in the hall? How would he know when to rush in? Her fears leaped about like animals trapped by fire.

"Guess you'd look O.K. in any color," said he, with that air of unselfconscious crudity which she now saw was not without its charm.

"Won't you sit down?" She pointed to the couch. It was unfortunately just out of sight of the front door.

"Cats and fish. And canaries. You're surrounded by friends, huh?" His camera was on his shoulder again.

"Would you like a drink? There's some bourbon and a little vodka, I think. Or wine. Ouch."

A thorn on the stem had jabbed her finger.

"Bourbon's fine. Dash of water .... O.K. place you have here." As he approached one of the walls, his voice deepened. "Pictures! You with celebrities. I'm impressed."

"As it happens, the people I really have to impress never are." And she marched into the kitchen.

He said something.

"What?"

"*I said,* isn't that always the way."

"*Isn't it,*" she yelled back.

She filled a glass with sink water and speared it angrily with the stem of the rose. Then she turned in his direction and, because the wall stood between them, jabbed upward in the air with the middle finger of her right hand. She made two drinks, added water to one and carried them reluctantly into the living room.

"Long-hair music, huh?" He stooped, drumming two fingers against the fish tank.

Tanya toned down the Rachmaninoff and carried the chiming drinks across to where he stood adjusting his rimless glasses. She found it difficult to look into his face though he stared at her quite openly.

"Their names," she began, trying to talk away her nervousness, "are Fish, Other Fish, Finch and Tuna Finch. Those little ones at the bottom, they're Quemoy and Matsu."

"*You* named them? You're a very clever girl."

"Won't you sit down?"

"The two birds. What's their names?"

"The one who sings is Eileen Herlie. The one who doesn't is Fifth Amendment."

"Ha, ha. Good, very good. Very clever."

She hoisted one end of a stiff and leaden smile. The couch, schmuck, the couch. And she dipped her palm toward the cushion she wished him to occupy. He elevated the drink she had just handed him. "Here's lookin' at ya," he said, and at last he did sit down. Relieved, she, too, sank into the couch, one cushion length away and studied his face as he sipped his drink.

He had the component parts of manhood but none of the accessories. No wit or charm to give some gentle touches to his temperament. He wasn't bald (which never bothered her in men) just balding (which always did). He wasn't casually or even poorly dressed but badly so, in what seemed to her to be the very worst of taste. He wore a crushed, bluish-white seersucker jacket (once part of a suit), black chino trousers and brown shoes. The blue T-shirt of Sunday was missing or covered up now by the addition of a white shirt (purchased this morning for the occasion but with a collar that kept scratching) and a black knit tie (also new). There was, however, something vaguely fascinating about him. She traced it, finally, to his manner of utter directness. Whether bluntly admitting his own shortcomings or bragging freely of what were, to him, his strengths, there was an honesty as well as a crudity to his nature which also revealed, without his knowing it, his enormous lifelong self-doubt.

"You look O.K.," he repeated, making her shiver. "I'm not kidding."

She caught him appraising her legs, and she lurched upward, yanking at the lower end of her dress.

"You read maybe the papers today?" was the way she began.

"Nah, I almost never read 'em. They're all lies. Utter lies. I'm not kidding."

"That's very funny," she replied, solemnly. "That's deeply humorous."

"You just lost me."

"Listen, what were you doing on the field trip yesterday?"

"Having a lark. I'm serious. Getting away from it all."

She stared at him, shaking her drink to make the ice ring. "What line of work you in?"

"Varies. You name it, I've done it. But I'd rather talk about…"

"What work are you doing now? Like right now."

"I've been asked to manage my brother's restaurant in Jersey." He ran his finger along the inside of his collar. "Or I might…"

"Then you're out of a job now, right? Is that it?"

He looked up quickly."Got plenty of money, though. We can paint the town red."

"You know what I think?" She was unable to hold back. "Like I think you're a liar."

"No, I'm not kidding. I really have money."

"You, I'm talking about—you. You're low and vile, the lowest thing going. Like there isn't words for what you are."

His lips parted, joined by a bubble of disbelief.

"What do you have to say to that?" she asked.

"All right, I'll bite. What in hell do you mean?"

Make nice, she reminded herself. Don't get angry. Soon Val will be here.

"Mr. Benjamin Reno," she said, "you were mentioned in the paper today, did you know that? You didn't exactly get top billing, but it wasn't bad for a supporting role. Detective Benjamin Reno, it said. So it appears you had a job all along. Good casting, too, cause you look the part. Like do you ever. You seem so surprised? I'm talking about those stories about the arrest. You're right not to read them, the papers. They lie, all right. You could like hire me for a testimonial."

He tilted his head as an animal does listening to an odd sound. "Mentioned me? Huh? Did they?"

"Ya vold."

Reno slapped the arm of the couch, looked around in exasperation, then punched the place he had slapped. "What can I say?"

"Repeat after me. I am low and vile and nasty and ..."

"Come on. I'm serious and I want you to accept my apologies. Don't look at me like that. Apologies for having been on a job which involved you in a mess. I'm sorry that I had to meet you this way 'cause you're something special. I don't meet types like you, normally. And when I do, they look down on me. Who am I, I'm nothin'? Really. But you didn't look down on me, not even when I got off on the wrong foot with you. The bum luck is I had a job to do. I met you. I was glad. Then things got messy. I'm sorry."

"I'm supposed to be emotionally all choked up now, is that it?"

"O.K. Rub it in. I'm sorry. What can I say?"

"It was a lie, all of it was. No one could see us from the road."

He lifted his whiskey to his lips and stopped. "Well, I don't know anything about that."

"Could we be seen from the road or not?"

"I don't know. I wasn't concerned with that. I'm not kidding."

"We couldn't be, like we could not be seen from the road, friend."

"Look, I know Keith. He doesn't work that way. Arresting people who are innocent. You people have been up there before, I understand. He had received complaints."

Tanya leaned toward him, eyes wide, tapping the cushion with her finger. "The paper says there *were* no complaints, fella. It's in the paper."

"Well, I don't know. Like I said, I wasn't concerned with that."

"You were concerned only with sliming around with the women."

"I liked you, that's the God's truth."

She leaned back, arms folded, glaring. "You and that whole lousy crew up there. I'd like to…"

"You have every right to be angry."

"I am exercising that right, thank you."

"But the fact remains… You see, well, it was left up to Keith to relay the story to the press services. I personally asked him to put in all the names *except* those of the women. You may not believe me but it was only now, from you, that I learned what he had done."

"You're right. I don't believe you."

"Understandable," he admitted, lifting the whiskey to his lips.

Don't get angry, she warned herself. You're getting angry. Then she caught his eyes at her legs again.

"Understandable, he says. Oh, you bastard, I could puke. You and that D.A. That cheap, two-bit potpourri of every politician I've ever listened to. Oh, God, here I go again. Tsh, to hell with it. Yes, that's what he is and you too. Conscienceless bastards. Do I sound bitter? I shouldn't be bitter, should I? Hell, why be a sore loser, huh? Your boss just ruined my life to make his prosper, is all. Like why be bitter."

He looked for a place to put down his glass and finally did so on the arm of the sofa. Instead of bitching, she reminded herself, you should be playing up to him. That was the plan. Reminders were no good, however, for thoughts of Val only made her feel that much more alone. Where the hell was he anyway? Well, up yours, she decided. Never, like *never* rely on a man.

"Look," he said, now leaning toward her. "Why don't we start over again. From scratch. Just you and me, huh?"

"Oh, God, you heartless bastard," she stormed. "You don't care, do you? Not about me or anyone? Do you?" She lifted her glass, found it empty and slammed it down again. "I bet you even..." Eyes shut, a hand over her mouth, she held still while everything firm and reasonable in her world melted in a hot flood of helpless rage. "OhGod... Ohdear." She stood up, walked a few steps and stopped. "Oh, I *do* hate you." Then she bit her lip and held herself as though chilled. She whirled to scream, *get out*, when the sound of the doorbell stung her into silence.

"Who's that?" he asked, uncrossing his legs.

"Stay," Tanya shot back. "I'll get rid of him. Whoever it is."

Rushing to meet her lover with a warning finger held to her lips, she swung open the door to find herself facing a pale, placid youth wearing dark framed glasses and holding a shabby brown briefcase. The rest of the hall was empty except for the smell of fried potatoes.

"Good evening, Mrs. Lando. I've been asked by the parish to speak to every good Catholic in the community. You are Catholic, isn't that right?"

Trying to close the door. "No, thank you."

"May I ask then what denomination you are, Mrs. Lando?" recited the lad with a swift and brazen calm.

"I'm Jewish and busy." Again she tried to close the door.

"You're in luck, Mrs. Lando." He bent over and stood up again having produced a large book from the briefcase. "We are also making available to our good non-Catholic friends this beautiful leather-bound edition of the Jewish Family Bible. Isn't it lovely? Why don't I step in and show it to you? It won't take but a jiffy."

"Seems you have a little something for everybody," she said in amazement, holding her ground at the door.

"Yes, ma'am. We feel that irregardless of a person's..."

"Like what do you offer athiests?" she asked, sarcastically.

"The same thing. The word of the Lord." And his sober, bloodless reply reminded her of the one waiting on the couch.

He opened the book. "Notice the paragraph heading, Mrs. Lando. In this way Scriptural words are as easy to follow as the writing of your favorite columnist."

"I'm sorry. I belong to a rare Hebrew-Christian sect and it's against our religion to even *read* the Bible."

She slammed the door and leaned her brow against it. Why must she always become entangled with the foolish and uncaring? She wanted to kill Val. She wanted to kill all of them. Meanwhile, Rachmaninoff continued as though nothing was amiss in the world. A hand rested on her shoulder and she jumped.

"Sorry, did I startle you? It's a real racket they have, these Bible salesmen. I understand the people they work for make a mint of money. Say, I did frighten you, didn't I?" He reached out to touch her cheek.

"No, get away." And she fled past him into the living room. What was she to do? Her snake bracelet had slid down to her elbow and she tore it off, wondering why the hell she had dressed up for this clown in the first place. Her new shoes were killing anyway and so she marched to her bedroom, stopped, turned in the doorway and ordered him to: "Wait there. I'm not through with you." Then she entered the room and found herself face to face with Val De Franco.

His left arm held the strobe flash from which a wire dangled to a battery box that hung by a thick strap from his left shoulder. Another wire from this box made a sagging spiral bridge to his Rolleiflex which was suspended at his stomach by a long neck strap. At the sight of her, he began bouncing on his heels, his face grimacing and his arms flailing. All she wanted to do was hug him, but he backed away flailing and grimacing while she advanced, arms outstretched, as though his very presence had saved her life. In a burst of pique, he snatched up a lipstick and wrote VAMP HIM in tall letters on the wall. He was underlining it for the seventh fierce time when she slapped at his hand like an outraged mother. He pointed at the message with manic desperation and shoved her toward the living room. When she shook her head with equal desperation, he pointed a stiff arm at the door in a kind of pompous Biblical rage as though disowning his own daughter and ordering her out into the night. She noticed the open window at the fire escape and realized that he had climbed down to her from the roof. He had been there all the while, and she wanted to hug him more than ever. Val, however, now resembled a near-hysterical stage manager silently ordering her back to work and then for some reason she didn't mind at all and smiled and mouthed the words *all right, already.*

An unlikely-looking hussy in a garish dress gaped unbelievably at herself from within the mirror. How was she to get up the fire to vamp someone when she could barely look him in the face? Simple. She thought of all those names in the papers and that one in a lifetime chance that had been taken from her and with these ready weapons she marched back into the living room smiling with all her vengeful heart: a huntress with herself as bait.

But he was gone. She called and ran into the empty kitchen. She reappeared with a moan, ran for the front door and burst into the hall to spot him striding away.

"Hello," she called seductively, "didn't you forget something?" As always when she tried to tantalize, her voice sounded to her disarmingly comic. Yet he stopped, though he said nothing; didn't even turn around. She moved up to him along the wall. "The initiation is over," she whispered. "I was just feeling a bissle hostile. It's all over now, you dig? To get it out of my system, I had to draw a little blood. I have Band Aids inside, O.K.? I'm nothing if not a sporadic hostess."

He looked as hurt as a scolded child. "There's no reason to stay."

"There's *every* reason to stay," she insinuated.

"*Every*... reason?" One eyebrow rose like a flag of combat.

"Well," she added with a fluid look, "at least there's *one* reason."

The eternal table tennis had begun.

"And what reason is that?"

"To have another drink?" She made it into a little girl's cautious question.

"That all?"

"No, man, you can have all the drinks you want." And like a nurse demonstrating her fearlessness in the face of leprosy, she took his arm and led him back.

"Come. If I disappoint you again, I give you strict orders like you should leave in a huff. That is if you can't find a cab. 'cause huffs are expensive. The question is, can fair maiden beguile handsome detective type to have another bourbon on the rocka-roonies? Huh?" They entered her living room together. "You know something? I never realized what a boyish and beguiling detective type you really are. I actually never noticed. Come on, now. Sit! Sit! Goot. Is lovely picture." She vanished and reappeared with refills. He hadn't moved an inch, his camera propped prudently in his lap, his face maintaining a suspicious suspension of belief.

She lounged beside him. "So tell me, you know, like what's new?"

"You're quite humorous."

"Oh, quite. We British types are swingers once you get to know us."

"What made for the big change?" he asked, sipping her liquor again. His eyes never left her, taking in with a steady poker-faced interest her odd, off-the-cuff, summer stock performance.

"Why? Penitence. Like I said. I was cruel to tall detective type because tall detective type was mean to slinky me. Now that all my anger is spent, slinky me and tall detective type can start from like scratch. The truth is that I just love impressive, pseudo-quasi-authority-figure types. Any questions?"

He raised his hand for permission to speak.

"You dere in da front row."

He gave her a slight juvenile smile. "Just one question. Kiss?"

She looked down into her drink and spoke soberly as though weighing the decision. "He wants a kiss." Then after a moment and with her old fire. "Well, like nobody's perfect."

"You're still making jokes. Why?" His reprimand brought her back down again.

"You're right. Yes, it's a bad habit. O.K. Slinky me will behave."

She took a full swallow with a sour face and placed her drink on a paperback copy of six Strindberg plays that lay face up on the already liquor-stained lamp table. She swiveled toward him and looked up into his eyes, but he had turned away to put the camera on the table. She tried to tuck her feelings away, and yet they lingered on despite her pretense at numbness. She felt, in part, a true and proper prostitute: this she couldn't quell. Yet the actress in her was unable to resist playing that challenging role of a devious and delicious Mata Hari.

He circled her with his arm as though they were sitting in a dark movie house, and she felt his hand cup her shoulder and draw her toward him. God how many damn times have I gone through this bit and I'm still doing it. Always with the wrong man on the wrong couch or in the wrong car. Still and all, she felt that imminent and exciting moment of danger. It was about to happen. Revulsion and lust had joined in a kind of pitiful joke. She waited. It was happening. His lips moistened her exposed neck and as luck would have it he was wearing her favorite men's cologne. Her vacant stare took notice that his shoelace had a double knot. His hand was on her flank where her vaccination lay hidden. A full kiss with his horrid mouth and she all but gagged. Worse yet, his fingers moved out of sight, crumpling back her red dress, exposing her light brown legs as his damp palm slid over her vulnerable flesh. Where was Val? The door was vacant. Lovingly she turned Reno's face with her hands so it could be seen in its full, unphotogenic profile. He looked dumbly at her, engrossed in his clumsy progress. She tried to smile. Only half her mouth rose to the command. Val! Now, Val. *Now!*

And out he popped, crouched and peering, his eyes deep in the ground glass, his arm holding the strobe light on high. Then came that deadly paralysis of time when the pose was perfect yet the camerman fiddled; that pause that turned spontaneity into a living stone, muscle into wrought iron and any expression whatsoever into a parody of itself.

At last there was a click, and at once disaster. No light. Just a click. No flash. *Nothing.* Reno lurched away as the intruder cursed aloud. He wound the film (a split-second forward-backward semi-circle swit-swit) and though the shot was spoiled, he shot again in a perfect repeat of that abrupt, lifeless, empty, black, barren click.

A three-sided silence lasted for a moment.

"What's this, huh?" Reno demanded, standing up. All eyes were on the camera.

"Oh, Val!" She tossed her head peevishly. "Can't you do anything right?"

"Well, up yours."

"I'll have to ask you…" But Reno was cut off.

"Well, thank God it's not my fault," Tanya said.

"It is your fault, damn it," said Val.

"My fault? How my fault?"

"I'll have to ask you not…" Again Reno was cut off.

"Yes, *your* fault cause you took so goddamn long setting it up."

"So what? So I took a while?"

"And the battery died waiting."

"Cut it out," said Reno, as he advanced on the photographer who was still fiddling with his equipment while squabbling with his accomplice.

"Damn strobe," Val ranted, his hair falling in his face. "Only piece of equipment I own that I didn't steal. Serves me right."

Reno disconnected the strobe plug from the socket of the camera.

"Hey." And Val reinserted the wire which his opponent just as quickly pulled out again.

"Stop it, will ya?" he whined, turning away.

Reno said: "Cut it, I'm not kidding."

"Just keep your hands to yourself there, buddy." It was Tanya scolding him while Val fired the camera once more, aiming at the floor, and again there was no light. "Tsh, damn these things."

"Oh, no you don't," she cried, darting to the entrance of the foyer to stand with outstretched arms blocking Reno's attempted escape.

"Oh, no you don't," Val shouted in conjoined alarm rushing up to relieve her of her post. He cursed his way out of the tangle of equipment and placed them on the floor.

"No pictures?" she asked.

"No pictures," he said. "The shot's lost anyway."

Again that three-sided silence. The prisoner's own camera now hung from his hand by its strap. Val swept his hair from his eyes. Tanya nudged Other Cat out of the way with her right foot. There was a concluding click from the corner of the room and the turntable rotated to a slow dead silent stop. Somewhere in the building a door went off like a cannon as Tanya stood, mouth open, staring at Reno.

"What'llwedowith'im?" Val asked in great excitement, bouncing on his heels. "What'llwedowith'im?"

"We'll think of something."

"You're making a mistake," said the prisoner.

"What mistake? What? We ain't done nothin' yet."

"Damn that strobe," Val grumbled. "I'll get my money back."

"How 'bout callin' the police?" she suggested. "And I'll accuse him of rape."

Like a teacher complimenting a student for originality: "Good, good."

"No good," the prisoner countered. "I *am* the police. They'll believe me, not you. As it is, he's out on bail. I'll say I came here to get him to plead guilty and get a lighter sentence."

In anger and disgust, Val turned away and turned back. "The bastard's bluffing."

"That's O.K.," she said. "So was I. What else will we do to him."

"How's about calling his wife?"

This time it was Tanya who said, "Good, good."

"Ha," said Reno, standing stock still. "Not married."

"Call his mother, then," said Tanya, viciously.

Tom Tom took a swipe at one of his shoelaces and darted off in ecstacy.

"You're shootin' wild," he said.

Val advanced on him in full fury. "You know something? I hate your creepy guts."

"Yes, isn't he grand," she agreed.

"I'll make you a deal," Reno delivered abruptly, backing up a step or two. He rubbed his mouth with the back of his hand and looked about as though for an exit.

"Go on," said Val, "I'm listening."

"I'll return your bail. Right now. You lost a lot of money yesterday, huh? Money needed to hire lawyers, huh? I'll return it."

Val paused to tap a tassel hanging from the lampshade. He returned his eyes to Reno's waxen face. "By check, no doubt?"

"Well, I didn't bring much with me."

"Isn't he grand?" she repeated.

"I'm good for it, I'm not kidding." Idly, he fixed the tangled flap of his jacket pocket.

Val was nodding. Not at what the other had said or at anything she had said. Just nodding slowly, staring at their prisoner, chewing his lower lip and nodding until she looked at him and frowned.

"Chase Manhattan Bank," Reno added, by way of assurance.

With his palms together as though in prayer, Val bumped them thoughtfully and rhythmically against his lips, still staring and nodding. Then he clapped his hands once and dropped them to his side.

"Noo?" she asked.

"I got it."

"Got what, baby?"

"What we'll do to him. I got it." He nodded twice more.

"What? Like what'll we do?"

"What we'll do is we'll kill him."

They stood like three actors uncertain as to who had the next line.

As if trying to wake him without a jolt: "Val?"

"We'll *do* it. Yes, we'll *do* it." His voice was excited, and he began bouncing on his heels again.

Reno rubbed his mouth. "Be careful what you say."

"We'll slit his throat," said Val.

"We will?" She frowned at his tight smile and felt her temperature drop.

"We will," he asserted, and with that he picked up a pair of scissors lying open on the lamp table.

"Think twice," the prisoner said, his confidence dwindling. "Attempted murder, that could get you twenty years. With you out on bail, could get you life, maybe. *Life*. I'll yell. They use the electric chair in this state. Look out. I'll yell."

Val gripped one of the handles with his fist, holding the scissors like a knife. Reno shifted his Bolsey camera to his other hand and erupted with rage. "*You hate me don't ya?* Well, I'm no different than you are, I swear to God. You can't scare me. And I won't try to bribe you, either."

Val moved forward with his knife and his thin smile, brushing his hair back and still nodding.

"Hey, be careful, huh? You're putting him on, aren't ya? Val?" Her timid fingers touched his sleeve. "Baby? Wait a minute. Baby? Is he the one we're after? Is he worth it? Baby?"

Reno flew into motion. With both hands gripping his camera by the strap, he swung it at Val in a swift wide arc which, as Val ducked, caught Tanya squarely at the side of the head. She lurched like a puppet, tumbled in a clumsy sprawl over the Carole Lombard chair and fell to the carpet in a heavy, gut-quivering thump. Both men studied her in horror, and then one made for the exit while the other fell frantically upon the writhing form, grasping her head, pressing it against his chest, calling her name and wincing at each of her groans until the sound of the slammed door registered.

"Are you all right?" *Val yelled.*

She nodded with an angry grimace, and he leaped to his feet, lunged toward the foyer and sprawled face forward hearing the screech of a cat instead of the sound of his own body hitting the floor. Up again and out into the hall where a plump woman in hair curlers sat on the cold tile clutching a large brown half-spilled bag of groceries. The diamond-shaped window of the elevator door went from light to dark as someone descended beyond reach. "Did a man just go in there?" Val shouted at the stupified lady, and then missed her reply as he clattered down a musty cliff of stairs, swung with the help of a banister post down another flight to another banister post down another flight past an unshaven janitor mopping the landing and on in an endless descent in an endless spiral with the vibrating amplified sound of Tanya's voice screaming at him from above.

The street lay bare beneath areas of lamplight through which people strolled in innocent apathy. Startled by the darkness, Val snapped his head this way and that looking for seersucker, and found it retreating toward bright Broadway's black mass of life. Should have brought the scissors, he thought, and then found them in his right hand. The cracks of the sidewalk passed beneath him as he dashed forward. When he looked up again, the target was gone. At the corner, amid the dissonance of a hot Manhattan evening, he stopped and craned his neck. He rammed one man and then another until he broke into the clear beneath a marquee of yellow light, rushing in great strides up cluttered Broadway, keeping his eye on the bluish-white cloth, losing it, finding it, causing a car to brake to a halt as he flew past the headlights, dashing on, breathing deeply, hearing his coins clatter, and losing it again. He stopped, was about to run some more when he glanced down a side street in time to see him, still holding his camera, making quick strides away from the crowd. Val followed his prey until he saw a distant cab with a bright roof-bulb come to a stop. The door opened and Reno slipped inside. Val ran with all his strength and then slackened his speed when he realized that the cab was coming toward him on a one-way street. He waved and moved into the road as the taxi gained frightening speed. He stood in its path. He threw out both his arms in the oncoming flood lights but they swung away from him and for a brief moment he saw the frightened, exhausted, waxen face staring at him from inside, watching as Val pounded once with his fist on the glass and then the cab raced up the street with Val following in long heavy strides, seeing Tanya running toward him, carrying her shoes, her dress hitched up and she not understanding his desperate signals as he indicated the cab which had just passed her. Then the taxi stopped. It was a red light. Val ran faster, almost colliding with Tanya as she came toward him from the other direction, hearing her voice but not her words, racing on with all his strength

toward the cab, seeing Reno watching from the rear window, stroking his hair into place, turning to say something to the driver and
back again to study the approaching runner, and then the light
turned green and as Val made a sweep at the handle of the rear
door, the cab moved out into Broadway, heading west across town.
It was beyond reach again, growing smaller in one of the crowded
side streets of the theater district, and as Val stopped to watch it go,
it disappeared and the sounds of New York returned.

There was a wastebasket at the corner, and he strolled over to
grasp it with both hands, leaning forward as though to vomit.

"What's the rush, Charlie?" said a dark blue suit. It was a tall
policeman with a long night stick.

"Catch…inga…friend," Val gasped.

"Oh? What's the scissors for?"

"Cutting…things."

"S'nothing…sir," gasped Tanya as she came hurrying up. "He's
with…me."

"What are you barefoot for, lady?" He eyed the rest of her, as
well.

"To catch…him."

"Should be the other way around, if you ask me. O.K. What's
the name, lady?"

"Tan…yaLan…do."

"What?"

"Lando."

"Whatcha running' fer? What's the rush?"

"Catch…ing…him."

"What's the scissors for?" he asked her, pointing at Val's hand.

"Cutting…things."

"Put your shoes on, lady. And get the hell out of here. I think
you're both cracked."

"Yes. Sir."

As Val kept his eyes in the direction of the side street down
which the cab had gone, she led him first through the crowd that
had gathered to watch them and then across Broadway to Duffy

Square where they sat on the ridge of the monument, she still in her bare feet and he still holding the scissors and looking once or twice behind him to where the cab had gone.

"I would have dressed differently if I had known it was a track meet," she said, pushing his hair out of his eyes. The touch of her hand seemed to bring him back.

"Are you O.K.?" He caressed her cheek.

"O.K. Headache only."

"Jesus, you were lucky." And he kissed her temple.

"Val, I was afraid you'd kill him."

"I would have."

"No! Really?"

"Yes, really." He looked up and saw people watching them.

"You're not putting me on?"

"No, I meant it."

"Why? 'cause he hit me?"

"And for a few other things. Jesus, will ya look at them standing around staring at us."

"T never knew a man who would kill for me before."

"Well, don't expect it every day. It's tiring."

He opened and closed the scissors.

"Oh, I won't. Like will I never ever. Wow."

Val loosened his tie and opened his collar. "Why did you try to stop me?"

"Why?" Tossing her hair with a queenly lurch. "Well, he was, you know, correct. You're on parole and all. You hurt him and you get screwed for good. Well, hell, he *was* correct."

"*Shit!* Am I sick of all the correctness in this world." With a groan he tossed a bottle top into the street.

"Ou, so angry," she said, pushing away her sorrow. "I love it when you're angry."

"Go screw."

"That, too, I love." And she kissed his ear.

"You know, you're pretty chipper there, young lady, considering you lost just about everything including nearly your life."

She gave him a sad smile. "Easy come, easy go."

He was unable to think of anything to say.

"Baby, come on, let's go home. I'll cook us up a victory feast."

"But we didn't win anything, for crysake."

"Yes we did."

"No we didn't."

"So like I'm wrong. You said yourself you didn't care for people who were always correct."

Raising one eyebrow, he thought about this and then said: "What's for dinner?"

"Chicken, I think. I'll have to look in the freezer."

"Chicken? And what else?"

"Keys and parrots."

He looked at her in amazement. "Jesus, you're too much, you know that? You are *simply* too much."

"Vot are you implyink? Vot? Dat Hy don't feel deeply da feelings vot dis voild offers dere? Puy on you."

"We're attracting attention, dear."

"So darlink, let's attract."

Patting one of her bare knees. "O.K., slim, you asked for it."

She held him by the sleeve. "Vait, vot? Vot you gonna do? Vot? Vait."

Val jumped to his feet and addressed those who were watching.

"Ladies and Gentlemen, a funny thing happened to me on the way to the fallout shelter."

In an instant she was beside him, and now all eyes were on the nut with the scissors and the lovely thing in the bright red dress. "Here we are folks," she growled in a down-and-dirty huckster's voice, "the Midtown, Cross-Country, Cab-Chasing, Student Conservatory Singing Society. Step right up."

"Presenting," said Val, "for your listening pleasure, a dual rendition of..." He looked at her. She looked at him and shrugged. "...of that great American favorite 'Swanee River.'"

"Again?" she asked.

And so, despite everything, they sang, each trying to outdo the other while parading arm in arm, she mugging with an assortment of comic faces and he bellowing it out in a loud imitation of Al Jolson. Tanya borrowed a gray fedora from a grizzled gentleman and, passing the hat, collected several coins which she gave to the grizzled gentleman in mock mistake, wearing the hat herself in a roguish tilt until, realizing her mistake, she claimed the coins and returned the hat while Val, on one knee, was bellowing: "Swaneeee, how I love ya, how I love ya, miiiiiy dear old Swaneeee," until a cop pushed his way into the center of the gathering and broke it up.

The End

www.ingramcontent.com/pod-product-compliance
Lightning Source LLC
Chambersburg PA
CBHW070626260626
47161CB00007B/2606